PENGUIN BOOKS

LATE CALL

Angus Wilson was born in the south of England in 1913. A part of his childhood was spent in South Africa, and he was then educated at his brother's school in Sussex, Westminster School and Oxford. He joined the staff of the British Museum Library in 1937. When the War came he helped towards the safe storage of the British Museum treasures before serving the rest of the War in Naval Intelligence. It was while trying to emerge from a period of depression and near-breakdown that he began to write short stories in 1946, a collection of which, *The Wrong Set*, was published in 1949. This met with immense critical acclaim and was followed a year later by a second collection, *Such Darling Dodos*. In 1952 his short critical study *Emile Zola* was published and was followed in 1953 by his first novel, *Hemlock and After*, one of his best known works. In 1955 he resigned from the Museum in order to devote his time to writing, and in 1963 became a part-time lecturer at the new University of East Anglia in Norwich, subsequently becoming Professor and Public Orator. He was made a CBE in 1968 and knighted in 1980.

His other novels are *Anglo-Saxon Attitudes* (1956), *The Middle Age of Mrs Eliot* (1958), *The Old Men at the Zoo* (1961), *No Laughing Matter* (1967), *As If By Magic* (1973) and *Setting the World on Fire* (1980). His third volume of short stories, *A Bit Off the Map*, was published in 1957 and a critical autobiographical study, *The Wild Garden*, appeared in 1963. Many of his books, including his *Collected Stories*, are published by Penguin.

Angus Wilson died in 1991. Among the many people who paid tribute to him on his death were Malcolm Bradbury: 'He was brilliant in the real sense of the word. He shone and he was very theatrical. Lectures were packed'; Paul Bailey: 'He was the kindest of men. I am not the only younger writer who is indebted to him'; and Rose Tremain: 'Angus Wilson was a great novelist and a profoundly lovable man'.

Angus Wilson

Late Call

Penguin Books
in association with Secker & Warburg

PENGUIN BOOKS

Published by the Penguin Group
Penguin Books Ltd, 27 Wrights Lane, London W8 5TZ, England
Penguin Books USA Inc., 375 Hudson Street, New York, New York 10014, USA
Penguin Books Australia Ltd, Ringwood, Victoria, Australia
Penguin Books Canada Ltd, 10 Alcorn Avenue, Toronto, Ontario, Canada M4V 3B2
Penguin Books (NZ) Ltd, 182–190 Wairau Road, Auckland 10, New Zealand

Penguin Books Ltd, Registered Offices: Harmondsworth, Middlesex, England

First published by Secker & Warburg 1964
Published in Penguin Books 1968
10 9 8 7 6 5 4 3

Printed in England by Clays Ltd, St Ives plc
Set in Monotype Baskerville

For Jean and Martin Corke

Prologue
The Hot Summer of 1911

Everywhere the clayey soil was baked as hard as rock, even in the farmyard and the pigsties where normally the least shower of rain kept the usual thick seas of mud churning. Great cracks had appeared in the flower bed that faced the front door of the farmhouse – an oval filled with bedded-out pansies and small pink begonias. Even the short stretch of gravelled drive that led to the cart track that in turn led to the roadway was fissured as though the many creatures beneath the earth's surface had at once decided to break their way through to the air above them. The dust pervaded everything: it was scratched up by the speckled and buff hens and raised into clouds as the sows rolled on their backs; it was puffed into brown, gritty smoke plumes as the disconsolate white ducks twisted their beaks in the almost dried-up pool, grubbing for deeply hidden worms; it filled the whole air as Derek Longmore sailed round and round the flower bed, doing bumpy wonders on his new bicycle.

Mrs Longmore, who, on their farm holiday, liked to dress peculiarly sensibly and simply, had nevertheless put on a white net veil to protect her face from the dusty air. In a large white straw cartwheel hat and a white linen dress with only a cluster of large pink roses as ornament (this very summer had at last come that end of the hour-glass waist, an end of the dangerous whalebone tyranny over Woman, that her good sense had so long wished for), she carried a green-lined unbleached linen parasol with a green bone handle curved like a parrot's head. Skirts were more sensible this year, too, at last, just above the ankles, so that they fell – thank Heaven – short of the dusty ground; yet her equally sensible white shoes, with square toes and a square bone buckle, toppled and corkscrewed in the most precarious fashion, despite their low heels, over the high, hard dried ridges left by the farm carts' wheels. It was like miniature mountain climbers, she thought imaginatively, and most disagreeable. She hoped that she looked cooler than she felt, for she was a great believer in the influence of Mind. If others thought her looking cool, then she would soon feel cooler.

But what others were there to think? Derek was absorbed in his new bicycle as, boy-like, he should be. Mr Tuffield, who thought no further than his cows and his wheat (or, at any rate, any other thoughts he might have were best not pondered upon), was away with the farm hand among the wheat, whose unseasonable dryness so agitated him. As to Mrs Tuffield, she thought only of doing the house and making tarts – which was a comfort as far as boarding at the farm was concerned (although another gooseberry tart in this hot weather and one might scream), but she provided no interested observer. Indeed Mrs Tuffield's eyes were at this very moment directed upon and through one, as she leaned out from an upstairs window, competing ineffectually with nature by launching small clouds of dust from mats that she beat against the outer windowsill. Pleased that her thoughts should be ordered with a certain elegance, even on holiday, even in this heat and dust (the thermometer had touched 100 last week), Mrs Longmore yet felt the need of an audience. Her own little Myra at seven years was rather young (or was it inattentive? For really a girl cannot have a dress sense, in proportion of course, too early). As to the Tuffield children, that brood of straying, whining indistinguishables that one met on the stairs like the farm's many cats and kittens, or at some unexpected corner of the farmyard or the orchard like the innumerable hens or ducks which scattered before one's coming with the most startling suddenness, if *they* had some comment to make it would be as incomprehensible as the clucking or quacking of poultry, so broad was their dialect. But they certainly had none, indeed very little speech at all, so cowed were they.

Mrs Longmore very much hoped they were not ruled by fear (her own childhood had been a nightmare for that very reason). But nice though it was to think of country children as rosy cheeked, and skipping and hopping in innocent play, the truth was that the Tuffield brood were pink cheeked, yes, but sad and listless, and neglected. Their mother was too occupied with the house and the chapel, their father too occupied with the farm and Heaven knew what, for his eyes had sometimes a quite horrid look. Ignorant and old-fashioned, in fact; Mrs Longmore could hardly bear to think what horrors of Bible reading and canes those children might be ruled by. She only hoped that it was all right for Myra to play with them all day – but such were the penalties of farm holidays, penalties outbalanced by plenty of fresh air and fresh eggs and pints of healthy milk straight, almost steaming, from the cow. And then there was the eldest little Tuffield girl. In her hands Myra would be all right; old head on young shoulders, poor little thing, everything was left to her. She had to be mother to the whole brood – not more than twelve years old and responsible for heaven knew how many little indistinguishables. She made a very good job of it. And she was surprisingly bright and intelligent; she had a sense of beauty, of wonder, yes, that was it, of wonder; how excited she was when one put on a new shawl or a new hat, or one evening, absurdly, just to feel nice, a crimson watered-silk, Liberty tea gown with a little broderie anglaise coat. Yes, she was a child who noticed. She seemed so pleased to be made a fuss of. She clearly lacked love, as Mrs Longmore could tell, when, once or twice, she had kissed or hugged her and called her, 'a funny little dumpling'. Mrs Longmore set out to find her.

But seek where she would – and in this intense heat she wouldn't very widely – the little Tuffield girl was nowhere to be found. Nor indeed was her own Myra. There were little Tuffield indistinguishables all over the place, chewing twigs from the plum trees or sucking stones that had fallen from the dilapidated old flint barn, pressed on the ground on their stomachs, grubby knickers upwards, teasing kittens, or bent over the dried-up water butts pushing snails with stalks of grass backwards into terrible headlong falls. One child had tears running from her eyes down her cheeks, and another mucus running from his nostrils down on to his lips. From none could Mrs Longmore learn the whereabouts of their eldest sister or of her own little girl. Some were too young to use words and those who were old enough spoke words that she could not understand. Exhausted and a little out of temper, she almost called her son Derek to her aid, but boys of thirteen must be left to themselves in the holidays; instead she went into the little parlour that was their rented sitting room, took Maeterlinck's *Life of the Bee* from the dresser where it was propped against the cruet, and finally settled herself in a rocking chair, specially put out for her by Mr Tuffield under an old apple tree in the orchard. There she read a few pages of that stimulating book and then fell asleep.

It had taken a lot of persuading on the part of Myra Longmore to get the little Tuffield girl to leave her charges, her brothers and sisters, and to wander away, not only out of the farmyard and the orchard, but right out of the farm into one of Knapp's meadows – somewhere, indeed, where she had never been, for it lay on quite the other side of the farm to either the village or the church, and neither Mother nor Father were friendly with the Knapps. But Myra was used to getting her own way; with either Mummy or Derek it was only a question of asking for long enough; and so it had proved with the little Tuffield girl. She had gone on repeating, 'Let's go away from the others. Let's play on our own'; and in the end, the little Tuffield girl had given way. For all that Mummy called her little, she seemed really more like a grown-up person, like a nanny only small.

If Myra had but known, it was not only her persistence that had overcome the little Tuffield girl's sense of duty, her long training in obedience and her fear of the consequences of doing wrong. It was much more something to do with all the Longmores, and especially with Mrs Longmore and the effect she had. They had only been staying at the farm ten days, but from the very first the little girl had felt her influence. Mrs Longmore had somehow singled her out, and, in doing so, had given faint yet definite outlines to her personality for the first time in her ten and a half years. The very fact that the grand and beautiful lady could not tell Bertie from Ted, or Rosie from Violet, made her singling out and talking to the eldest little girl something quite special. It was true that some of the things she said were the usual remarks of visitors, pats on the head that spread a crimson of embarrassment from the little girl's already rosy cheeks right down her neck – 'Quite the little mother', or 'Such an old head on young shoulders'. This was the stuff that Mr Bentall, the minister, addressed at her, or the governess who came with the Easter lodgers, or Mrs Clark, the rector's wife from London, who had come with her family each summer until this year and who, indeed, had this year sent instead Mrs Longmore herself. But Mrs Longmore had said a lot more to the girl than these public embarrassments; she had shown books to her and asked her to hook up her dresses at the back; she had given her a cherry silk ribbon for her hair; she had asked her the name of some birds in an apple tree and, when she did not know, they had looked together in a picture book and found that they were warblers; she had told her how to say some words properly like 'down' and 'pot', and also not to say 'little old'. Above all, she had asked for her to play in the parlour with Derek and Myra at 'Happy Families' or building Meccano; and though Mother hadn't liked it because six o'clock was Violet and Ted's bedtime and half past six was bedtime for Bertie and Rosie, she'd had to let her go in there at least on the Wednesday and the Saturday, for Mrs Longmore had said that every good nanny had her evenings off. But it was above all the things Mrs Longmore said in the parlour as they played at their games – 'Don't bother with it if you don't like it', 'Take off your shoes and be comfortable', 'Never mind if it is marked. We can always get another table, but you'll never be ten years old again in a cool room in the hottest summer England's known for half a century', and especially, 'Of course you must have it, it suits you. It makes you look quite beautiful.' And Mrs Longmore had said, 'Doing something different is the thing. Not all the time, of course, because then it wouldn't really be different. But every now and again, when people least expect it.'

It couldn't be said that Mother and Father would have least expected her to leave the others and go off with Myra right out of the farm on *this* morning more than any other; they just wouldn't expect such a thing at all. But perhaps it could be said that leaving the others to play and wander at will, and leaving the washing in a pile on the dairy floor instead of hanging it on the clothes lines, was a double negligence that her Mother in her wildest nightmare would hardly have dreamt of. The little girl had thought of all this; and yet, from the moment she and Myra had slid down the dusty bank of the ditch that divided the farm from Knapp's meadow and, grasping each in turn an old oak tree root, had hauled themselves up on to the other side, she had ceased to give any thought to her wickedness or its consequences. She began to do all the things that she had wanted to do for years – things for which there was never time because there were so many duties in the day, or things she could never do for herself alone but had always to do to amuse and quieten her brothers and sisters. And she did them straightaway as though they had all been waiting in a line ready to be done for years – things, many of them, that yet seemed to occur to her for the first time.

In the meadow she didn't have to pick any buttercups or daisies just to split their stalks with her nails and thread them together as a necklace for Violet; she didn't have to hold the golden flowerheads under Bertie's chin to see if he liked butter; she didn't have to watch for fear that Rosie might eat the minute toadstools that sprouted here and there in the grass; she didn't have to stop Ted from making mud pies with the huge dried cowpats. She lay flat on her back and stared at the cloudless, harshly blue sky; and, when the sun's glare became too blinding, she turned over and lay on her stomach, pressing her face close among the daisies so that her eyes could follow almost at its own level a reddish ant that seemed to her as it hurried through the grass to trot like the pony in Doctor Osborne's children's cart.

Myra was busy picking daisies.

'I shall only pick the ones with lots of red on the petals,' she announced. She always spoke like that. When they played games in the parlour, at halma, she said, 'I'll have the yellow men', and, at 'Happy Families', 'I shan't collect the Bungs or the Bones. You can have them.' Sometimes Derek would complain,

'Myra's getting too uppish, Mater. She'll jolly well have to be squashed,' and then Mrs Longmore would say, 'Glorious Myra! She knows her own mind.'

Now Myra said, '*You* can collect all the white daisies. And the buttercups too. Yellow wouldn't match at all with the reddy coloured daisies I'm collecting.'

Usually in the parlour, Myra's tones, backed by Mrs Longmore's approval, impressed the little Tuffield girl greatly, but now she felt Myra's presence only as a bother. But not a serious bother, for Myra, after all, was no part of her duties. She got up from the ground very slowly and then deliberately began to pick not daisies or buttercups but minute pieces of snail shell that lay scattered on the hard earth beneath the tufted grass. She sorted them very carefully into greyish-coloured pieces and brownish-coloured pieces and put each separately into the two pockets of her pinafore. As she did so, she knew that when she searched in her pockets at the end of the day and found them, she would perhaps be surprised, but certainly she would throw them away, scatter them in the farmyard. Yet that didn't seem to matter; for the moment she was collecting some things that she had never noticed before, that probably nobody would have noticed, some things that were almost part of this meadow where she felt so free. So free that suddenly she began to dance, although she had no very clear idea of dancing, having only read of it and heard Auntie Beatie, who had been in service, describe a ball. She held up the sides of the skirt of her washed-out blue cotton dress so that the black cotton stockings showed to above her knees. Her dance was a sort of glide followed by a hop. Myra paused in her daisy search.

'Oh, that's not how to do it!' she cried, 'Look. First position, heel to toe.' And she demonstrated her dancing class exercises. 'And you must smile when you're dancing,' she added, showing her even little white teeth. (Mrs Longmore believed that teeth and bowels and fresh air and self-expression were the four primary considerations with children.) The little Tuffield girl's square-jawed, rather heavy-cheeked face remained set and solemn. She stopped her dance as soon as Myra spoke; she walked on across the meadow towards the ditch and the beech hedge that separated them from another meadow where she could see that cows had collected around what the summer's constant sun had left of a stagnant pool.

Ordinarily she hated the sight of cows, those lumbering, barrel-shaped, ill-smelling causes, with their erratic milk yield, of some of her father's worst rages, the objects of some of her own most frost-nipped, numbed early morning winter chores. With their dismal liquid eyes and henna-coloured dung-caked flanks, the cows before her now exactly recalled her Father's, as they flipped their great heads to ward off the tormenting flies. But they were not Father's cows, they were part of a whole new adventure; and at once she wanted to explore the plashy meadow and even beyond. She could hear Myra behind her, out of breath, out of patience now with her unwanted dance, cry.

'Stop! Stop! Oh, why don't you watch me? Don't you want to learn?'

The little girl knew that she was learning without Myra's help. Once more she scrambled across another dusty ditch and through the tight beech hedge without a scratch or tear. Although neat, she was a stocky little girl and not usually lissome or agile, but her mood seemed to lighten her small, heavy body. Arrived in the meadow, she sat down in a flat, clay-chalked hollow that had until this summer, perhaps, been a never empty puddle. The grass around was coarse and there were clumps of spiky miniature bullrushes, but to the small girl, as she lay on her back, the harsher feel seemed no less delightful than the softer buttercup meadow – just a new and delightful delight.

But the exploration was proving no delight for poor Myra. Getting no answer to her cries, she had ceased her little dainty pirouettes and followed carefully her companion's path. Too carefully, for the slope where the little Tuffield girl had slid across the ditch was now cleared of dust to expose a slippery tree root. Myra fell heavily on her bottom, tearing a long strip of the lace hem away from the skirt of her dress and laddering one of her white cotton stockings. She was near to tears when she reached her friend. For a moment the little Tuffield girl was recalled from her new happiness; but then she thought of what Mrs Longmore would have said. The day was more important than a skirt.

'That'd be best to take off th' dress,' she said, and to encourage Myra, she took off her own cotton sunbonnet and pulled her blue cotton dress with its pinafore over her head. Folding it, she carried it under her arm. Some of the authority she normally exercised over the indistinguishables must have been communicated to Myra, for after a moment's hesitation she, too, took off her fine blue-ribboned straw hat and her lace-trimmed dress.

Myra was secretly afraid of cows, but she did not like to say so to anyone on the farm (or indeed to her mother, for Mrs Longmore, in her abhorrence of fear in children's lives, did not like her own to mention that emotion). Now, to keep up her spirits, Myra showed off her petticoat, explaining how it was made of handmade lawn, and how the insertions and the top were of handmade Brussels lace passed down from her Cartier grandmother. The little farm girl listened and even felt the material with a look of interest, but not with what Mrs Longmore would have called 'wonder'. Or certainly no wonder for Myra's having such a fine petticoat, for her attention had been suddenly and entirely caught by the real likeness between the Brussels lace and the flowers so long familiar to her that Mrs Longmore had told her were called Queen Anne's Lace. She had brushed her way through high-standing clumps of these as she came from the beech hedge into the meadow. Now she ran back and fingered the creamy flowerheads.

'Look, that crumbles,' she called. With difficulty she broke one of the tough stems and held the flower out towards Myra; as she did so, clouds of pollen flew up from the mass of little florets.

'Stardust,' cried Myra, and then, because she longed to attract the Tuffield girl back into her own orbit, she started to pirouette again, 'I'm the Princess of the Stardust,' she sang. She whirled round and round, moving towards the farm girl – she did not want to be separated from her in a field where there were cows, yet she did not want to seem to be at her call. 'Scatter the stardust for the Stardust Princess,' she cried.

The Tuffield girl threw the flower away into the hedge. She wanted to tell Myra not to be a softy, but it seemed better to say nothing.

In any case the Stardust Princess was soon in grief. Absorbed in her pirouettes, less sure-footed than the farm girl, she swung round into one of the few plashy, muddy patches in the field, where beneath the coarse grass an underground spring defied the months of sunshine. Brown-yellow clay mud spattered both her white stockings to above the ankle, splashed her snowy petticoat; the mud seeped, squelching, from her shoes. Discomfort and fright made her cry. The little Tuffield girl was always prepared for tears, they were so much part of her daily chores. If they were 'temper tears', she tried to copy her mother's roughness with shakes and slaps; if, like Myra's, they seemed 'real', she could express her own nature, one at once practical and tender. She wiped Myra's face with her handkerchief; she cleaned the mud from the stockings with handfuls of long grass, and, when this only smeared the dirt, she tried to scrub it off with an end of her own pinafore soaked in spittle. The sunshine, a slight soft south-westerly breeze, freedom, a sense of happiness not to be lost, loosened her imagination. She said,

'Stocken and shoe 'd best be taken off.'

Before Myra knew where she was, she had been seated on a molehill, long since dried into a hummock, and before her was the small Tuffield girl on her knees removing the muddy white shoes, lifting up the petticoat to unloose the suspenders, peeling off the long white stockings. The sense of being served quietened Myra; she felt herself once again a princess, although she voiced no more royal commands. The farm girl hitched up her own faded and patched white cotton petticoat and, unclipping her suspenders, slipped down her black cotton stockings, and removed them with her shoes all in one movement. Barefoot, gingerly, the two girls stepped out across the field.

Myra, remembering her mother's actions, slipped her arm round her companion's waist, and, raising her lips to the other girl's cheek, kissed her. The Tuffield girl seemed surprised, hesitated, then returned the kiss. Taking Myra by the hand, she ran across the meadow. Past the cows they went (whatever other result, Myra Longmore never feared cows again in her life, so reassuring was the hand that led her on), down to where the spikes of yellow flags shone in the sun.

'There's water runnin'. There's water runnin',' the

Tuffield girl sang out to a tune that came suddenly into her head. Myra joined in, and, dancing and singing, they came to a small brook. It was the Tuffield girl that led the way in, but both girls were soon paddling and splashing in the pebbly clear water. The cold was delicious to Myra after days of sweating heat, with (unlike home in Chelsea) no more than basins or hip baths to wash away the stickiness; to the Tuffield girl it was like discovering the Pole. But after five minutes or so, the intense cold of the water contrasted disagreeably with the intense heat of the sun; the pressure of the pebbles began to hurt their feet. They jumped from the brook and started to pick the long yellow-headed flags. Then Myra, leaning too precariously to break a sharp sheath, dropped her straw hat into the stream. At first, she was as delighted as her companion, to see how quickly the brook carried it away from them. Then she became scared as she saw it bobbing off, crown downwards, like some worn-out old shopping basket, its ribbons all soaked and bedraggled. The little Tuffield girl was clapping her hands with joy when she was brought back to reality by Myra's slapping her hand and crying,

'You've lost my hat. Mummy says the blue ribbons are adorable. It'll be spoilt now.'

Partly to astonish Myra into silence or perhaps to comfort her by sharing her loss, partly from delight at this reversal of all seemliness, the farm girl took off her sun-bonnet and threw it into the stream. Made of cotton, it sank immediately. But, of course, Myra's hat was not lost. It had come to rest in a shallow among some wild musk. At first, they were delighted with the newly-scented hat, but, then, when Myra put it on, water trickled all around her face and neck from its wide brim. The Tuffield girl ran back and fished her own bonnet out to share disaster once again. The results were unequal, for the cotton bonnet could be wrung almost dry, and, though unsightly, was wearable; nothing but misery could come from the watery straw, and the dye of its adorable blue ribbons had started to run down the lace top of Myra's petticoat.

It was the farm girl's idea that they should leave their hats to their watery fate, but Myra was delighted with the notion: for as hats, hers was clearly the greater disaster, but

17

as boats, hers was a stately schooner and the sunbonnet a shabby wreck. She began a long story of the straw hat's future adventures, in which the blue ribbons had become adorable princesses. 'And they sailed on and on and on until they came to a wonderful smiling lake where everything was still and beautiful . . .' For a little while the Tuffield girl stayed and listened to this story, because Myra's voice had become so strangely like Mrs Longmore's as she told it; but soon she tired of such tinkling – 'the princesses were so, so, so happy', and 'there swimming on the lake was a beautiful white, white swan' – when there was better noise to make for oneself as much as one liked and anything, even swans perhaps, to find. So she walked off on her own across the most soggy part of the meadow where the shade of overhanging elms allowed only zebra stripes of sunlight to pierce through.

Behind these elms stretched woodland as far as she could see. Here and there, where the earth was covered with low-growing ground elder, she could in fact see quite a long way down irregular avenues of even darker green splashed with sunlight; but in most directions her view was blocked by hazel nut bushes and tangles of wild rose and bramble. She thought it must be Paddock Wood, a huge wood of which she had often heard her mother give warning, for somewhere in a clearing of its trees there were sometimes to be found encamped gipsies. Gipsies were her mother's supreme example of idleness and wickedness; they were not only a bogey for the children but they offered Mrs Tuffield her chance, by ordering them off the farm premises or reporting them to the village policeman, of fighting the Devil made Flesh. But somehow the realization that she was so close to this famous occasional encampment of the Evil One neither drew the Tuffield girl towards the sinister wood nor sent her in panic running away from it. She merely turned her back to the trees and sat down propped against a huge knobbly hole of one of the elms. Above her she could see the smooth flat underside of a giant yellow fungus that protruded from the tree trunk. She gazed up at this for a while, and then turned her attention to the ground, to some woodlice that in idly scratching away a piece of bark she had set in busy motion.

But she was absorbed in neither the still fatness of the fungus nor the scaled scurry of the woodlice, they seemed merely objects helpful in crowding out thought or fancy. She was content, lying back in the warmth of the leaf-dappled sunshine, just to be; she could not remember such a thing before, she could only recall doing things or thinking about things to be done.

Myra was doing a great deal. Without any listeners, the story of the princesses and the swans soon began to sound empty, even though she tried to alarm herself by inventing a lake witch whose evil powers were unlimited; but she could think of no frightening thing for the witch to do that she had not thought of before. So she decided to make a princess's crown of wild flowers; it could serve by crowning her own head to compensate for lack of an audience and perhaps it would compensate her mother too for the loss of the straw hat (for she had already begun to long for and dread homecoming). Mummy was always pleased when she made beautiful things and showed imagination. She was, in fact, very skilled with her fingers and had soon threaded a chaplet of buttercups, daisies, vetch, and lady's slipper that would have satisfied most girls of her age. But her skill and the thought of Mummy's needed praise made her ambitious. She decided to weave not just a chaplet but a full crown of braided flowers two or three inches deep. Across and round the meadow she ran, now bending low for many minutes picking bare a whole patch of tough-stemmed marguerites, now dashing off to the far edge where the grass ran into a wheatfield and poppies grew in profusion and among them a few cornflowers. With all her blooms selected she sat herself on a dry bare patch in the middle of the field, emphasizing by her eminent isolation her independence of the farm girl, who was so unconscious of her. She was quite intent for half an hour before, with the sun beating down on her unfamiliarly bare head and arms and legs, she began to feel first flushed, then sore, and, at last, sick.

When she stood up, she became giddy. She began to cry, as she ran towards the other girl, ' I want to go to my Mummy. I want to go home.' In her distress, she dropped her clothes and shoes and the crown of flowers. The Tuffield girl picked them up and added the garments to her own bundle, but the crown of flowers had fallen in pieces. She would have left them on the ground, but, to distract Myra's fears, she gathered them up and handed them to her.

'That was a rare little old crown,' she said, then, remembering Mrs Longmore, corrected herself, 'That's proper beautiful, Myra. We'd best go into the wood. That'll be cool there for you to mend it.'

Myra was afraid to go into the wood; after the strong sunlight she seemed to be entering night's blackness; she blinked and stumbled. The elder girl took her arm to guide her away from the bramble thickets; but her firm grasp was painful to Myra's burnt skin. She broke from her crying, 'You hurt me. You hurt me.' For a moment a vision of Mrs Longmore's beautiful eyes distressed at the sight of her adorable Myra burned, and behind her the harsh condemning lines of her own mother's waxy face and, worse, the flashing black anger of her father's eyes, filled the Tuffield girl with sick panic, but her sense of well-being was strong enough to flood through her, washing all other thoughts away.

Myra meanwhile was almost hysterical; rage and fright and discomfort pressed on her so; she ran among the brambles and the briars, half hoping for disaster, half terrified at her own panic. Her ankles and feet were scratched, the precious lace of her petticoat hem was sharply torn. At first the little farm girl called after her by her name, but when she received no response, she changed to a soothing, clucking sound much like that she used when feeding the hens. Violet sometimes got out of control and then only such a sound could hush her. It worked now with Myra, too, for she came limping back to the pathway that the older girl had trampled out among the ground elder, and lay there, curled up, whimpering and muttering so that it was hard to hear her voice. It was still the sunburn and the heat she complained of, though she seemed quietened a little by the cool of the undergrowth. Most of her wounds were only grazes, but above her right ankle a thorn branch had cut sharply into the flesh. It was Mrs Tuffield's first aid method to ignore 'as fussing' all injuries unless they bled; but bleeding wounds she instantly bandaged, not with any aim to heal, for she never cleaned any wound, but rather to hide any tiresome evidence that her children were really in pain. Her eldest child had learnt these methods exactly. Her own rag of handkerchief she had discarded in favour of the snail shells; nor could she find any in the pockets of Myra's dress. Then a wonderful idea came to her. In her life of minding and doing she did not have much on which to sharpen her intelligence except the organization, the better ordering of her daily chores; all this last year she had been seized with a new pleasure – that of finding ways and means that served two purposes at once. It was this new thrill of killing two birds with one stone to which she had attached Mrs Longmore's frequent phrase 'a wonderful idea'. So now she took off her petticoat – it was an old one of her mother's cut down but not cut down enough, and, in any case, to bandage a wound was surely so important that her mother must forgive her – and unpicking the hem she tore it away in one long strip. With this she bound Myra's ankle. But that was only half the deed done; more important was to persuade Myra to follow her own example and take off *her* petticoat. In that way she would be cooler and what was more the Brussels lace would be safe from the thorns and spikes – oh, it *was* 'a wonderful idea', a kind of three in oner!

'Look,' she cried, and she stood up in her camisole and drawers and twirled round, 'Look! I'm *cool*, I'm cool!' and, indeed, she felt cool and free and happy as she had never felt before. Myra was horrified.

'Oh, you shouldn't, you shouldn't. Someone might see.'

'There's no one and if there was your mother said we was to "feel free".' (The phrase came from one of Mrs Longmore's defences of Liberty gowns, one of her diatribes against the deforming tyranny of the corset, but how was a farm girl of twelve to know the proper limits of *Kleidreform*?)

Myra felt the force of the other girl's joy, was drawn into imitation of the freedom of her movements. Soon the two little girls each in camisole and drawers, the smaller the proud wearer also of a liberty bodice, were seated among some cool-leaved clumps of wild arums mending the crown of flowers. When it was done and Myra acknowledged as Queen, both girls felt contented and friendly to each other as they had not done before on that afternoon. Not even Myra's highly-coloured, dramatic and menacing version of *The Babes in the Wood*, literally learnt at her mother's knee, with which she now appropriately entertained the elder girl, diminished in any degree their enjoyment of the dark wood's sun-splashed coolness; nothing seemed alarming there – neither the sudden clacking of pigeons in the tree-tops, nor the scuttling flight of rabbits in the undergrowth, nor the untimely nearby hoot of a barn owl disturbed in its rest. They kept along the winding path of low under-growth with the high elms and oaks and hornbeams protective above them. The Tuffield girl led the way, treading down the elder and garlic and loosestrife, bending back the fretful arms of bramble that barred their way. All thought of gipsies had gone from her mind, though she remembered with content that Paddock Wood was said to be so big, she hoped that it might stretch on for ever.

And then suddenly the dim light ahead of them grew brighter, until wish how she might, there could be no doubt that the trees were growing sparser, the undergrowth changing to scrub, the wood coming to its end. Soon they were making their way among saplings of hazel and black-thorn and at last on to a patch of rank grass that sloped down into what seemed a gulf across which they could see another grass bank. But the opposite bank was carefully fenced and mown; along its crest stretched a neat laurel hedge through whose yellow-spotted leaves she could glimpse a garden and the wistaria-clad ironwork of a verandah. For a moment the little Tuffield girl stood stock still as though she had walked into a dream, for here where Paddock Wood should have stretched on forever was a place familiar to her if not on every day, at least in every week. Then she knew – the unknown wood they had come so enchantedly through was not Paddock Wood at all, but a small copse very well known to her from the other side – the very side on which they were now standing. The verandah and garden belonged to the rectory, which she passed every Sunday on her way to church, the rectory where she was to go into service whenever (or if ever) Rosie grew old enough to look after the others. And the gulf between them was the Church Lane; from the back of the farm they had come by a way unknown to her to a place only a few minutes from their own front gate. She was about to turn as quickly as possible back into the copse, back to the happy land where her stay had been so short, but Myra had seen further down on the rough bank's slope the mauve of a rare patch of scabious and the Queen must have them for her Crown. Already in hasty descent to get what she wanted she had slipped on the bank's surface and was sliding contentedly down the slippery outcrop of chalk. The eldest Tuffield resigned herself to following. But now Myra sent up a wail of distress, for the sharp descent of the bank carried her on relentlessly past the scabious, on to bump painfully on the dusty road below. The Tuffield girl, doggedly setting her heels in one after another of the bank's many rabbit holes, managed to avoid such a precipitate slide, stopped herself by the clump of flowers and picked a handful as an offering to allay Myra's misery. And so they did. The mauve pincushion heads were worked into the front of the crown like some semi-precious stones. And then, since they had arrived at the road, and the shortest way back was so directly before them, Queen and lady in waiting must set off for home. But even into Myra's royal fantasy and the farm girl's sudden Grace there crept some prudential sense of their daily world, of policy and pleasing and deportment. Even royalty must be robed to walk down Church Lane, however spattered and tattered the robes might be – as to the hat, the floral crown would surely in its beauty compensate Mrs Longmore for its loss (Myra was sure it would), and the Tuffield girl counted on Mrs Longmore's powerful intercession before the doom seat to save her. But they *must* be decent for fear Father or Mother should chance to see them before they found Mrs Longmore to present her with the crown.

As though to warn them to hurry, there came the sound of a lumbering cart echoing down Church Lane. The Tuffield girl moved speedily to divide the articles in her bundles – first Myra's clothes, then her own. Her alarm passed to Myra, who began to jump from one leg to another.

'Quick, quick,' she begged, 'Oh, it would be awful if

anyone saw us. Awful, awful.' She echoed her mother's horror at all things *mal élevées*. She tried so hard, Myra, even at the age of seven to capture grown-up emotions, her mother's, that the parodies came out disjunctive, chaotic, creating havoc with her body, her movements. Now in caricature of distress, she snatched her clothes so quickly from the farm girl that all were tumbled in the dust of the road. 'Oh, heavens,' she cried, 'oh dear, what a fiasco.' It was a triumph of unconscious mimetic art and brought to the Tuffield girl a first intimation of the possibility of Mrs Longmore thrown from her usual poise. She picked up the clothes and began to beat the dust out of them.

'Your mother wouldn't be angry, surely,' she said, 'Why, she told us Wednesday she didn't mind along there were no fuss. We mun not fuss.'

'Oh, darling mummy, she's always kind,' Myra cried. She was Mrs Longmore now at histrionic heights the Tuffield girl had seen nothing of.

But Mrs Longmore kind or no, here was Snushall's cart bringing muck down to his field along the churchyard side. Luckily Mr Snushall with his occasional penny gifts after chapel was, though so different from Mrs Longmore, kindness itself. The girl could see his happy absent smile as he sat there holding the reins of the cart horse, and his young Albert standing up among the muck leaning with both arms on the handle of a great rake. The farm girl quickly held her dress up in front of herself, and she tried, too, to cover Myra, but the young queen was now in too wild a pantomime of distress. She jumped on the roadway from one knickered leg to the other.

'Oh dear. Oh dear. This is quite terrible.'

Albert Snushall saw them first. He burst out with a guffaw; then uncertain, blushed scarlet and looked solemn. His laughter had roused his abstracted father. Snushall's round surprised eyes stared out of his clownish, seal-like countenance. At first he just looked, then he too burst into laughter, and soon Albert had joined in, freed from all restraint.

All Myra's grandeur was outraged at this reception. 'I'm the Queen,' she shouted pointing to her crown, but they only laughed the more. The Tuffield girl, too, did not quite like this reaction to a freedom of behaviour that should either have shocked or pleased; however, her good sense told her to be happy that the first adult reaction had not been anger. She was about to explain their predicament to Mr Snushall before the cart had passed out of earshot when, suddenly, around the corner from the direction of home came Derek Longmore weaving brilliant circles on his bicycle from side to side of the bumpy, rutted road, increasing twofold the dust already raised by Mr Snushall's cart. When he saw the girls he stood up so high on the pedals that the Tuffield girl thought he would fall over the handlebars.

'Myra,' he shouted 'Oh, you absolute little beast,' and he swung his bicycle across the road and whizzed back homeward again, calling 'Mater! Mater!'

It seemed only a second before Mrs Longmore herself appeared from around the corner, still strolling gracefully as she had intended when she set out to follow Derek on his bicycle for a little walk before luncheon. She was there before Snushall's cart had moved on. At the sight of this gracious lady in white with her elegant parasol, Mr Snushall's laughter died away; he even turned and gave his young son a cuff, telling him to stop his 'gibble gabble'. Mrs Longmore's reactions to the unexpected sight were also affected by the presence of a man. For a moment, however, she could not see the two girls clearly through the shade cast by her parasol.

'What are you two doing out here?' she called.

'But Mater,' shouted Derek, 'they're being beastly.'

'Oh, do stop shouting, Derek. What are you doing here, Myra?'

'I'm the Flower Queen,' Myra began. Then something told her that her mother's reaction would not be as gentle as they had expected. Immediately she began to cry. 'She made me do it, Mummy, she made me do it,' she said, pointing at the farm girl.

Now Mrs Longmore could see clearly. 'Good heavens!' she cried. 'You little horrors! Put your clothes on at once. What do you mean by taking Myra's clothes from her like that? And she's hurt her leg! Put your clothes on, both of you.'

'Oh please, Mrs Longmore, ma'am,' the eldest Tuffield began, 'we din't feel free in them.'

'Didn't feel free in them! Didn't feel free in your clothes!' Mrs Longmore was indignant at the position she had been put into – alone in a farm lane with two small girls in their drawers and a yokellish sniggering farm labourer looking on. 'Well, don't hang about, Derek,' she cried. 'You don't need to let these little sillies spoil your ride!' Derek's whizzing on up the lane was, as she had hoped, a signal to Mr Snushall, who drove the cart off as briskly as his old horse could trot. Mrs Longmore herself now felt a little more free; she began to remember many humorous principles of child management, she recalled the little Tuffield girl's admiration and wonder. She said, leaning down towards the little girls, and speaking in a very soft voice, 'Now, whatever have you been up to?' She meant to inject into her serious tones a touch of mockery to which, if the little Tuffield girl had any sense of humour, she would respond, but somehow she could find no mockery to allay her seriousness. Responding to this severity of her mother's, Myra now passed from tears to desperate sobbing.

'She made me do it, Mummy. She made me take them off. She wanted me to take everything off.'

Now the mother in her turn responded to her small daughter's histrionics. She drew Myra to her. 'My poor, poor little Myra,' she cried, 'you're not to think of it ever again.'

The farm girl's bewilderment between the two of them was complete.

'If you please, ma'am,' she cried, 'Myra got herself proper hotted and I thought it best' – she sought desperately for the right words – 'to give her a change. Something as she'd never done before. Like you said.'

Mrs Longmore's clumsy efforts to pull Myra's clothes on quickly were chafing the girl's sunburnt flesh. Anxious not to cry out and upset her mother further, she chose instead to bawl more loudly against the farm girl. 'She's a horrid girl, Mummy. She's nasty.' The little Tuffield girl attempted to aid Mrs Longmore in dressing Myra, indeed so quick and neat were her efforts that, despite Myra's screams, she had her stockings and shoes and her petticoat on before Mrs Longmore pulled her away fiercely by the arm.

'Leave Myra alone,' she cried. Attracted by the noise, Violet and Rosie, Ted and Bertie arrived on the scene and were standing in a knot. 'They're rude,' they cried, 'they're rude. Ooh! They're rude.'

The uncomprehending prurience that underlay Myra's complaints and the small children's taunts touched something in Mrs Longmore. For her a bad old world was being replaced by hygiene and fresh milk and elastic belts and continental breakfasts and Mind; the enemy was ignorance and brutality and fustiness and gross, heavy meals and narrow-minded Sundays and dirt – not so much clean dirt, as the sort of dirt that she feared to see in Mr Tuffield's eyes. She had suspected that she was paying too high a price for the farm eggs and milk, too high a price in Tuffield fustiness and ignorance, and, despite all Mrs Tuffield's cleaning, in Tuffield squalor. Now she knew it. At the base of all the sensible, up-to-date teaching that she professed for the bringing up of her children there lay one principal tenet – let there be beauty, especially beauty of mind. And now from this Tuffield squalor, from the least suspected member of the family – but corruption like fever is inescapable – something nasty, something beastly had come out to touch her children. She gathered Myra up in her arms, 'It's all right, darling,' she said, 'Mummy's going to take you away from here.' And she walked off down the lane towards the farm.

After a few steps she turned and said coldly, 'I shall have to tell your mother, you realize that. What she does about it, of course, is her affair. But it is only fair to her as a mother to know what has been going on.' As she looked at the grave, square face in front of her, it did, indeed, seem difficult to think that anything terrible had been going on; but, then, what could not ignorance and poverty (Mr Tuffield was a very unsuccessful farmer, otherwise they would not take summer boarders) do in the way of corruption? If only the girl were to make one little graceful gesture of appeal, to recall for one moment that sense of wonder she had seemed to show in Mrs Longmore's presence, it might have been possible to relent (and Mrs

Longmore ached to relent, for somehow she felt that she was heading for all sorts of ridiculous, even incommoding behaviour), but the stocky little figure stood quite stiff and stubborn – how easily the wrong sort of environment could harden even children! Mrs Longmore turned away in anger at such stubbornness, such refusal to help herself, or indeed, oneself in a dilemma that threatened absurdity. She set off with Myra to announce to Mrs Tuffield their intention of leaving: she would go to nearby Felixstowe, they knew her there at the Grand; it was hardly exciting, but the children enjoyed the beach, and she could wear something a little bit frivolous in the evening now and again which would be amusing. But, before she left, it would give her a real satisfaction to bring home to Mrs Tuffield how little, for all her chapel going and her cleaning of the house, she had kept clean her children's minds.

The indistinguishables ran before Mrs Longmore in a chirping, clucking, grunting quartet; out of their general noise, their mother, who understood them very well, learned that the eldest had deserted her charges, had done something 'rude', and above all, involved 'the lady'. Mrs Tuffield was on the scene before Mrs Longmore had turned the corner out of sight of the corruption, indeed before the corrupt girl had been able to do more than put on her petticoat. Mrs Tuffield walked straight past the elegant though anxious figure of Mrs Longmore, and hit her little daughter twice very hard across the head. The girl cowered down into the ditch by the bank. 'That's no good cruddlin' down there,' her mother said. 'You've got a proper good few things to hear, you bad, gatless little girl. Leaving Violet and them to play around and leaving the linen when I'm everlastin' working to keep things together.'

Mrs Longmore said, 'I'm afraid it's not just that, Mrs Tuffield. If only it *were* just that. After all, all work and no play . . .' She left Mrs Tuffield to finish the proverb, which she had only produced as a means of communicating with the semi-literate.

'I'm afraid that's just what it *is* for her, ma'am. *All* work. That's what the Almighty made for her. That's been the trouble, as I doubted it would – all that crubble and playin' 'em air games. That's all right for the gentry, but that's not for 'er.' She roughly pulled her daughter up from the ditch and hit her again. 'Wicked little thing,' she said, 'that'll be lucky if the Devil don't take you.'

'Oh, don't!' Mrs Longmore cried. 'What she did was bad. But she wants talking to, not hitting.'

'Ah, talking, she'll get a mobbin' all right. And more 'an that. She'll get a bastin'. A real bum bastin' from her father. That's what you'll get, my girl. 'Es angry enough, the wheat being crackly and that.'

Satisfied with having contradicted Mrs Longmore and sufficiently frightened her daughter, she now felt ready to ask what had happened. 'What's she done then, ma'am?'

'She took Myra's clothes off.'

'What she want to do that for?'

Mrs Longmore, faced by the question, felt more sure of her sophisticated, sinister fears, yet quite unable to put them into clear words. Woman to woman, it should have been so easy, but there were certain crudities. . . . Mrs Tuffield grew impatient with waiting for an explanation, she turned to her daughter. 'What you want to do that for? Muckin' them up! and where's your bonnet?' Myra immediately began to cry loudly for her adorable ribbons, but Mrs Longmore appeased her growing guilt by a certain stylish lavishness about straw hats.

'My dear Myra! You're not too young to acquire some sense of proportion. Never fuss about lost possessions. It has a mean look.'

'Well, you'll not get another bonnet,' Mrs Tuffield was saying to *her* daughter. She felt no such sense of lavishness. 'That went in the water to keep company with 'ers,' the girl explained.

'Water, what water?'

'In Knapp's meadow hinder.'

'What you go there for? What you *done* all this for?'

'I wanted to do something different.' The girl looked towards Mrs Longmore in hope. But Mrs Tuffield was in full spate before anyone could intervene.

'Different! You'll be different along of when your

father's finished with you. You'll be as God made you, you scringin' little thing.'

'Oh, don't talk to her like that, Mrs Tuffield,' Mrs Longmore cried. 'I know she's done wrong. But she *can* be good. She can be quite a special little thing when she likes.'

'Special! There's nothing special about 'er! Nor about none of us, ma'am. God put 'er here to work for others. That's what's she's to do. Special!' Such a rage against Mrs Longmore and her foolish wicked ways seized Mrs Tuffield that she turned away from her for fear she should lose control and strike her. She concentrated on her daughter. '*You* wanted to be different! Well, you're nothin'. And you always will be.' With each word she pulled the girl roughly by the arm.

'Poor little thing! You'll dislocate her shoulder or something. Let her put her dress on at least.'

'She won't need no dress where she's going, and that's bed. And if I were you, ma'am, I'd send that one to the same place. She's old enough to know better than what she's done.'

'Well, you're *not* . . .' Mrs Longmore began when she detected a shockingly shrill note in her own voice. She started again in her quietest, most reasonable tones. 'I've no wish to quarrel, Mrs Tuffield. How you manage your children is your affair. But it is evident that I can't have my children here when things like this can happen. We shall leave tomorrow. I know that we spoke of a four-week stay, and, of course, you'll receive the full four weeks' money.' If Mrs Longmore's 'of course' had expected any disclaimer from the farmer's wife, it misfired, for she made no reply at all, but dragging the eldest girl by the arm and driving the rest of her brood before her with her apron, she made off back to the farm. The eldest Tuffield girl looked back once; she had shed no tears, only she was shivering a little; Mrs Longmore began to smile a little smile of comfort, but something in the girl's eyes froze the smile and she turned instead to call to Derek, who had had a spiffing ride.

It was late – about nine – when Mrs Longmore heard Mr Tuffield come in. There was something in his step that suggested that he was what Mrs Tuffield had apologized for on their first evening as 'a bit foggy'. At the time she had wondered whether it was his 'fogginess' that drove Mrs Tuffield to the chapel or Mrs Tuffield's grimness that drove him to the local inn. But the rector and his wife, whom she had visited that afternoon to telephone to the Grand Hotel at Felixstowe and to order a taxicab to take them to Woodbridge Station, had said that it was six of one and half a dozen of the other. Such charming people – the rector and his wife – not at all old-fashioned; she had the prettiest collection of Hokusais and he was most interested in Maeterlinck. They had been always shocked, it appeared, that Hypatia Clark (a Church of England clergyman's wife) should have boarded at the Tuffields' at all – the Tuffield reputation in the village was a terrible one. It was just as well that it had all come to a head and that they were leaving. But the whole incident had completely exhausted Mrs Longmore – in this heat! She was only so happy, having got Myra and Derek to bed, to relax on the little plush sofa in the parlour.

But her relaxation was not to be complete. For, first, Mr Tuffield was shouting and lurching up the stairs; and then, suddenly, there were screams so loud and terrible that Mrs Longmore thought that all she had imagined about fear (that emotion which had ruined her childhood) had indeed been but a child's imagining, and that only now did she know what real terror might be. She walked up and down the stuffy little parlour in an agony of hatred and disgust – for the wicked man, for the vile cruelty of an ignorant, squalid world, for herself. She went to the door once or twice with the intention of intervening, but physical fear drove her back to the sofa each time. Finally she sat there, rigid, her forefingers pressed into her ears, feeling disgusted and infinitely ridiculous. But she could still hear the screams. At last they died away.

It was about ten minutes later that someone knocked on the parlour door. She could not find any words in her alarm; but the door opened all the same, and there stood Mr Tuffield. Mrs Longmore thought if he were more like a gipsy now, a Heathcliff of a man, one could perhaps find some meaning in his violence, but as it was his flashing black eyes were set in a little dried-up, pursed-mouthed toad's face. She looked away from him in disgust.

'Mrs Tuffield says you're leavin', ma'am. I'm sorry for that, I'm sure.'

'There's nothing to discuss about it, thank you, Mr Tuffield.'

'Ah, but there is ma'am. If it's that girl that's been botherin' you, that won't bother you no more. That weren't only you that complained, I 'ad my neighbour Snushall laughin' at me on account of 'er. I've bum basted 'er proper.'

'Please, Mr Tuffield, I don't want to hear about it. It's all wrong to beat a child like that. Unfortunately she's your child and I can do nothing about it.'

He seemed to her to grin. 'That's right, ma'am,' he said.

'But I can and do tell you to get out of this room.'

Something malicious came into his eyes as he looked at the lady. 'Till the blood run,' he said, and went out of the parlour, closing the door quietly behind him.

All that evening Mrs Longmore debated what she could do. She heard Mr and Mrs Tuffield go up to their room. She heard their snoring. Finally, exhausted, she went upstairs herself. Derek in his little cupboard of a room was fast asleep. In the room they shared, Myra in a cot, was turning fretfully. Mrs Longmore put on her white silk nightgown, unloosed her long black hair and sat brushing it before the little stained dressing-table mirror. Then suddenly she thought of something. She opened one of the trunks she had so painfully packed in the afternoon, and rummaging at the side, pulled out a long lemon-coloured piece of tulle. She had worn it one evening round her head, to the little Tuffield girl's great wonder. Now, tiptoeing across the corridor, she entered the Tuffield children's bedroom. She had not somehow expected to find them all sleeping in one large bed with the eldest girl lying on her stomach in the middle. She was moaning still, but it seemed, in her sleep. Mrs Longmore bent down and placed the chiffon scarf on the hump which she guessed to be the little girl's feet. She was glad to get out of the stuffy, ill-smelling room. It was little enough she had done, God knew, but it was something.

1. Leavetaking

Sylvia Calvert hated being the centre of any public show; it made her face hot with blushing and she always felt she wanted to go somewhere. But on an occasion like this when she knew everybody, there was no reason‧ to feel shy. So she had made up her mind to be made a fuss of for once in her life. She had sent Arthur down to his club so that he shouldn't spoil things for her by monopolizing the occasion or giving way to a lot of false sentiment. It's only the fakes that carry on in public. Not that Sylvia had to restrain any strong emotions herself at leaving Palmeira Court or parting from its residents. She'd left so many other hotels, known too many people in her life to get upset by such things now. Keep your feelings for your own flesh and blood was what she had come more and more to think. And even then the Calverts were not a sloppy family – Arthur's nonsense these days was just old age. When the boys were going back from leave in the war, she'd never done more than chaff them a bit. She'd say, 'Remember me to Hitler when you put him up against the wall.' To Harold who spent his war at a desk! Or, 'Think of my pillow slips next time, Len, with that fancy hair cream of yours.' Len was quite struck on his own good looks. And Harold would reply, 'A fond farewell, people all,' and Len, 'I'll be back again like a bad penny, Mum.' Only he didn't come back. So there was more to fuss about in life than leaving the place you've worked at.

Yet this evening was an occasion; and she hadn't had so many of those in her life. She had put on her black velvet dress and her long ear-rings, and the day before she'd had a perm and a blue rinse. She had thought to sit back and enjoy being the centre of attention for one evening. And now they had chosen old Miss Hutton of all people to deliver the farewell speech. And not only did Miss Hutton spit when she spoke so that little beads of moisture settled on Sylvia's dress, but she had a marked hump. A hump that thrust whiffs of camphor at Sylvia each time the old girl jerked nervously forward into a new sentence of her speech. Sylvia hadn't let other people touch her except to shake hands for years – oh, of course, she'd kissed the children and grandchildren when they were kids, but Judy, her youngest grandchild, was already seventeen – yet who knew with these humps whether you could always avoid touch? That and the spit. There was no sense in getting steamed up about it. That was the first rule the doctor had given her – avoid all fuss, relax. So, surprising herself by admiring her own plump white arm as it showed through the slashed black velvet sleeve, she took a sip of gin and it, and then relaxed with a puff of her cigarette. And the doctor's orders worked too: for exhaling slowly, she so put Miss Hutton off the end of her speech with a cloud of tobacco smoke that she had to smile to herself at the old girl's startled expression. The smile turned to suppressed laughter and that, giving rise in turn to a rumble in her tummy, made her by association feel comfy and contented as though she had had a rich meal.

'I know you'll forgive me,' Miss Hutton was saying, 'if I recall my own retirement. We old people become very egotistical. But on that occasion I said to my girls "Always make time your slave, never let it be your master". And so, dear Mrs Calvert,' Miss Hutton was ending, 'just in case it may seem to you that Time has caught up with *you* now that you're retiring, we've decided to give you an electric clock. You won't have to be an early riser any longer for the rest of your life, you'll be able to ask for a late call. And we shall picture you, defying Time, lying snugly in bed when this clock strikes seven; just turning over and going to sleep again, knowing that you haven't got to worry about all the troublesome residents of Palmeira Court to whom you've been so very kind for so many years. And if when the clock strikes, you do think of us, don't remember all our little grumbles and grouses; just remember that you brought a lot of comfort to people, many of whom were old and most of whom were lonely.'

Crooked, grey and forbidding, she sat down, her hands

trembling a little from the strain of the forgotten pleasure of public address. Oh Lord! Sylvia thought, that's put the fat in the fire. She could see Mrs Streeter stiffen, and Charlie Webster, they were both under sixty and didn't think of themselves as lonely at all; Commander Anderson was sunk in gloom so that when he gave one of those involuntary groans that his arthritic pains forced from him he seemed to be protesting at Miss Hutton's exposure of his loneliness; and little Mrs Tyler, who might soon have to go to an old people's home because she could no longer care for herself, had shrunk down behind one of the vast leather armchairs as though Miss Hutton's words might summon the dreaded uniformed attendants to take her away.

'Thank you very much indeed,' Sylvia said loudly. If it hadn't been for the need to repair Miss Hutton's gaffe, she wouldn't have been able to speak above a whisper. She never could in public; at her wedding breakfast she couldn't even get 'Cheerio' out so as anyone could hear. 'I knew my own dial had got a bit battered,' she went on, encouraged by the firm tone of her own voice, 'but I didn't expect to have it replaced quite so soon.' Seeing that somewere puzzled by her joke and others disapproved of it, she subsided into a whisper, 'But thank you very much all the same.' She buried her nose in her now empty glass.

Miss Hutton began to explain the gift to her for all the world as though electric clocks had only just come on the market. As if Harold's house would not have all the latest equipment of every kind! But Sylvia listened quietly, for the old girl didn't have so much opportunity to hand it down nowadays. Then, as one after another the old dears came up to thank her for being 'so thoughtful', 'making just that little difference', 'bothering with an old man', 'always having a jolly word', she began to feel increasingly embarrassed, and finally impatient, even annoyed. Of course it was nice to know that she'd done her job properly and made them all comfortable, but this personal note. . . . She almost felt that she was being mocked. After all she'd never done more than her duty. But that was it, people were so insincere, they exaggerated everything. Well, whatever they felt she knew for certain that she'd have forgotten most of their names and all their faces within a few weeks. Embarrassed by all the fussing, she found herself studying her nails although she'd only just orange-sticked them, or staring over the shoulders of those who came up to her; anything to avoid looking at them. Old and lonely – well, of course, it was true, but so were most people, one or the other or both. It certainly did no good to talk about it. It wasn't doing her any good either to get all steamed up. Abruptly, so abruptly that she cut Mrs Dyer off in full gush of gratitude, Sylvia got up, mumbled a few inaudible words about tomorrow's tiring journey and walked out of the lounge. Perhaps it was her paste and emerald ear-rings, her newly blued hair and her black velvet dress, but she felt quite aloof from them all as she left them. She was no longer the manageress.

Upstairs in her small private sitting room in dressing gown and slippers she did not feel aloof at all, just weary and disappointed. She ought, of course, to have shown more pleasure, but she was impatient to begin her new life. She was always one to get on with what must be. Also the scene had somehow disappointed. What was it that she had expected when they first spoke of 'a presentation'? A picture flashed before her, from long ago – she couldn't exactly place it. Shy faces, comic ones, well known they were, peering, or rather 'peeking' round a door; and one of the figures coming forward very timidly, elbowed on by the others . . . the present – yes, to present a gift to a tall, fine-looking woman, majestic but not superior. Of course! It was Marie Dressler . . . and the others peeping timidly round the door were a whole lot of film comics, or rather 'characters' – Donald Meek and May Robson and Edna May Oliver and Zasu Pitts. A lot of old actors they'd been in that film honouring a famous star on her retirement. Marie Dressler had played the star. Oh well, she wouldn't have minded being Marie Dressler with *her* handsome looks and superb figure, and yet with no airs, just an old trouper as they called them. But that was how it should have been this evening – all the old things peeping round the door too shy to come in. Not that she wanted to queen it. Only that it would have been more of an occasion, more like a real presentation. But there you are, they've time and money enough on the films to make things real.

Sylvia was not, in fact, to leave Palmeira Court without people peeking round her sitting-room door. Three of them, to be exact. First – very shyly – Mr Martineau, retired from the building trade, with his own sitting room at the hotel, indeed with his own large comfortable house if his wife had not recently died, making housekeeping impossible. 'Oh, excuse me Mrs Calvert, I'm sure, I thought the Captain might be here.' Nice old thing he was, but lonely without his wife; you had to keep him at bay. And then it all came out, somewhat timidly, because Mr Martineau, having put away a nice little pile, didn't want to appear grasping. 'If it wasn't that I'm afraid the Captain's forgotten about it and I know you're off early tomorrow. . . .' Sylvia did not, in fact, blame him for wanting his money back, but when she learned the amount that Arthur had borrowed, she decided to make no immediate promises. Ninety pounds would be a large sum for them in retirement.

'I'll speak to Captain Calvert as soon as we're settled in at my son's.' She said nothing about future repayment, because she held in horror the making of false promises or the telling of lies.

The old man had hardly gone, mumbling apologies, when Pat Reynolds breezed in. Sylvia often thought of Pat as the kind of girl . . . well, not that she would have liked to have been herself, she would never have had the brains . . . but the girl that Iris would have been if she had lived. The same quiet good looks – dark hair, creamy skin – and the same easy, jolly, chaffing manner that Iris had shown even as a schoolgirl of fourteen. Pat was already chief staff supervisor with the people that made radio sets out at Arkley and she couldn't be much more than thirty. Sylvia only hoped she wasn't letting all her chances of marriage go by.

'Hullo, dear Mrs C. I didn't come to the Great Occasion. I couldn't face the Hutton on the soap box. I was definitely anti the clock anyway. So I brought you this. May you smell nice wherever you go.' She gave Sylvia a bottle of Chanel No. 5. 'By the way, not to worry about the twenty pounds. Any old time'll do. But I do think you could have asked me yourself, not sent the Cap. round instead.'

Sylvia tried to disguise her surprise, but Pat's present had softened her so that her emotions were near to the surface. 'Oh, it's too bad of him,' Pat exclaimed. 'I'll give him a piece of my mind when I see him. I like the old boy, but why couldn't he say he wanted it for himself? Not to worry, Mrs C, definitely not to worry. Just stop his pocket money from me, that's all.' She leaned towards Sylvia as she spoke; and Sylvia automatically turned her head away. Straightening up, Pat said, 'Well, cheerio Mrs C. Best of luck,' and was gone.

To have had her last talk with the only resident she really liked so spoiled brought Sylvia near to tears. And why had she to turn away like that? It would not have hurt her if the girl had kissed her. Yet that, too, was Arthur's fault, for if Pat had not suddenly pitied her so much, she would never have thought of kissing her. She wasn't a sloppy sort of a girl at all.

The culmination of these nasty surprises (not that, knowing Arthur, she could really say she was surprised) came when a few minutes later a knock on the door introduced Mrs Amherst. Luckily Sylvia's desk was open, the flap covered with old letters she had been sorting out earlier that evening, so that she immediately sat herself before it, only worrying that her dressing-gown might give her away. She would never do her correspondence in a dressing-gown, but how could the woman know that?

'Yes, Mrs Amherst, what can I do for you?' Pretending to be busy like that was something she could hardly remember in her life before, but she could sense disaster (they say women can foretell these things). She had decided over a year ago, when all the unpleasantness with Arthur happened, that relations between her and Mrs A should be strictly those of manageress and guest. Sylvia had been the wronged party, and had determined not to have anything out in the open, for being wronged means being an object of contempt.

Mrs Amherst's words scuttled round the room – sweet yet explosive. As though she had let fall a basin of loaf sugar on to the floor, Sylvia thought, and if there was one thing she hated it was sugar, even in tea or coffee. She tried not to look at the little woman's scrawny, grimacing face with its silly dabs of rouge on the cheeks; and when she realized that the hard, sugary words being poured at her were intended to melt and coat her with false intimacy, she tried resolutely not to hear. Some words, of course, got through – 'so appreciated all you've done . . . so busy we see nothing of you, sometimes felt I've not been a favourite . . . natural enough you should have them of course.'

Sylvia pressed her hands firmly on the desk flap to prevent herself from crying . . . on her last day, on her last day. She would have thanked God that she was going, if it weren't that she couldn't tell about the future. She drove the woman's words from her consciousness, but into the vacuum swelled other images and other voices. Arthur's hand, white and vein-knotted now that he was old, with freckly, yellow patches spreading each year on the loose skin, his hand scrabbling under a tight skirt. The Company's letter. 'Dear Mrs Calvert, It is with particular regret we have. . . . Of course all our sixteen hotels, we have no hesitation in saying that the Palmeira Court has under your management . . . and this at a time when the trade of sea-side hotels has seriously deteriorated' . . . scrabbling among all that scrag and bone, scrag end of mutton done up as lamb . . . 'letters from a resident . . . unfortunately only too certainly confirmed by inquiries among other guests . . . persistent talk, obscene language, sufficient in a visitor to justify giving notice, totally impossible in the husband of the manageress. . . .' She had been up to London to see the Company's secretary. 'We wouldn't show the letters of complaint to anyone else, Mrs Calvert. And even so I must insist on absolute secrecy.' . . . 'To be perfectly frank I can only excuse some of his habits in the belief that he must be getting senile, but that doesn't make it any more pleasant for us ladies, sincerely yours, Lois Amherst.' And finally the Company's decision –' must insist that he doesn't enter the public sitting rooms. . . .'

'I've sometimes wondered if I've offended you in some way, Mrs Calvert. I'm afraid perhaps that the Captain's making a fool of himself about me – it seems silly to talk about it even, but I wondered if you'd taken it a little more seriously than I ever did. I soon put him in his place, you know.' Sylvia's legs started to shake beneath the desk, soon the trembling would seize her whole body. I'm too fat now to disguise it, she thought, the bitch is bound to notice. I must throw her out of the room, fell her with a blow, anything to get rid of the woman before my body betrays me.

'You opened your legs out to his hands,' she said, 'I saw.' She felt a hot flush spreading up her neck; she knew that if she stood up she would fall. One of her giddy spells. This sort of scene was just what the doctor had warned her against. Her anxiety drove her amazement at what she had said from her mind, but Mrs Amherst's appalled expression recalled her.

When the sugar poured forth again, it cracked and clattered against Sylvia's plump body like hail. Mrs Amherst intended to freeze, but her agitation broke her attempted dignity up into an absurd spluttering.

'Filthy! How could you? Captain indeed! Common cockney! I've always said, never touch pitch.' With effort she controlled herself to add demurely, like a small girl giving evidence, 'He's old enough to be my father.'

It was quite true, Sylvia decided; for all her yellow chicken-skinned neck, she could be no more than fifty. How could he have let himself stroke such a scrawn? She remembered the feel of his hand in tenderness upon her own body in their early married days. And now the same hand had itched after that rubbish. And the woman, too, must have wanted it pretty badly at fifty, to encourage a man of seventy. Realizing the contradictory conclusion of her thoughts, Sylvia gave a loud, scornful laugh.

'There's nothing funny about it, Mrs Calvert, let me assure you of that. I felt sorry for you at the time but I can see I needn't have wasted my pity. Let me tell you'll be very lucky if that dirty old man doesn't land in the courts. Some young girl, I expect. That was why I made my complaint. Not for myself, but in case some young girl should suffer.'

Mrs Amherst stopped, realizing with alarm the involuntary revelation to which her anger had driven her; but Sylvia showed no sign of comprehension. Although she would dearly have loved to rub the woman's face in the filth of her behaviour, the whole subject carried too much humiliation for herself and Arthur; best let it die. 'I've no doubt at all,' Mrs Amherst, emboldened by the silence, went on, 'that that's really why you're going. Ritson Hotels have reached the limit of their patience. He's been in the public rooms again. I've noticed it. High blood pressure indeed! You're well enough to shout filth at me. You've been dismissed. That's the truth of it, isn't it?'

Sylvia's flushed excitement died away into a leaden despair at the hopelessness of trying to control Arthur. She had made him promise solemnly not to speak of her illness. People only have contempt for sick folk.

'Who told you I had high blood pressure?' she said.

'Your precious husband.'

'Well, I'm afraid Arthur wasn't telling the truth.'

There were times when you had to lie outright; and, as for Arthur, he deserved to be made the scapegoat.

'So I can see. "Don't worry my missus with it", indeed. A very good way of wriggling out of paying what he owed. Well, I want my twenty pounds back.'

It was a big sum to repay on the spot, what with the expense of moving and that, but Sylvia pulled out her cheque-book from its pigeon-hole in the desk and wrote out the cheque.

'I'm surprised you lent your money to a dirty old man,' she said, as she handed it over.

'Well,' Mrs Amherst hesitated, 'I suppose I felt I owed him . . .' She stopped in mid-sentence. Sylvia looked her straight in the eyes – china blue they were like a silly doll's, whites speckled with blood.

'Captain Calvert rose from the ranks,' she said, 'and gave his health for his country. We all owe something to men like him.' She felt at once proud as though she were standing on a platform as 'God Save the King' was being played, and also ashamed, because these were things not to be boasted of. 'And now, come on, get out,' she said. And Mrs Amherst went.

Sylvia decided to calm herself by reading through the letters on the desk. It was the Company's desk and whatever happened she musn't leave any personal letters behind for the new manageress to find. Not that there would be anything very intimate or that she would see the new manageress again; but if you let strangers meddle with your personal things, you put yourself in their power.

She could not forbear reading Harold's letter again, although she had read between the lines so many times now, and anyhow there was nothing to be done about it, they were committed.

DEAR MOTHER,

This letter is just to welcome you and Dad to 'The Sycamores'. You will find it very different here from 529 Enright Avenue. To a degree both Beth and I were unwilling to move from the old house. It was so much what we had hoped for when we came to the New Town – a spacious road, a house modern and yet neighbourly. We were also, of course, sorry to leave Craighill. It was, you know, the first district of Carshall to be completed after the Town Centre. And the first to have its own shopping centre and community hall. And we were the first residents. But the world can't exist on pioneer sentimentality. Especially the England of Mac the Knife (don't breathe these revolutionary sentiments to Dad); the whole country seems to be dying of a surfeit of nostalgia. But you'll hear H. C. on that theme when you come to live here: the children blow a whistle now for what they call TFFTST (Time for Father to Stop Talking!) So – you have been warned!

Anyhow I think you'll like Melling. It's on the far side of Carshall away from the trunk road; almost into the country, but, of course, facing towards the town. 'The Sycamores' is a good modern house – E. and S. T. Burman White Ltd, the people who did the new kiosks on Brighton front that were illustrated in the *Guardian* a month or two back – with its own two acres of garden – but, of course, not isolated; it conforms to the Carshall neighbourhood principles. Beth and I were very hesitant about buying a fully detached house like this (I mean not in a street); it went all against our principles. The last thing Beth wanted was to be taken off her essential work here on committees and on the bench by houseproudery (a Family word – used by the children with great contempt!) But automation solved that problem. And now Death has solved it for us altogether. But about Beth's death I can't write; perhaps I may talk about it when you're living here or again I may not be able to. I'll only just repeat what I said in my last letter, that one of Beth's last hopes was that you would move in here sometime. We had no idea of this blood pressure of yours then. So you see, you don't have to worry about 'intrusion' (quote yours of the 4th December); Beth wanted it.

The truth is that the house has been a bit big for us from the start. I'll feel much less conscience with you and Dad here. Then, too, children grow up and out of the Family world; though you'll find us a closely knit group of individuals (the best sort of society, in my humble opinion). You'll have your own big bed-sitting-room and your own things. In fact (if you want it that way, but I know you won't), you can just think of 'The Sycamores' as a hotel without the responsibilities.

Truth to tell it's a most unsuitably opulent residence for the headmaster of the local secondary modern, as I am sure any worthy snoopers, who don't know about my text-book income, think. You're probably laughing and saying what's he fussing about having a nice house for, anyway; but the New Town and what it stands for were the centre of all Beth and I believed in, and now she's dead, it's all I have.

That sounds a bit harsh about the children. And, of course, they've been fine and we have grand times together – it's a mad house I warn you. But as Ray has just said, 'Tell Gran it's just the first certifying that hurts, after that it's all over.' Mark's going through a phase of adolescent rebellion – C.N.D. and so on – I'm glad to say. Judy's school friends incline towards the 'awfully county, don't-chyaknow' which gets me down at times. Having her Gran here will help her a lot, I'm sure.

About Dad. Don't worry. I didn't mean to sound childish. I've come to terms with all that years ago. It's not like when we were kids. Beth taught me. She said if your mother can put up with him, it's not for you to grumble. Of course, he's welcome here. I only meant to read the Riot Act in case. I have got a responsible position here and I can't have him trading on it. But as you say the years have sobered him down. Tell him from me the

43

Cranstons (some very nice friends we've made in Melling) hope to have him as a regular fourth at bridge – they're just a bit scared their bridge won't be good enough for him. And, of course, it won't be. Has anybody ever been quite good enough for the old man? But enough of that.

Sylvia put down the letter with the others, and, gathering them into a bundle, took them to her bedroom to pack in the last-minute suitcase. Then she undressed and got into bed. Harold was so clever. It was difficult to know. She'd never been close to Beth or him for that matter, or the children. And as to Arthur and Harold! Well that was how life went. Of the two subjects on her mind she really preferred to let Mrs Amherst come to the surface.

The old bitch had felt ashamed of what she'd done, but you'd need a sensitive measure to tell how much her shame cancelled out her spiteful action. Sylvia had no such measure; she could only think that she need never see the woman again. There was no point in bearing grudges, life was too short. Yet it was lucky that she was on pills, she thought as she took one, for Arthur's behaviour was enough to bring anything on. Not only to have told the old cow that his wife was ill when he'd promised faithfully . . . no, that wasn't so blameworthy, after all in doing so he'd thought about sparing her; it showed the doctor's remarks hadn't gone completely over his head, it showed he still had some tenderness for her. Sylvia checked her thoughts; she'd been bitten too often not to know how unsafe were any sentimental feelings for Arthur. Anyhow she was disgusted with him, borrowing money from a woman who'd had him turned out of the public rooms. And then she remembered that she couldn't justify even this charge, because, of course, she'd never let him know that there'd been complaints against him. After forty odd years of marriage you can't let your husband be humiliated; she'd simply told him that Ritson's had made a rule 'no staff in the public lounges', and had kept out of them herself to give the lie colour. And so he'd never been taught his lesson, and no one could blame him for not learning it. She had to laugh again to think what a muddle life could be – you do the right thing or try to, and it only leads to worse. 'I don't know,' she said aloud in the nearest to a Midlands accent she could get, 'I really don't know.' The quotation from her favourite character old Mrs Harker in her favourite tele show 'Down Our Way' made her as usual feel warm and relaxed. It was sad in a way how little you *could* know in a busy life, but repeating the tag in Mrs Harker's comic voice somehow made it seem all right, something everyone felt. You could stretch your legs, scratch where it itched, and go to sleep.

She was woken from her sleep by his impossible singing at an impossibly late hour. Another wife might have immediately thought – drink; but that, thank God, she never had to fear, with *his* lungs and heart, smoke and drink had been almost strangers for the last thirty or more years. Just five a day and two half pints or one whisky – that was the complete limit. This enforced abstention always made her feel lenient towards him, for everyone has a right to a good time at least if he can get it. Arthur's singing, however, had no such excuse; it was just a complete lack of consideration for anyone but himself. She pretended to be asleep. He was singing one of his old favourites, and, angry though she was with him, she wanted to hear it to the end, for it was one of those old songs that came home to you – the words were so true.

> 'It'll be just the same,
> All the same,
> A hundred years from now.
> No use a-worrying,
> No use a-flurrying,
> No use a-kicking up a row,
> You won't be here,
> I shan't be here,
> When the hundred years are done,
> But somebody else will be right in the cart
> And the world will still go on.'

Well, that was true enough, there was always someone in the cart and there always would be. She ought to have it all out with Arthur here and now, not let him get away with it; but what would be the good? I'll be all the same a hundred years from now. The same rows leading up the same blind alleys. The doctor had said avoid worry; and Pat Reynolds, 'not to worry, Mrs C'; and the song, 'no use a-worrying'. And she was so sleepy and warm.

And then Arthur farted twice very loudly. He said automatically 'Pardon!'

'Oh, for God's sake, Arthur, get into your bed.'

'I said "pardon", didn't I?'

'Pardon! You always say "pardon" and then think everybody'll forgive and forget what you've done. Like a spoilt child.'

'God Almighty! What's all this about?'

'Nothing. Go on, get to bed. We've got a tiring journey ahead of us tomorrow.'

'And a nice one, I can see, if you're going to use that martyred tone all the way. I go out to the club on a bloody awful wet night because you want to have your little presentation to yourself and this is all the thanks I get. God knows, I try to do everything I can for you . . .'

'You don't have to do anything for me, Arthur, except not to deceive me and tell lies. You know you have only to come to me if you want money. That I'll always do my best to make your pension go further. Goodness knows I scrimp and save as it is. But to go to strangers and tell lies about it . . .'

'What do you mean "lies"?'

'You told Pat Reynolds the money was for me.'

'Oh, so that ruddy cow's come mooing to you, has she? I thought she was supposed to be so fond of you. A nice way to show her feeling for an invalid . . .'

'Arthur, I will *not* have you telling people that I'm an invalid. Not when we get to Harold's. Do you understand that?'

'Who the hell's been telling people? Who the hell's interested for that matter? You've got a damned sight too self-centred here, Sylvia – let me tell you that. People at Carshall won't care whether Mrs Arthur Calvert has high blood pressure or not. You'd better get that into your head.'

Sylvia kept her eyes closed as she talked with Arthur. Now she guessed that this was goading him to fury, for he came and stood over her.

'Are you bloody well listening?' he shouted.

'Yes, Arthur, I should think the whole hotel could hear you now.' But she didn't open her eyes; she couldn't bear to see his face with its familiar distortion of rage.

'Damn the hotel! We've slaved ourselves to the bone for them. We don't owe *them* anything!'

Sylvia burst out into laughter. 'You owe Pat twenty pounds and old Martineau fifty and heaven knows what beside that I don't know of.'

His tone changed. 'Honest to God, Sylvia, that's all there is. Anyway Martineau's loan was between two gentlemen. I don't know how the bleeder has the cheek . . .' He sounded aggrieved.

'Oh, Arthur. I've just paid Mrs Amherst her twenty pounds.'

'All right, so you know everything. What the hell's it got to do with you, anyway? They're my debts and I'll settle them. I don't know what you wanted to pay old mother Amherst for. She's got plenty enough in alimony. She could wait. Anyhow I only borrowed the money so that you wouldn't be worried with a lot of small bills. All this moving costs more than you think.'

'Arthur, don't be childish. You've had nothing to do with the moving, as you know. You didn't even pack your own clothes. Go on to bed. I'm tired.'

'*You're* tired.' His voice was so violent in tone now that she wondered if he *had* perhaps taken a drink too many. She felt his finger nails tightening into the flesh of her arm. 'You ruddy cow. I wish to God I'd never seen you.'

As always he was obviously ashamed of his sudden brutality, for through half-closed eyes she watched his shadowy form slink away in the dim light to his own divan on the other side of the large room. She remembered a jackal, or a hyena was it? In some travel thing on tele. How easily Arthur could be hunted, she thought, but instead of feeling protective towards him, the idea of his cowardly slinking away from pursuit filled her with disgust. She snuggled into the mattress to shut out such silly fancies. From the other side of the room she could hear the terrible wheezing and groaning of one of his coughing fits. As she laid her head back on the pillow suddenly the black emptiness before her closed eyes turned red and wheeled round twice. The giddy spells frightened her more at night or when her eyes were closed, for then she was swung helplessly out into a void; whereas by day objects familiar to her, however much they reeled and danced, remained things known.

A couple of crocks the pair of us, wasting our little bit of breath in stale rows.

She felt a welcome cosiness when a few minutes later he said in his chatting voice, out of the darkness, 'Another accident at Rushman's corner. Young chap on a cycle thrown off the esplanade in that bloody great gale. Broke his hip, poor blighter.' She clicked her tongue against her teeth in compassionate disgust.

'The council ought to be ashamed,' her voice found the same chatting level. 'Accidents year after year!'

'Break your bloody neck before they'd spend their precious money. They're all the same. "Write to the Ministry" old Harry Leighton said to me at last year's dinner, "tell them your colonel says that the country should do better by the men who fought for her!" Write to the Ministry! Bloody good that would do. "The Minister has instructed me to inform you . . ." Inform my arse.'

'I read the other day that they're going to raise the war pensions.'

'Ah, you read. If you believe all you read . . .' and his voice subsided into wheezes and groans.

'Well, I expect if we get a new government they will.'

'Governments! What do they care about us? We don't belong to the great future. We're not teenagers. We only stopped them on the Marne that's all. We ought to be bloody dead.'

'The young ones wouldn't have an England if it hadn't been for the tommies like you, Arthur.'

But she wanted to go to sleep, or at any rate sink into the warmth and forget. In the ordinary way she would have worried herself into sleep with the next day's little frets – telling Concepcion not to put toast on the table until it was asked for, persuading old Birdie to deal with the mess in poor Mrs Tyler's room, getting on to young Pablo about that back-door lock, blowing Mayhews up about the tough beef . . . but tonight there was only a past you couldn't change and a future you couldn't see into. You needed all the warmth you could get to help you into sleep. It might have been some sort of transference of thought – it does happen, especially with people who are close, and Arthur and herself were close, whatever the bitterness, just through forty odd years spent together.

'You're not to worry, Sylvia. If it doesn't work out at Harold's, we can always go elsewhere. We're not tied.'

It wasn't true, of course: they were tied, they couldn't afford to refuse Harold's offer. But that was Arthur all over – black could be white as long as it made him feel more comfortable for the moment. He lived for the moment. The warmth of her cheeks gave her warning. I musn't get worked up and bitter. A man who's been badly gassed and become a life-long invalid couldn't do other than live in the moment. All the same she musn't encourage him to any uppishness at Harold's, and seventy-two years was a long life to have lived from minute to minute.

'Now, Arthur, you know you'll be happy at Harold's. You like the local there. And the buses are easy. Harold wrote that some Mr Cranston wants you to make up a four at bridge. They're only afraid they don't play a good enough game for you.'

'How do these blighters guess these things? They're bloody right every time.' But he was pleased. A few moments later: 'Now if we'd had Len to go to,' but before he had finished his sentence, he was asleep and snoring.

Len to go to! He knew as well as she did that Len would never have had a home of his own. Anyway, before Len had been killed, he and his dad had fought every time they met. And then, after the telegram came, for months Arthur had carried on about it in public – 'my youngest's given his life for his country. "If what Winnie says on the radio's right, Dad, I've got to go," he said. And he went' – until she had burned with shame. First of all, Len would never have listened to Churchill; Bing Time more likely. Then he hadn't gone, they'd come for him; and then, again, he'd been killed when he wanted to live, and surely that was enough without using him for a show. 'If we'd had Len to go to . . .' You couldn't be cosy with Arthur without his building it up into something false; he just hadn't got the truth in him, as the Bible said.

Stale rows leading nowhere; intimacy that did not signify. Yet in novels you read of family feuds that went deep enough to kill young love for ever, and that the brush of a hand roused tenderness enough to mend the fiercest quarrel. But books and life were not the same; there was no sense in expecting such a thing.

Arthur wore his greenish gaberdine raincoat over his sandy-coloured tweed jacket, his grey flannel trousers were always hitched so high, revealing his suspenders above his thick grey woollen socks. One thing he still did with patient care was to polish his light-brown leather brogues. He carried his ashplant and his old reddish sandy tweed cap. Sylvia was happy with her beige nylons and her black suede shoes. She was wearing her new dress and jacket of mulberry bouclé rayon with a bow at the neck and a black patent leather belt; her big black patent leather bag wouldn't stay shut; her hat was a darker, wine-red ruched ribbon. Did the dress clash with the hat? She had never been sure since she had bought them. But they were both nice warm colours. Her beaver lamb coat was old now, but still serviceable.

She had woken to her usual overcrowded day of chores, and she had known a full five minutes of confusion as the day gradually changed into a whole diary of blank pages – her new life. This shifting, swirling prospect had left her quite fuddled, otherwise she would have taken better precautions to keep Arthur from talking to strangers on the train. It was indeed folly, her own, she realized even as she did it, to distract him from the sporting pages of the newspaper she had bought for him, by suggesting a move to the restaurant car.

First, of course, he would be bound to chaff the waiter about the food – 'This chicken must have crossed the road a bloody few times.' 'This must be the cheese that beat the Derby favourite by a short head in '31', and so on. The waiter's laugh, she expected, would grow more and more hollow, as Arthur's chaffing grew louder and more condescending. But all this she was prepared for. What she hadn't bargained for were Mr and Mrs Lionel G. Hoppner who sat down opposite them at the table. Mr Hoppner looked at the menu and said, 'May I make so bold as to ask what you folks advise?' And Mrs Hoppner added, with a smile that banished any suggestions of egotism, 'We don't care too much for fried foods.' After that they were all four soon on naming terms. When Sylvia knew that they were Americans she heaved a sigh of relief. Lots of people didn't like Americans; most of the retired people who were residents in the many hotels she had worked in were anti-American – but then the poor old things were jealous, they couldn't afford to travel or keep young like American visitors do. No, so long as no questions of their children's diet or fear of being cheated over tips were involved, Americans were perfect guests. Of course, sometimes, they talked too much when you were busy supervising the bed-making in the morning or doing the flowers, for example. But still nobody had to listen to them; they were quite content if you put on an interested face. And at this moment Sylvia thanked God that the Hoppners were Americans, for only Americans would feel free enough to silence Arthur. Everything indeed looked promising.

'We're certainly delighted with the improvement in British services. There seems to be a new spirit abroad in this country since we were here in the fall of '58. On that vacation Mrs Hoppner coined a new phrase, "If it's British, it's likely to be off." Or rather I think your cockneys say "awf".'

'Now, for pity's sake, Lionel, don't get going on one of your awful burlesques' she put her hand on her husband's. 'Save it for the Bob Hope Show, darling.' They smiled at each other in happy content. 'No, but what Lionel says is true you know. Something has happened to Britain. Now, when we were here in '58, if you wanted room service you had to . . .' And so they went on: each tried to out-talk the other, yet each had obviously learnt over the years how to give the other a chance. Sylvia only feared that people in the carriage might be staring at such a noisy table, but still so long as Arthur was not the centre of the attention . . . she felt free to look at what interested her – the badly cleaned cutlery, the stained table-cloth, the slopped soup plates.

It was Mrs Hoppner's meat that set Arthur talking. 'That muck's no good to you. You asked for it rare, didn't you? Not that charred rubbish. Waiter! Waiter! The lady asked to have her beef underdone. Yes, I know she said "rare", but that happens to be what Americans call "underdone", and the sooner our famous British Railways get wise to the modern world a little, the sooner we British taxpayers may find ourselves out of the red.'

Despite Mrs Hoppner's protests, her beef was taken away; and, indeed, to Sylvia's surprise she seemed pleased rather than annoyed at Arthur's fussing.

'Why, thank you, sir, you're very kind.'

'It's a pleasure, my dear lady, a pleasure.' After that he got going on slang. It was one of his favourite topics. 'I'm a cockney, born within the sound of Bow Bells. Now I bet if I was to say that your trouble and strife was well worth another butcher's hook, you'd think I was off my chump, wouldn't you?' Mr Hoppner said, no, he was familiar with those phrases and he translated the compliment to his wife who said,

'Well, butcher's hook is certainly a strange kind of compliment.'

Encouraged, Arthur told them of 'apples and pears', 'pot and pan', 'plates of meat' and so on. Sylvia's muscles grew more tense, her smile more fixed. She dreaded, as always, that some genuine cockney might chime in who was really fluent in rhyming slang; and more absurdly that Arthur's birth certificate would suddenly be flourished before the company – 'Arthur Calvert: Date of Birth July 7th 1888. Place of Birth: Southampton.' And then she imagined Bow Bells would ring mockingly as they slunk away – like in a tele-play.

But, of course, it didn't matter really. Mr and Mrs Hoppner were smiling away, as though they'd been given a complimentary ticket to a Punch and Judy show. Some people at the table across the gangway had been brought into the audience by Arthur's showmanship and carrying tones. Indeed Sylvia heard a man's voice whispering loudly to the Hoppners, 'You may not realize it, but you're getting a private view of the genuine old England in our friend here.'

Sylvia could not bear to look up to identify this patronizing voice; but she told herself that if Arthur didn't mind being treated like a performing seal, there was no reason for her to be embarrassed.

And then suddenly of course he did mind. Whether it was Mr Hoppner's 'Could you just give us a few moments, old timer, while we order our dessert?' or whether it was Mrs Hoppner saying could he speak a little softer, she guessed it must be this noisy railroad, but her head ... anyhow Sylvia could tell from the tone of Arthur's voice that he was working towards a row. 'The best thing, I may say, apart from your pretty women, that has come out of God's own country has been your slang.' He smiled down the gangway at the English passengers. Sylvia pretended to be looking for her handkerchief in her handbag. He gave the Hoppners a number of examples of their national slang that particularly pleased him such as, 'Baby, you're all wet'. Mr Hoppner remarked that he had not heard some of the expressions since he was in knee pants. Mrs Hoppner added that she guessed that they came from way before *her* time. Arthur again winked at the English party across the gangway and said, 'Sez you.' For a moment Mrs Hoppner froze into silence. Sylvia fixed her attenton on the countryside passing outside the carriage window.

'Look how the river's swollen, Arthur,' and 'Four weeks to Christmas and they're lifting the beet.'

In this Arthur saw only a fresh opening to draw the Hoppners back into the conversation.

'My missus was country born and bred. You want to go to her if you like the up in the morning early lark. Give me the good old London pavements.' Mrs Hoppner received the information with a cold smile and a little bow, but Mr Hoppner, not wishing perhaps to include Sylvia in any snubbing, said,

'I certainly would like to see more of the English countryside. Mrs Hoppner and I usually visit at Scarborough, Yorkshire, where she has a cousin; but otherwise London about does it all for us. What part of the country are you from?'

Sylvia told him, Suffolk, but added that she had not lived in the real country since she was a girl.

'No,' Arthur took it up, 'we've been too busy running the hotel industry of the country. We're the people who've been putting England on the tourist map. In fact, if you'd met us on any day before today, we'd have offered you free

53

board and lodging at the Ritz or the Savoy, whichever you preferred. And bob's your uncle. As it is you'll have to doss down at the Hilton. And like it! No, but seriously this is a big day for my wife. Her first day of freedom after running some of the finest seaside hotels in the country for longer than I'd like to say in front of her. And running them damned well too. I can say so, because she's done the major part of the work all the time. I'm very good at getting in the way.'

The Hoppners murmured their dissent. Sylvia could feel them thawing again. With luck they would all leave the table now without a row. She loosened her belt a little with her thumbs, but she did not dare to relax. If Arthur really got going he was bound to land them in some embarrassing lie or other.

'As a matter of fact, I've been a bit under the weather for some years, dicky lungs. The Huns had a spot of poison gas they wanted to get rid of in '17 and I took a basinful of it.' The Hoppners' murmur became reverent. 'The wife has got the business head. She saw the red light in time. We've got these Butlin people over here, you know. Holiday camps instead of hotels. Bloody awful things if you ask me. But nobody is asking me. Apparently today's public like them. Anyhow Mrs Calvert got out of the business just at the right time and at a very nice price.'

Sylvia intervened, to cut him short. 'I wasn't the proprietress really. I was the manageress.' He retreated at once into sulky silence, and even the Hoppners punished her insensitivity with close attention to their apple charlottes. She should have done it more tactfully, she knew; but better a sulky Arthur than one who made a public fool of himself. He would get over it, she thought, and buried herself in a copy of the local rag she'd brought to show Harold. There it was – a short paragraph announcing their departure from Eastsea. 'Mr and Mrs A. Culver leave Eastsea this week after fifteen years' residence in the town. Visitors to the Palmeira Court Hotel where Mrs Culver was for many years manageress will miss her friendly attentions. Mr Culver was a well-known and popular figure at local sporting events. We wish them happiness and good health in their retirement.'

She remembered that Arthur had not yet seen it and thought the reference might restore his good spirits. 'Look, dear.'

Reluctantly he put on his horn-rimmed spectacles.

'Culver? Who the hell's that?'

'It's a mistake, dear.'

'So I should bloody well think. I'll write them such a stinker they'll never get up again. Culver after all these years!'

'Oh, don't be silly, Arthur. We're not important people.'

'You'd sit down under any damned insults, I do really believe.' He was beginning to shout.

'Let's go back to the carriage, shall we, dear?' But they stayed, of course. He wanted his coffee and he wanted attention. He had crumpled the *Eastsea Advertiser* into a ball in his anger, so she turned to the *Daily Mail*. Answer to last week's puzzle; it is probably easier to answer the question by eliminating those whom you would *not* save. First, sorry for her, the Captain's wife will have to go overboard. She's fifty-five. Her children are all grown up. She's not particularly bright, she doesn't even get on very well with the Captain. In fact their relations if anything rock the boat. In any case she's had her life. Not so easy to decide with the men. And for the other women, they are all under thirty. If the ominous radio messages picked up by the *Dauntless* just before the explosion was correct, then those girls may be the only hope for the future survival of the human race ... No point in reading answers to puzzles you'd never seen, so she looked at the woman's page. There were two articles; how to plan your Christmas office party, and 'giving a new look to Santa'. In default of something better she was about to turn to the news pages when she heard Arthur say:

'I'd like to tell you a story that may interest you as an American, of something that happened to me near Poperinghe in the winter of seventeen/eighteen. Or are you like most of the younger generation, bored stiff with a war that took place before the flood?'

'Younger generation!' said Mrs Hoppner. 'This is certainly your day, Lionel.'

'I don't know about that, Alice, I wasn't even in first

grade when World War One ended. But yes, do go on, please. I respect and esteem the veterans of those faraway campaigns.'

Sylvia could see that he was wanting Arthur to acknowledge his teasing smile, but she could have told him that Arthur never noticed any chaffing but his own.

'I was acting major at the time and not acting too badly for an ex-ranker either, let me tell you. I'd just come back from Blighty leave after the spot of gas I told you about earlier. Look, here's the certificate of disability I still have to carry around with me.'

Mr and Mrs Hoppner examined the grubby paper with the attentive concentration Sylvia had seen from strangers so many hundreds of times. If only she could send the certificate to the cleaners with his suits, she thought. And 'have to carry around' anyway, who said he had to? Then ashamed of herself,

'Captain Calvert oughtn't to spend the winters in England with the bronchitis he gets, but there, you're a hero one minute and forgotten the next in this world.' Arthur was evidently pleased. He carefully replaced his certificate in his inside breast pocket.

'Ah well, we can't ask the public to have too long a memory. There's been a whole generation of new heroes since then. Mrs Calvert and I had the tragedy of losing our youngest in the last war.' But his little dark eyes were twinkling impatiently to get back to his story. 'Anyway, to cut a long story short, I was living like a gentleman for once back at brigade headquarters. The colonel sent for me. La-di-da sort of chap he was, all Eton and Oxford, but I got on all right with him. "Calvert," he said, "You're something of a diplomat. I want you to go over and represent the brigade at a dinner in the Yankee officers' mess." Mind you, that was no compliment to the Yanks. Catch that la-di-da lot sending a low fellow like me to dine with any of their own pals. However, I wasn't going to refuse the chance of a good blow-out, and orders is orders. So I went.'

Sylvia became conscious of a subdued restlessness on the part of Mrs Hoppner. She probably wanted to retire, yes, that was it. One lady can always tell that sort of thing about another. She wondered now how she could hurry Arthur on without angering him. But at least he'd reached the American mess. She had heard the story a hundred times, but of course he never told it in exactly the same form, which meant that she couldn't relax and be sure that there would be no offence.

'I shall never forget it. We had some awful thing called pumpkin pie. There was one chap turned to me and said, "Well, Major, I reckon, guess and calculate you never had a pumpkin pie before."' Arthur's imitation of an American accent was not good, yet to Sylvia's ear it had an embarrassingly grotesque echo of a voice she had heard only recently. Then she realized that Mr Hoppner was as restless as his wife. But Arthur was in full flow. '"I certainly never have," I said, "If you lads live on this stuff, the American Army'll soon be gone with the wind."'

'Pardon me,' Mr Hoppner interjected, 'that best seller didn't appear until around 1936.'

Arthur ignored the correction, 'He was some sort of brigadier and he didn't like it at all. He said, "It's one of the customary dishes of the United States, Major."' Sylvia had to laugh because Arthur sounded so like Mr Hoppner when he had been offended; but she tried to make amends.

'I think Mr and Mrs' she mumbled the name because it always worried her to say strangers' names in a public place, unless, of course, she was in charge of things, 'want to go, Arthur.'

'I guess we ought to get our check, honey.'

'Yes, if you will excuse us, sir.'

But Arthur wouldn't. 'No no, laddie. You can wait a few moments to hear the end of an old sweat's story. Well, as I was saying this brigadier blighter or whatever he was, you can never tell with Yank officers, had got right up on his high horse. But I've never been a respecter of persons. I believe in the old French saying "Toujours la tack". So I simply said very quietly, "Thank you very much for the information, sir. Now I understand why your poor blighters all march on parade as though they wanted to pump ship. It's the effect no doubt of the pump ship pie!" For not to be crude, that was what the filthy stuff looked like.'

Of all the hundred embarrassments the joke caused Sylvia, the uppermost was the thought that Arthur was getting senile, else he would never have made a feeble joke like that, even a year ago. Her second anxiety was lest Mrs Hoppner might feel that the joke made any reference to her present condition. But mercifully Mrs Hoppner, though still restless, looked quite blank; not so her husband, whose sallow cheeks had flushed with the pink of annoyance or embarrassment or probably of both. He clearly understood English slang a good deal better than his wife.

'Oh, Arthur, really.' But he did not hear.

'I will say that for your chaps, they all roared with laughter. They've got a great sense of humour, the Yanks. Second best to the English. But this brigadier bloke, of course, didn't like being laughed at by his own mob. So he turned on me sharp, "To what do you attribute your famous guards' parade order then, Major," he asked, "plum pudding?" Well, if there was to be any leg-pulling, I was going to be the one to do it. "No," I said, "the British army marches on their spotted dick." Of course they'd never heard of spotted dick so the joke fell flat. But to show there was no ill feeling I promised to send them one.'

'It's a sort of light suet pudding with raisins,' Sylvia explained. If he had to tell the story at least it should be understood.

'Oh, really?' Mrs Hoppner looked so unhappy Sylvia nearly said, 'You're excused.' Arthur was impatient.

'Yes, yes, yes, we don't want to listen to pages of old Mother Beeton's Cook Book. As soon as I got back to Brigade Headquarters I wired to my old aunt – Mrs Calvert and I hadn't then entered the holy state – and told her to send me one of her best spotted dicks. Of course parcels took a bit of time to travel then. We were fighting a war, you know. Anyway as soon as the thing arrived, I bunged it off to this brigadier at the American Headquarters – "With Major Calvert's compliments." Didn't hear anything for weeks. Then one day the colonel sent for me. "What's this?" he said, "Will you thank Major Calvert for the spotted dick? I guess we understand very well now how the British Army comes to march on its stomach. Another spotted dick or two and we'll be hard bellied enough to do the same." The damned thing had been travelling for weeks of course and then they'd eaten it cold. Anyway the long and short of it was, I wasn't sent on any more diplomatic missions. Which goes to show that only a bloody fool thinks he can pull the leg of an American.'

Mr Hoppner burst into roars of laughter, 'Well, you certainly can tell a story against yourself, old timer,' he said. And Mrs Hoppner, who perhaps hadn't followed very well, said,

'Oh, spotted dick! Oh lord! Isn't that the British for you!'

Even Sylvia, who had heard the story so often, could see the charm of the twinkle in Arthur's eye as he sat back. Then Mr Hoppner was impelled to order two brandies for the men and a crème de menthe and a crème de cacao for the ladies. In fact it was Arthur who insisted on paying for them.

'No, no, we're hosts here. The missus and I'll drink you out of house and bourbon or whatever the bloody stuff's called when we come your way.'

When the drinks arrived Mrs Hoppner said, 'Excuse me, please,' and slipped away and didn't return to drink her crème de cacao. Sylvia dared not swallow its creamy richness on top of the sugary heaviness of her own crème de menthe. She felt quite depressed at an expense they could ill afford wasted on people that they would never see again. When Arthur and Mr Hoppner reached the exchange of addresses stage, she could not bring herself to join in. She fell into silence.

Arthur said, 'We're off to live with my son in Carshall, one of these New Towns. You ought to see it. I don't know what I think, myself, but it's one of England's showpieces. My son's a big pot in the school world; writes all these how-to-do-it books. He'd be honoured to entertain you and your missus.'

Back in their carriage, Arthur was quite short with her. 'A fine advertisement you are for Anglo-American friendship.' However, the encounter had put him in very good spirits. He was full of it when the family met them at Carshall old town station in Harold's new Zephyr. He couldn't listen to any of the family news, despite all Sylvia's hints. 'Charming people with pots of money. He's one of these American tycoons. I made them laugh a bit. It's all a question of give and take.' In the end Harold said a little crossly,

'They sound fascinating people.' However he was clearly struck with Arthur's eupeptic mood. 'The old man seems on top of the world, Mother,' he said when they were alone together, 'I'm glad for your sake.'

'Oh, he's impossible, quite impossible.' Sylvia immediately regretted saying it. She was determined not to let her troubles with Arthur impinge on Harold's life; and then again Harold received her answer with a frown that seemed almost as much directed at her as at her information.

'Well, we won't let you upset yourself here. You can relax here, Mother. Although, of course, we shall make use of you. You can't give up a lifetime of being made use of all in a day!' And he laughed to show that he was teasing her.

2. Trees Without Leaves

If she could judge from her first morning at 'The Syca-mores', Sylvia felt that she would never be made use of again.

She woke to a gentle tap on her door. The bright yellow of the room bewildered her. Then she saw the typewritten notice signed by Beth, it read, "To all bed-makers. Remember that you have to lie on it." Now she recalled Harold's remarks the previous night, 'I only hope Beth's choice of mustard with white isn't going to prove too much for you, Mother. It wasn't altogether intended to be lived with for life.' Arthur had looked round the room quizzically, taking in the hard yellow curtains and carpet.

'Rather hot stuff, isn't it?'

'My dear Dad, if there's anything you don't like, it goes out. It's your room. Though as far as I can remember you were never very choosy about how Mother's rooms were furnished.'

'Oh, Dad'll be all right with the yellow. He isn't going to have any hangovers here, anyway.'

'How do you know what I am going to have or what I'm not going to have?' Arthur had fallen in with her teasing note, but Harold had still seemed not quite happy.

'I've left the minimum of furniture in here so that you can have plenty of space for your own stuff when it arrives.'

Looking at the little black tubular chairs with yellow seats, she had wondered if that was what he'd meant by minimum. She'd hardly dare to try her weight on them. 'It's very nice, dear. I don't know how we shall live up to it. Do you, Dad?'

'Oh, we'll live up to it all right. Your Mother's as pleased as punch with it really, Harold. And so am I.'

Harold had gone away happy. After he'd gone, Arthur

61

had grumbled for the whole half hour it took him to get to bed. 'Like a bloody tart's room.'

Now he was snoring happily. Before she answered the knocking, she got out of bed and shook him. His snoring embarrassed her so in front of people. 'Wake up, Arthur, it's after nine.' Then, 'Come in,' she called.

'What the bloody hell . . .' Arthur was beginning, when Judy came in with a breakfast tray. What a pretty neat little girl she was, Sylvia thought. Arthur said, 'Ah! How's my pretty little granddaughter this morning?'

'Breakfast in bed!'

'Well it's a Sunday, Gran. And anyway Dad thought you would be tired after the journey.' She arranged the special little clip on the bed tables. 'Three-minute eggs. I hope that's right.'

'Just right, Judy. But I ought to have been downstairs getting breakfast for all of you. After all, you're working the whole week.'

'Yes, you don't want to spoil your grandmother, you know. I never have.' Judy didn't smile. Harold said she was studying hard in order to go to University. Sylvia only hoped she wasn't overworking; her little, finely shaped face was very pale.

'I'm sorry about this awful jelly marmalade. But that's Mark's terrible taste. When *I* do breakfast you'll get proper Oxford marmalade.' She was very much the little lady, Sylvia thought, even at seventeen; whatever she said, just about marmalade and that, she made it sound quite grand. '*Bon appétit*,' Judy said and went out of the room, but not before Arthur had farted loudly.

Sylvia decided to say nothing. She didn't want to nag Arthur, and then, even if she did tell him off, as likely as not he'd only do it the more. She concentrated on her breakfast; everything was so neat and dainty – a special little pink china tea set for her and Arthur's a blue one, the toast was wrapped in a paper doyley, and the eggs had little covers of pink and blue suede. Arthur couldn't get his off, it was fitted so tightly to the egg cup.

'Buggering nonsense!' And then when she'd got out of bed and taken the egg cover off for him, 'I've never seen such bloody fiddle faddle.' His egg proved to be very lightly boiled; the yolk ran down the sides of the egg cup. 'I can't eat this dribbling muck.'

But when later they were downstairs, it was, 'Very nice breakfast, Harold.'

'Oh, it was Mark's doing. First Sunday in the month you know.' They didn't know, but Sylvia said, 'Oh, Mark, you shouldn't have. A young man cooking for me.' Mark only scowled at her from beneath his fringe – the boy was so odd he quite scared her.

'Yes, you ought to have seen your grandmother, sitting up in bed all la-di-da like a Hollywood film star.'

Harold had seemed rather impatient; now his face brightened. 'I'm afraid your social examples are a bit out of date, Dad. There's rather a good article here on the decline of the Hollywood star.' He picked up the *Observer* and read a long article to them. While he was reading, the three grandchildren got up and left the sitting room. Before he'd finished Arthur had picked up *The Sunday Express* and was reading the sports news. Sylvia, left alone as the audience, tried very hard to concentrate on what Harold read. But two things worried her: the clock said after half past ten – surely she ought to be getting on with something; and then she really didn't know anything about what Harold was reading – she only went to the cinema once in a blue moon nowadays; all the names had changed, supposing he asked her a question. But he didn't. When he had finished reading the article, he said, 'This only confirms what I've been saying for some time. More vulgarized popular taste, increasingly remote minority culture. The polarization of the two cultures, in fact.'

Mark had returned and was oiling a hinge on a side table, 'The two cultures doesn't mean that at all, Dad. It means science and the arts.'

'I'm perfectly well aware of that. Words are for use, not for labelling as museum specimens. Anyway, don't bring oil cans into the sitting room.'

Mark flushed red, but went on with his task, muttering 'Humpty Dumpty had a great fall.'

'As so often happens,' Harold said, 'the little microcosm of our world down here reflects very accurately the country at large. We have no cinema at Carshall. If you and Dad

63

want westerns or horror films, you'll have to go to Carshall old town, I believe. On the other hand, the Film Society flourishes. They show the classics that we all knew before the war – Earth, Potemkin, Mother, and that sort of thing, Mother . . .'

'Mother, Mother,' Mark mumbled.

'And the post-war stuff – Italian, Swedish, Japanese.'

'Japanese? I shouldn't know what to make of that, I'm sure, Harold.'

'Well, come along some time and give it a trial. The Seven Samurai, wonderful blood-curdling Lyceum melodrama stuff. You'd love it, Dad.'

'No thanks, old boy. The tele's good enough for me.' Arthur was but half listening.

'Oh, Dad,' Sylvia said, 'You used to be such a picture goer. Maurice Chevalier and Jeanette Macdonald.'

'I go a good deal to the Film Society,' Harold announced.

'Remote minority culture,' Mark murmured.

Harold laughed. '*You* take your beastly oil can out of the sitting room.'

Mark laughed back. 'Why should I?'

His father's mood changed. 'Because your mother wouldn't have permitted it.' Mark blushed scarlet, snatched up the oil can and walked out of the room, slamming the door.

'Well, there it is,' Harold put down the *Observer*, 'all these chaps with the right names have strings to pull, but they have very little to say that I couldn't have said better for them. Or many others like me, of course.'

Sylvia, still troubled by Mark's violent departure waited a few minutes, then she said, 'Well, I musn't sit here idling, Harold. If you and Judy can just show me what needs doing, I can get on.'

'There's nothing for you to do, Mother. Judy's cook today.' Before Sylvia could protest, Judy herself came into the room.

'Will you all prepare to eat at half past one?'

Harold stroked his toothbrush moustache with his index finger and looked at his daughter quizzically. 'I was just telling your grandmother that you were cook today. You

64

couldn't have dressed more appropriately to impress her with your capacities.'

Judy was now wearing a hacking coat and riding breeches.

'Caroline Ogilvie is going to let me take Punch out after lunch.'

'Caroline Ogilvie, whoever she may be, no doubt *lunches*. We low common people have dinner. Don't we, Mother?' For a moment Sylvia could not understand what he meant – all her life of hotel managing she had eaten lunch – so she smiled.

Harold got up from his armchair.

'I said last night I would initiate you into the mysteries of the household, but I'm wondering, in view of the weather reports, whether we shouldn't go out and have a look at the Calvert Estate instead,' he smiled at the absurdity of the phrase. 'If the weathermen are right – and at last they seem to have some scientific accuracy – we're in for a deep freeze from tomorrow which may well keep you indoors for a while, Mother.'

'I'm not an invalid, dear.'

'No, but we're going to treat you like one for a bit. But this morning we could take a chance. It's quite warm once you get out of the wind.'

'Oh dear. Have I got as old as that? That's just the phrase I always used to say to all the old residents.'

Harold ignored the remark. 'Tell the boys they're wanted to show their grandmother the family demesne, Judy.' Once again he laughed, then turning to his father. 'Are you coming, Dad?' Arthur, buried in Huddersfield v. Arsenal, was impervious to Harold's voice, so Sylvia touched his shoulder,

'Harold wants to show us the garden, Arthur.' She gave him a look to urge acceptance.

'Oh, all right. I don't mind a toddle round the family estate.'

The joke didn't seem to make Harold laugh when Dad made it.

When, all wrapped up, they assembled on the front lawn, Harold pointed out the main features of the architecture. 'Ashlar blocks, you see, give it strength. And the white weather boarding preserves the local character. I'm all for picture windows, aren't you, Mother?' Sylvia didn't really know what to say about it – parts looked quite pretty and old-fashioned like a farmhouse, and other parts looked quite light and airy and modern.

'It's very unique, isn't it, Harold?'

'It's a ranch-type house,' he said.

'There you are, Sylvia, you'll be expected to round up a couple of steers before breakfast. Your grandmother's a bit heavy for rodeo.' You could see the boys found Arthur's chaffing to their taste, for they both laughed, but when they saw that she wasn't smiling, they stopped. Sylvia quickly laughed to put them at their ease. They must have thought she was hurt by Arthur's legpulling, how could she explain that it was years since she'd listened to him? And anyhow she was busy thinking of what she was meant to say. It was easy enough for Arthur, he was already established as the old clown, but she was supposed to make comments. Luckily Harold was too busy talking to expect more than the fewest words.

'Yes, ranches for the Carshall tycoons. They were built to try to persuade our industrial executives to stay in the community. But, of course, they prefer to buy up the local rectories and manor houses. However, there's enough of us to fill them. Being rather small fry compared to the millionaires of Texas and Arizona, we actually live all the year round in ours. And there's a slight difference in acreage,' Harold pointed mockingly round the small garden, 'a matter of a few tens of thousands of acres difference. But be that as it may, we *are* the local tycoons. As tycoonish, I'm glad to say, as Carshall New Town intends to accommodate. Among them your ever-loving son, the textbook tycoon.'

'Can we place your order for genuine feelthy books, Modom? Sex in the schoolroom, that's one of our most successful titles. Or the Head and his Harem.'

'Calvert's corrupters. Guaranteed a dirty word on every page.'

Harold appeared to take his sons' teasing very well. Indeed it looked as though he was more annoyed than pleased when Judy sprang to his defence.

'I suppose you think you're the mostest being clever about Daddy's books. Well, at least school-teaching is an educated profession.'

'Thank you, Judy, for that testimony of status. But I think I'll belong to the modern world of electronic engineers and fabric designers rather than pretend to gentility with family solicitors and private school headmasters.'

Judy snapped back at her father, 'Oh, I wasn't suggesting that being a secondary school-master was a real profession. Anyway, talk of pretension! What about describing Ray as a fabrics designer? He's in the rag trade.' She began to dance round the garden calling out, 'Ray's in the rag trade! Ray's in the rag trade!' Sylvia was glad to see that she could be such a nice, unaffected schoolgirl. She'd be so pretty with her shoulder-length blonde hair and slim figure if it weren't for her mouth, such an unhappy, missish mouth, like Beth's, if it were not too mother-in-lawish to think it. Now her brothers were chasing her, more like kids than twenty-year-olds. Such an odd contrast, Ray so goodlooking and Mark such a freak. No doubt at all Beth's strictness when they were small had not made the children one jot less lively, quite the opposite, it seemed. It just showed one should not judge what one didn't understand. Clever people like Beth and Harold knew better.

But Ray and Mark had caught their sister now and were scragging her in a jolly, ragging way, when Arthur stepped in.

'You leave my little Judykins alone. I'll have to be your protector, Judy, I can see.' And he scragged her neck too, but in a different way, in a grandfatherly way.

Sylvia said, 'Now, Arthur!'

Harold was addressing the garden at large,

'The Girls County High suffers from a peculiarly virulent form of conjunctivitis – status snobbery meets there with social snobbery. I'm afraid it sometimes affects Judy's vision.'

The girl broke from her grandfather's hold and ran indoors.

'I like my little granddaughter, Harold.' Sylvia noticed the two boys smile at Arthur in approval. She wished that she had said it, even if she was not sure that she really did understand Judy.

'There used to be a high fence on this side of the garden. The architects made these concessions to the English mentality in their efforts to woo the executive group. Beth and I had it taken down at once. After all, if the New Towns have done nothing else they've taught us the one valuable lesson the famous American way of life has to offer – good neighbourliness. Now we're no more cut off from our neighbours than we were at 592. There!' pointing down a road of white weather-boarded houses each with a door painted a different bold colour, 'that's Higgleton Road. And that road to the left, which by the way will take you to the shops, is Mardyke Avenue.' The houses in this street were set on top of a grass slope; their concrete porch roofs were supported by black painted metal tubes. To Sylvia it all seemed strangely like the other parts of Carshall that she'd seen on previous visits; but she could tell from the proud note in Harold's voice as he said the names of the roads that she must not say this. She sought for an observation to make. 'It's very quiet, isn't it?' Harold frowned. However, a moment later two young men in black leather jackets and white crash helmets came out of a house in nearby Higgleton Road and started revving up their motorcycles. As the noise became more deafening, Harold's frown changed to a friendly smile. As soon as the motorcyclists had roared off, and they could speak again, 'I like these ton-up types,' he said.

Nobody answered him. His sons were busy with some private conversation. Neither Sylvia nor Arthur had any comments to make.

The other side of the house was the surprise. Through a screenwork of leafless sycamores you could gaze far away across rolling countryside.

'We're on the very outer edge of Carshall here. The very last house in the whole New Town, Mother. There's a circular road in the dip there that joins up with the trunk road, but you can't see it. All you can see is the country.' Sylvia, checking his statement and finding it correct, said, 'Yes, that's right, Harold, you can't see any road.'

Harold frowned.

'On the other side of those hills,' he pointed straight ahead, 'is the Midlands.'

Sylvia thought that he said it rather as though he had put them there. She had lived in many parts of England but always by the seaside; even as a country girl she had not been more than twenty miles from the sea. The idea of 'The Midlands' struck chilly upon her; looking before her at the vast fields, she imagined them stretching on and on across the middle of England. She saw them as one huge ploughed plain and herself on an endless, lonely walk across it, rather as in the far distance she could see a solitary tractor at work, its sole moving companions a flock of rooks and seagulls that fed in its wake. The leafless sycamores high above her seemed suddenly now more dried up and sad than when she had glimpsed them from her bedroom window the night before. Under the heels of her fur-topped bootees cracked dead leaves and withering, winged seed pods. She pulled herself together.

'You've got a lovely home, Harold.'

'*We* have,' he corrected her and put his arm round her waist. The embarrassing physical gesture seemed to underline something in what he had said that had already made her uncomfortable. She shifted her large weight away from him, turned her gaze from the awful Midlands, and looked back to the front gate.

'I like the front side of the house best though.'

Harold seemed unexpectedly pleased at this. 'Oh, I knew you'd like Melling. It's much more convenient here for the shops than at 592. And we've got a coffee bar of our own. Not like dear old Craighill where the 'coffee cats', as Beth used to call them, had to go all the way into the Town Centre to slake their thirst.' He looked tenderly at Sylvia. 'That's my chief memory of you and Beth together, Mother – clucking disapproval at the idle housewives who had time to spend gossiping over cups of coffee.' He laughed affectionately at the memory and then, looking at Sylvia, abruptly became silent. After an embarrassed pause, he went on, 'Of course, when you want to go to the Town Centre on your own, Mother, we're wonderfully situated for the bus. It stops at the corner of Prideaux and Higgleton. Not a hundred yards away. I usually rely on the Zephyr

69

to get to work, but Judy can tell you the bus times. Judy!' he looked round, 'Where's she got to?'

Sylvia could hardly believe that he had forgotten Judy's departure, yet he seemed genuinely surprised at her absence. Arthur, who was holding forth to his grandsons, ended his sentence, 'Of course, I told him exactly where he could put it.' Then, 'She's grown into a very pretty kid, that.' Harold frowned, but to Sylvia's relief, Arthur added, 'She's very like Beth, Harold, very like,' and almost imperceptibly he winked at Sylvia. She had to give it to Arthur that you could never tell when he would turn up trumps.

'I wish she were a bit more like, Dad. However, I'm glad you think so.' Harold gave an approving smile at his father. But Arthur had already returned to his story, 'After that there was what the nobs call a marked coolness between the padre and yours truly . . .'

'I do hope Dad's not boring the boys too much,' Sylvia said.

'It'll do Mark good to listen for a bit.' At once he shouted across the lawn, 'You sometimes deign to use public transport, don't you, Mark? Come and tell your grand-mother the bus times.'

'If you're so bloody keen on church parade,' I said. Arthur stopped a little grumpily in mid-sentence at the noise of his son's shouting.

'Oh, sorry to interrupt you, Dad. But it's good for Mark to come down to earth and be useful now and again.'

'Buses for what and where?' Mark's forehead beneath his Beatle fringe was red with an eczema and his cheeks pitted with past acne. With his frown and his slight stammer, Sylvia didn't know what to make of him. She could well believe that he was going through a difficult phase. Young people were so touchy now. Look at Tom Colman. In the other night's episode when Mrs Harker said, 'I don't know. I really don't know,' just like everybody expected her to, instead of laughing at the funny old thing, Tom Colman had shouted at her, 'That's your trouble, and you never will.' The poor old thing had been so hurt, until Miss Dinneford – that was a new character, some sort of social worker – had explained that it was all due to young people growing up more quickly 'in that way' nowadays and the crushes on the evening trains and that. Yet it was young Tom in another episode who got up the collection to replace old George Lampson's cornet when it was stolen, although the boy seemed to hate cornets and played a guitar himself. It was certainly a case of 'I really don't know'.

Harold's voice raised in anger brought her back from 'Down Our Way' to down her own way.

'As I was responsible for the completion of the gazetteer of Carshall Streets, I suppose I may be expected to know the difference between Tidsbury Avenue and Tidsbury Crescent.'

'Yes, you *may* and one glance at the gazetteer shows that you don't.' Mark had put his chin down as he argued with his father so that his face was almost buried in his dirty suede jacket. Sylvia could see that Ray was afraid there might be a family quarrel. Still smiling brightly at Arthur's story, he half turned in a comic melodramatic posture towards Harold and Mark.

'Who dares to attack the faithful gazetteer? Oh, Mark Calvert, my lad, you'll come to no good. The book we studied at our dear old mother's knee . . .' He stopped in mid-sentence, his handsome, squashy, tom-cat's face flushed with embarrassment.

'Ray's made a gaffe.'

'It's hardly polite of you to point it out if he has, Mark. In any case your mother was the last person who would want a special hush round her name when she's dead. Do try to be natural.'

'Being natural, I now point out that when it comes to a sense of locality, you haven't got one. You'd send poor Gran half round Carshall if she followed your routes.'

'Oh, don't worry about me. I can find out the bus times for myself, I've still got a tongue.'

But Harold raised his voice and drowned hers.

'And I suppose you're going to produce computers that make perfect maps and foolproof gazetteers?'

'How did you guess? We're working on them at the moment. *And* to replace headmasters. Eliminating the purely hackwork type of manpower in fact.'

Sylvia found it difficult to know exactly what was happening, for although they both laughed all the time as though the whole thing was a leg-pull, yet from the look in their eyes and the edge in their voices she guessed that they soon might lose their tempers.

'Oh, indeed, well if you want to be in at the death you'd better buck your ways up a bit and get through your exams, Mark. Otherwise you may find Electrometrico have eliminated you before your apprenticeship's finished.'

Mark's voice rose now, almost hysterically.

'Don't worry, we'll probably all be eliminated long before then.'

'Oh, no! Oh no! Not again! Not the same old cry! And you call yourselves the cool generation. Can't you even discuss the times of buses without whining about the bomb? Have some sense of proportion.'

Once more Ray intervened,

'That's what they told the customer at the geisha, Dad. When he complained about the radioactive fish.'

Mark brushed aside his brother's assistance.

'Oh very funny. Ha-ha! Excuse me if I don't laugh.'

'It's a good try, but not you at your top form, Ray. It's a *non sequitur*. It lacks that logic that is the basis of all good jokes. You see, no sense of proportion would help a Japanese gentleman, however honourable, once he'd consumed radioactive fish.'

'Oh God!' Mark cried, 'oh, wonderful! And he doesn't even realize what he's said.'

Harold was blushing now; Sylvia hadn't seen that happen since he was a boy.

'If you're so content with a cheap debating point, you can hardly expect me to believe that you're much in earnest. Of course a sense of proportion won't save a radioactive world. I never suggested it would. But it *will* save us from panicking and so . . .'

Arthur interrupted,

'Well, if you won't think it rude, Harold. I shall toddle in. This cold air isn't exactly what the doctor orders for an old geezer like me.' He gave the brave smile that Sylvia knew so well.

Now perhaps they could all go quietly indoors and forget this quarrel about politics or whatever it was. Surely there must be some work to get on with, and, if not, the best thing would be a nice book. She followed Arthur's move.

'I think I am a little bit cold, too.'

'I'm not surprised. Once Mark gets on to his hobby horse we could all freeze to death before he'd notice. That's a point, by the way. With all your apprehension of total atomic annihilation, Mark, you have no concern for the many *natural* disasters that might eliminate three quarters of the human race. It's all or nothing with you. Your morality seems to be a simple matter of the counting of heads. . . .'

Ray went quietly up to his father and whispered loudly in his ear, 'TFFTST, or even TFFTSU. That's to say, if you haven't heard, Dad, Gran and Granddad are freezing to death.'

Coming from Ray, Harold seemed to take it. He laughed. 'Well, there it is, Mother. The Calvert Estate. As to the garden, as you see, we don't have any. Just the little apple orchard and the rest is lawn, and that's electrically cut. By the way, it's lucky for you, Dad, that you've come at this time of the year, otherwise you'd have to add the electric mower to the many infernal machines we're going to instruct you in. Beth and I were very un-English about gardens. We were far too busy to bother with one. Far too extrovert, I suppose you'd say.'

'I don't believe Gran would say that at all,' Mark mumbled. And then he and his brother began a pantomime of military drill.

'Introver – shun. Extrover – shun,' they cried.

Arthur was delighted.

'Good lads,' he said, 'they know their drill.'

And so, laughing, they all moved indoors. Sylvia thought what a happy lot they were really; although she didn't understand them very well. Someone had said about Mark being a pacifist and here he was playing at soldier's drill. Well, of course, you had to admire pacifists but only so long as they really had the courage of their convictions. She hoped that she wouldn't have to think too much about such difficult questions. She and Arthur had never been clever, never been anything really, although Arthur talked so big sometimes.

When they had all sat down to their beers and sherries before dinner that morning, Harold said, his eyes twinkling just like his father's,

'You may have noticed, Mother, that in the opinion of the younger generation, I'm a monster of obstinacy and insensitivity. As a matter of fact, strictly between ourselves, I have a strong suspicion that they've got a point there. But unfortunately there it is. That's the nature of the beast.'

Sylvia wondered whatever she was supposed to answer. Of course, Beth would have known. She could not help wishing that Beth were there, and then, of course, she herself need not be. She was quite ashamed of such ungrateful sentiments. Ideas like that came into her head, no doubt, because she had too little to do. Harold was making her too comfortable.

'I think you'd find the whole thing would come to you much more easily, Mother, if you really tried to grasp the basic principles on which electric cooking and heating rest,' Harold had said this on the two previous evenings; he was looking content patiently to say it again on a third. All the same Sylvia thought she could detect an extra edge in his voice that evening; and who could blame him? She was so horribly slow to learn. Heaven knew she'd tried hard! But there was such a lot to know and Harold talked so much, so fast, and so indistinctly with his unfilled pipe waggling at the corner of his mouth that she really could hardly remember feeling more uncomfortable than she had on these three last evenings in that spacious modern kitchen.

'I'm awfully stupid, Harold, you know. But I've still got a very good memory. I think, if you were just to show me the various switches, with that chart you gave me I could pick it all up by myself. I've got a very good sense of timing.'

'My dear Mother, with an autotimer, there's no need to have a sense of timing.' He laughed and, wiping the saliva from the stem of his pipe on the corner of his blue and white plastic apron, he put it away in the apron pocket. Sylvia wished that she could get used to these aprons on men.

Pablo at the Palmeira had worn a plain white chef's cotton apron, as had Giuseppe before him, but they were not only professional cooks but foreigners. Here Harold had this blue plastic thing, Mark a green one, and Ray one in orange and white. And all the aprons had frills.

'We've relegated instinctual cooking to the lesser breeds without the law. And *they* aren't going to put up with it for long. Now take this meal we're cooking this evening. Of course, it's not a normal meal. I've specially designed it to illustrate all the equipment,' he smoothed his moustache with a certain pride. 'The goulash in your top oven. And just for this evening – an example of conspicuous waste – an apfelstrudel in your lower oven. Of course, that's really reserved for the big fellows, turkeys and such and for any fiestas. We'll bake there for this little party we're giving for you before Christmas. Then, on the drop-in hob – soup for Dad on the simmerstat, and on the two hob points two veg, also for my conservative-minded parents' – he winked at her – 'and then a special treat for Dad whose true blue palate can't take goulash – a half chicken for the grill. Frankly I shouldn't have pandered to him like this if it hadn't been a very useful way of demonstrating the roto-roaster.'

Sylvia felt she ought to say something if only to check Harold's flow of words so that she could concentrate.

'Well, you know what Dad is, Harold.'

'Yes. Though I must say that the leopard seems to have got rid of some of his worst spots, doesn't he? Now set your top oven here and your lower oven here.' He turned the knobs.

'I don't see the numbers very clearly without my specs, I'm afraid, Harold. But . . .'

'Well, it isn't the end of the world if you don't. That was exactly what I explained last night. With this heatview you've got a double check – this marker is going up and down the whole time, it's just as if you had your beloved gas flame . . .'

'*I* didn't want to have gas, dear. I told Mr Hopper at the London Office ten years ago when they modernized the Palmeira that electricity would be cleaner. But it was a question of economy. . . .' She had not liked to tell Harold that, in any case, they'd only installed two gas cookers at the hotel and those reserved for breakfasts, otherwise they'd kept the old boiler type ranges.

'Modernized!' Harold gave a snort.

'Well, they concentrated on the public rooms, you know. The lounge was re-done in contemporary ten years ago. And then putting in the Lobster Pot Bar cost such a lot even though it was all fish nets and anchors. The kitchens didn't matter so much really. The guests never see them. And we've never had any trouble getting Spanish and Portuguese. Before that it was Hungarians and Italians. There's always somebody wanting to come to England to learn, isn't there? Apart from the Irish, I mean.'

Harold looked at her. 'You're like Rip Van Winkle, Mother. . . . Now, we must concentrate on the job in hand. What do you do with the autotimer? Think now, Sylvia.' He'd never used her Christian name; and although it was meant to be some kind of a joke, she felt most uncomfortable. However she must try to play up to him. Some vague, long-forgotten memory of school came back to her: it spelt 'catch'. She would not be caught. She said,

'I don't need it at all, do I? Because we're not going out.' She really felt pleased with herself and she smiled. She hoped the face Harold pulled was one of mock sternness.

'Wrong.'

'But you explained about the clock yesterday. It starts the meal and turns it off when you're out. I remember.' She felt near to tears.

'And I did explain another little thing to you: this pinger timer that warns you when the meal is ready when you're in.'

'Oh, of course. I'd forgotten. The little bell. The ringer timer.'

'Well, no, Mother. I did explain that too. Neither Beth nor I particularly cared for a loud bell in the house, so we had the telephone and the autotimer fitted with muted pingers instead of ringers.'

'I don't know whether I shall hear it in that case, Harold. I'm not deaf you know, but I don't exactly hear as I used to. Not that it matters. I don't think I should need it. I've got a very good sense of time.'

Harold sighed.

'As I explained, it's a five-hour pinger.'

At that moment Arthur shuffled into the kitchen in his bedroom slippers. He'd established his daily wear for 'The Sycamores' now – pyjama coat under a cardigan, grey flannel trousers hanging elephant-like at the seat and tied with an old pyjama cord, and bedroom slippers.

'Bloody racing cancelled at Wincanton, but down at Kempton Diocletian won the last race by a short head,' he announced, 'thirty-three to one when the betting closed. What a turn-up for the book!' He had not for many years expected Sylvia to be interested in his nightly relays of the sports results, he was not, therefore, put off by Harold's blank expression. But once he'd made his announcement he was happy enough to hear the household news of the day.

'How's your Mother getting on with all this electric lark?' he asked.

'Harold's showing me how to use the five-hour pinger timer.'

'Pinger!' Arthur guffawed until a fit of choking brought tears to his eyes. 'Pinger Ponger, the town's dead wronger,' he said. When nobody laughed, he looked cross, 'Five hours! I don't want to wait five bloody hours for my grub, thank you.'

'Oh, Arthur! Don't be so silly. Of course dinner won't take that long to cook. The clock hasn't anything to do with five hours. That's just its name, isn't it, Harold?' She saw from her son's expression that she was mistaken again.

Harold, as though to mark his mother's greater culpability in error, said,

'You're going to have a half grilled chicken to yourself, Dad.'

Arthur took the treat lightly.

'Good. Don't forget the Worcester Sauce. But what I'm looking for now is a bottle of beer. It's a bloody awful substitute for my evening pint, but if I toddle down to the local on these icy roads I'm liable to fall arse over tip.'

Really, Sylvia thought, he made it sound like a world catastrophe. Harold was quick to throw open the door of the huge refrigerator.

'There you are, Dad. Help yourself.'

After a good deal of muttering, Arthur selected a bottle of Whitbread's. 'Why the hell you don't put all this stuff outside in the frost, I don't know, Harold, if your aim is to freeze the taste out of it.'

'Oughtn't we to warm the plates, Harold?' Sylvia pulled out the drawer at the bottom of the cooker. She added proudly,

'Look, Dad, all this space for plates.'

'Very nice. Where do you keep the beer mugs, Harold?'

But Harold was intent on instructing his mother, 'Well, and what do you do now?'

Sylvia's pride was broken. She could not think.

'You've forgotten your warm drawer switch, of course.' Arthur roared with laughter.

'You musn't do that, Sylvia. Whatever you do in this weather, keep your drawers warm. That's very good. What do the Yanks say? Hot pants! I don't know that I like them as a nation, but you have to give it to them every time when it comes to slang.' He had found a mug and was pouring out his beer. 'Got a bloody great head on it, this stuff, hasn't it?' and he left the kitchen.

Harold pressed his lips, 'The old man's a bit crude at times, isn't he. Well, we've got an hour to kill before we grill the chicken. Do you feel up to a general run through the whole works?'

It seemed to Sylvia at that moment that perhaps Harold was enjoying all this as much as she was not, despite his very reasonable impatience; but the idea was as absurd as . . . as Harold in a frilled apron, and she dismissed them both from her mind as effects of the temperature of the house – it was so beautifully warm, almost stuffy – upon her too pressing blood stream.

'Now show me how to work the washer. Look, here's a pile of Judy's stuff, panties and things. You can demonstrate on those. Serve my lady bountiful right for leaving them about.'

'But I said I would wash them for her. She was going to do them when she came in, but she's so busy studying.'

'Oh! She's not out with her grand friends then. The frost has saved the fox no doubt.'

Sylvia looked out into the blackness. 'They don't

hunt at night, Harold dear.' Some things she did know about.

'Well,' said her son, crossly, 'now's your chance to wash the stuff.'

For a moment Sylvia felt herself flushing with annoyance. He was really so absurdly inconsiderate, as bad as his father. Seven in the evening wasn't a time for doing washing. However, she controlled herself and did as she was asked. While the clothes floated round like some crazy fish in an aquarium, Harold pointed out the special virtues of their machine. As he was speaking Mark rushed in, seized one of the many glass jars from the white shelves and took out a packet of biscuits.

'I shan't be in to supper, Dad.'

'Why not?'

'Evening school.'

'I thought we were agreed that we'd fixed supper time to suit evening classes.'

'Yes; well, it doesn't.'

'Kindly be civil, Mark. *And* truthful. You're trying to fit in some meeting to save the world from devastation before you go to the Tech. That's it, isn't it? My dear boy, can't you tell me? We can agree to disagree, surely.'

Mark did not answer.

'Do you always wash your frillies at supper time, Gran?'

Sylvia started to laugh, but Mark's frown was so severe that she stopped.

'Those happen to be Judy's that milady had left for her grandmother to do.'

'She's studying hard, Harold.'

'When she's got a few moments off from hobnobbing with the county.'

'Oh, if that's the sort of stink she likes, let her breathe it, Dad. Anyway what are *you* doing in here?'

'Giving your grandmother a few lessons in the basic principles on which electric gadgets work.'

'Oh, take no notice of him, Gran. Just push the knob you like and hope for the best. Don't let him treat you to his little hobbies. We never do. The great student of social trends! Bugger the principles of electricity. As if he understood them anyway.'

'Not that language before your grandmother, please, old man. As I was saying, Mother, the great advantage of a smooth-sided agitator is . . .'

His words were drowned by Mark's raucous laughter. 'Smooth-sided agitator! You've said it! Don't you trust him, lady. You does what you wants how you wants.'

When Mark had gone, Harold said, 'It's been the greatest happiness to me that young Mark should have turned out such a rebel.' But Sylvia thought that he looked depressed.

'What about a glass of sherry?'

'Oh, not for me, dear.' She thought how dearly she would have loved her evening gin and it.

'Well then, one to keep your instructor company. He who talks too much and too fast.'

As they sat with their glasses, Harold said:

'Well, there it is, Mother. The safety valve that Beth in her wisdom found for all the ill-gotten gains the textbooks have brought us.'

He waved his arm around the room with its walls of dark green (Forest Green he said it was called, but that didn't make it less dingy – kitchens ought to be bright – cream or primrose) and its array of shining white shelves and machines.

'Everything from the deep-freeze down to the mixer was Beth's choice.'

And that was the real cause of her depression, as it had been every evening. How could she listen to him when she was wondering desperately whether the moment had come, the moment she had known must come ever since she and Arthur had accepted his invitation to live there, the moment of intimacy between them when they must talk of Beth, of her long and cruel cancerous illness, of his agony, of the children's loss.

Every evening as Harold had held forth, her attention had been driven from his funny, kind, prosy ways to thoughts of Beth; every evening she had tried to forget her daughter-in-law's brusquerie and hardness and remember only her courage and efficiency; but these qualities so quickly became mixed up together, good and bad going round like the panties and bras in the spin dryer, the cups and saucers in the washing-up machine. How could she talk and what could she say? But there was no need, Harold was in full spate.

'Beth saw at once that as we'd got to spend this textbook money, the best thing was to use it to rationalize the sort of chores that don't really enrich life. You see, Mother, neither of us was a conspicuous spender or a notable saver; nor did we want the children to be. The truth is that Beth and I are misfits in the affluent society. Or rather Beth was.' He corrected himself so casually, that, for a moment she did not realize what he had said; then, although she tried to feel for him, she could only think how Beth would have hated to be a subject for social embarrassment, especially before her mother-in-law – not that it was the sort of old joke about mothers-in-law; no, they got on all right, when the family used to come to the hotel at Christmas – but almost as strangers, related strangers. With such dead feelings about the dead how could she start their little intimate talk?

In any case, she was given no opportunity, for Harold bumbled on in his eulogy of Beth. 'Mind you, she was no slave to labour-saving devices. Beth always had taste. No mayonnaise was ever made in a mixer in this house. . . .' And, 'She had an infinite capacity for patience, she never seemed tired. After a whole day on the bench, with cases that rent her heart and wore out her patience she still gave the rice six separate rinsings – there was never any starch left in Beth's rice . . .'

How to speak through such a flow? How to lead him away from all these little everyday things on to the tragic loss so that he could take it out of himself as the old folks used to say? Suddenly the black night outside, the heat, the dark green walls, the white machines, all closed in on her. The washing-up machine, the quick grill, the deep freeze, the cooker, the spin dryer, and all the other white monsters stood in line against the green wall like so many marble tombstones. It only wanted the crematorium oven. Beth's memorials? Beth's grave? She looked round for some escape from this enveloping whiteness but only a tiny angry red eye glared at her from the smooth white surface warning her off sacred ground that was not hers, off a dead woman's home. She felt herself shrinking away to nothing as Harold filled the air with the blaring trumpets of praise.

She shook herself for a moment to recover from her giddy spell. It was this central heating. Luckily Harold had not noticed. She told herself not to be morbid. As though in answer to this injunction, the door opened and Ray appeared. Ray was always a tonic. With his fair curly hair and his wonderful smile he was like Owen Nares that she used to queue for in the old days – only up-to-date, of course, more like one of the pop singers, but never grubby. And so full of fun, too; last back from work in the evenings, yet never tired, always off out somewhere.

'Where is it tonight, Ray?' she asked. In only these few days, she already felt that she could talk to him as she could not to the others.

'Works dance,' he made a grimace. 'Dawncing with awah Directah's wife. Come along, love, and be Twistatulle's dancing grandmother.' He sniffed the air, 'Goulash! And I'm missing it! If I'd known you were Hungarian, Gran, I'd have practised my czardas.' He did a step or two with a pretence tambourine and ribbons.

When Sylvia had stopped laughing, she said, '*I* haven't made it. It's your father. He's showing me how to use all these wonderful gadgets. Only I'm so slow to learn.'

Ray's large eyes narrowed as he looked at his father.

'You've been holding forth again, Dad. I know the look. Word drunk, that's him. Father, dear Father, come home from the soap box. The Principells of Electricitah.'

Sylvia looked sideways at Harold to see if he was taking it all right; but she needn't have worried. No one could be offended with Ray. He said everything with such a smile and, even with his father, he gave him such laughing looks. You could tell what a flirt he must be with the girls.

'Never you worry, Gran. I know all the magic words to charm the monsters. I'll bring my wand along and teach you all the spells tomorrow night. Anyway these monsters will be out of date in a year. So that's for you.' He made a rude gesture with two fingers at the cooker. 'You're dismissed,' he said to Harold. 'Gran's beginning a new course from tomorrow night and it will all be done by flair.'

82

'That's all very well for you ex-art school blokes,' Harold laughed. 'You can use mumbo jumbo. The artist's intuition! But your Grandmother's never studied art.'

'She doesn't need to. She's a picture all to herself. Aren't you, lovey?' Ray bent down and kissed Sylvia and she didn't even feel a bit silly. 'Well, that's settled,' he said. 'Six thirty in the kitchen and the password's spaghetti bolognese. How do I look?'

Sylvia surveyed in turn his well-pressed dark suit, shining white shirt and short blue overcoat with fur collar and double cuffs. 'You look really smart, Ray,' and then because she felt that she knew this grandson, 'Lucky her!' Ray frowned slightly, then smiled again,

'Ah! You mean awah deah Directah's wife. "What's this I hear, Calvert, you and my Monah eloping." "It's no good, sir, I won't take a quid less than five hundred for the job." "Thank you, my boy. Cheap at the price to get her off my hands."'

His imitations were so funny he had them both roaring although Harold disguised his laughter by fiddling with his moustache. He looked sternly at his son's feet.

'Those elastic-sided shoes look more like a children's dancing class to me. I suppose you dandies have given up the Italian style altogether.'

Once again Ray looked at his father with narrowed eyes, then turning to Sylvia,

'There you are, Gran. Where else would you get a father like him? Up to all the latest styles.'

'*I* liked the Italian style,' Harold announced.

Ray patted him on the shoulder as he left them. 'I know you did, Dad. Always almost with it.'

Sylvia couldn't quite tell what he meant.

'He's a good lad, isn't he, Mother? Anybody else with all that charm would have been spoilt years ago. There isn't an activity here he doesn't take part in – sports, dancing, acting, the lot. Of course, he has a natural ease. I watch him walk into a room sometimes, and then I think what an effort it always cost his mother or me to go out to parties.'

'Arthur's got it,' Sylvia said.

Harold frowned. 'Yes,' he looked very solemn. 'All these

tools. They can only be judged by how we use them,' and he started the roto-roast turning.

In the following days Ray took her in hand. But the fact remained that even when with Ray's easy, jollying along tuition she had in a few days become mistress of all the electronic monsters, she still felt herself of no real use to the household. They clearly didn't like the old-fashioned English cooking that was all she knew, and even that came back to her somewhat hazily, for it was many years since she'd cooked except in staff emergencies. She'd have to learn from them to do what they could do better. But learn she must, for she'd always believed, always would, that the men of the family, the breadwinners must have things just as they like them. That was the only reason that she saw to it that Arthur sometimes had the things he fancied so that he could forget now and again that he'd not been the real wage earner for so many years.

It was just such an attempt to keep up Arthur's morale that led to all the trouble over the central heating.

She had been reading Leslie Gericault's new novel all the afternoon; but somehow she hadn't liked it as much as most of hers. It was about Miss Clitheroe, the old spinster in the village, who appeared so simple, but was really so wise, and solved all the villagers' problems for them. She liked the Miss Clitheroe books as a rule because the old girl said such funny things in an old-fashioned way. But this one was different, not so good as the others. In it Miss Clitheroe had a sort of heart attack and, although of course in the end Doctor Manly, the old village G.P., said that there was no real reason to worry, he did add that we must all remember that we are none of us getting any younger. Sylvia had found it hard to finish the book. The piece about it on the cover said, 'In *Miss Clitheroe's New Neighbours*, Leslie Gericault gives a further dimension to life in Pensworth-cum-Astbury. To her wonderful true life vignettes of everyday village comedy she has added a new note – a note of gentle gravity.' Sylvia wished she had not.

When Arthur came down to join her in the sitting room, she could not remember when she had felt so pleased to see him, although she also could not prevent herself from saying,

'Oh, Arthur! Really! Half past three. Half the day's gone, and you've got your pyjama jacket on again under your shirt.'

Happily he too seemed anxious to preserve a pleasant atmosphere, for he did not reply to her criticism with his usual battery of curses.

'How about a pot of tea, Sylvia? This damned central heating dries up my mouth.'

She made him a nice fresh pot and brought it to him with some ginger nuts on a tray. Sitting there opposite him in front of where the fire should have been, she felt so glad of his company that she even said nothing when he dipped the biscuits into his tea.

'Well, I suppose Harold knows what he's doing. He's meant to be so brilliant. But I've never seen such a god-forsaken hole as this place in my life. All this talk about bridge, I haven't smelt a card yet, let alone a bridge player.'

'We've only been here a week, dear. And the weather's been so bad.'

'A bloody week too much as far as I'm concerned.'

'Oh, now, Arthur. I feel a bit lost too. But it'll be all right as soon as the furniture's arrived. We can make our room like home then. You'll have a nice comfortable chair. Then you won't want to stop in bed all day.' She added quickly, 'There I'm nagging you again.' She laughed. But she saw that Arthur wasn't laughing at all. He had got up from his chair and was staring out of the window, then he came back and stood over her. He was trembling with one of his sudden angers.

'It's no good Sylvie. I can't live here. You'll have to tell Harold. We'll leave as soon as ruddy Christmas is over.'

She had to say firmly: 'Now, Arthur, you know you'll never live within your pension. We must just make the best of it. We're very lucky old people really.'

His familiar rage had brought back memories and she feared that she would cry from sheer nostalgia. But her own words soothed her. In him they produced the feeble storm she expected.

'I wish to Christ you'd have me quietly put to sleep. It would be far better for all of you to have me out of the way. Serve your country, lose your bloody lungs, and they can't even give you a decent enough pension to live on. Ruddy charity, that's what we've had to take . . .'

Sylvia waited for it come to an end and so, abruptly, it did. He sat down opposite her again and said,

'I wouldn't mind so much if it wasn't for this blasted central heating. Dries you up to nothing.'

'They say it gets rid of all the draughts, dear.'

'Draughts! You can always have screens, can't you? Give me the old-fashioned coal fire every time.'

'I like them better too. But they do mean more work.'

'Well, *we've* always had them, haven't we?'

'Yes, but we've always had a hotel staff. And I must say it's warmer here in the passages.'

'Warmer in the passages! Who the hell wants to sit in the passages? I don't know.'

Sylvia laughed. 'I don't know. I really don't,' she put on Mrs Harker's accent. Then because he looked so forlorn, 'I'll put the temperature down for you. Ray showed me how to do it the other day. Of course it'll take some time to have any effect.' When she opened the little gauge she clicked her tongue. '70. Well, really! Anyone would think it was summertime. 60 will be quite enough, won't it Arthur?'

'Quite enough. What does Harold think we are. Ruddy monkeys in the jungle?'

Just the fact that they'd altered the temperature to suit themselves made them both feel more at ease. Sylvia had to smile, for only ten minutes later, Arthur said, 'Ah, that's more like it. I can breathe now.' She knew the temperature hadn't changed that much yet. But they said so much is in the mind, didn't they?

They sat watching television together quite happily so that when Judy, always the first home, came in, they were content not to call her to them as they usually did, but to let her go straight upstairs to her room to study. They watched a whole Western and for once Sylvia didn't complain about the noise of the shooting and Arthur didn't say that it was all kid's stuff. They were pleased to see Harold, of course, when he came in, but at the back of her mind Sylvia thought how nice it would have been if the family had been out – just Arthur and herself with the tele and a nice Welsh rarebit on a tray.

But Harold was in very happy, friendly form. He had received the proof of the family Christmas card back from the printers. The Calvert Christmas cards were famous in Carshall and even farther afield. Harold and Beth had invented such amusing ones. One year it had been a drawing of Harold wearing wings and singing in the bath like he always did – 'Hark the Harold Angel Sings', it had read. Another year, there'd been a picture of a great Christmas pudding, and, in reproduction of Harold's writing, an inscription, 'Our monster pudding – but we shan't give Beth Any', and then, in Beth's handwriting, 'God forgive him his puns.' Always something original and personal. Of course, not everyone liked them. Sylvia remembered how when old Miss Mitton at the Palmeira had seen one of them on the mantelpiece in their room, she had said it was a mockery of Christ's birth. Sylvia had tried to explain that they weren't a religious family in the strict meaning of the word, but there was obviously offence given.

Harold handed the proofs to his mother.

'There you are, and you too, Dad.' And he smiled slyly. It took Arthur and Sylvia rather a long time to read the card because it was in verse and the first letter of each line was sort of oldfashioned in colours with little drawings inside the spaces.

It read:

> Calvert's Yule-Tide News announces:
> Harold's Hastings still not come.
> Ray still shines, the King of Rayon.
> Judy's Punch, it seems, is dumb.
> Sylvia – what is she? Our granny.
> 'The Sycamores' is now *her* home.
> Mark got lost at Aldermaston.
> Arthur's here no more to roam.
> So happy Christmas to you all.

Sylvia's mind was still with the Western – she'd guessed the girl's brother was a bad lot even before they'd taken the mask off the dead cattle thief. She found the poem so difficult to understand, especially the pictures, although probably they were clues. She wasn't too happy either about having her Christian name and Arthur's sent out like that to strangers; and then nobody knew them, why should they? It looked so forward.

However, Harold was waiting. 'Well?' he asked.

'The picture of the house is ever so good dear. Who drew it?'

'I made rough sketches,' he said rather impatiently, 'and Ray and Judy did the final drawings between them.'

There was a silence. 'Well?'

'It's lovely, dear, though I don't understand it all. Fancy putting in Arthur and me. I don't know what people will think. Two old nobodies,' she added, 'Your father did his bit in his time, but they won't know that.'

Harold took the card from them and laid it on one of the many coffee tables.

'They'll think, as I intended, that we're happy and proud to have my mother and father living with us at "The Sycamores". Or, at any rate, anyone whose friendship I care about will think it.'

Arthur rose to the occasion, 'God bless you, my boy. You've made two old people very happy.'

To Sylvia's amazement he got up from his chair, and, drawing Harold's head down in his cupped hands, he kissed his balding crown. There were tears in his eyes.

Sylvia was glad she had some knitting to bend down over so that no one could see she was not weeping. She supposed she was wrong not to feel as strongly as that; she was pleased, just as pleased as Arthur if it came to that. But family feelings aren't just for Christmas, they're for every day. And the Calverts weren't a family to show emotion. The affection was there, there was no need to speak of it. What was it Mrs Harker had said the other day to that silly sister of hers who was always having hysterics? ''Tisn't tears, my girl, that's needed. More water than tears can make has flowed under our bridge through all these years.' Or something like that; it wasn't quite clear. But she had so agreed with the old thing. And now . . .

'I don't quite get what this bloke with the hockey stick's got to do with your mother.'

Sylvia signed to Arthur to keep quiet, but, in fact, Harold was delighted.

'Yes, that drawing does want a bit of touching up. What you reasonably call a hockey stick is a shepherd's crook, Dad. You know, "Who is Sylvia? What is she; That all our swains commend her."'

'I don't, but I'll take your word for it.'

Harold seemed so pleased that Sylvia ventured to ask some questions about the drawings too; and, of course, when you heard the answers, it seemed silly not to have known them all along. Arthur remembered perfectly well about King Harold at Hastings when he was told; and Sylvia remembered well about King Arthur and the sword, she'd heard it as part of Iris's homework in the old days. It was more confusing about Mark, because she'd read about the Aldermaston march, but she didn't know that he'd been on it; and it seemed he hadn't, it was a sort of joke to tease him. As to Punch and Judy there was more to it than just that, but they couldn't have known because it was a horse's name.

'For once,' Harold said, 'Judy's snobbish equine attachments came in useful. Thank God! Because it would have been difficult to find anything to say about her. She hasn't the personality of the other two.'

'She's got a very pretty little figure has my little grand-daughter, let me tell you that.'

'As long as you don't tell *her*, Dad.'

'Mind you,' Arthur said, 'the card's very clever. But I don't exactly see you as poet laureate, Harold. After this.' Harold was delighted.

'I challenge anybody to write nine such feeble lines between interviewing a paranoid parent of a cretinous child and telling one of Her Majesty's Inspectors just how bad I thought his report on the School's mathematics performance was.'

Arthur didn't exactly understand, but he recognized the tone of his son's speech.

'That's the stuff to give the troops,' he said.

'Well, Mother,' Harold bent down and kissed her cheek again, 'I've tried to tell you how happy I am to have you here. I hope you're not too disappointed with the place. It's a poor thing, but mine own. Or rather not exactly that because as you know the philosophy of the New Towns precludes freeholds. But who knows? Today's heresy is tomorrow's dogma.'

Sylvia made every effort to sound enthusiastic.

'I'm very happy, dear. It's a lovely home.' Then she felt the pulses in her temples throb as a sudden courage welled up in her. 'But I shall be happier still if you let me do more. I don't like you and the boys, or Judy while she's studying so hard, doing housework and cooking while I sit about all day. It's bad enough my not being able to get out and do the shopping.'

It was a hard struggle for Harold. At first he tried holding the untenable front of her blood pressure, but –' 'Oh, no, Harold. The doctor was most anxious that I shouldn't be idle. Worry – that's the thing to avoid; that and back-breaking work. Well, the work here wouldn't break the back of a mouse. As long as I get my afternoon rests. I'm much more likely to worry, sitting about.'

Arthur broke in to help her. 'Yes, you'd much better let your mother get on with it. She's broad enough in the beam without sitting about on her b-t-m all day.'

Then Harold fell back on stronger defences.

'I know this may sound silly to you, Mother. But it's really a matter of principle. From the very start, as early as they could be useful, Beth brought the children up to live the co-operative way. We all did a full day's work *and* we all ran the house. Anything else, as Beth said, belonged to the era of slave and owner, wives and chattels, and the rest.'

'But I don't do a full day's work, Harold.'

'My dear Mother, everyone's a right to retirement some time even in Utopia. To be frank, it's the children I'm thinking of. Of course Ray and Mark are adults, they'll choose for themselves; though I think I know how they will. But Judy isn't, and she's got enough false notions already.'

He was so agitated that Sylvia could only say, 'Very well, dear.' But she couldn't keep a quaver out of her voice. When Harold saw that there were tears in her eyes, he filled his pipe embarrassedly.

'Now, Mother, we're not a family to give way to tears.' But then suddenly he agreed to compromise; Sylvia could run the house on weekdays, the rest of the family on Saturdays and Sundays.

'Well, that's all settled then,' Arthur said comfortably.

And indeed his parents' content reached Harold, for any annoyance he had shown soon gave way to high spirits.

'All this problem of retirement and families has been grossly worked up by the professional sociologists,' he said. 'While they've been arguing, some of the more practical of us have been solving it for them. The basic answer's simple enough – the notions of freedom and companionship that we've stood for, and still stand for, are by no means incompatible with our grandparents' ideals of responsibility and manliness.' Sylvia couldn't make any sense of it. His grandparents! Her parents were not much of an advertisement, and Arthur's had been dead since the year dot. Nor could Arthur; and he changed the subject.

'Your mother and I have got something to show *you* this evening, Harold. We've made the house a bit more like an Englishman's castle and a little less like the snake house at the Zoo.'

It was Harold's turn to appear puzzled. Sylvia's heart was in her mouth; she signalled to Arthur with her knitting needles to say no more. But out with it all he came. 'So you see,' he ended, 'that your mother's perfectly competent to tinker about with all these blasted machines.'

Harold swung round on her. 'Who showed you how to alter the thermostat?'

'Ray did, dear, but . . .'

'Well, he had no right to. The temperature of the house and, for that matter, the barometer are the affair of the head of the house. They always have been.' He cut himself short. 'In any case, these gauges are very delicate mechanisms. Unless absolutely necessary they should not be altered except in October and March.'

'And your mother and I, I suppose, are to be dried up to bloody dust.'

'Of course, if you find the house so uncomfortably hot, the temperature must be lowered. But I should still prefer that you should ask me before you . . . In any case we'll leave it as it is now and hope that we shan't all catch our death of cold. But when you've got your own room fitted up, Mother, perhaps you'll be good enough to get me to set the temperature there as you want it and we can restore the rest of the house to some degree of modern comfort.' He laughed, 'I'm being absurdly pompous. It's a matter of generations – you live in the glorious age of draughts, we don't.'

But it was too late to pacify Arthur, despite Sylvia's frowns. 'As soon as our bloody furniture comes, Harold, you won't see me again in your posh lounge, I can tell you that. Not a comfortable chair to sit on.'

Sylvia felt she must back up Arthur a little. 'We're in the house all day, you see, Harold. You wouldn't want us to be uncomfortable.'

For answer Harold cut himself off behind a barrier of evening newspaper and thick pipe smoke. Yet the feud was not ended. It flared up between Arthur and Harold later at supper with all the family present. As Sylvia was refusing a second helping of risotto from Mark, Harold said in his announcing voice, 'Well, Ray, it seems your grandmother's out of your tutorial clutches.'

'Yes, you've got your "L" plates off, haven't you, dear?'

'The question then comes, who's to teach your grandfather the elements of domestic economy.'

Arthur, intent on his chump chop, looked up in surprise. 'Count me out, laddie. I'd only . . . well, I won't say what I'd do to the works in front of my pretty little granddaughter. But they wouldn't be the same after I'd messed them about; that's all.'

'My dear Dad. You've always wanted to live by pressing a button. Now's your chance.'

'Thank you very much, Harold. Unless you'd let me look after the barometer,' he winked at the boys. 'Your father runs the weather here, you know, as well as the temperature. No, I had enough blasted buttons in the ranks to last me a lifetime. Unless you can produce Alf's button.'

The grandchildren had never heard of this, and addressing himself to them, he told the whole story in Old Bill tommy's language. '"Strike me pink, Alf said, and so the genie blighter struck him pink."' They all laughed with him except Harold.

'Don't you agree with me, Mother, that a little house-work would work wonders with the old man?'

It wasn't so much that Sylvia wanted to be on Arthur's side, although that came into it, but more that the absurdity was too great for her.

'Oh dear, Dad hasn't got out of doing everything all these years to start now, Harold.'

She saw that Judy thought it a bitter remark to make about her granddad, for she turned to him and said, 'I know what I'd do, Granddad, if I had Alf's button. I'd wish us two absolutely super horses to ride off together on.'

But Harold was angry, 'Very well, Mother, I wash my hands of it. You've preferred to spoil him all your life. You must take the consequences.' His hand shook as he helped himself to more sugo.

Mark said, 'Any more news about the Inquiry Commission on Goodchild's meadow, Dad?'

'Oh, so the machinations of the N.A.T.O. war machine haven't entirely blinded you to local affairs,' Harold answered, but he was smiling.

Sylvia felt a flush spreading up her neck. Perhaps it was only the effort of suppressing tears. Then she felt a hand on her arm.

'We had a lovely new design in today, Gran. Just made for you. You know, dowager's stuff. The full purple. But just right with your hair.'

Ray spoke to her now in an almost intimate whisper, steadying her in no time. She felt quite happy as he told her about the new long tweed evening skirts that they were all wearing now. Upstairs in their room, Arthur said, 'I told young master Harold off, all right.' Sylvia, rubbing cream into her face before the dressing-table mirror, decided that it would be wiser not to respond; then an anxious look in his reflected eyes made her feel that she ought to support him. She smiled 'Oh, Arthur.' But her tone was admiring.

He came over and kissed her; he put his hand on her bare thigh where the dressing gown had fallen apart. It seemed years since he had made such a gesture. In her imagination it took her back to their early days of marriage, to their first boarding house in Bognor – it must have been

1920. Of course there had been times since . . . She returned his kiss and the pressure of his hand.

'Well,' he said comfortably as he got into bed, 'don't say I never stand up for you, Sylvie.'

At breakfast the next morning, Harold stood up as though he was going to offer a prayer. 'With the Christmas holidays about to begin, I want the family opinion on whether this isn't a good moment to revive a lapsed custom – one of Beth's most cherished. I mean the family roster. Ray?'

'Whatever you think, Dad.'

'Mark?'

Mark scowled, but nodded his agreement.

'All right then, Judy?'

'Yes, of course, Daddy.'

'Very well. Now this is just a rough draft that I typed out in the witching hours. It needs the family approval.' He passed a typewritten sheet around to his three children. Sylvia could see that they were more resigned to whatever it was than delighted by it. But they all, even Mark, smiled as in turn they agreed. She thought that, whatever Harold's faults, he must be a good father to command such affection.

It was Judy who said, 'You've seen it, Gran, I suppose.'

'No dear. Should I?'

All three of her grandchildren seemed to blush at once, but it was Mark who pushed the paper towards her. 'You should have seen it first,' he mumbled. It was a difficult list to follow. It was headed:

ROSTER FOR HOUSEHOLD DUTIES,
FOR JANUARY, FEBRUARY, AND MARCH

Then across the top were a list of duties: Breakfast, Washing Up, Housework, Shopping, Dinner, Supper, W.U., Laundry. And at the side were the days. In each column were initials for the person responsible for duty.

'You're "G", Gran,' Judy said.

'That's for gorgeous,' Ray told her.

'G' appeared only as often as the other letters, and not at all under shopping.

'I've left you out of shopping for the moment, Mother. On the other hand, as you see, dinner's a blank except at weekends because the boys are at work. I thought you'd get whatever you wanted for yourself and the old man. Now the school holidays are here, Judy and I can take on when we're in. Laundry falls to you in the third week of every month. Supper washing up I've kept as a dual act. I think it's a necessary concession to human gregariousness. As Beth used to say, solitary confinement ought to be a thing of the past.'

'But surely the housework . . .' Sylvia began.

'I think you'll find it works out best as it is, Mother. Oh, and please notice, everyone, the highly coloured addenda.'

Indeed, there at the bottom of the page in large red type was: Temperature Control 1st Jan, 1st March only – Harold; and in smaller green type: Car and motorcycle washing 1st of each month R, 15th each month M; Garden duties: Jan, Feb: none. March: Prune the roses – Judy.

'You don't know anything about roses, do you, Mother? Beth's aunt gave us three bushes. A fearful nuisance they are. However Judy's an adherent of gracious living . . .'

Sylvia couldn't believe that he'd done it. After promising! She had only three meals a week to cook, including breakfast; that and her share with the others in the washing up. She tried to tell herself that she'd been selfish in over-persuading him; after all an Englishman's home is his castle. But the weeks, the years ahead, stretched out in front of her in empty uselessness. All that day she kept feeling herself too big; she seemed to have to squeeze between coffee tables, she knocked a tobacco jar off the hall windowsill, her body filled the rooms she entered so that she revolted herself – a superfluous, fat old woman. Oh, it was mean of him!

During that day she rejected the idea of a direct appeal to Harold from pride mixed with fear. At last, when the evening came, she asked Ray for his help. He was quite put out by her story. His full red lips pouted and he closed his long eyelashes over his big eyes like, yes, almost like some embarrassed beautiful girl, except that, with his square, chunky build and his sailor's roll, no one could be less girlish.

'Oh dear!' he said at last in a mock horrified voice, 'oh

dear! This is a nice little caper.' He looked at her for a moment, then flashed a smile, 'What do you want to cook for anyway, Lovey? When you've had a basinful of it like I have ... I know what it is. Modom's blasée. Weary of the round of pleasures, she wants to go on a new jag – house-work. You idle butterflies!'

Sylvia didn't know what to make of it. 'I wasn't exactly idle at the Palmeira, Ray dear. If you'd seen my day's work ...'

He kissed her cheek. 'I know, Gran. I was only having you on. As the salesman ... Well perhaps what the sales-man said isn't quite for the ladies' ears. God bless 'em! I'll see what I can do. Trust your beautiful blue-eyed grand-son.'

But he couldn't do much, it seemed, for in the end it was Mark who came to her. He mumbled so low that she had difficulty in hearing him.

'Look, Gran. What I'd do is agree with Dad. I mean it's ... Well, the roster means a lot to him. I mean, we don't want it either. But now Mother's gone and so on. Well ... Would you come and look at something, please?'

He took her up to his bedroom and pulled out an old typewritten sheet from a drawer.

'That was the last one Mother had to cope with. In fact she didn't keep going to the end of it. Then Dad stopped them. But you see everywhere he put B then, he's put G now.'

So there wasn't anything she could do but accept. Nevertheless she still remembered that he had agreed to her wishes and then gone back on her promise because of a petty grievance. It *was* mean of him, she couldn't help thinking it; even though, of course, she should never have forced him into the position of behaving badly by fussing him with her troubles. And at least the roster gave her the courage to insist on her own diet so that now she and Arthur shared supper of a grill which she cooked. This separation of diet seemed to restore them to their original apartness from the family.

There were times when Harold tried to make it up to her. With the revival of the family duty roster, he had also brought back a sheet headed 'Comments' which was stuck to the Forest Green kitchen wall with sellotape. Here he and the children exchanged remarks on each other's cooking. Harold's tribute to her was long and personal. 'How that treacle tart took me back, Mother, to "Seaview" at Littlehampton, "Mrs Calvert's wonderful treacle tarts." How Len used to wolf his down so that he got three helpings to my two. And your hand hasn't lost one inch of its skill.' Perhaps it was the effect of his fulsomeness, but none of her three grandchildren made any comment but, 'Excellent, thank you, Gran.'

On Monday Harold took 'Comments' away. He said shortly, 'It would be absurd to pretend that, without Beth, we're up to this sort of thing.'

Sylvia cursed the new manageress who'd written from the Palmeira to say that there'd been some muddle in the despatch of their furniture. But it was on its way now, and she longed intensely for its arrival so that if there was to be this division it might be made complete. 'The best of friends are best apart.' It sounded hard but that was how life was.

In fact she felt more embarrassed than hurt by Harold's snub; it was like when Mr Hooper of Ritson Hotels had asked all the manageresses to Head Office for an interview and then announced that he'd decided to select the Catering Supervisor from outside. You felt stripped in public. Everyone knew.

Even Arthur had noticed. 'Don't look so down in the dumps, for God's sake, Sylvie. Because young master Harold's turned out to be the little twister he always was, we don't have to worry. You cook for me and I can't want anything better. If they prefer a lot of greasy Eytie mess, let them get on with it.' He'd patted her on the back. But, of course, that didn't really help.

One evening that week, however, a chance to please Harold did come.

'Do you still enjoy dolling yourself up, Mother?' Harold asked. 'Because if so we might accept the Bartley's invitation for cocktails. Carshall's very hospitable at Christmas time. As a matter of fact if I liked to accept all the invitations I'm sent . . . As it is, as you see, I'm out almost every evening in the ten days before Christmas . . . I haven't suggested asking you and Dad, though you'd be welcome at any of our friends' houses. But I thought that you'd prefer to settle in first. And anyway the weather . . . But the Bartleys happened to know you've arrived and they've specially asked for you to come. They're extraordinary people really. Quite a young couple. He owns all Carshall's greengrocers' stores. No education, but, in my opinion, a very high I.Q. indeed. Their boy Derek's one of my brightest sparks. I'm putting him in for G.C.E. next year. She looks like a mannequin, but she's most public-spirited. Beth admired her enormously, they were on many committees together. Beth always said you could forgive anyone looking like a doll who could do the hard day's work that Muriel Bartley did. Theirs was the only house she would dress up for. She hated that sort of thing, as you know. Would you care to go there?'

Arthur laughed, 'Care to go? Of course she would. Have you ever known a proper woman refuse an opportunity to wear her glad rags.'

Harold frowned, 'Don't consider going, Mother, if you don't want to. As to the weather, there's no sign of a thaw. But you'd only have the distance from the door to the car and back again. I shan't disguise that I'd be pleased if you would come. Apart from anything else Muriel Bartley's my right hand among the school governors. Oh, and by the way, Dad, the Cranstons will be there. Jack's ashamed of not having fixed any bridge up for you yet, but what with the weather and the Christmas rush . . .'

There was no doubt it could be a new beginning all round. When Harold took Sylvia aside and said, 'You'll see the old man smartens himself up a bit for the Bartley's, won't you, Mother?' she promised that she would and she did.

As for herself, Sylvia really did her best. She was worried about whether she should take a taxi down to Madame Greta the hairdresser for a blue rinse and set (she'd got the salon's name by subterfuge from Judy), but later the same morning Judy said almost casually, 'Isn't it lucky your hair is just right for the Bartleys, Granny? Caroline Ogilvie's grandmother's got lovely white hair like yours. She was saying that she dreads having it done down here. It seems you only have to nod off for a minute and they send you out all terrible perms and purple.' So that was a helpful warning. She wore her mulberry twinset and her beaver lamb, but, for this frozen weather, she was pleased to feel that she had just the right hat – an ocelot high crowned cap in Russian style. Of course, it wasn't real fur, she hadn't been able to afford more than nylon, but it did look quite good. As they assembled in the hall, Ray said, 'There's my lovely. All you need's a sledge.'

'A damned big one,' Arthur laughed. He'd been given a red carnation by Judy for his buttonhole and he was as pleased as Punch.

'You go away,' Ray said, 'Gran'll make old Muriel greener than all her groceries. It only wants a touch.' And before Sylvia could protest, he'd draped a piece of some silk material round the neck of her dress – an odd silvery pink it was, patterned with an acid green. At first she thought it would clash horribly with the mulberry, but at a second glance in the hall mirror she could see he was right. She was about to thank him with a kiss but he quickly clicked his tongue in protest. 'You'll spoil your lipstick. Well, I must say, the girls are doing us proud.' And certainly Judy looked charming with her long fair hair swept down to the shoulders of her scarlet mohair coat. Even those hideous old black stockings they'd revived looked nice on her shapely legs.

'You look sweet, dear,' Sylvia told her. And Harold, who hardly ever noticed such things, said,

'Very nice, Judy.'

Judy smiled. 'Thank you, Daddy. I'm afraid it's only copy-cat from something Caroline Ogilvie's aunt bought for her.'

Harold said, 'Hm!'

It was glorious to be outside again, even though the frosty air bit one's cheeks. Harold offered Sylvia an arm down the path, but she evaded it and he went on ahead to start the car. She wanted to feel her freedom to the full. She took two steps and thought – yes, really, it was a pretty district; she could see that many of the houses down Higgleton Road had those holly wreaths that people liked so much nowadays on their highly coloured doors, and in every window she glimpsed the silver frosting and coloured witchballs of Christmas trees. She took two steps more and her heel seemed to slide from under her on the glassy stone. She tried desperately to steady herself. Ray and Mark both ran towards her but too late. She had fallen, cutting her outstretched hand, and grazing her left knee, and bruising her bottom most agonizingly.

The pain and the shock were not enough to drive from her a dreadful picture of herself – a fat useless old woman dolled up to no purpose, a sprawling ugly furry mess on the pathway. She could sense that the cheap imitation hat had fallen rakishly to one side, and that the white hair straggling down her face was spattered with blood from her hand. Ray's lovely gift lay on the gravel, torn and bloody.

Despite all Mark's and Ray's gentleness she felt herself to be a huge sack of coals as they lifted her up from the ground and supported her back into the house. Pain and shame apart, she was too shaken and giddy to take in much of what was happening, but she guessed the ridiculous little procession behind her – Arthur muttering random blasphemies, Judy holding disdainfully the pink and green scarf, Harold with she dreaded to think what expression on his face, but certainly there because she could no longer hear the car engine. In fact when she looked up from the sitting-room sofa where they had laid her, she was right as to the procession, for they stood in a row before her, but quite wrong as to their expressions, there was nothing in any of their faces except concern for her. She felt so ashamed.

Mark cleaned her hand and leg with Dettol and bandaged them as gently and professionally as any nurse. It seemed that as part of his pacifism or C.N.D. or whatever it was, he believed that everyone should be equipped in First Aid. He looked so solemn as he bent over her and his doing it at all so much surprised her that, despite her pains, she tried to thank him with a little joke. She smiled, and putting on Mrs Harker's voice said, 'Mark, the nurse of the family! Well, I don't know. I really don't know.' But he'd never seen 'Down Our Way', and, when she began to explain, he told her to hush and rest.

As soon as it became clear that no bones were broken,

that the doctor was not needed, that all she required was rest, Harold said loudly, as though the remark might not otherwise penetrate a fading consciousness, 'Well, I'd better telephone Geoff Bartley and say we can't get there.' After that it was Sylvia's task to persuade him that they should go; and to do so as quickly as she could so that they should miss as little of the party as possible. The more it became clear that they could go, indeed would go, the more did Harold seem to need persuading, so that, at one point, Sylvia found herself with some agony rising from the sofa. 'I'm perfectly all right, perfectly all right to come.' She only hoped that she could keep up the performance long enough to persuade Harold that he ought to go at once to prevent her insisting on joining them. Her fear was of fainting so that he would once more be delayed, and this time for long enough to miss the party altogether. But luckily Arthur was not one to be 'all dressed up and nowhere to go'.

'Your Mother'll be perfectly all right here. Of course we must go, Harold. We can't be rude to these friends of yours. Besides, my little Judy's got to show herself off.'

Finally Harold agreed that, if only not to worry his mother, they should go. 'We needn't stay for more than a courtesy visit.' On some sacrifice, however, he did insist; Judy must stay behind to look after her grandmother. 'She's not exactly a ministering angel yet, but the sooner she learns to be one the better.'

Sylvia lay on her bed, to which Ray and Mark had helped her, and tried to think what to say to Judy to make up to her for her disappointment.

'I expect your father seems a bit strict to you sometimes. But I dare say that he forgets that he's your Dad and not your Head. It's more his manner. And then he's only strict because he's so fond of you.' She thought suddenly of her own father who had been so strict because he wasn't.

Judy looked her right in the eyes for one second, but without any expression, as though she were looking at nothing; then, 'Are you all right with just the eiderdown over you, or would you like me to help you get right into bed?'

Sylvia realized she'd said it all wrong; but really her

bones ached so and she felt so shaky that it was difficult to concentrate.

Judy began to minister by tucking the eiderdown all round Sylvia so that she was confined in one cramped, painful position. 'There! That's more like it, Gran. I'm only too glad not to go to those awful Bartleys. Mrs Moore-Duncan, that's Caroline Ogilvie's grandmother I was telling you about who has such lovely white hair, says it doesn't matter what kind of people people are as long as they're genuine and don't pretend to be something better. Do you agree, Gran?' She didn't wait for an answer. 'The Bartleys are terrible show-offs.' Picking up Sylvia's hair-brushes and scent bottles, she examined each in turn. 'Granddad's frightfully genuine, isn't he?' she observed. 'How did you come to meet?' Sylvia explained that she'd been working at the great country house where Arthur was convalescing. 'Lady Pembroke had given it for a hospital. Your grandfather was badly gassed, you know. He wanted nursing all the time.'

'Oh, you were a nurse, Gran? Daddy never said anything about it. You'd think he would have done when he and Mummy were so keen on me going in for nursing. Not that I'm against nursing. Lots of the girls at school are going to be nurses. Some of the nicest ones too. But of course it's a vocation, isn't it?'

Lying on the bed, trying to suppress her shivering, Sylvia had a sudden intense memory of the awe with which she used to look up from scrubbing the floor to see the starch of the matron's or a V.A.D.'s uniform. She would not lie to little Judy, but, seeing her smart, trim little figure, she could not tell her the truth. She need not have worried. Judy was in a mood to talk rather than to listen.

'Would you like me to cook you something? A boiled egg? Or some soup? Shall I refill those hot-water bottles? You must be longing to have your own things around you, Gran. Of course, in a way Mummy was right to have this modern décor in a house like this. If one's got to live in awful Carshall. I do look forward to your furniture coming. I love old things. It will be exciting.'

'I'm afraid you know our old sticks all too well already, Judy. You've seen them nearly every Christmas at Eastsea.'

'Oh! Have I? I thought that was hotel stuff.' Judy's face clouded. 'All the same I'll bet they'll be nicer than all this. I mean they *will* have character. Mrs Ogilvie has some absolutely lovely old pieces that have been with the family for generations. Wasn't it awful some American or something, at any rate some terrible show-off who was brought there to tea, offered to buy them? Caroline said you should have seen her mother's face. Of course, she said at once that he must have made a mistake, because they weren't showpieces or anything, just family things that they'd always had. Wasn't it a super-snub, Gran? Am I tiring you? You must say.'

Sylvia longed to say exactly that, but she had had so little chance to talk with her granddaughter; and for all the girl's assurance she couldn't help believing that Harold's manner had hurt her. A phrase came back to her from something she had read last summer – could it have been in one of Denise Robbins's – 'The absurd little subterfuges of sophistication with which we try to ward off life's first hurts.' Yes, that was it. She had thought then how true it was of many young people today like Pat Reynolds. She liked young girls. She had always been so much closer to Iris than to the boys. She mustn't be put off just because the girl was clever like her mother – book learning could only be a small part of a girl's life. She must try again, only less directly this time.

Shifting her great weight as best she could beneath the tightly tucked in eiderdown, she eased the pain in her buttocks. She said: 'What subjects are you taking for your exam, Judy?'

'Oh, Botany, Geography, French, German, and ghastly Latin.'

'Don't you like Latin then, dear?'

'Oh, I would. But Miss Mackie, who teaches it, is so awful! Everybody hates her. She's so old.'

'Well, I'm old, dear.'

'Oh, I know, but not like you. I mean she's never been married or anything. Honestly I think when she has to stop teaching irregular verbs she'll just crack up or something. I mean she's never been anything. Just taught Latin all her life. Isn't it awful?'

The subject of Miss Mackie made Sylvia more conscious of her aching limbs. She sought in her mind for a change of subject; but Judy made the change for her.

'Wouldn't it be lovely if I could do like Caroline and go for a year to a finishing school in Switzerland and then come back and just live in the country and ride?'

'I think that would be a pity, dear, with your brains. Your father's so proud of you. He's sure you'll get all sorts of A's and O's.'

'A's, Gran darling. Did he really say that? I wish he'd say it to me.'

'And then it'll be nice to follow in your mother's footsteps.'

'Oh, Mummy didn't do a proper University degree. She was only doing some sort of Social Science Certificate when Daddy met her. All the same it would be nice to live in the country. Oh, I know Daddy thinks he has to stay in awful Carshall. But look at Chantry Farm, Mrs Moore-Duncan's house! After all, that's only eight miles away.'

'You wouldn't have the same comforts in the country, dear. I know. I used to live there as a girl.'

'Comforts? Oh, you mean central heating and all that. But most houses have that now, don't they? Chantry Farm has. But Mrs Moore-Duncan only has it on at the very last moment in winter. She has lovely log fires all the year round. She says England doesn't have a real summer. And, of course, it's the open fires we all crowd round when we come in from riding. Were you really on a farm when you were a girl, Gran? Did you have those wonderful great coppers for washing?'

Sylvia desperately sought to recover her girlhood wash-days from beneath decades of soiled hotel linen. 'Yes, I think we did, dear.'

'Well, there you are! Mrs Cartland, Caroline's great-aunt, Mrs Moore-Duncan's sister, has coppers for washing and she bakes all her own bread. She says that it's the only way to make sure that it's really crusty. I think that that's what's so marvellous about your generation. You still had contact with shapes and forms through your fingers and hands. People say we've all gone dead now. But surely that's bound to be so when we let machines do everything for us.'

Sylvia's bruises hurt her so much that she gave an involuntary scream but she managed to disguise it as a yawn.

'I think I'll have a little snooze now, if you don't mind, dear.'

After Judy had gone, it took her a long time to find a position that did not cause her pain; but at last she fell asleep. She awoke to the lively return of Harold and Arthur. They had been on to the Cranstons, it seemed, and Arthur had won twelve bob at bridge.

'Well, Mother, how are you? You missed a good party. Dad's the social success of Carshall. He kept them all in fits of laughter.'

'I simply told them a few chestnuts that were already old when Noah took his little cruise in the ark. But they seemed amused by them.'

'I've never seen Jack Cranston laugh like that in my life, Dad.'

Sylvia tried to sit up to express her pleasure at their successful evening, but her muscles ached too much. Her movements drew Harold's attention.

'Muriel Bartley was most disappointed that you weren't there, Mother.'

Sylvia could think of no answer to this, so she closed her eyes.

'I think the old lady's sleeping,' Harold whispered. 'What about you and me having a nightcap downstairs, Dad?'

3. Settling In

'Now Mother, how *do* you feel?' Harold asked a few mornings later. He had brought in the breakfast tray, for a late breakfast in bed was a panacea for all ills at 'The Sycamores'.

She smiled in answer, wondering if the morning mail had brought her any news from the outside world.

'Truly?' And again a little sharply, 'Is that really the truth, Mother?' for she had not yet answered. She had seen a letter balanced against her teapot, and the thought of it held her enchanted. She came to at his brusque tone.

'Yes, Harold dear, truly.' Then to convince him, 'I don't say I could do the twist, but short of that . . .'

'Splendid! Then I think I can let you into a little secret. I haven't said anything up to now . . .' He paused, for his mother had begun opening her letter.

'Yes, Harold dear?'

'No, no, read your letter, of course.'

'It's only a bill, I think. You were saying . . .'

'I was going to show you this.' He produced a card from his pocket. Sylvia looked at it vaguely.

'It looks like the railway at last,' then catching his puzzled look, she quickly added, 'What a pretty card, dear. Who sent it?'

'I did, of course.'

'Oh!' Sylvia was bewildered. She found her glasses on the side table. '"A Nip and a Nibble",' she read aloud. 'The picture of the roast chicken and the bottle of wine or whatever it is quite makes one's mouth water, doesn't it?'

'Yes, yes, Mother, read on.'

'THE CALVERT FAMILY INVITE YOU
TO MEET THE OLD FOLKS AT HOME'

'Oh!' she said, 'Oh!' and then, 'Oh! That *is* sweet of

you, Harold dear. I don't know what to say. I'm afraid your friends'll be most disappointed. I'll do my best to entertain them. But what about catering? Do you have someone in Carshall? Or should I go up to London and see what Barker's could do for us? Mrs King in the catering department knows me so well. I could easily manage the journey.'

Harold laughed. 'Caterers, Mother! You'll have to forget your grand hotel banquets now. Calvert and Company are giving their services free for this occasion. But you'd better look at the date on the invitation . . .'

'Thursday 19th. But, Harold, that's tonight. Oh dear . . .'

'Now don't fuss, Mother. Everything's under control. It's only a small party anyway. The boys did their stint of baking in the witching hours. Judy and I are at the good work now. When you're down, we shan't refuse a helping hand. . . .'

Sylvia wondered how a small party could need so much preparation, but then she really knew nothing about private entertaining. And anyway she wanted so much to see what was in her letter. She fingered it lovingly.

Harold said, 'Well, I'll leave you to your correspondence.'

He sounded a little hurt. She called after him, 'I am looking forward to the party.'

Her voice sounded light and happy, for she knew that the Railway Delivery note had come at last to announce the arrival of their furniture. As she looked round at the yellow walls and white hangings (now a bit Arthur-stained and crumpled) she had a moment's fear about how their few old-fashioned sticks would fit into such bright, exotic surroundings. But the main thing was that at last they would have their own room, a bit of their old life as they were used to living it. And then . . . she stared in horror: the furniture was due for delivery that morning. She only knew one thing: that she must stop it coming lest it upset all Harold's preparations for his kind party. To the familiar rhythm of Arthur's snoring, she dressed as quickly as she would have done in the freezing draughts of their Palmeira bedroom – here, with the central heating she had become as slow and torpid as a giant tortoise. To descend the stairs without a creak seemed an impossible task – she saw herself as one of those hippopotamuses dancing ballet steps in that Disney cartoon and almost broke the silence with a fit of giggles. But at last it was done. She was in Harold's little study and on the telephone without anyone knowing. As she gave the station number, she had one awful panic thought that, if she refused the furniture today they might postpone for weeks, for months, for ever. Dismissing the superstition, she made her request; only at last, after much delay, to be told that it was too late, the delivery van was on its way.

As she came out of the study, Harold emerged from the kitchen, a pair of steps under one arm, a black portfolio under the other. 'Ah! There you are, Mother', then he frowned in double take as he saw where she was coming from; she could see him take a breath in order to put all questions aside, and she spurred herself to speak before he recovered.

'Harold, dear, I'm afraid' . . . But she got no further.

'I don't believe you've ever seen these caricatures that Beth did of the family. She was too modest about her gift. But I thought I'd pin them up the stairs. People can see them when they leave their coats.' He put down the steps and produced a drawing of Mark, all fringe and jeans, standing in the pouring rain, above him loomed a gigantic column. The caption read, 'England expects . . .' 'That was where Beth was so good for him. "If he really cares," she used to say, "then a bit of healthy laughter won't destroy his faith."'

'Well, that is clever. I'd no idea . . . Harold, I'm afraid . . .' Judy's head appeared round the kitchen door.

'Oh, Gran. There you are! Could you come for a minute and watch the milk for elevenses. I've got to take out the meringues.'

Harold turned away towards his reverent task. There seemed no choice. And, of course, when among the ivy and polydendron Sylvia broke the news as they sat down before their earthenware coffee mugs it was too late – the doorbell chimed; the furniture had arrived.

Sylvia's first thought was for waking Arthur and getting him out of bed, which she did to a cannonade of curses that resounded through 'The Sycamores'. 'You must go and

have your bath, Arthur . . . and you must manage it yourself this morning.'

'But I don't understand these damned water heaters . . .'

'You don't have to. Just turn on the taps.'

Downstairs she found Harold already in furious argu-
ment with a square broken-nosed boxer-like man in a
turtle-necked sweater. A very pale, fishfaced young man
stood looking on, swaying alarmingly as though he were
about to have an epileptic fit.

'It's perfectly unnecessary for you to telephone. You
have my orders to return with the delivery tomorrow.'

'Tomorrow! You've got a hope, sir, if I may say so. With
Christmas deliveries!'

'Well, the day after tomorrow then. There's no immediate hurry.'

'My orders are to deliver. And unless they counter-
mand those orders when I get on to depot, which I should
be very surprised, deliver I shall.'

'You're not bringing anything in here today.'

'Then the stuff'll stay in the garden, if that's where you
want it.'

Sylvia told herself that she musn't be selfish and intervene; she must let Harold manage it in his own way. The
young man said to her confidentially, 'It's a pity their
rowing about it, isn't it? It's not as if it was anything much.
Just a few old bits and pieces. They'll take no time to move.'

'You happen to be talking to my mother about her
furniture. Kindly mind your manners.'

The broken-nosed man intervened, 'Don't you talk to
my mate like that.'

But the young man's pallor was suffused with blushes.
'I'm ever so sorry, they're very nice bits and pieces.'

Throughout the next hour as they clattered and struggled
up and down the stairs Sylvia could hear the young man's
adenoidal voice saying, 'They're ever such nice pieces,
really, aren't they?' and 'You've got some lovely pieces,
here, haven't you?' He hissed on all his s's.

'Oh, so it's your stuff, is it, lady?' the boxer said, 'Well,
what's it to be?'

'I do really think, Harold, now that it has come . . .
I'm sure these gentlemen could bring it in without getting

in your way. My son's busy. You see, we're giving a party.'

'Oh, a party's nice,' the young man said.

'Well, I'm afraid I can't lend a hand. I shall be too busy,' Harold was firm.

'Lend a hand? Oh, that's the trouble is it? You don't have to worry. We don't need any help with this little lot. In any case, you're not exactly the health and strength type, are you? I shouldn't like to take the responsibility of your lifting anything.'

The young man said, 'He's a nice gentleman, though.'

Harold glared at them both, 'Well, I wash my hands of it, Mother.'

He continued to sellotape Beth's caricatures to the walls above the stairs. As each piece of furniture was brought in, the men had to wait while he came down the steps, folded them up and either descended or ascended the stairs. At least twice he was almost squashed to death as he stood majestically on the landing to let the men pass. Sylvia could also hear him shouting testy orders now and again to Judy in the kitchen.

Upstairs in the disordered bedroom, Sylvia had no time at all either to clear away the little black tubular chairs and the mustard leather pouffe, or to decide where each piece of furniture should go. And then as each piece was carried in, one emotion succeeded another of recollection, of affection, of pride, of doubt, sometimes of shame as the stains or chips or tears showed in the strong sunlight of a frosty morning that glared in through the picture window. The two armchairs in their pretty powder blue rep seemed so faded beside the mustard, and the sagging sofa in its chintz cover looked more like the sort of thing rag-and-bone dealers leave outside their shops in all weathers. She had never noticed before the chipped varnish on their old sideboard – it was French, and looked quite an antique. That Colonel Chamberlain at Bay View in Scarborough, who knew all about furniture, had said that although the lion's heads on the drawers were beautifully carved it wasn't worth a lot of money. One of the feet shaped like claws had broken off coming up the stairs, but far worse (or was it?) the stair wall's kingfisher blue had been badly scratched (she had heard Harold's voice raised in anger).

All the while she was thinking where each piece should go and trying to forget what Harold might be feeling. Arthur's voice came bawling out from the bathroom in one of his favourites, 'What was it the colonel told the adjutant? What was it the adjutant said to Sergeant Brown?'

'I don't know cock!' the boxer man commented. The young man said, 'Don't he sing nice, Leslie?' and later to Sylvia, 'One of the old numbers, isn't it?'

When she dusted over the sketches of Ilfracombe that Miss Priest had given her she found they'd broken the glass of her favourite one of the High Street. Leslie (that must be the boxer's name) put her sewing machine down so heavily on a tubular chair that one of the thin metal legs fell off and the whole thing clattered to the ground. Then came a parcel of cushions – some square, some round, some sausage-shaped – all in shot-silk they were, gold and orange, green and red, blue and violet; she'd always been fond of bright cushions. But now the mustard walls killed everything.

'Only a few more pieces,' Leslie announced as he and his mate shoved Arthur's card table out of the way against the wall. It had once been such a fine piece of walnut, but the wood was deeply marked with cigarette burns and in some places it was swollen and cracked. When Sylvia went to move it away from the wall she found that by mischance the back edge was covered in tar which had come off on the yellow wall.

'And the sergeant told the private and the private told his girl.'

'Oh, Arthur,' she shouted in protest.

But the answer came bawling back, 'And they're looking for Mademoiselle from Armentières.'

But now she could hear angry voices on the stairs. As she looked down, Harold held up a paper covered in footprints and torn by a boot. 'Beth's drawing of me as Napoleon, that's what your damned men have done, Mother.'

'Oh dear! I am sorry, Harold. This is the last piece to come up, dear.'

'I very much hope so.'

She was too excited to do more than smile vaguely in answer. It was the old dresser from the farm, the only thing she had from her girlhood. It really *did* look nice. There was something for Judy to see.

'Judy! Judy!' she called. 'You'd like to see the old dresser, dear.'

'Later, Mother. She's busy with the cheese straws.'

But Judy, if only to prove careless of her father's continual orders, was upstairs in a minute.

'Oh, it is charming, Gran! A real farmhouse piece! Won't it be lovely when all the old pewter pots and pans are set out on it.'

Sylvia avoided any comment. The two removal men stood by admiring the dresser too, as she signed the receipt book.

'What was it the colonel told the adjutant? What was it the adjutant said to Sergeant Brown?' As though in answer to his own questions, Arthur's voice came in a loud yell. 'Bugger and bloody damn!'

The boxing man gave a whistle and he and his mate began to pack up.

Sylvia shouted, 'Arthur!' in reproof.

In reply, he burst out of the bathroom stark naked and shouting curses.

'Now then!' the boxing man said, 'there's ladies present.'

'I don't care who's bloody present. I got a shock from that damned hot rail that might have finished me off.'

'Well, it hasn't, Dad,' Sylvia said.

Judy turned away to look out of the window.

'Now, Arthur, get in there at once,' Sylvia pushed him by his scrawny old buttocks into Harold's bedroom. She looked at the hand he held out. 'There's nothing wrong,' she said. 'Don't be such a fusspot.' She went to the bathroom and got his towel. 'Dry yourself, and don't come out of there until you're decent.' When she returned to her room, the men were going.

'That wasn't very nice for the young lady, was it?' the young man observed.

'Oh, she won't fuss about that, will you, Judy?'

But she was fussing. She was standing quite tense, her face white. 'Oh, Gran, wasn't it awful? And I had thought of asking Caroline to come in to see your antiques. She might have been there.'

'Well, dear, I don't think she'd have seen much to hurt her if she had been.'

And really, she thought, with Arthur's pot belly and the way his Jimmy Jones seemed to have shrunk now he'd got old, there wasn't much to see. 'Oh, said the petticoat, you make me laugh, you don't cover your rumtum up not by half.' It was an old saying of cook's in the days when she worked at the rectory, though what could have made her think of it now, let alone say it aloud. . . . The effect on Judy was instant; she gave a whimper and ran downstairs. The boxing man looked fiercely at Sylvia.

'Well, I must say. This is a nice set-up and all.'

As they went away his mate looked back. 'Wasn't it a shame?' he said.

About a quarter of an hour later, when Arthur at last was dressing, Harold came up to their room.

'What's upset Judy?'

Sylvia was determined that Arthur should deal with it. She busied herself trying so to combine the shot-silk cushions on the divan beds that their colours would not fight with the mustard walls. After a short silence Arthur said, 'I'm afraid she saw me in the buff, old boy.'

'Try to be careful about that sort of thing, Dad.' When Arthur made no protest, Harold softened. 'All the same, there's no need for our Victorian miss to have the vapours.'

'Well, I'm a pretty fearful sight, you know, without my clothes, Harold. But it was your bloody electricity that did it. I got a damned great electric shock.'

'Oh, Arthur, don't exaggerate.'

'That thing does give a slight shock occasionally,' Harold said judiciously. He laughed, 'I did say leave the gadgets alone, Dad.'

To Sylvia's surprise, Arthur once more accepted the reproof. 'Your mother, of course, was too bloody busy with this furniture lark,' he ended with a deflated grumble.

Harold smiled kindly at his father in recompense. Then he looked round the room. 'All the old pieces, eh? It's like two worlds really. Not that your things don't go well with the mustard walls, Mother. Or they will when you've got them all in place. Beth always said it was one of those clean colours that make a good background for almost anything. Well, I'll leave you to it. I'm due back on the kitchen front.' As he went out he walked over to the tar stain and touched it lightly with his finger. 'Pity,' he said.

When he had gone, Sylvia sat on the sofa, looking so dejected that even Arthur noticed it. 'What the hell's the matter now?'

'It'll never be right. Everything looks so shabby and awful.'

'I don't see what's wrong. I'm very fond of this comfortable old chair of mine.'

'It all looks awful against this bright yellow.'

'Well, for God's sake, we can't ask Harold to repaint the walls. He said himself Beth chose the bloody colour.'

'No. We'll have to get rid of some of our furniture. Look how awful that old sideboard looks! It doesn't even fit into this room at all.'

'Don't you criticize that sideboard. It's worth a lot of money.'

'Oh, Arthur, you said that before and Colonel Chamberlain told us it wasn't.'

'I don't care what Colonel Chamberlain, whoever he may have been, said. It belonged to my old aunt Lucy Tamberlin. It's French.'

'Belonged to fiddlesticks, Arthur. I remember when we bought it at that sale in Clovelly.'

'My dear girl, I suppose I know the bits and pieces that came from my own family. That sideboard came from Charlie Tamberlin's family. He was half French.'

'You've never mentioned him before.'

'Never mentioned Charlie Tamberlin! Of course I have. He was a real bastard to poor Aunt Lucie. Used to kick her under the table as soon as the pudding came on.'

Sylvia began to laugh, 'You're making it up, Arthur.'

'What do you mean, making it up? Old Charlie Tamberlin! He was only a little fellow, but he made a packet out of selling plover's eggs up at Leadenhall Market. Started with a stall, ended with his own business. But he never learned manners. . . .'

'So it would seem! Kicking his wife when the pudding came on.' Sylvia laughed until she had to wipe away the tears. 'But it's no good, Arthur. None of your talking'll make the room look like our own.'

'All right. Sell the bloody stuff, then. But don't touch my armchair. That's all.' He was silent for a moment, then, 'You know what, Sylvie. You want to let yourself enjoy life for a bit. Before you kick the bucket.'

Later that evening when Sylvia, finally ready for the party in a gold lamé blouse and long black evening skirt, was coming out of her room, she heard her grandsons' voices down below.

'Well, why ever didn't you tell us their stuff had come, Dad?' It was Ray. She didn't hear the answer, but Mark said, 'That doesn't matter. Of course, we must go up and see it. Gran'll be terribly hurt otherwise.'

She tried to ward them off. 'It's all a mess yet.'

But Ray wouldn't have it. 'What's the use of having a grandson with an eye for design?'

As the boys looked round the room, she could see that they shared her feelings.

'It's awful, Ray, isn't it?'

'No, not awful, Gran lovey. Just a bit of a mess.'

'But Ray, there's a castor off that table and the sideboard leg is broken. And look at all the chips and stains.'

'Chips with everything,' said Mark, then he added, 'Sorry, Gran. There isn't anything here that I can't repair in a couple of days.'

'It's quite true. He's a busy boyo with his fingers. But it's the colours really. Mum's mustard does fight with everything. But honestly, lovey, I do think you'll have to stay with it. It'll upset Dad so, if you don't.' He looked around gloomily; then seeing her depressed expression, he brightened up. 'Oh, don't worry. Now look, how much do you want to keep that chintz? I mean, it's seen better days, hasn't it? . . .' And in a few minutes he had sketched out a programme of cheap but good new fabrics he could get for her, so that she went downstairs for the party, shy, but more lighthearted than she'd felt for weeks.

'Your grandmother's furniture looks very nice, doesn't it?'

His sons didn't answer. Harold, as though to apologize to her for this, said:

'With your permission I'll show one or two old friends your bed-sitting-room, Mother. I don't believe they've any idea how these rooms can be adapted.'

'Her permission's not granted,' Mark said.

'What's it got to do with you?'

'TFFTST,' Ray said. There might have been a row if the door chime had not sounded.

At first Sylvia did not know how she was going to bear it, she felt so shy. How could she stand around and talk with all these people? She knew nothing about them, and they knew nothing about her. After they'd said how glad they were to see her there, two or three of them said, 'Of course you must be a great student of human nature, Mrs Calvert.' She couldn't think what they meant at first, but then she discovered that it was because of all the hotels and residents and so on. They didn't seem to know that running a hotel was a job. And then, at the end, there was nothing left to say but which of the boys took after her or whether Judy featured her, or was she at all like Harold? After a bit she wanted to giggle. All these total strangers! As if she were a baby in a pram. Up they came to her, one after another, saying, 'Now *you're* Harold's mother! I'd have known it at once!' or 'Well, you're not like the rest of the family, are you?' She was proud, of course, to be part of the family, but it made her feel a bit of a cheat. She could hear Arthur's voice across the room – 'I don't know whether it was because they wanted to get rid of me, but they didn't leave me long in that cushy job. No, yours truly was earmarked for what the blighters called a position of greater danger and responsibility. I didn't mind the danger but . . .' She thought, like fun you didn't, my boy. But they didn't know Arthur and as far as they were concerned he might be King Kong himself. But she . . . Well, she *was* Harold's mother and no saying she wasn't, yet if that meant they thought she would be or say anything special, it was 'nothing doing'.

Then suddenly Judy came up, her face quite pink and flushed against her white dress.

'Oh, Gran, can you give me a hand? Mrs Burrows who's come in to help really isn't at all bright, and my friend Caroline Ogilvie might arrive at any moment. She's never been able to accept before, but this time she said she'd be sure to come. Oh it *is* so important that she and Daddy should get on. Daddy's prejudiced against her. But I know they'll adore each other if they meet in the right way. Quietly on their own. Caroline's so shy.'

'Don't you worry, dear. Off you go and enjoy yourself.'

From that moment the whole party seemed to come alive. True, Mrs Burrows *wasn't* very bright – with those rabbit teeth and that flycatcher mouth, Sylvia would never have taken her on – but getting good work out of people like that is part of the game. Luckily the poor creature was very willing, and there was one rule Sylvia always made – never turn off anyone who shows willing. Not only was there the serving up of the soup and the risotto to organize, there was all the waiting to be arranged, for Harold seemed to have big ideas of what a small party meant. So Sylvia got as many of the young people together as she could and kept them on the move passing food round. She had them circulating like professional waiters in no time. When Judy brought up a tall, rather ambling sort of girl in a green jumper with long awkward arms and said breathlessly, 'Gran, this is Caroline Ogilvie, my friend,' Sylvia just answered, 'Nice to see you. Have a good time,' and immediately gave the girl a tray of risottos to take round. 'Be sure to say there's plenty for second helps,' she added.

Judy cried, 'Oh Gran!' But you could see the girl was glad to have something to do with her hands. After the hot dishes to warm up with, there were plates of cold turkey and ham, and of cold sausages, and of salads; and of course cheese straws and lemon meringue pie and mince pies and home made coffee layer cake. And then there was the drink: mulled Spanish red wine and pineapple punch and beer. 'Help yourself, everyone,' Harold had said, 'for if you don't nobody else will do it for you.' But Sylvia had known that it wouldn't work without supervision – the greedy guts got everything and the shy went hungry. She'd seen it again and again with buffets where there was no wary eye to keep watch.

But even then, with waiters and organization, you still need one thing more: a really good assistant who knows the company. And Sylvia was lucky, for by chance she found just that. A funny sandy-haired, long-faced little man he was; with red blotches on his cheeks and long hands that were all blue and purple from bad circulation. Ray brought him up. 'This is Wilf Corney, Gran. Give him something to do to keep him out of mischief.' But there wasn't any need, or rather you couldn't. He worked like a beaver, and knew exactly what everybody wanted before they were asked, and who took sugar, and who shouldn't have another drink. And all the time he kept up a whispered commentary that held Sylvia in fits. He made fun of everyone and was a marvellous mimic. As she circulated round the rooms with food or drink, she would meet him coming the other way and you couldn't tell what he'd say. 'Pardon me, duchess, shall we sit this one out?' or 'Please to come quick, Mum, Master's took bad in the pantry.'

Harold saw her laughing, 'Enjoying yourself, Mother?'

'It's that Mr Corney, dear.'

'Oh, Wilf Corney from the Bank. Not a bad little chap at all. Quite a clown.' Mr Corney must have heard, for the next time round Sylvia saw he'd made a clown's paper hat for himself and was walking round with a string of raw sausages over his arm (Heaven knew where he'd got them from). 'The Headmastah wants me to learn biologah, but I want to go on believing in the stork.' And he burst into mock crying, 'Boo hoo! Boo hoo!' It was funny enough for tele – the Billy Cotton Band Show or that.

And so she went from group to group laughing, for everybody likes to see a cheery face. And after all, if you've got nothing to say for yourself, you can't say better than, 'let me get you some more' – they all want to hear that.

In this way she came to know quite a lot of people; there appeared to be more of Harold's friends than the kids', a nice cheery crowd on the whole, not at all school-teacherish. Yet more than once she was glad to have an excuse for moving on to another group. People get so worked up these days – it's the pace of living – and then, if you don't know what they're arguing about, you feel a bit silly.

Harold seized upon her early on. 'This is my right hand, Mother, Chris Milton. I'm headmaster. He runs the school. I find it most convenient.' He stroked his moustache. Sylvia was about to say something to this tall broad-shouldered youngish man who was squeezing her hand so painfully and laughing so loudly, when a stout greying-haired woman with a sweaty red face pushed herself forward. 'Be careful, Harold. The truth will out, you know. There's many a jest . . .' Sylvia thought how silly not to get the quotation straight. But Harold said, 'Oh, sorry, Lorna. This is *Chris's* right hand – Lorna Milton.'

'Glad to know you, Mrs Calvert. Of course, *I* run the school really . . .'

'Especially now that Beth's . . .' Chris Milton began, and then drowned the words in embarrassed laughter. His wife laughed loudly too. 'We must have a get together, Mrs Calvert. These men need keeping in order.'

A tall dark woman with a lot of costume jewellery and jade green eye shadow intervened. 'Introduce me to the guest of honour, Harold. Geoff!' she called across the room to a young pale-faced man in a very expensive looking dark suit. 'Here's Harold's mother. They don't feature each other a bit, do they?' The man approached and looked round the room in general.

'Like as two peas, Muriel. Which is she?'

They all laughed.

'Don't take any notice of Geoff, Mrs Calvert,' the woman called Muriel said, 'he's Cockney. He doesn't know any better.'

'As you will have gathered, Mother, these are the Bartleys – Muriel and Geoff.'

'No less!' Muriel agreed.

Sylvia hadn't really gathered. Looking at the lines round Muriel Bartley's mouth, she thought, they've all married women old enough to be their mothers. But then as she got older she found herself thinking that other women looked old.

'The Bartleys, eh?' Geoff said, 'so there's been talk already. What's he been saying about us? There might be money in it. I've got a good lawyer.'

When they'd all laughed again, Muriel Bartley turned to Mr Milton. 'What's this I hear, Mr Milton, about your turning traitor?'

Chris Milton laughed so loudly in reply that some of his beer splashed from his shaking mug on to Mr Bartley's suit.

Muriel Bartley sponged it down with the silk handkerchief she pulled out of her husband's breast pocket. 'Yes. Well, now the damage is repaired, we're waiting for an answer.'

Lorna Milton took up her husband's cause. 'Don't bully my man, Mrs Bartley. We've thought it all over and we don't agree with you.'

'Can I take it that that's the official view of Melling Modern, Harold?' Muriel asked. Her eyes had narrowed to green slits of eye shadow.

'It certainly is not. I'm not surprised that Chris should get the wrong end of the stick, mind you. He hasn't seen Carshall grow up as we have, Muriel.'

Mrs Milton turned to her husband, 'There you are Chris, what did I say? They've turned on the sob stuff.'

'To believe in a serious social experiment like New Towns,' Harold said. 'Do you call that sob stuff? It seems to me clear thinking.' Sylvia could tell he was getting worked up, so she moved on with a jug of pineapple punch. But when she came back to his group five minutes later, they were still at it.

'We've driven you away, Mrs Calvert,' Chris Milton greeted her. But Muriel Bartley was too engaged to care. 'We've helped to make the place, we intend to see it keeps its character.'

'Hear, hear,' Harold cried.

'It's the Ministry that decides, surely,' Lorna Milton said.

'Right,' Muriel answered, 'but who makes up the Ministry's mind? Public opinion. That's democracy.'

'Some of us have put a lot of money into this place,' her husband added.

'Oh, I see,' Lorna Milton exploded with teasing laughter, 'I thought it was an experiment in a *new* way of living.'

Muriel Bartley ignored her, she spoke chaffingly to Chris.

'Well, don't start canvassing the kids. Teachers have an unfair advantage.'

'Is that an official threat?' Lorna demanded.

Sylvia couldn't really tell whether the women were shaking with laughter or with temper. She felt she couldn't walk away again. She said, 'Arguing's thirsty work. Who wants another drink?' But they didn't respond. Luckily

Ray, who seemed to be everywhere at once, was suddenly with them.

'Hullo, Muriel. Don't you look gorgeous?'

Muriel Bartley ignored this. 'Where do *you* stand over Goodchild's meadow, Ray?' she asked.

'I can't remember, Lovey. Looking at you's put it right out of my mind.'

'Ah! Mr Tactful as usual. Well, you won't get around me, Ray Calvert.' But he did. As Sylvia felt free to move on she heard him say, 'Where did you get the jewellery? Off the Christmas tree?' and Muriel, delighted, answered, 'Do you mind, Mr Ray Calvert? I'll hit back at you one of these days. You wait, you bully.'

Mrs Milton said, 'Ray, Chris and I want you to judge the prelims of the kids' art show.' And Geoff Bartley said, 'Now that's a firm date to run out to the Old Mill Christmas Eve, Ray. . . .'

It seemed to Sylvia as she moved away that Ray gave her a slow wink. He'd certainly got them all sorted out.

Arthur was holding forth to a delighted audience. Sylvia kept away from him, partly out of embarrassment, partly because after all wives always spoil their husband's form. But he hailed her. 'What the hell's that filthy stuff in that jug. This is Jack and Renee Cranston – my Missus. How about getting something proper to drink for Mrs Cranston, Sylvie? I know Harold's got a bottle of Scotch tucked away somewhere in his study.'

'No really, thanks, I'm ever so happy with this.'

'That's what you say now, you wait for the morning after. Have it your own way. Mr and Mrs Cranston, Sylvie, are the robbers who took his last penny off an old man at bridge last Thursday.'

'Robbed you! I like that. I'd have to get up early to rob your husband, Mrs Calvert.'

Mrs Cranston was as bright as a little bird; her husband was big, redfaced and jovial. '*Old* man!' he said, 'I *should* think! What do you feed him on, Mrs Calvert? Meat?'

'We're taking your husband in charge,' Mrs Cranston said; then jerking Sylvia to one side by the elbow, she whispered confidentially, 'You don't have to worry about him finding friends here. We all love him. He's just an age to get along with my dad that lives with us. Dad'll come for him in the mornings and they can go down on the bus together to the British Legion or have a look in at the Crown. Dad likes a bet and a game of cards, too. They'll make company for each other.'

Sylvia didn't know quite how to take this, but Arthur said loudly,

'Well, as I was saying when my old woman interrupted me – this old girl at the estaminet, as they call them, got to know me well. I don't say I parleyvoo like a native, but I can get along when I have to. . . .' Sylvia saw that his eye was fixed firmly away from hers, so she took that to be a signal to get along also.

Of course, it wasn't as easy to get away as that. She was going along to the kitchen to see if there was any more risotto for two latecomers (latecomers are an eternal problem) when in the dining room a woman's hand came out from the leafy darkness and grasped her arm. It gave her quite a start because they weren't using the dining room. A voice said rather intensely, 'Mrs Calvert? It is Mrs Calvert, isn't it? I wonder if you've heard of me? Sally Bulmer.'

Looking down into the gloom Sylvia saw a big, handsome middle-aged woman seated on the low bench seat against the trellis partition. She was dressed in a black dress with a large black lace shawl round her shoulders and an artificial red rose pinned in her hair. Sylvia nearly said 'Sandeman's Port' but stopped herself in time.

'Oh yes – you're Carshall's Welfare Officer. Harold's often spoken of you.'

Miss Bulmer gasped and her great round dark eyes widened. 'I can't really believe that. Once or twice. But not often. But I'll try to believe it because it will raise my morale. You see our Harold does such marvellous work for the community here that I sometimes feel the rest of us just give up. I know that sounds contradictory but it isn't. Am I keeping you?' she asked, though Sylvia hadn't even tried to move her arm away.

'I was getting some risotto for two latecomers. They don't like soup.'

'Oh, take the nasty soup away, I won't have any soup

today. And we all know what happened to Augustus. If they really won't take any soup, they'll get thinner and thinner until they vanish. And then you won't have to worry about them. No, but seriously, stay and talk to me. I've been so anxious for this talk. I looked for you at the Bartleys . . . .'

'I fell down,' Sylvia said.

'Oh, how right you were! But now we can talk. You see, you're his mother. And he's overworking. Someone's going to tell you that sooner or later. So why not me? Of course, the children do their best, but the young have to be selfish. In fact, since she died. . . . Not that Beth didn't have her faults, but still she was what he looked for when he got back in the evenings. And now he'll have you. Oh, I think that's so good. Well, we all do. Most of us, that is. I won't disguise from you that there is the anti-Harold group, but they're simply the jealous ones. And then . . . I know I'm keeping you but I believe you'll feel it's been worth while . . . he isn't getting the backing from his Number Two at the school that he should. The wife should never wear the trousers, don't you think? Oh! I know you can't do anything about all this. But just knowing it may help you to help him. Because this I can say,' and Miss Bulmer pushed her great face up into Sylvia's, 'he'll never, never tell you it himself. Wild horses wouldn't make him do it. And Carshall, as you may believe, is without wild horses.'

Sylvia didn't know what to say. 'Thank you very much. It's very good of you to tell me.'

'Well, not really,' Miss Bulmer blew smoke rings up from her mysterious darkness, 'because, of course, there's the other side. We don't want our Harold running the school in one of his states. And his states are bad! That criticism I have to make. But what about this *Look Back in Anger* business? Of course he'll do it superbly. But why, why on top of everything else? It's bad enough all this over Goodchild's meadow! It's a righteous cause. We all know that. But why our Harold? He's got a hobby in the survey, let him keep to that.'

Miss Bulmer's tones were those of challenge, and indeed, Sylvia felt ashamed of her ignorance of all these things in

Harold's life. She said uncomfortably, 'We left school so early, you know, when I was a kid.'

Miss Bulmer looked at her as though she was mad; but luckily for Sylvia, Mark's face appeared at the dining-room door and Miss Bulmer pounced on him. 'Hey you there, Mark!' she called, 'Or should I say Jimmie Porter?' Mark looked at her contemptuously.

'I never know why you say any of the things you do,' he said.

'Of course you'll be first rate in the part. If you deign to speak up so that we can hear you. But I suppose you'll refuse to do it. No doubt you've got to march or lie down somewhere.'

Mark ignored her. He went into the kitchen and returned stuffing a sausage roll into his mouth. 'Anyway, isn't *Look Back in Anger* a bit square now, a bit for the mums?' He walked past her. She called after him, 'I told Harold straight off, if you ask him to take part he'll refuse.'

'I haven't said I won't.'

'But you will. The young never do what they're asked. It wouldn't be natural if they did.'

He turned on her, 'What makes you ask a lot of daft questions if you know all the fatuous answers to them?'

Sylvia clicked her tongue in disapproval of his tone; but Miss Bulmer roared with laughter. 'You've shocked your grandmother. Don't worry, Mrs Calvert, Mark and I always have this battle. Hip versus square. We like it, don't we, Mark? The young love a fight. But don't you stay to be embarrassed. Go and feed the latecomers with rice!'

Sylvia found herself dismissed.

'By the way, I hear great things of you at the Tech, Mark,' Miss Bulmer cried. 'It looks as though our Jimmie Porter's got his eye fixed on some room at the top.'

To Sylvia's shocked surprise, Mark pushed his way past her out of the room without taking any notice of Miss Bulmer's remark.

Back at the party, she saw that Judy and her friend were talking alone in a corner. Oh dear, wallflowers. A job half done was never worth doing! She'd set Judy free from the chore of entertaining, but she could do more for her only granddaughter than that. She felt really quite elated with how easy the party had proved after all her shyness at the start. Shyness at sixty-four! It just showed how silly she could be! She heard Harold's voice in his study. He was holding forth to a group of younger people. 'I've chosen it because I think Osborne's hit off exactly the sort of old-fashioned, industrialized, unneighbourly jungle-world Midland town that the New Towns are going to replace. The very sordidness of it all may make Carshallites count their blessings a bit. They need to be reminded . . . .'

Sylvia saw at once that she would have to interrupt him or give up her mission. She touched his arm.

'What is it, Mother?'

'Something you can do for me, dear. There's someone I want you to meet.'

He would have resisted her claim, if the group he had formed around him had not seized the chance to break up. She led him to the sitting room; Judy and her friend had disappeared.

'Well, really, Mother. What is all this about?'

Muriel Bartley called to them. 'Come and talk horrors; what do you think of this awful Ibiza murder? No more Majorca for me, I can tell you. If only he'd killed the old girl and not the niece. Selfish old thing probably, with all that money, dragging the niece round from hotel to hotel. Well you must know the type better than we do, Mrs Calvert. What do you think about it?'

Sylvia looked so much at a loss that Muriel Bartley went on: 'Oh, you're like Harold probably. Disapprove of reading murder cases. Even so you can't have missed the Priest case, it is all across the front page of today's *Express*.'

A black shadow fell momentarily across Sylvia's happy mood. Was it something that Mrs Bartley had said? Or was it her loud voice? Or was it her green eye shadow? At that moment she heard the voice of Judy's friend in the hall. Once again she took Harold's arm. 'This way,' she said.

'You're tiddly, Mother.' He preferred to laugh rather than to protest before Muriel Bartley. There in the hall Caroline Ogilvie was whispering goodbyes to Judy. 'No, honestly, Judy I *have* enjoyed myself. It's just that Mummy has a thing about my being late. Oh! And Saturday we'll take Stingo and Punch out.'

'Harold. This is Judy's best friend, Caroline. Caroline, this is Judy's father.' Judy glared at her grandmother.

Harold said, 'You're a little late, Mother. However, I'm sure there is something in this theory that we're bound to be friends at sight, Caroline, since both Judy and my mother hold it so strongly. Perhaps you will come to supper one evening if such a meal isn't too vulgar.'

Caroline blushed. Her reply was too softly spoken to be heard. She looked so gawky and uncomfortable that Sylvia in her buoyant mood felt suddenly as though Harold were once more a small boy who needed taking down a peg.

'Don't you take any notice of the headmaster, Caroline. You come and have dinner with me. And he can have his old supper on his own.'

The girl blushed and stammered this time, but Judy burst in: 'You mustn't keep Simmonds waiting. Fancy, Caroline's mother had Simmond's cars to take her to parties long before the New Town was ever thought of.'

When the girls had disappeared through the front door, Harold asked, 'Can I go back now, Mother?' He had a twinkle in his eye that reminded her of Arthur.

'Yes, but don't be so naughty another time.' She laughed too. He made his escape while she waited for Judy. 'You musn't worry, dear. Your father was very naughty. But he knows it.'

Judy rushed past her. 'Please don't criticize Daddy,' she shouted back down the stairs.

Some time later Sylvia treated herself to a nice long talk with Mrs Burrows while they washed up. After all, she'd done her full stint of entertaining, she had a right to relax now. Mrs Burrows turned out to have a sister-in-law who worked in the Electrometrico canteen and some of the things she had to tell were really a revelation. At last Sylvia had to apologize for keeping her after eleven, but the woman said not to worry, she'd properly enjoyed their chat. After she had gone, Sylvia sat in the kitchen on her own with only the light from the dining room, the half darkness was quite soothing after the tiring evening. She smoked a cigarette and allowed her contentment, despite the little bother with Judy, to lap warmly over her tired body.

She came to from her dozing to see Ray with that Mr Corney come into the dining room. They were both laughing. And then, 'Oh! look what Carmen's left behind, the gipsy's warning.' Mr Corney picked up Miss Bulmer's black lace shawl and draping it round Ray's shoulders capered round him in a little dance, '"Imagine a tomboy dressed in lace, that's Nancy with the laughing face,"' he sang.

Sylvia remembered the number well. She laughed, and then, because she felt so pleased, she sang '"She takes the winter and makes it summer. Summer could take some lessons from her. My Nancy with the laughing face."'

The effect on the two men was immediate, they stood tensely still. 'Who's there?' Ray called, as though he were in Maigret, or something.

'Only Gran.'

'Oh! Are you all right, Gran?' His voice was still strained.

'Yes, why shouldn't I be? I was laughing at your larks. Did my singing make me sound ill then?'

She switched on the kitchen light. Mr Corney gave her a funny sideways look. 'Ray tells me you've been living at Eastsea,' he said, speaking very quickly, but with a sort of grand drawl, 'I know it quite well really. At least I stayed there for a few weeks three summers ago. In lodgings with Mrs Crutchley. I wonder if you know her.'

Sylvia didn't, but this in no way checked the flow of his talk.

'She was a splendid old body and looked after me jolly well. We ate like fighting cocks. You ought to go there, Ray.'

'It sounds smashing, Wilf.'

Sylvia couldn't understand it. 'Well, I'd better take this back to that Miss Bulmer.' She picked up the scarf. '"The gipsy's warning!"' She chuckled as she left the room.

Most of the guests had gone or were about to leave. Miss Bulmer was talking to Harold. 'I managed Mark tonight,' she said. 'Didn't I, Mrs Calvert? He'll be Jimmie Porter because I said he wouldn't. And now, what a marvellous opportunity to put the questionnaire to your Mother, Harold.'

He looked a bit surprised, but turned to Sylvia, 'If you would, Mother. It might be rather interesting. It's part of the survey Sally and I are conducting. A piece of amateur sociology to confound the professionals. You see we're convinced . . .'

'No, Harold. Explanations are quite out. And I'm not sure that a close relation should be present at the interview anyway. Mrs Calvert,' she turned to Sylvia, 'these are just a few questions that you may find it fun to answer. Now, first, how do you think of yourself? Don't worry about class, age or job – just how do you think of yourself?'

'Mother's in rather an intermediate position. As a result of the Butlinization of the seaside . . .'

'Now, Harold, keep quiet or go away. It's so interesting. Just because of the close emotional relationship with her, you've immediately objectified. That's according to our prediction. It's a triumph for our system. But I'm afraid you've spoilt the question. Look, forget that question, Mrs Calvert, and answer this one – what are you?'

Sylvia laughed, 'I'm very fat.'

But neither Miss Bulmer nor Harold smiled. She tried again more seriously. 'I was a manageress, but I'm nothing now.'

'The atmosphere isn't right.' Miss Bulmer reminded Sylvia of that Mrs Maugham who'd been a medium at Clovelly. 'Your mother's tired. She isn't finding this fun and that of course is fatal to the answers. You aren't finding it fun, are you?'

Sylvia could think of no answer but friendly laughter. It came out as a snigger.

'*We* aren't doing this just for fun, Mother, you know.'

'Goodbye,' Sally Bulmer's face came very close, 'and remember my careful indiscretions.'

'Goodbye,' Sylvia answered, 'but it's really true, you know, I'm a nobody. I always have been.'

When Miss Bulmer had gone, Sylvia found herself alone with Harold.

'She's a quaint one, isn't she, dear?'

'Oh, Sally's a bit of a crank. But that shouldn't be held against her. After all most people think of Beth and me as specimens of the family Crankidae.' Perhaps to wash down the pill, he asked, 'What about a last quiet nightcap in my study?'

They sat for some minutes in silence with their whiskies. 'My friends gave you a good welcome, Mother.'

'Indeed they did, it was a lovely party. I only hope I was useful.'

Harold said nothing for over a minute, then he spoke in a faraway voice. 'Parties aren't the same without Beth.'

At last the moment had come. Sylvia thrust aside all her tiredness and a slight sense of deflation. 'Of course they can't be, dear. I know how much you must miss her. I've wanted to talk to you about it, or rather to let you talk to me.'

Again Harold was silent, then in a low but violent voice, he said, 'I ache for her so at night!'

Sylvia sat dazed at the statement. Harold rose. 'Well. I shall be off to bed. The old man was a great success. He's quite a citizen of Carshall now. Good night, Mother.'

They'd had their intimate talk and Sylvia felt exhausted. She went up to the bedroom. Arthur was in bed snoring loudly. As she saw the Ilfracombe sketches piled against the wall, Muriel Bartley's voice screamed, 'If only he'd killed the old girl!' But it couldn't be – her Miss Priest was independent and not old. She felt stifled suddenly and took off her dress. She then stood looking out of the window. The moon above the bare sycamores was at its full. As far away as she could see the country stretched, empty and lifeless. A lorry rattled in the distance. She strained her ears to listen until the friendly sound finally died away. Although she was shivering she could not leave off staring at the black emptiness of the Midland hills, when suddenly Arthur's snoring seemed to creak and clatter in his chest. She was intent at once. She knew the sound so well. He was in for one of his bad bronchial attacks. She turned almost eagerly back into the room. A period of busy, familiar nursing was ahead of her.

4. New Year   New Town   New Life

'They don't need to bring the Crazy Gang back, do they? Not with these two,' Renee Cranston whispered to Sylvia. And certainly Arthur and Mr Tucker had the whole bus shelter in fits. It was the same each morning. The more her father was scored off to the delight of those waiting for the bus, the more Renee Cranston laughed. It made Sylvia turn hot and cold. She said, 'I shan't see you off tomorrow, Arthur. You re well enough to manage the bus yourself now.'

'That's right. Leave your old pot and pan to sink or swim.'

'Now that's not fair, Captain Calvert.' Renee was stern. 'After Mrs Calvert's been nursing you all these weeks.' She addressed the general crowd. 'Pneumonia! Gassed in the first war! He jolly near popped the hooks. If it hadn't been for her nursing, the doctor says ... And *she's* not well either. It's the blood pressure with you, isn't it?' The bystanders clicked their tongues. Something like this happened every morning too. Sylvia, blushing scarlet, decided that cost her what it might, she would give up shopping in Melling and go each day into Town Centre.

'The temperature of the blood is 98.6,' old Mr Tucker said, 'that's only human, mind. Fish are a very different kettle of fish.' As nobody laughed, Sylvia's laughter sounded loud and hollow.

'Dad knows everything,' Renee Cranston winked.

'Temperature of the blood!' Arthur joined in. 'What's the use of that sort of knowledge, you miserable old devil? Now if you knew what was going to win the 2.30 at Windsor, there might be some use to you.'

Mr Tucker looked serious. 'That's not knowledge. That's prediction, Arthur. Mind you, up to a point you can make a scientific forecast, even in racing. If you know the horses' previous form, that is.'

'If they knew your form, Stanley, the odds'd be about two hundred to one against.'

Everyone laughed; and, as usual, Mr Tucker laughed obediently after them, which brought about a second peal of laughter all round.

But now the bus had arrived and the two old men were hoisted on to the step.

'They look a couple of proper charlies,' Renee said. And really Sylvia had to smile at the sight of them side by side on the lower deck – two white faces, with red blobs for noses, identical grey wool mufflers and dark overcoats. Mr Tucker had a greenish cap, and Arthur his sandy one. Perhaps it was Arthur's ashplant that made him look so much the grander figure of the two. Indeed he had once been an officer and a hotel proprietor; whereas old Tucker's feet had kept him at home in '16 and then he'd been a commissionaire or messenger or somebody who stood about in the City.

'Best foot forward, Mrs Calvert.' And, true enough, once out of the bus shelter you could tell it was still only February, even though the weather had turned mild. But best foot forward or no, Sylvia saw that Mrs Cranston had often to slow down her pace for her; after all, what age was Renee Cranston – thirty-five? – and as lively as a cheeky cockney starling. How Sylvia longed to suggest that each should do her own shopping on her own! Mrs Cranston had so much more shopping to do. She bought almost everything for her family at the Melling self-service store – they seemed to live on tinned stuff and breakfast foods; whereas Sylvia only had a few items to get – eggs, oranges, bacon – all the rest the boys brought back in the evening from the Continental grocers in Town Centre. Then Renee Cranston knew all the customers and shop assistants and liked to have a bit of a natter with them, even at the self-service store, where you'd think the dead-pan faces of the girls serving would have told anyone that they didn't want to talk.

'Washes whitest of whitest, does it?' she said today, 'Well, that's too posh for us.' And when the smudgy black eyebrows rose a fraction in the chalk-white face and the near white lips parted to express boredom, she still went on, 'Oh, I know that stuff, it turns your hands into water lilies. I'd like to see Jack's face if all I could put round his neck was a couple of water lilies.' The white face was turned away from them and they were presented with the swept-up back of a blonde bouffant. 'Miss! If you please, Miss!' Renee was not to be easily defeated. But the girl only half turned and with a long opalescent fingernail indicated one of the wire baskets. 'Use the container, please,' she said, as though Renee Cranston was about to be sick on the floor.

It was no different at the greengrocer's (one of Geoff Bartley's chain), or rather only a different tune, for here all was jolly exchange with the young chap that sold the fruit. 'Tangerine, tangerine,' Renee sang gaily, 'tastes delicious and so clean, if it's' – she opened her arms wide like the little puppet Tangegirl on the tele – 'TAN-GE-RINE,' the young man shouted in reply. They both laughed.

'Renee's my name, you know, so it fits ever so well.'

Sylvia felt herself a dreary wet blanket not joining in the fun. But, after all, everybody knew the commercials if they all started singing in public. . . . Her ankles, too, ached so with all this dawdling; the doctor had particularly warned her against standing. It was all such a disappointment. After years of ordering by telephone, one of the things she'd really looked forward to had been pottering around the shops. What made it so silly was that she felt sure Renee Cranston, a woman young enough to be her daughter, only accompanied her out of kindness. But there it was; they were friends of Harold and they'd been so good to Arthur.

'Ready for elevenses?' They came out of the green-grocer's to the dead brown grass and leafless ornamental cherry trees that decorated Melling shopping centre in winter.

It had happened for more than a week now – this daily coffee chat at Renee's house. Sylvia did not know how she could face any more sessions, trying to find things to talk about, for in her own home Renee became quite passive and silent.

Once again: 'You come back to "The Sycamores" this time.' But as usual Renee refused.

'I must be at home to have everything ready when they come back for dinner. I don't believe in kids getting back to an empty house. That's why Jack won't let me go back to the office. Not that we need the money.'

Sylvia, remembering how Harold admired Renee for this, felt ashamed to have tried to lure her away. In desperation, 'Why don't we go to the coffee bar? Harold recommended that when I arrived. He said it would save me going all the way to the Town Centre.'

'The coffee bar?' Renee giggled. 'Oh, I don't think that'd do. It's all teenagers and ton-ups there, and sometimes even lorry drivers. Look,' she led Sylvia to the lilac-painted doorway. The café was almost empty. Three youngsters in jeans were standing by the juke box and two men were eating egg and chips.

'Dube dube doo. Dube dube doo.' The juke box sang loudly at Sylvia, 'Dube doo dube doo doo doo doo, that's the language of love.'

'Oh! That's an old number,' Renee hummed it. 'Of course it's only full evenings and Saturdays.' All the way back to her house in Higgleton Road Renee met neighbours as she had at the shopping centre. She always stopped a few minutes and chatted. Only once or twice she dismissed a neighbour more perfunctorily, 'Hullo, Liz, how's your Mum getting on?' 'Well, Diana started work yet?' 'Kids,' she said in explanation. But save that Liz and Diana were wearing jeans, Sylvia couldn't see much difference between them and the other housewives; everybody in Melling was so young.

Settled in Renee's front room with the February sun coming through the triangle of window left clear by the crossed muslin curtains, Sylvia felt quite warm and happy. Wherever the sun shone in the room there was no speck of dust to be seen – not on the cocktail cabinet, not on the dining-room suite, not on the Austrian dolls that Renee and Jack had brought back from their Vorarlberg honeymoon. Sylvia could relax amid the high polish and the neatness, to the cheerful chattering of the sulphur budgie cock from the kitchen. If only she'd known what to say when Renee, now silent and expectant, sat down before the tray of coffee and biscuits.

'I can't think what can have made Harold recommend that coffee bar to me.'

Renee disposed of this easily. 'Oh, well, everything to do with Melling or Carshall is perfect for him. But of course he doesn't know much about what goes on, being in school all day. It's more in the mind, really.'

After a long silence Sylvia asked 'Do you think Tom Colman's serious about Janet Paulton?'

'Who's she?'

'Mrs Covell's niece.'

'Oh, I didn't know she had one.'

'Oh yes. She came to live with them about a week ago. She's got a job at Madame Paula's.'

'Oh. I haven't followed for over a week now. I've been too busy. And then it comes on at the kid's bedtime in the winter. I don't like Tom Colman anyway. Conceited lump.'

Sylvia tried to keep it going. 'You're like Mrs Harker. She doesn't know what to make of Tom.'

'I don't know,' Renee could imitate well.

'I really don't know,' Sylvia added. And they laughed longer than Sylvia felt was quite natural.

'Harry Worth was funny last night.'

'Oh, was he? We don't watch much now of an evening. It's all bridge now with Jack. That's why we were so glad to have Captain Calvert. It's difficult to get a four round here. Everything's bingo or whist. Of course it's natural. But now Jack's got this new job, they told him he ought to learn bridge. He'll be more in the bridge set now. I enjoy it. It keeps you on your toes.'

'I used to like bridge. You need a good head for figures. But I've got that doing the hotel accounts and so on. But I never play now. It only get on Arthur's nerves.'

Renee found nothing to say to that, and Sylvia was about to take her leave, when she was given a second cup of coffee. Even drinking it quickly she needed to find some more conversation.

'I'm reading a book about Mary Queen of Scots.'

'Oh, really. I don't have much time for book reading.'

'Of course they know now she wasn't altogether innocent. She was plotting all the time against old Queen Bess. But still it was a tragic death. When they lifted the head up, everyone could see she was a haggard old woman for all her rouge and paint.' She shuddered. 'And old Queen Bess too lying there on the floor, waiting to die. She'd broken all the mirrors. At Greenwich it was.' Renee wasn't really listening. She clicked her tongue, 'Terrible times'; then looking away from Sylvia, 'Don't tell Harold, but I think we shall move out next year or the one after. Of course we shall wait until Sheila and Mick have finished school. But then I think it'll be a country cottage for us. Heating's no problem nowadays. Now Jack's promoted, we shan't want to go on renting. We could buy a house here like "The Sycamores", but Jack reckons it's best to get right out. Only don't tell Harold, he'll call us traitors to Carshall.'

'I'm very glad, Mother, that Renee Cranston has taken to you. People like the Cranstons are the basis of Carshall life. Jack came out from London because they couldn't find a home. And now he's been made sales manager, which means of course that he's backwards and forwards from London a good deal. But that's all right. That's what the New Towns are for. Villages that are big enough not to be afraid of the metropolis. Does Renee say anything about their moving?'

Sylvia made a noise and relied on Harold's loquacity to save her.

'I ask because he must be doing quite well now. It's typical of them not to put on any airs. All the same I hope they look out for something larger. Like this perhaps, if a little less formidable,' he laughed. 'If the older executives are too snooty for the Town they work in, we've got to breed our own. Carshall must develop its own mixed society – status wise, I mean, nothing to do with class – or it must die of atrophy.' He talked on, but the dangerous corner had been turned. However, Sylvia felt more than ever resolved to rescue herself from the daily dose of Renee. She had never been driven to subterfuge with her family – of course it had been necessary with the residents and their confidences, but then that was business – and she was not going to start now.

'... that, of course, is the fundamental issue that the Goodchild's Meadow business presents us with.'

This sounded to Sylvia the sort of sentence at which intervention was possible. 'You know, Harold, although Melling's so convenient, I think I shall go to Town Centre for the morning shopping. For a bit anyway. I've been rather shut in since we've been here, with all this bad weather. ...'

Harold seemed surprised at the interruption. 'You're eager for the busy world. Well, as long as you think you can stand the bus journey, Mother. In that case the boys may as well hand all the shopping over to you. For a while at any rate.'

So the next day found Sylvia on the bus for Town Centre, passing that wide ribbon of pastureland called Goodchild's meadow than ran right across Carshall. She looked at it on each side as she passed. At the moment the grass looked dry and there were pools where heavy rain had fallen. Badly drained, she thought, and remembered her father's fields. Perhaps that was what all the trouble was about. She must ask Harold, after all she would soon be a Carshall citizen, once she'd got her bearings. Shopping in the Town Centre provided something more like, and she ambled around, taking her time. Her purchases made, she watched the metal arms of the fountain jerkily dropping their loads of water; it was clever but you couldn't say that it played. Staring into the basin, she wondered what sort of supervisor they could have that would let it silt up with chocolate wrappers and ice-cream cartons like that. She looked for a while at the twisted bronze called 'Watcher' that Beth had so admired. Although it was difficult and modern, you could admire the way the metal had been twisted so cleanly. Then she studied the lilac and pink mural with its emerald background – she didn't like that so much, because the two girls had such long necks and sheepish faces, and why was the young man with a kind of big brimmed velour hat standing naked on the bank of flowers, with his head turned away from the girls? It didn't have the clean lines that you looked for in modern things, and yet it didn't make any sense either. Someone had chipped the lower mosaics too, which ought to have been attended to. After that she sauntered past the shop windows in the Arcade, and then past those in the gallery above. She was disappointed to see how they had packed goods into the windows; it was not the kind of clean, modern display you could expect nowadays, but more like the little drapers and that in Paignton back in the twenties when they'd lived there. She decided to ask Ray why this was so; he would know. She went to the Public Library, too, and changed *Fotheringay Pilgrimage* for a new book; she chose a novel this time, something light after the history – *A Winter's Holiday* by Martin Home. The library she really could look forward to, she thought. Changing her own books was so much more satisfactory, kind though Mark had been. She didn't know anyone here, of course, as she had known Miss Dillon at Boots in Eastsea before they closed the library section; but you really didn't need assistance here, everything was so well set out and clean, and so light with all the big glass windows. She particularly liked the bowl of anemones on the table in the reading room; it took away that cold official feeling. All in all, she thoroughly enjoyed the morning in Carshall, although by 11.30 she would have been glad to get her bus back to Melling if she hadn't agreed to meet Arthur for a sandwich at the Falcon at lunchtime. So she spent the interval sitting with a coffee in the snack bar part of the Ten Pin Hall. Unfortunately, after ten minutes of real peace and quiet, some young chaps came in to bowl, and, as she didn't understand the game it proved more of an upsetting noise, like bombing, with it's continuous booms followed by crashes. However the Ten Pin Hall was nice and light and clean.

Arthur was already seated in the saloon bar when she arrived; with him was old Mr Tucker and another man, not so unlike them, but a bit younger and wearing a bowler. It was all men in the bar except for a mannish-looking lady with a suede hat who ate a plate of toad in the hole at a table by herself and seemed to be adding up bills. Sylvia chose a gin and it, as she always did, but it seemed to put Arthur out. 'Bloody woman's drink.' He brought it for her with a tongue sandwich. 'Though why the hell I should give any woman a tongue sandwich I don't know. As if they hadn't long enough tongues since the days of Eve.'

The man in the bowler didn't have much to say to her. He and Arthur were too busy working out the afternoon's winners.

'Melachrino!' Mr Benson said, 'I rather fancy Melachrino, Arthur, for the three o'clock.'

'Melachrino!' Arthur's eyes narrowed with contempt, 'I wouldn't trust that spavinlegged bastard in a selling hurdle after his performance at Doncaster last week.'

'He's got Mick Robinson up,' Mr Benson said.

'He'll need to have and all. Look at the handicap he's carrying. Anyway Mickey Robinson's finished as a jockey. What race has he won this season? I ask you that.'

'He won the 3.30 on the second day at Aintree.'

'Aintree! I don't know why I bet on this bloody steeplechase stuff.'

'Melachrino,' Mr Tucker announced, 'that's a Turkish cigarette. Or used to be.'

'Turkish cigarette!' Mr Benson echoed contemptuously.

'Turkish cigarette!' Arthur almost exploded with irritation into Mr Tucker's face. 'I don't know why they let you out, Stanley. You Turkish twit, all you need is a veil and a yashmak, and with your pot you could do a belly dance.'

Mr Tucker joined in wheezily but heartily at this joke.

'Do you like horse racing, Mrs Calvert?' he asked.

'Oh, a little flutter on the Derby and the Grand National, yes. And you?'

'Oh, I'm very fond of it. Yes. I like to win, you know.'

'I hope I'm not keeping you from picking the winners.'

'Oh no! Not at all. I'd like your opinion on what will win this race.' He spread out the racing edition before her and pointed at the 4.0 starters. She read down the list. Such a nice old man, she thought. 'Well, Lad O'My Fancy sounds a good one.'

Arthur was on to it at once. 'Lad O'My Fancy. Sort of bloody choice a woman would make. Look at the form!' He jabbed the entry with his forefinger. 'Three times out in the last month and never in the first three! Lad O'My Fancy!'

Sylvia was relieved when the men had to go off to the bookie's and she was able to get her bus back to Melling.

Three days later she left for Town Centre again with quite a sense of familiar pleasure. No meeting with Arthur this time; just shopping, perhaps a cup of coffee, and then the bus home, but at her own pace and thinking her own thoughts.

When she had made her purchases she had a quarter of an hour to wait for the bus, so she decided to walk down to the big church – St Saviour's was it? – not that she often went into churches, but it was quite famous as a modern church Beth had told her and you couldn't help wanting to know what such a strange building was like inside. Yet despite the odd metal steeple more like a piece of children's Meccano and the funny slots in the side of the building, it was rather plain inside – spacious and light enough, but more like a lecture hall with unpolished wooden chairs and little tie-on cushion seats covered in jade green American cloth. Apart from a long thin silver crucifix that stood on the altar steps, you'd hardly know it for a church – not that it was at all like chapel; it was just a big room with everything very simple and quiet, especially the thin slotted glass windows through which the sun poured with a lovely sky-blue light. She picked up a card and read the prayer that was printed on it – 'help us to avoid the easy jibe, the grouchy mood, and the martyred smile. Help us to forget ourselves in doing what we can for others and in doing it cheerfully. . . .' It all seemed sensible enough; lots of people found a great deal of comfort in religion. Yet Sylvia wasn't too sure that she was looking for comfort.

She came out of the church later than she had intended, late enough to see the Melling bus leave without her. To make sure of the next one she determined not to stray from the Town Centre. She looked again into the basin of the fountain, there seemed to be more paper, someone had dropped a whole *Daily Express* and its soggy pages had separated and wreathed themselves clammily around the ice-cream cartons. She followed the bronze twists of the 'Watcher' more closely – it was like a maze, once you'd seen how the twists went, you could do it with your eyes shut. She looked to see if she could find any title to explain the mural, and, sure enough, tucked away in a chipped lower corner of the emerald mosaic there was some writing. She went up close to look at it. 'E. Oicker', it read.

'I had no idea you were an art lover, Mrs Calvert.' The loud voice was like a cheery gale. Sylvia turned guiltily round to see Mrs Milton. She looked redder and sweatier in the face than ever; and no wonder, for under her zipped leather jacket she was wearing at least two heavy woollies. Sylvia noticed that she had a slight dark moustache, which you couldn't like.

'How do you find our Ernie's work?' And when Sylvia looked blank. 'It's a Dicker. The Country Idyll. Chris loathes the thing. He calls it the Country Piddle. I've named it Dicker's fiddle. There are so many good young craftsmen who needed the commission. But of course the Corporation went out for a name. Trust them! Don't tell the Headmaster I said that. I'm in his black books enough already over Goodchild's meadow. Let me buy you a coffee.'

'Thank you very much, but I think I should get my bus, Mrs Milton.'

'What, and have the Headmaster saying I couldn't even do the honours of the town to his mother. No thank you. Which shall it be – the Ten Pin Hall or the Black Cat?'

Sylvia chose the Black Cat, because she had been so fond of the Black Cat at Eastsea when she'd had the afternoon off. The Black Cat here was quite different – no dolls or handmade jewellery for sale; it was like a mixture of a coffee bar and an old-fashioned confectioner's. There were only three tables crowded in between the bar and the busy shop front. The constant hum of customers asking for Eccles cakes and loaves and sponge fingers as well as the noise of the Expresso machine only roused Lorna Milton to louder gales. Her talk was like being blown along the sea front, Sylvia thought, and smiled.

Politeness and curiosity united to help her out this time. 'What exactly is this trouble about Goodchild's meadow, Mrs Milton?'

'Oh no! Oh no! You're not catching me. I've had one of the headmaster's straight talks about that already. "No propaganda, Lorna, please." To Sylvia's dismay, in imitation of Harold, she stroked her own moustache. Then discretion satisfied, 'It's a storm in a tea cup. The truth is that if our Harold could, he'd like to oppose the whole thing, but as they're going to build these posh houses and he's so keen on multi-status Carshall, he can't very well take the usual "only over my dead body line". What he and Muriel Bartley and all the other old stagers have got up to though is a sentimental campaign about the meadow. You've seen it, I suppose, by the way. . . . Well, I ask you! Of course, it looks nice with the cattle in summer. And the original idea was a good one. But . . .' She stopped in mid-sentence and offered a plate of heavy cakes. Sylvia took a parkin, Lorna a bun with a lump of lemon curd on top. 'This'll stop my big mouth,' she laughed.

Sylvia was quite bemused, 'But what can Harold do?' she asked.

Lorna laughed again, 'You tell *me*. Oh, Mrs Calvert, I oughtn't to say it, but can't you stop him? It's such a waste of his time. He's a wonderful headmaster. Well, no, that's not true. But such a wonderful teacher! He knows more about teaching the backward than anyone in the country.'

'He's certainly done well with the textbooks.'

'So he should. He's got a genius for it. And he wastes his time on these outside things! Oh, I know *de mortuis* and so on, but it's her fault. She wanted to run everything. And she wasn't content until she had pushed him into it all. And the poor kids too.'

Sylvia crumbled her parkin nervously. 'I think Harold and Beth had every reason to be proud of the way they've brought up the children. They're wonderful.'

'Oh, of course, they're nice youngsters. And they'd be nicer still if they weren't put on show. What about *Look Back in Anger*? I'm all for it. A spot of culture in Carshall. What do Chris and I run the art show for? We don't expect results; we're pleased if two or three come along. But this 'all Calvert cast' stuff. Produced by Mr Harold Calvert, starring Miss Judy Calvert and Mr Mark Calvert. And I've no doubt Ray's sunny face will be seen some-where, if it's only over the top of a bouquet.' She looked at her watch, 'Time for your bus.' When she'd paid the bill, 'Well, this *has* been a red-letter day for me. I've put my big foot in it everywhere I could. Chris is going to like me for this.'

'I'm sure you don't have to worry with me. I don't really understand . . .'

'Look, Mrs Calvert. I'm famous for saying the wrong thing. It's just that . . . well, I get a bit upset. Old Chris works damned hard. And nobody seems to . . .'

'Harold thinks the world of Mr Milton. He's told me more than once how he relies on him.'

'And so he can,' Lorna's tone was grim, but her brown eyes were those of a stroked nervous dog. 'By the way I do all my shopping in the Town Centre. Craighill's no good for anything but baked beans. So we must have another coffee natter soon. Next time we'll talk about you.' She stretched out a fur-gloved paw and shook Sylvia's hand like a friendly tame bear.

Harold raised his eyebrows when he heard of his mother's encounter. 'I don't wish to fuss you, Mother, but you want to be careful what you say to our Lorna. I don't mean that she's a mischief maker. But she's rather embittered. She's got it into her head that old Chris is headmaster material, and, of course, he isn't. He's a very good second in command, with careful guidance. But Lorna will never accept it. She's for ever pushing poor old Chris. It's pathetic.'

For the next few days she had no need to shop. She made herself cosy up in her own room. Mark had repaired all the damaged furniture, and Ray had found some chaircover material which she'd run up while Arthur was ill. It was a sort of rough unbleached linen with stripes in ochre and dull red – an Arab design, Ray said. At first she hadn't felt a bit happy about it; but there was no doubt at all that the colours toned in well with the mustard and white. Not that she'd have ever chosen such a combination as the foundation for her room – a pretty blue, delphinium or cornflower, more like, with perhaps a suggestion of mauve, a wisteria pattern or a lilac – but still when everyone is so kind you mustn't ask for the heavens. After all they hadn't had their own place since the big smash up with those debts of Arthur's in 1929 when they'd had to sell 'The Fuchias' Guest House in Paignton with its pretty veranda. So this was as much their own place as they had had in any of the hotels; or more so. Arthur was clearly happy enough with it. On such evenings as he was in, he made straight for his old armchair.

She buried herself deep in *A Winter's Holiday*. It was all to do with a red-haired girl at an office who'd been ill, after a broken engagement. She got an anonymous present of £250 with which to take a winter holiday abroad. At first she felt too numbed to use it. To her surprise, however, her employer, who was usually a grouchy sort of man, urged her to go, and even recommended a holiday hotel in Sicily. You could tell the author had been there because there were descriptions of the almond trees in blossom and of those Greek temples – 'honey coloured against a deep blue sea'. Just as the heroine was feeling really strong again and getting a bit restless because there were very few visitors in Sicily at that time of the year – although the natives, it seemed, were very kind and lively and made her smile with all their talk – who should turn up but her boss? It was he who had sent the money, it seemed. Sylvia wished she hadn't borrowed quite so light a novel. She made herself read on. The boss hadn't intended to follow the heroine there at all; but he was so unhappy, his wife who had always been a bad lot was in a home for drunkards, and obviously he'd fallen in love with Yolande – that was the heroine's name. And quite reverently without any attempt to press his love upon her, although she had guessed, he set himself to give her a wonderful time – motor trips to Mount Etna and wonderful fish lunches on terraces covered in morning glory. At last, ' "You've done all this for me," Yolande whispered. "You've brought me alive, darling, after a long dark winter sleep." "Like a little red squirrel," Rodney said. And he smiled to think how apt his comparison was. His own little precious rare red squirrel!' Sylvia shut the book. She reminded herself not to get any more of Martin Home's. They had become too silly.

She busied herself with moving the cushions around, but it was no good, she did not feel at home. She felt shut in, and, closing in upon her like the doors of a jail, came first the thought of Melling, with its crowds of children on bicycles and kidicars and tricycles, its ton-up boys and girls in jeans, its endless lively houseproud young couples producing more and more kids, what place had an old fat woman there drowned in Renee Cranston's cheeky certainties? And then, like the clanging of the outer door, came Carshall with its prams and arcades, and queues of teenagers for the Mecca, and churches like halls, and ten pin she didn't understand, and murals she could make nothing of – bang, this outer door clanged, blown shut in the gale of Lorna Milton's buffeting words. It was unbearable to go about where strangers discussed and criticized your own flesh and blood; especially when those strangers knew all about the family and you did not. But of course they were *not* strangers; *she* was the stranger. Perhaps she had been forcing the pace. She decided to give the New Town a rest. She would go into Carshall Old Town to shop tomorrow – it would be more what she was used to and it would be somewhere new. She felt pleased at her decision – you never got old as long as you kept your curiosity alive.

The clock said only four o'clock. She longed for the first member of the family to return. As if *she* had anything to grumble at! Now poor Miss Priest – for the photo in the *Daily Express* showed her clearly that it *was* her Miss Priest although of course she was an old lady now – *really* had troubles. Even the newspapers seemed to imply what Mrs Bartley had said openly. It must be bitter for her to know people were wishing her brutally murdered instead of her niece just because she was old. She had been such a lively and sensitive woman. She almost decided to write to her; but you couldn't really write to say you were glad someone hadn't been murdered instead of her niece.

She went downstairs and made a Victoria sandwich in order to fill in time, although, to tell the truth, Ray's sponges were much lighter than hers. And it was yet only just after five. She looked out of the window into the fading light to where shadowily the fields lay hidden in that damp white mist which rose each evening from the clayey soil. There would be nothing moving now above that sodden yellowish earth, unless it were a few late roosting peewits or an early stirring owl, breaking the cold clammy air with their melancholy cries.

The journey to Old Carshall next morning was tiring,

involving two changes of buses, but she alighted in a charming market high street before a row of old-world houses with their black-and-white beams. By the village green stood a stone cross and they had preserved an old ducking stool where the poor old women used to be punished for gossiping. Unfortunately it turned out to be early closing day, so she had to shop immediately. Even then they didn't have the packets of ravioli that Mark had asked for, so that she must shop in the New Town on her way home. The sun was shining quite brightly for February, and, after she'd had a pot of tea and a boiled egg, she decided to stroll around the old place for half an hour. She went into the church – it was all churches now, she thought, laughing – which was really ancient with a lovely old organ painted blue and gold, and real stained glass windows, one of them very interesting to her because of the tommies and hospital nurses shcwn in it. When she came out again it was raining hard. A little ashamed, she went into the cinema with a queue of school kids. There was only one picture – about King Charles II, before the time of Nell Gwynne and all that, when he was running away from old Oliver Cromwell. He was hiding in the cellar of a famous castle which had been taken by a Roundhead colonel. The colonel's daughter found him there, but she didn't betray him; instead she helped him to escape by sending a dove with a message or something. It was quite difficult to follow – one of those very complicated pictures with nothing to them – and then every time a man was thrown from the walls or knocked off his horse, which was very often, the kids all cheered; and when anybody kissed, which wasn't very often, the kids made a sucking sound. Sylvia came out before the end, but very quietly so as not to spoil the children's pleasure.

She went to the Crown for tea. It was a beautiful old Trust House. Sitting in the lounge before the great open fire admiring the beams and the horsebrasses, she ate her piece of shortbread with a real relaxed pleasure. For a moment she forgot everything, and fancied that she was having her weekly afternoon off. The manageress – one of those smart women with white hair but very young faces – came up and asked if she had all she wished.

After Sylvia had told her how good she thought the set tea was, she couldn't resist asking if they were always as quiet as this at that time of the year.

'We don't do a big tea trade in the winter. It's not the tourist season. Although you'd be surprised how many casual visitors we do get for the night. I mean apart from regular business representatives.'

They discussed the difficulties of providing for casual visitors. The manageress was amazed at someone understanding the position so well, so that Sylvia had to tell her how she herself was in the trade, or had been up to a couple of months ago. The manageress – Mrs Thwaites her name was, her husband had been killed in the Battle of Britain – wasn't sure how far she would care for seaside work, with all those children in summer, and only the regular old residents in the winter. Sylvia had to say that she never had any difficulty; she loved young people about the hotel, the noisier the better. The old residents, it was true, could be a bit more difficult, but you had to remember that the poor old things were often very lonely. Mrs Thwaites then complained about the servants you got today; she didn't think foreigners really ever understood how we did things in England. But Sylvia didn't agree at all; she'd found them very quick to learn and real hard workers, which – perhaps she was old-fashioned – was what she admired. Mrs Thwaites yawned, 'Well, speed on the day of robots, I say.' There was a short silence, but Sylvia didn't want to let the conversation lapse. 'Do you do much catering for weddings and big parties?'

The manageress must have heard some noise in the hall.

'Excuse me a moment.'

It was a quarter of an hour or so before she came back.

'The reception always need supervision, but I needn't tell you that. You were saying?'

Sylvia repeated her question. 'Oh yes, we do most of the parties for the directors and senior executives in the New Town. There's nowhere of the right kind in that terrible place, of course.'

So Sylvia decided not to tell her that she was living at Harold's, and then even she could hear voices in the hall.

'Don't let me keep you, I know what a nuisance gossiping visitors can be.'

Mrs Thwaites smiled. 'How rare to meet a customer who understands.'

Sylvia told her what a treat it had been to talk to someone in the trade. She had stayed so late that the shops in the New Town were closed and she had to return without Mark's ravioli.

At supper Harold frowned at his spaghetti bolognese. 'I thought you were giving us ravioli, Mark.'

'It's the same sugo.'

'Yes, but not the same pasta. I'd looked forward to ravioli. I don't know what the rest of the company think, but I suggest we pass a vote of censure on the cook for a culpable, misleading menu.'

It was not for Sylvia to comment on this vote, for she and Arthur were eating liver and bacon, but she did feel it necessary to explain that it was her fault and why.

Harold was amazed. 'Old Carshall! Apart from occasionally using the station, I don't believe I've been there for six years. Some idiot at the County Council wanted me to give a lunch last year at the Crown for a visiting group of educationists from Yugoslavia. I refused to lend myself to that sort of vulgar deception. If our school meals are good enough for the boys and the staff, they're good enough for visiting V.I.P.s. I was amused in fact to find that the British Council chap who came down with them thoroughly agreed with me.' He was smiling now, but as he forked up another twist of spaghetti. 'Old Carshall! What on earth did you find to do there? Really, Mother, if you're going on country jaunts, I think we must hand the shopping back to the boys.'

'Why is spaghetti ever so much nicer than ravioli?' Judy asked.

'All that has nothing to do with it. The fact is that if your Gran . . .'

But Harold was called away by the telephone's ring. As head of the house, he liked to answer the telephone. Ten minutes passed before he returned. Red in the face, he pushed his plate of now cold spaghetti away from him.

'That telephone call concerned you, Judy.'

Sylvia wondered if the girl had been expelled from school or something, he spoke so grimly.

'Your headmistress apparently feels that your chances of a distinguished career are put in grievous peril by your proposed appearance as Helena in your father's production of *Look Back in Anger*.'

'Oh, Daddy! How absolutely mad! She really is! I mean . . . Lots of people think she's going right round the bend. Apparently ever so many of her family were completely crazy. And they say . . .'

'Who says all this, Judy?'

'Well, I mean, Mrs Ogilvie, Caroline's mother, says that she's the most unsuitable headmistress.'

'Then Mrs Ogilvie, Caroline's mother, ought to be ashamed of herself. There are many things over which I cross swords with Miss Castle, but we heads of schools have quite enough difficulties without uninformed parents wilfully undermining our authority. Miss Castle had a quite remarkable university record.'

'Oh, I know she's brilliant at biology and botany and all the rest of it. But as a headmistress! Well, I mean to begin with she has absolutely no social manner. You should have seen her when Lady Anthea Warren came to give the prizes. "Girls" – you know how she speaks with her teeth out for an airing – "Lady Warren has come here . . ." Lady Warren! Wasn't it awful?'

'I don't know quite what issue of Tatler etiquette you're trying to teach us, Judy, but in any case it has nothing to do with the point. Miss Castle believes that rehearsals for the play are not advisable in your A level year. That must be enough. It's inconvenient, but it's not irreparable. Luckily we've only had the read through and one rehearsal.'

'But, Daddy! You said you wanted me in it. You said I was the only person round here who could play Helena.'

'I said that there were certain affinities between the egregiously priggish Helena and yourself that made for type casting. But this sort of thing can't possibly interfere with your A levels.'

'But I don't want to go to a university anyway. And *you* don't want me to go. Just because I happen to be good at languages.'

'That's not true, Judy. I have my views about the present dilution of the universities and I have a right to them, I suppose. Also, looking at some of my brighter pupils and thinking how much more they would benefit from a university education than the stuffed geese of the grammar schools, I have my doubts about the infallibility of the examination system. All that doesn't mean that I should for one minute stand in the way of my daughter's getting to the university, if her headmistress believes she's the right material.'

'But *Mummy* didn't want me to go.'

Harold banged on the table so that the spoons and forks jumped.

'You will kindly never say that again, Judy. Whatever she may have thought, your mother was the most generous-minded woman living.'

Judy burst into tears.

'Don't worry, Judykins. You'll be the belle of the ball wherever you go.'

Judy didn't even look up at him. Since the bathroom incident, she had avoided her grandfather. He got up from his chair, 'Well, if we're to get three rubbers in tonight, I must be toddling. Excuse me, Harold, old lad.'

Harold grunted at his father's departure. 'I'm sorry, Judy, if you're disappointed. Of course I should have liked you in the play. But such disappointments are a part of life, you know.'

Judy sat red-faced and tense.

Sylvia asked: 'What's the play about, Harold dear?'

Harold laughed. 'To be honest it's strictly not for the mums. It concerns one Jimmie Porter, the most likeable unlikeable youngster who ever wanted to set the world to rights if he knew how. The part's a natural one for our Mark.'

Mark looked down into his suede jacket and said, 'Who isn't, by the way, going to be able to play it after all.'

Harold stood up. 'Did I really hear what I thought I heard?'

'I'm afraid so, Dad.'

Harold sat for a few seconds in silence, save for shaking his head in refusal of either fruit or cheese that Ray offered him. Sylvia noticed that his hands were trembling.

'Oh, I shall be so sorry not to see you, Mark dear, on the boards.'

Mark had taken an apple and he filled his mouth with carefully peeled quarters each time he spoke. Sylvia had to strain to understand him.

'Well, you won't, I'm afraid, Gran. You'll probably have old Ray here instead.'

'Oh no, she won't! I've never looked back and what's more I'm never angry. Besides, there's a lot of smooching with our Priscilla. And that can't . . .'

Harold interrupted in a loud voice, clipping each word with restrained fury. 'May I inquire your reasons for evading your commitment?'

Mark continued to talk to his brother. 'Oh, most of the time Jimmie Porter beats her up. And then Terry Knowles is playing the friend Cliff. He's almost as important as the wife. You ought to do it, really, Ray. You'd have fun.'

Sylvia could tell how anxious he was to persuade Ray; she'd never seen his usual scowl turn to such a lively grin.

All the plates and spoons and forks jumped for a second time as Harold brought his fist down heavily upon the table.

'I want an answer, Mark.' Then he gave an answer himself. 'I'm not unreasonable, you know. If it's the evening classes, well, of course, I must accept it. But I thought we'd fixed all that when we scheduled the rehearsals. . . .'

'It isn't the evening classes. Anyway, if I'm a natural for Jimmie Porter, I'm not going to be cast for *Room at the Top* as well, you know. No, the local committee's chosen me to go to this unity discussion with the 100 people. The dates clash.'

'Oh, for God's sake, Mark! I've never been against you following lost causes, but you've said yourself again and again that you C.N.D. people and the 100 group can never agree.'

'Yes. I still doubt it, but I'm afraid you believe only in unlost lost causes, Dad, just as you believe in likeable unlikeable youngsters. That was your phrase, wasn't it?'

'Oh, this is too easy, boyo.' Ray appealed to Mark.

'Mark isn't in it and it's the end of the world. But anybody can play Helena, I suppose.' Judy ran out of the room.

'If you work that girl up much more, Dad, she'll die of starvation. She takes most of her meals at the run now.'

Harold ignored Ray. 'I'm waiting to know your serious reasons for letting me down, Mark.'

'Such disappointments are a part of life. Isn't that it, Dad?' He swallowed his last piece of apple and was gone.

Sylvia didn't know after supper whether to stay with Harold or go up to her room, but, as everyone had left him, she decided to remain downstairs. She would have liked the tele-play – 'something just plain funny, and a bit saucy into the bargain for those who want to get the taste of the kitchen sink out of their mouths' the *TV Times* said about it. But Harold didn't look in the mood for anything funny, let alone saucy. She had no library book, so she looked on Harold's shelves. They were mostly educational books, and that, but she found a volume of murder trials which would do to pass the time away, although she wasn't a great detective-story fan.

'You won't like that, Mother.' But when she began to replace the book, 'Oh, read what you like, please.'

The trial part was difficult to read – all those questions and answers. But then she got absorbed in it; Sydney Fox it was. The way he and that old mother of his went from hotel to hotel, running up bills and then doing a moonlight flit. Of course, she'd come across cases like it once or twice. But nothing as bad as this. She felt quite angry that the proprietors and manageresses didn't catch up with them – a couple of rogues. And then suddenly the story took on a terrifying intensity. The stout old mother with her white hair and rosy cheeks and her fur coat, and the son so softly spoken, so adoring. You could see what was going to happen as the net closed in on him – the one cornered rat turning on the other. She read of the insuring of the old woman's life and she became so afraid for her that she had to put the book by. In Bournemouth it was – she remembered the hotel quite well, more a boarding house really. Harold was busy writing on the backs of old envelopes; he seemed absorbed and more relaxed. And then the paraffined paper burning the bedroom; the old woman's heavy body, only her underclothes on, no night clothes, just the one dress and the fur coat all she had in the world, and the sheets she lay in all pee-ed on. At the very end of his tether, what could the loving son do but sell the old woman for the best money he could get for her? The question she had conjured up from the book presented itself so unexpectedly, so directly to Sylvia that she shivered, lit a cigarette and inhaled deeply. Harold looked up.

'Well! I've recast it. Ray to replace Mark, June Mackie to do Helena. It's not typecasting this time, but so much more room for an interpretative production. I was being lazy.' He laid down his notes. 'Do you know, Mother, I often think of something old Len used to say. "Harold needs a bit of a setback to make him show what he can do." Old Len understood us far better than we realized.'

Sylvia couldn't remember Len's saying it, but she answered, 'Yes, he did, dear.' She could not help thinking how convenient dead Len was to Arthur and Harold.

The school hall was very large, yet the first-night audience filled it, although the small metal chairs had been packed together as tightly as possible. Sylvia felt herself overflowing at both sides on to Judy and to Muriel Bartley. Arms and thighs were pressed as closely as in the rush-hour London Tube.

'Harold's got his audience all right.' To Sylvia's discomfort Muriel's voice attracted as much public attention as her make-up. 'It's disgraceful that he wasn't allowed the Community Centre. I gave them a good dressing down at the Corporation Offices. But half the trouble's been the C.A.D.S. themselves. They've never given him real backing. Not enough fat parts it seems.'

People were chattering all around them. Sylvia only hoped they wouldn't whisper during the play – it was such an important occasion for Harold, and, of course for Ray, too, but he'd take everything in his stride, as he had taken on this part at such short notice. These local things were always more social occasions for the audience. Judy and Muriel Bartley kept on drawing her attention to people whom she'd never seen before. It seemed rude to turn and stare at strangers, indeed she could hardly do so at all, without swaying three or four people along from her in the row, so crushed were they all; yet she hesitated to remove her fur coat which enveloped both her neighbours, for the hall, so packed to immobility, was yet vibrant with mysterious draughts from its many exit doors and long metal windows. Whenever she did look round it seemed to her that people were whispering and pointing her out; and so, no doubt, they were, for Harold was a big local man, this was his big day, and she was his mother, seen in public for the first time. Such a sense of being watched from behind did not make it easier to sit in the second row and give the full attention she was sure this play would need. But once the lights were down.... If only nobody asked her what she thought of it all afterwards; but she would be too busy seeing that the little party went well, and this time it really was all her own, for everyone had been too busy to give her a hand.

'So our Harold's pulled it off. Chris and I are delighted.' And as if to echo his wife's declaration, Chris Milton burst into a general coverage of laughter. 'Our poor little art show drew twenty-four. But then we can't *shock* them into coming can we, Chris!' She didn't look at Sylvia, thank heaven, for they'd never had their little natter and Sylvia had hidden from her in the Arcade once or twice in Carshall. She began to worry about how much she had offended Lorna Milton, but Muriel Bartley's loud voice kept her from thinking.

'No, I'm afraid you're right there, Mrs Milton. I did wonder this time, Mr Milton, whether you aren't guiding them a bit too much with their art work. Oh, I know you wouldn't do it consciously, but this year's show did lack that sort of smack in the eye that the kids' imagination usually gives us.'

Sylvia could tell from the little beads of moisture that had gathered on Muriel's shiny mauve eyelids and at the corners of her cyclamen lips that she was working up for a row. She turned away from such troubles to Judy, sitting so neat and quiet in her first black evening dress. Now Judy deserved a medal if anyone did, taking her disappointment so well!

'Isn't that your friend Caroline, dear? She looks so pretty . . . well, not perhaps pretty, but handsome. Cherry's certainly her colour. Is that material marocain, do you suppose? I can't see well enough from here.'

Judy screwed her handkerchief up into a ball. 'Oh, I do think Mrs Ogilvie or one of them might have come with her, whatever they think of the play. After all, Daddy's doing something really important. . . .'

On the other side Muriel Bartley's voice had risen high – you could tell now that she was cockney. 'Oh, it's nothing to do with me! If you want to judge all that's been done here in fifteen years from a six months' residence. . . . Anyhow, shush! Here are the big pots!' She dismissed the Miltons and turned to Sylvia. 'That's the General Manager, Colonel Rigby, and his wife. And the thin one is Jock Parsons, the P.R.O. This is a triumphant turnout for Harold all right.'

Sylvia had only time to see a flurry of bald heads and tight corsages with carnations pinned to them before the house lights went down and the curtain with its strange design of young men with hooves playing the pipes – all drawn and painted by the boys – rose to reveal such an ugly little sloping room and Ray, wearing old jeans, was talking.

Truth to tell she couldn't follow it very well, although Ray and the other boy were very funny about the newspapers, and the way they larked about with each other was very natural. She couldn't quite get what sort of people they were; the room was so shabby and yet they talked so well – Ray had ever so many lines and said them beautifully, of course, if a bit loud – probably they were students. The heat from the flood lights was intense, she wished she had taken off her coat; and then the girl spoke her lines rather monotonously; and that iron going backwards and forwards. Harold had produced it very well, you could see that; yet surely he should have made the girl throw herself into the part more, have got her to move away every now and again from that ironing board. As it was everything was so lively when the boys were doing their bits, but the talk between Ray and the girl seemed a bit dead. No doubt it was because Harold knew the girl would move awkwardly that he'd kept her stuck in one place. He'd been talking the other evening about the difficulties of position and movement with amateurs. Yet what with the hot lights and no pretty clothes to look at and Ray's shouting all the time a bit on one note and the iron going backwards and forwards, backwards and forwards. . . .

She was woken by the pressure of Judy's elbow. Ray was still talking. She concentrated very hard on his words. Likeable unlikeable, Harold had said this Jimmie Porter was; but she couldn't recognize Ray in the part, because whatever Ray said was done to please and now he seemed to shout his words and look grim as though he were imitating Mark, except of course that Mark mumbled.

'That old bitch should be dead! . . . I said she's an old bitch, and should be dead!' It was about the girl's mother that Ray was speaking, but only the boy Cliff said anything to check him. The girl seemed too intent on her ironing to stand up for her mother. And then terrible words came pouring out of Ray's mouth, as though the comic things Arthur said about worms and a dose of salts had got mixed up with the dreadful brutal things he also said in his rages.

'I say she ought to be dead,' Ray shouted. 'My God those worms will need a good dose of salts the day they get through her! Oh, what a bellyache you've got coming to you, my little wormy ones! Alison's mother is on the way!' There was a shocked drawing in of breath from some of the audience and nervous titters from others; but then that's how it had been all through. No one appeared to feel, as she did, that the blackness of night had closed in quite suddenly. She tried to attend carefully to the rest of the scene, but across her vision there ran and stumbled and fell a line of fat naked old women – some haggard and ancient as witches, others with rouge and peroxide hair and earrings – and in their eyes was the uncomprehending terror of cows going to the knacker's yard. In the background she could hear Ray's voice ranting on with its endless jeering. She knew who they were – Jewesses that she had read of going to the gas chamber; yet it seemed only a terrible story when she had just read it in the *Dispatch*. And now suddenly Ray's voice came through as tenderly as when he explained the mysteries of the kitchen to her. 'It's Hugh's Mum. She's had a stroke. . . . I think she's dying. . . . It doesn't make any sense at all.'

She sat through the act and on through the interval with its silly chatter and nervous, tittering questions about the play, through the offers of coffee and of cup ices; but she was intent to reconcile these two voices of Ray's – or, of course, not really his, but of this Jimmie Porter's – the brutal and the tender. She could find no answer. Perhaps this was what Harold meant by 'likeable and unlikeable'; but it seemed to be beyond a question of liking. She listened throughout the play and the voice came again to her in tenderness and yet again in brutal jeering – was it just that sometimes this Jimmie Porter loved himself and that sometimes he hated himself? So much of the time he seemed to be talking to himself and not to the other characters. That might be so, but it didn't really concern her. All the talk about squirrels and bears, the way that Ray didn't seem quite real in the part when playing with the two girls, yet came alive in all the back chat with Cliff – none of this had to do with her; these were things that concerned the young people, imaginary characters or real actors. For her there were only certain words that mattered: 'She thought that Hugh's mother was a deprived and ignorant old woman who said all the wrong things in the wrong places, who couldn't be taken seriously', or over and over again, 'Oh, what a bellyache you've got coming. . . . Alison's mother is on the way.'

At last it was finished amid loud clapping, although there were here and there glum disapproving faces, and the ostentatious departure of a few of the audience allowed Harold to smile amusedly before beginning his speech of thanks.

Sylvia made herself listen carefully to every word he said, though they came to her through a muffling fog of horror. He spoke most professionally, with a quiet humour, and little unexpected pauses that kept people on their toes.

'. . . I am naturally pleased to think that a Carshall audience, despite all appearances to the contrary, has the intelligence required to appreciate a play of this calibre. But then a producer should never make the mistake of judging his audience by the sheepish expression on their faces. . . . I am not going to single out any of the cast who have so nobly fought out the battles of their generation for you this evening. But I will say that if any of the younger members of the audience felt that there was a touch of the square about everything, that is the fault of the producer, who as you all know is an old square, and not of the actors who are one and all hip. Oh, excuse me, Tom, I had forgotten you. Thanks to Tom Staddon for suggesting in his playing of the colonel that some of the oldsters are neither as bad nor as dumb as they seem. I should however like to say a word about why I chose this particular play for performance in Carshall, because, as many of you know, I fought a few battles to get it put on. For me the whole thing centres round young Jimmie Porter. You may hate him, you may love him – and judging from the sounds of the audience tonight Carshall's verdict inclines to thumbs down – but you can't deny that he brings you all alive. I shan't say anything about tonight's performance of Jimmie, as you may have guessed from the programme the casting of this part was a disgraceful piece of nepotism. I would just add, like every parent who ever got up in the witness box – "You may not believe it, but he's a good boy at home." So much for the actor, but what about the role Jimmie Porter? Disgraceful you say; wordy young do-nothing; brutal young cad. As a headmaster I should like to say, please go away and think a little about the world we've made for Jimmie – yes, you and I, sir, so respectable and level-headed – a world that has nothing to offer to a generous, intelligent, warm-hearted young chap like that, a world that has soured and embittered him. But isn't everything done for them, you will say? That's just it, as any secondary schoolmaster can tell you, the nice neat England we've built doesn't leave any room for participation. It tells you to take your bit of welfare from the experts on a plate and be thankful for it. But not in the New Towns, you'll say; not in Carshall. We've got a new hopeful young world here of uncrowded leisureful happy living. We've got a cause to fight for – something that Jimmie couldn't find in his squalid cramped surroundings. Yes, we have. But, for God's sake, let us remember that New Town living, like anything else that's worth having, has to be fought for by alertness, by caring. We have a first-rate administration here, but even the best of administrations can err. If any of you believe, as I do, that Goodchild's meadow, that expression of the country running through the town, is an integral part of Carshall's way of life, then don't just sit on your hands and hope for the best, or grumble over your pint at the local. Get out, and say or write what you think. We have, as I said, a fine administration, but they need your voices and mine – the voices of the people who live here – to make sure that the ideal of the New Towns, the ideal on which Carshall was founded, shall not be forgotten and neglected through reasons of expediency, or economy, or so-called commonsense. Carshall is a place where we all look forward in confident hope. Don't let us through funk or laziness allow it to become a place where we have to look back in anger. Thank you.'

Muriel Bartley rose from her seat and called out 'Good old Harold!' then leaning down she whispered to Sylvia, 'I bet it was an afterthought, but he's put the cat among the pigeons all right.' Indeed many members of the audience were silent; and some few had left at intervals throughout the speech. The big pots in the front row clapped, but sedately. And then, as Sylvia was folding her fur coat around her and Judy was collecting her scarf and bag, the heavy bald-headed man whom Muriel Bartley had named as Jock Parsons rose amid calls from the bald heads and tight corsages around him of 'Ssh!' and 'Speech!'

'Ladies and Gentlemen,' Jock Parsons began, 'it's not normal, I know, for the audience to reply to the producer's speech of thanks. But this is not quite an ordinary occasion. So as the Town's P.R.O. I'm going to reply for you. We have been given a fine performance of a remarkable play – a play which, whatever some of us may think of its characters and its language, comes, as Harold Calvert has rightly said, to challenge any easy self-satisfaction that we may happen to feel. Although I am sure we're not more self-satisfied in Carshall than in the rest of the country . . .' Sylvia had lost some of his words because Muriel Bartley was whispering, 'We are, of course, we are. He knows it.' 'As Public Relations Officer here, and I know that our General Manager agrees with me, spontaneous cultural activities like tonight's production – I don't mean of course that we should want to look back in anger every evening –

are the sort of things that make our job on the Corporation here so rewarding. The houses are here, the factories are here, the shops are here, the gardens are here. But it's in the dance hall and in the community centre and in the Ten Pin Hall, and in the amateur theatre, that people get up and sing. And only by reponse can we know that the whole thing's working. I said that a show like this happened spontaneously. But of course, it doesn't. In this particular case, we owe the evening's entertainment to the determination and hard work of Harold Calvert. There is always a lot of talk about the difficult relations between the County Council and the Corporation. It is said that the New Towns have been saddled with a lot of County Council red tape. Well, there may be some truth in that; but so long as the County Council goes on sending us headmasters like Harold Calvert who really care for Carshall and what happens to it, I for one shall thank the Lord for the County Council. But since our friend has raised the subject of Goodchild's meadow, I feel I must just correct what he said – for in this matter I'm afraid an employee of the County Council, however loyal a Carshallite, can't quite know all the facts as we of the Corporation do. The decision about Goodchild's meadow when it's made, will be made at the Ministry level. Of course, we hope and I believe we can expect that that decision will reflect the interests and wishes of the residents of Carshall, will not depart from the spirit that actuated the founding of the New Towns, but it is a decision which inevitably involves a mass of legal, economic and administrative elements that cannot be decided, that should not be decided in the emotion of public controversy or debate. . . .' Mr Parsons paused for breath. The first notes of 'God Save the Queen' came *fortissimo* from the radiogram at a nod from Harold. Immediately he made a pantomime of apology for the interruption and gestured to stop the music; but he had achieved his purpose, many of the audience were already standing, and the Public Relations Officer refused the offer to proceed with a shake of his head. As they stood bunched in loyal homage, Muriel Bartley whispered 'Good Old Harold', and Judy said under her breath, 'I knew Daddy would win.'

The two speeches had caused a sensation that threatened to put even the controversy about John Osborne's play in the shade. Muriel Bartley could talk of nothing else as she drove Sylvia home. Sylvia debated with herself whether Harold had done himself harm or not, and, mingled with her misgivings for her son, went a running calculation of the number of sausage rolls and cakes and sandwiches she had provided for the coming party. But both the unfamiliar, half-comprehended anxiety and the familiar domestic concern were muddled sequences of thought, for through them all the time she could feel the shame of Jimmie Porter's foot kicking at her naked buttocks as he had at the cistern in that squalid little room and could hear him calling in his jeering, mock Northern accent, 'Can you hear me, mother?'

The party was not altogether an easy one. The cast sat together. You could tell they felt it all a bit of an anti-climax. Of course, for the first quarter of an hour people went up and congratulated them. Lorna Milton said, 'I'm not praising you, Ray. This is enough of a Calvert jamboree without that. In any case I thought you and Terry hogged the stage. No, I'm going all out for the girls. Jolly good, Priscilla! Jolly good, June! Though I don't believe for a minute that two pretty girls like you would tie yourselves with an oik like him.' But Chris Milton, for once, didn't altogether agree with his wife. 'No, no, Jimmie Porter was the only one who was trying to express himself. I suppose it's square of me, but if only he had played some instrument that called for a bit of team work. Not the trumpet.' Muriel was full of praise for them – they really had put the cat among the pigeons. But it was Sally Bulmer who gave them the most attention. 'Good for you, Ray. I didn't know you had the guts. Mr Sunshine willing to play the unpopular. And as for you, Pris, you put up a good exhibition of battle by ironing. But what was this good-looking lout doing sitting around the house?' She dug Terry Knowles in the ribs. 'What a household! Oh! It's a clever enough play. But a decent social worker could have cleared up the whole mess in a day and a half.' Harold came in for a good deal of the praise, but that soon shifted from the play to his battle with Mr Parsons.

Sylvia, seeing the cast sitting on their own, was a little worried. She made herself remember little things that each of them had done on the stage, and although it cost her a lot, saved her praise of Ray to the last. 'I thought that was very good, Miss White' – Priscilla off stage was a nice-looking blonde girl, not at all embittered or sad looking – 'when you came back in the last act. You stood at the door and I think all the audience felt the drama of it.' 'Oh, thank you, Mrs Calvert. Mr Calvert's going to be furious with me. I stood there much longer than he told me. But I didn't see why the men should hog all the attention.' 'We did not, did we, Ray?' 'They did, didn't they, June?' 'I must say I rather think you did, Terry.' June was as prim in real life as she was playing Helena. 'Well, we can't help it if we got all the attention, can we Terry?' 'Oh, it was quite a male beauty chorus, of course.' 'It was the acting, you slut. Isn't she a slut, Ray? You ought to have bashed her bonk a real good one.' 'I tell you what, boyo, we'll do the whole play again without the girls.' 'Oh, so that's how it is. Come on, June. . . .' 'We'll meet you birds after the show's over, won't we Ray?' 'You'll be lucky, Terry Knowles.'

It was all fun with shrieks of laughter. But there was a little crossness too; but then of course they were overtired. Sylvia, if she did not altogether understand the causes of the strain, could sense it; but she could see no way of assisting beyond giving her share of praise and then stoking up the guests' energies with food and drink so that they could reach boiling point, subside and go home as soon as possible. She succeeded admirably, for the last guests had shouted themselves hoarse and left by a quarter past midnight when Arthur returned from cards at the Cranstons'.

'Well, I hear I missed a bloody good show. Congratulations, Harold, old boy. And not only on this *Look Back in Anger* stunt. What's more important, I hear you fought a couple of rounds with that pompous ass Jock Parsons, and everyone seems to think you won on points. Good lad!'

'How did you hear all this, Dad?' Harold was smiling.

'Ah! Muriel Bartley looked in as we were playing our last rubber.'

'You don't want to believe all Muriel says. She's

partisan. But I think I did give them the sense that they won't necessarily have everything their own way.'

'Good lad!'

'After all, there are times, I think, Dad, when tact is only another name for cowardice.'

'I wouldn't know. I've never practised either.'

The heat and smoke of the room threatened to turn Sylvia's exhaustion into giddy sickness. She moved to retire to bed.

'Well, what did you make of it all, Sylvia?' Arthur winked at Harold. Sylvia realized that she had said nothing to Harold in praise of his production; she felt a desperate need to make some communication to him.

'I think I did understand what you meant, Harold, about that boy. His being likeable and unlikeable, I mean. But it wasn't really for him to say that the one old woman shouldn't have died or that the other would be better dead. They were human beings. . . .'

She could see that he didn't understand what she was talking about and that she had entirely failed to reach him; but she could do no more now, shut in by the heat and the smoke. She had to escape or fall. As she stood for a moment in the purer, cooler air of the hall to regain her balance, she heard him speaking.

'The old lady's getting a bit out of touch these days isn't she, Dad?'

'I don't believe you kids ever realized how difficult your mother can be.'

She waited for Harold's answer to his father and, when none came, she dragged her heavy body upstairs to bed.

5. New Leaves

It was the second time that Sylvia had been caught by Renee Cranston in Melling. This time they met face to face outside the self-service store; but Renee only said, 'Well, you certainly are a rare bird these days. Keeping all right? Cheerio!' and flashing her bright smile was gone. Sylvia couldn't tell whether she imagined a hurt look in that cheeky bird's eye or not. In any case she was too resigned to worry. She had rationalized the shopping now to once a week in the Town Centre and three quick tootles to the Melling shops. The quarter hour's rush shopping in Melling was almost over; soon she would be home to pack Arthur off to the British Legion and the bookies, and to begin a long day of nothing at 'The Sycamores'. Or not really nothing, for there was always the tele and books, and then she was determined to see that she had a proper lie down on her bed each afternoon as the doctor had recommended. After all, she had retired from work because she was an invalid, and it was absurd to start getting steamed up now just because she had to lead an invalid's life.

She'd quite scared herself the evening of that play. Having high blood pressure gave people these morbid fancies; but you had to be careful because a lot of worrying like that would send the blood pressure rushing up. Anyway, with all their religions and philosophy and that, they hadn't solved these problems in thousands of years, so what price an ignorant old woman like her taking them on? It would all be the same in a hundred years, that's all you could say. That and do your best, which she'd tried to do. She'd done her stint of hard work in her day. Arthur seemed as pleased as Punch with life – she'd spent her £200 gratuity in paying all his debts, but what did he care about that? As to the family, with all that education what did they want with her? She was grateful to them for being so kind and she tried to do a good part by them where she could; for the rest she could repay them best by keeping her trap shut. She'd thought this again and again as she watched some of the old residents fretting their days away with nagging and groaning, and what was sauce for the goose was sauce for the gander.

Morbid fancies apart, one problem did vex her at spare moments – as now when she had got back from shopping, or between programmes and books, or in the evening interval just before the family returned. Should she write to Miss Priest? She knew the address now – the hotel's name had slipped through into the newspaper reports. A woman reporter had interviewed Miss Priest there. 'A tall well-dressed white-haired woman looking younger than her years, Miss Priest laughed at my suggestion that many in her position would have fled from the scene of such tragic association as soon as they were able. "I can't answer for many, can I?" she told me. "But I shan't miss Theodora less by leaving Ibiza. The best I can do for her is to stay here and help the police as much as I can in their investigation."' Sylvia had recognized immediately in this the good sense and courage she had so liked all those years ago. But the reporter had added a comment, 'It was a point of view certainly. But as I looked back at the hotel up to the balconies with their showers of purple bougainvillea pouring down in the harsh sunlight, I didn't envy Miss Priest her continued stay even in so romantic and comfortable a luxury hotel.' 'Don't cast nasturtiums' – it came back to Sylvia from the Rectory days where cook used to say it; she would like to have written it on a postcard and sent it to the reporter woman. She was quite sure that Miss Priest would never be callous. But you can't write and tell someone that. What could she write? To thank Miss Priest for having offered an ordinary working woman like herself friendship; to apologize for not having accepted it; to explain that she had been held back by shyness, and something else, caution – if you don't hold your hand out you won't get it bitten? As if Miss Priest, who had travelled everywhere and had hundreds of friends, would have cared about the silly reserves of a manageress of a little hotel – yet now, perhaps, even if she didn't remember Sylvia's name, any letter of friendship . . . She went up to her own room and took out her writing pad. The telephone rang. She almost decided to let it ring unanswered; as like as not, by the time she got down to Harold's study, they would have rung off. But after all it was Harold's house and Harold had a right to his messages.

'Hullo? Oh, Mrs Bartley. I'm afraid Harold's left for school. Well, you knew that. Oh? Yes, of course. Well, anything I can do. I see. Yes. Yes. Oh! Oh dear, I don't know! I'm not at all clever, you know. Of course, I don't understand about it, but if you and Harold both take that view, I'm sure there must be . . . Well, I'm good with figures. Oh, I see. Not really. I very often used to type the menus and that, and if the receptionist was away . . . All with two fingers, you know. If it would really help. Oh, I don't think that would be necessary. Well, we could talk about that later. I'd like to think about it. Shall I ring you up again? About seven. Yes. Of course.'

So there it was. And of course she must do it, since Harold was so concerned about this Goodchild's meadow business. But to be truthful she hoped the job wouldn't take long, for Muriel Bartley's smart brightness scared her a bit, and then there was her little afternoon rest to consider, and now that she'd become quite keen on some of the after tea children's programmes she didn't want to miss them.

Harold was delighted. 'I can't take too prominent a part in this little public agitation, as Muriel knows, with my position as headmaster. The County Council might start objecting. But I still feel I set the thing in motion. And to know that one of the family's helping . . .'

Sylvia was warmed by his obvious satisfaction. 'Well, I'll do my best, dear.'

'Oh, you'll do it perfectly. It's quite a routine little job. Or at least I know nothing about it, but I don't see Muriel slave driving you. I'm the last person, you know, Mother, to want you to strain yourself in any way. You're under doctor's orders. But I have been a bit concerned . . . Well, in general, you know retirement's not an easy thing and we don't want you getting net curtainitis.' He waved his hand towards the heavy flame velvet curtains with which Beth had gone splash in the sitting room. 'It's only an adaptation malady, of course, but . . .'

So the Zephyr dropped Sylvia each morning at Muriel Bartley's as Harold went to the school; and she walked back each midday through the bracing March sunlight, unless it rained, when Muriel took her home in the Vauxhall. She felt killed by kindness.

Muriel Bartley's home was certainly a strange setting to work in – a twin to Harold's, called 'Sorbetts' after some old farm that had been there; but not at all alike inside. Muriel in her morning attire of black trousers, striped silk shirt and golden Chinese slippers made that clear the first day.

'I'm afraid it's not contemporary here. I like old things, or more perhaps the old style. And then I'm a terrible collector. The things I've collected since Geoff and I have gone on these cruises in the last few years. Do you like my dolls? And the china? And my glass? Oh! I don't know. Sometimes I think I'll sell it all up and start afresh. After all, it's the collecting that's the fun. But I don't really get a lot of time for the house by the time I've finished bossing everyone around. That's my trouble, I'm a great bosser. You musn't let me push you around. Just hit back. Like all bullies, I crumple up quickly.'

Muriel had her own little work room, the equivalent of Harold's study. It was quite plain – all efficiency furniture, except for a little cocktail bar that she'd cleverly squeezed into one corner. 'I couldn't stand someone in the room I'm working in. It'd give me the jim jams. Especially another woman. I expect you feel the same. Two old hens together?' She laughed and Sylvia laughed too in relief.

Each day then Sylvia sat on a precarious little painted wooden chair at a precarious little painted wooden table in the drawing room surrounded by the French style suite – Louis something, Muriel said it was – upholstered in powder-blue figured satin, except for two deep chintz-covered sofas in which, as Muriel said, 'You soon sank never to rise again.' There was only just room for the typewriter on the table, so that the envelopes and directories and leaflets were all ranged at her feet on the thick pile, powder-blue, fitted carpet. On the first morning it took her some time to forget the distraction of all the objects that surrounded her – the blue satin oval panels each hung with Cries of London in white frames, the hundred or so dolls in national dress in the cabinet before her, the rows of ships in bottles, and Venetian glass swans and paperweights in the cabinet behind her, and to her left the china cabinet in which poodles and ladies in crinolines and rose-entwined country cottages all jostled together among white china baskets, see-no-evil monkeys and a huge china Cheshire cat with a long neck and one eye closed in a sexy wink. There was something interesting everywhere to distract her from the names and addresses which she copied from the directories to the envelopes.

However, as Harold had said, it proved to be a routine little job. There were three different printed leaflets – one for private residents, another for people in business and another for clubs and societies; Sylvia's task was to collect addresses from the directories and type them on the envelopes. She could in fact make only one mistake – that of putting the wrong leaflets into the wrong envelopes. Once she'd got used to working in such a fancy setting and had ceased to listen for Muriel's footsteps she found that she could work very quickly. Soon she was typing and sorting almost automatically, while thinking over yesterday's episode of 'Down Our Way' or of the new one about prison wardresses – how was that nice little Scotch wardress going to prove to the up-to-date and thoroughly fair Governor that she hadn't smuggled cigarettes into the sick bay when every one of the other wardresses was in league against her? The pleasure of yesterday's viewing and reading merged happily into the prospect of the afternoon before her. She knew of course from another book that the Queen eventually got tired of the Duchess's airs and graces and quarrelled with her, but this was a historical novel and you couldn't always tell how things would go in them, besides the heroine was a young lady-in-waiting torn between love for the poor bullied Anne and admiration for the violent Sarah; it was difficult to know which side she would choose when things finally came to a head. It was usually midday before Sylvia had time to turn around.

Time to go home – or almost. For there's always a fly in the ointment. Midday brought Muriel, changed from trousers into a suit for attendance at an afternoon committee or just in order to run down to one of the four branches of Bartley's to make things hum – she did all the firm's books in her little office at home.

'How about a little tipple for a good little girl? What! Seventy-eight addresses this morning! You deserve a double for that!' And off to the little bar they went, where Sylvia hoisted herself with some difficulty on to a swivel stool. From there she stared at the row of jugs on the back shelf. The first had a girl's head peeping out from the inside, then each jug showed a little more of her as she climbed out with no clothes on; at last the girl was completely out of the jug, clasping it in her arms and showing her sit-down-upon while she looked back saucily over her shoulder. Sylvia always had her favourite gin and it, and enjoyed it, or would have done had it not been for keeping up with Muriel's talk.

'So you haven't travelled abroad? Oh, well, I don't know that you've missed much. The sun's nice, of course. But every year I say to Geoff, "That's the last time". What with the food, and then some of the prices are daylight robbery. It's all much the same anyway – the Northern Capitals, Greek Islands, we've done the lot. But still you can usually get a good game of poker. And then Geoff and I enjoy dancing. Yes, it seems a pity not to travel.'

'The hotel always kept me too busy to travel.'

'Oh, well, business must come first of course. And then your old man being a bit silly about money. . . . Oh I know all about it, Harold told me. "Don't lend my Dad anything," he said before you arrived. Not that Geoff and I do lend. If you're going to give, give to charity is our motto. Do you do any work for the Red Cross? Or probably more for the Women's Toc H, with the Captain an Old Contemptible?'

'I know I should have done, but in the hotel business . . .'

'Not being your own mistress, of course. . . . Harold told me of the bust up you had when he was a kid. Shame! I really think I'd up and leave Geoff if he touched the business. . . . I don't know how it is, but Geoff and I have always been the same – we're both money makers. But we do try to give to charity. You can earn your lolly and have a good time with it, but remember the poor devils that haven't had the same break, that's what we always say. Now this afternoon, for instance, I'm on this committee for the orphans through the Townswomen's Guild. Poor damned kids that nobody wants. But you've had a hard life yourself, Harold told me. You'll know what I mean. Silly isn't it, really, gambling? I mean I like a little flutter. But when it breaks up the home . . .'

'I don't know what Harold's said, but you musn't think . . .'

'Oh, don't worry! We like the old boy, Geoff and me. He's a bit of an old rip, of course. But he's a good sport, you can see that. Oh no, it's more that we felt sorry for you. I said to Geoff that first night we met you at "The Syca-mores", "Harold's mother's been through it all right." You can always tell by the eyes.'

During the whole of that first week at Muriel Bartley's Sylvia found that she eventually sat down to her lunch-time snack hot with a mixture of shame and irritation. She could never quite understand it, for no one could be more lively and kind than Muriel. And no one did more for others – if it wasn't 'the damned kids that nobody wanted' it was sure to be 'the poor devils who can't see', or 'the blighters that are born a bit wonky in the head' – so many causes that Sylvia had never got round to helping. Not that Muriel was preachy about it, not at all, she always under-stood exactly why Sylvia had not had time – rotten child-hood, Arthur's gambling, the crash at Paignton, Iris's death – she seemed to know everything that had gone wrong in Sylvia's life, and some things even that she'd forgotten. Nobody could be more praising of the work you did – 'I've never seen anything like it. You eat the work up. If we don't save Goodchild's meadow after all your efforts, I'm damned well sure we never will.' She was always appreciative. And yet Sylvia had indigestion every day by the time she took her afternoon rest. Perhaps it was the gin and it; yet she hardly liked to refuse it, for Muriel would think she was going pussyfoot or something.

On the Wednesday of the second week, the last envelope

was filled, addressed and sealed. Muriel was a bit taken aback. 'What are we going to give you to do now?'

Sylvia felt most distressed. 'Oh, there's no need, I'm perfectly . . . Unless of course I can be of use.'

'Oh, I don't know what really. A promise is a promise though.'

'Now, Mrs Bartley, if Harold's said . . .'

'Nobody's said anything. Of course not. Besides, a good cause can't afford to lose good workers.' And sure enough she produced another little job that needed doing.

'Now don't let me down over this, Mrs C., I've stuck my neck out properly. But I don't see why you shouldn't manage it. You did the envelopes in double quick time. Of course, this is harder. Now what you've got to do . . .' And she explained to Sylvia that 'The Save the Meadow League' – for that's what they were called now – had made a counter proposal to the Corporation. They all agreed – none more than Harold and the Bartleys – that an extension of executive type housing was needed to give Carshall that mixed, all status quality that the new town pioneers had intended. They suggested that, to avoid encroaching on the meadow belt, the Ministry should be persuaded to agree to a small extension of the town into the surrounding country. As it so happened, Muriel explained, the farmer who rented Goodchild's meadow owned suitable land for building right on the edge of the town, so if *he* sold that to the Corporation nobody would be the loser.

Sylvia didn't quite understand it all. But that wasn't really necessary. The bright sparks on the committee had already been through the Reith Commission Report and Carshall Corporation's annual reports and those of the other New Towns. Muriel gave Sylvia a list of references to copy out from all the documents. She had only to arrange them under suitable headings: Agricultural Belts, Compulsory Purchase of Agricultural Land, Restricted Leases, Multi Status Housing, and so on.

'Harold's always talking about the need to settle you in here. Well, after this lot, you'll be able to teach the General Manager about his business.'

The new task cost Sylvia a most exhausting concentration. No doubt the division of subjects was clear enough to the committee, but she often found it difficult to decide whether an extract should be classed as 'Compulsory Purchase' or as 'Boundary Extension'. She compromised by the additional labour of copying it out twice. She tried hard also to believe that Muriel hadn't manufactured the job for her; but her good sense told her that there must be many faster typists available, and, as to the division into subjects, if the committee could not have made that when they selected the references, they must be exceptionally lazy. Disguise it how you may, a job made to take up time is a waste of time. And so try as she would to keep them out of her mind, the comforts of her own easy chair in her own sitting room, the thought of a nice long read (Deborah Forrester, although only a slip of a girl, had dared to warn the haughty Sarah that she was trying Queen Anne's patience too far), or even the warm sensation of just sitting lazing in her chair looking through Elsie Tanner's column in the *TV Times* (she always had some good tip about life to offer), all ran in and out of the web of speeches and figures and legal decisions that made up her morning's work. In the event of disagreements concerning compulsory purchase between the Corporation and a landowner, the County Council supporting the landowner, or in a direct dispute between the Corporation and the County Council, on appeal to the Ministry of Town and Country Planning, the Minister would appoint an inspector to hear in public session the objections of any interested individual or body of individuals. But in fact she was not interested. In her experience the Ministry people would settle matters on their own, however interested you might be, as they had all the problems of rationing in the years after the war, and goodness knows those problems had concerned her enough when she was running the hotel at Scarborough. As to bothering about such matters where you weren't directly concerned, she wondered that the people on the committee could have so much spare time. Look at that business about the widening of the Esplanade at Eastsea! A nice state the hotel would have got into if she'd spent her time going into all the ins and outs of that. Anyway the Town Council and the Ministry of Transport had got it all carved up between them before the public inquiry came on –

Arthur had been told the inside story of it down at the club.

However, Harold cared a lot about this Meadow business; so – Muriel Bartley apart, and bother Muriel Bartley if it came to that, she wasn't flesh and blood – she must try to do her best to understand. As she read of belts of ploughed land or of pasture preserved in this or that New Town 'to help the children grow up in familiarity with the natural rotation of the seasons' she forced herself to bring it all alive by recalling exactly how Goodchild's meadow looked; but if you'd been brought up in the country you couldn't take fields seen from the top of a bus seriously. She found it far worse anyway to think of the alternative of Carshall houses like Harold's and Muriel's eating further into that vast dark stretch of country that she looked out upon from her window each night. As she visualized the scene her pulse beat more quickly, and giddiness or shortness of breath intervened to save her from contemplating the struggle – the digging up of those gloomy fields, the bricks and mortar, the workmen with their transistors sprawling across the clayey land. Black desolate thoughts would creep in at such times that only made her more hungry for the penned-up safety of 'The Sycamores'. She would hurry the job on so that she could bring this new régime to an end, for she had made up her mind to challenge Muriel's bluff if a third task should be forthcoming when this one was done. But the work in fact could not be easily hurried along like envelope addressing.

So it was that one Wednesday when she got home she realized that in her haste she had filed away a report on compulsory purchase at Crawley in the 'Multi-Living' folder. The knowledge came to her as she was taking off her shoes to lie down on her bed, and despite the two aspirins which she now regularly swallowed after her snack lunch she couldn't banish her anxiety with sleep. All through the afternoon and evening's tele she fretted about it, so that a programme on the old Yorkshire sheep bells quite failed to engage her attention, although she liked that sort of thing as a rule, and even old Harry Worth fussing about his hot-water bottle couldn't make her smile.

The next morning when she arrived at 'Sorbetts' she discovered that Muriel had taken most of the extracts down to the committee room for the chairman, Mr Raven, who was soon to address the first public meeting. She passed a miserable morning divided between working with painfully slow concentration and summoning up enough courage to admit her silly mistake.

But when the tipple time came Muriel, ready in a pillar-box red moiré silk costume to accompany Geoff for a rare dinner and show in town, was in no mood for talk of work. She was bursting with the latest reports of the Priest case.

'It looks as though he'll swing,' she said, 'or whatever happens to them in Spain. Not that I don't feel sorry for him. The poor devil probably hadn't eaten for days. I know I said to Geoff when we were in Malaga, "I don't believe these sods have had a proper meal for months." And then a lot of these rich women flash their jewellery around. I'm surprised more of them don't get bumped off. Mind you, I expect there was a bit of sex in it somewhere, don't you?'

'I haven't been reading the details really. You see I used to know Miss Priest, the aunt, years ago, and somehow . . .'

'Did you? Well, I don't want to criticize, but I think she's a lot to blame. I mean that woman ought to have been married, not tied to an old aunt. What was she? Forty-three? There you are, it's not surprising if there was a bit of hanky panky with this waiter. They get desperate, you know, at that age. You wouldn't believe the stories that the Cook's chap was telling me . . .'

'I'm sure Miss Priest wouldn't have tied anyone to her. She was far too independent. Certainly in the days when I knew her . . .'

'Well, you know best, of course. But people change, don't they? I mean especially when they get old. You see, this old girl had got all the lolly. They're bound to get selfish. Look at the facts of the case. I mean, all she'd got to do was to give her niece a bit of dough and tell her to push off on her own. But no, money's power with these old girls. Nobody wants them, and they know it, so they take it out on people round them. Mind you, I don't say it was like that with your old girl. But that's the way it goes.'

Sylvia put her glass of gin and it down on the bar

unfinished, heaved herself off her stool, and collected her bag and gloves.

'I'm quite sure it wasn't like that with Miss Priest, Mrs Bartley. I really don't think you should say such things.'

Muriel's protruberant eyes seemed to leap even further out of their heavy green-shaded lids.

'Oh, when will I learn to shut my big mouth? I'd no idea you felt so strongly about it, I *am* sorry. I've offended you, I can see.'

'No, you haven't. It isn't that. Please don't worry.'

It was with the greatest difficulty that she shook off Muriel's distressed apologies. It was only when she got home that she remembered again the mistake in the filing. She couldn't bring herself to telephone about it.

The next morning she didn't come down to breakfast.

Harold called, 'It's getting late, Mother. Are you nearly ready?'

'I don't feel very well, dear. Will you tell Mrs Bartley I shan't be coming in?'

Once or twice during the day the telephone rang, but she did not answer it for fear Muriel might be at the other end. Sure enough that evening Harold said, 'I saw Muriel Bartley on the way home. She said she's been ringing you all day, Mother. She seems to be afraid that she's offended you in some way. Something to do with some murder. You women!'

Sylvia laughed and luckily Harold took this as a dismissal of the subject.

When Monday came round, she said quite deliberately, after breakfast, 'I shan't be going to Mrs Bartley's, dear. So don't wait for me.'

'Are you feeling ill again, Mother?'

'No, dear. But there's no point in my doing that job.'

'What *do* you mean? I hear you're the world's most efficient secretary!'

'I'm afraid Mrs Bartley's exaggerating. As a matter of fact I made a very silly mistake.'

When Harold learned the facts he laughed. 'Good heavens, Mother! Why ever didn't you tell Muriel about it straight away? Anyway, it doesn't matter. As a matter of fact, you're obviously far too conscientious. And why hasn't Muriel paid you for all this work?'

'I'm very glad she hasn't, dear, because now I needn't go on with it.'

'But, my dear Mother, the committee's depending on you.'

'I don't think so, dear. They can get any typist to do it.'

'Nonsense. In any case, I'm relying on you, Mother.'

'It's very kind of you, Harold. But you don't have to worry about me. I'll make my own life. I can't have little jobs invented for me at my age. That's silly.'

'Even if that were true, which it isn't, it's much sillier to sit about letting yourself get old.'

'I am old, dear. Oh, don't worry! I'll find plenty to do as I go along. It's just taking me a little time to settle down, that's all.' She laughed, 'I'm not used to doing nothing, like Dad.'

Harold pointed the stem of his pipe at her. 'Mother, I'm going to say something you may not like. Dad's been hopeless over the years as we all know. But you've let yourself get into the habit of nagging about him. I sometimes wonder if you really know what he's like by now.'

Sylvia looked at him in surprise. 'Oh yes, dear, after all these years, I think I know Arthur very well. But we musn't let all these trivialities make you late for work.'

'Mother! I'm a headmaster now, not a junior clerk. In any case the point is, are you going to help the committee or not? If not, you might at least let Muriel know.'

'Of course I shall, dear. I shall write to her this morning. I'll just say I'm not well enough. That's the trouble with muddles like this, they always lead to white lies.'

Harold knocked his pipe out angrily on an ashtray.

'Very well, I wash my hands of it entirely.' He banged the door as he went out.

During the day Sylvia did in fact write a short note of apology to Muriel Bartley. Immediately afterwards she wrote a long letter to Miss Priest. She didn't say much about how awful all the murder business must have been, instead she recalled some of the excursions they had taken together around Ilfracombe and some of the things that Miss Priest had said. 'I just wanted you to know,' she wrote, 'what pleasure it all gave me.'

None of the grandchildren was in to supper that evening.

Had it not been for Arthur's talk, Sylvia would have had to acknowledge openly that Harold was sending her to Coventry. As soon as Arthur went out – to the Bartley's, apparently they'd started up a poker game – she made her way upstairs, although she had particularly looked forward to Maigret. She did not want to embarrass Harold by forcing him into ostentatious silence. She had not long been absorbed in Mrs Masham's intrigues against the Duchess of Marlborough when the click of the study door told her that Harold too had isolated himself; but Maigret was half over by then.

Later she was woken as usual by Arthur's return. But this night he did not allow her to go to sleep again. 'Christ Almighty! What have you been doing upsetting Harold like this?'

'There wasn't any job there really, Arthur. It was silly...'

'What the hell do you mean silly? Harold wanted you to do it, didn't he? I've never heard such damned selfishness. After all he's been doing for us.'

He swore for a bit and then got into bed. Sylvia couldn't stop a kind of compulsive sobbing that had seized her. She had almost to stifle herself in the pillow so that he should not hear her. At last his snoring made her feel able to turn once more on her back. But she lay awake in empty desperation until after she heard the clock strike five.

During the last week in March the weather suddenly turned quite warm. Little artfully planted rings of daffodils brought spring to most of the gardens in Melling. Pink and white blossoms spurted here and there upon the trees that lined Higgleton. In Mardyke the Japanese quince covered one white house with masses of Knapp's scarlet blooms. With the start of the Easter holidays the children were kings of the streets – roller skating, kicking footballs, cycling, skipping, even the very smallest bowling hoops. Sylvia's almost daily outing to the shops at Melling now became more hazardous, more fearful, more challenging than the longer weekly expedition to Town Centre to change her library book, for the longer journey meant only a short walk through the shouting alien children to the bus. Sometimes in despair she tried to reach the shops by side streets, but they all proved to be alive with this strange, happy, independent, absorbed young life, and, worse, some proved to be cycle-jostled, noise-filled cul-de-sacs. However, once the gauntlet had been run and she was home again, with 'The Sycamores' saxe-blue front door closed upon the springtime, she gave herself up to shut-in safety. Some days she would sit still all day curled up with a book or in front of the tele like a dormouse in a cage. On other days she would hop from one book or programme to another. Now in her own room, now downstairs, now cutting herself a sandwich or making a pot of tea at the oddest hours when the schools Quiz Time happened to end or a chapter brought Melisa York from Natchez to her uncle's Charleston home for the first romantic meeting with the fascinating young Yankee officer – these were Sylvia's canary or budgerigar days. But whether torpid days or twittering ones, she always took her half hour rest each afternoon – a half hour that got longer, sometimes lasting on from two until half past three or four. She also ate a lot, in part so that she would not need supper, for when she was not cook for the evening, she often stayed upstairs in her room. Even the grandchildren noticed.

Judy said, 'You ought to eat, Gran. I know how frightfully difficult it is sometimes. Mrs Ogilvie says that she has long spells when food simply revolts her.'

Mark asked if there were some supper dishes she especially hated.

'I know my macaroni pongs a bit, but we can easily . . .'

What they could easily do, Sylvia, as usual with Mark's mumbling, never heard.

Ray sat down in a chair and said, 'Now, lovey, the family dials round the table are enough to make you bring it all up again, I know. But you must be a good girl and eat.'

She tried to respond to their kind anxiety, but the family talk at supper so jarred upon her thoughts, so interrupted the many stories she was busy following, that she feared to make matters worse by screaming. It was not long before they accepted her absence at the table.

Once or twice she woke in the night voraciously hungry and had to pad downstairs in dressing-gown and slippers to the kitchen, a more ghastly white cemetery than ever in the silent moonlight. On one such occasion she met Harold as he came out of his study after a late session of writing reports. They passed each other in silence. She felt impelled to look back at him as he went upstairs; and, turning, she found that he too had stopped to look back at her. For almost a minute she stared right into his eyes that seemed quite blank. After that she kept a tin of biscuits and some chocolate in her room.

That'll be quite enough of that, thank you, Wardress Webb. No, I don't want to hear any excuses. The rules about make-up for prisoners are perfectly clear. But Wiggin swore blue that she'd been out of the store room when this month's make-up packs were distributed. My dear Wardress Webb, if you're going to believe everything that women like Wiggin tell you! They don't happen to be very honest, you know. That's why they're here. Yes, I realize that, and I'm not half as trusting as I used to be, Chief Wardress. But Wiggin does seem a bit different to the rest; she's only a girl and . . . Only a girl who happened to think that she had a right to other people's property and who went on thinking it so many times that she landed up in prison. These women are criminals, Wardress Webb. But surely we're here to help them. We're here to see that discipline's kept. We wardresses are ordinary women doing a job of work. If you want all that high-falutin talk, Wardress Webb, you'd better go and have a nice long chat with our dear new Governor about the poor harmless, ill-treated convicts and penal reform or whatever she's always spouting about. But don't come to me with excuses of that kind again. . . . Oh, I say, Miss Webb, what's up? Chief Wardress doing her strong woman stuff again? It's nothing, Mr Varley, honestly. Look here, Miss Webb, I've not been a prison Chaplain for the last three years without knowing when people are unhappy; that old battle-axe has got a down on you. All right, if you'd rather not tell me. But I say, Miss Webb . . . Janet, have you ever eaten in a Chinese restaurant? Would you like to? Bird's-nest soup and all that! I'd love to take you to one if you'd care to come.

It was no good; whoever it was refused to stop ringing, although Sylvia had disregarded the noise for more than three minutes. She went to the front door. Sally Bulmer loomed large in the doorway, less gipsy-like but almost more enveloping in her daytime clothes, all bosom and lace blouse and huge uncut amethyst brooch.

As the noise of the voices came from the sitting room, she cried, 'Tele!' in a tone of proud discovery.

Sylvia ignored the cry. 'Everybody's out, I'm afraid.'

'Except you. Now, what am I interrupting?'

'It's "Wardress Webb".'

'Ah, the new serial. Can new viewers join in along the line? You'd better put me in the picture.'

Sylvia led the way back to the sitting room. 'The Chief Wardress has ticked Wardress Webb off again. And the Chaplain's asked her out to supper. He's quite young. And, oh yes, now that's Wardress Appelby. She's engaged to Jimmie. He's a student. And last time Mollie Green, one of the convicts, made it clear that she knew Jimmie. So . . .'

'Ssh! Ssh!' Sally Bulmer put her finger to her lips in pantomime solemnity. 'We must take our tele more seriously.' They sat and listened to Wardress Appelby fencing with Mollie Green about Jimmie for a few minutes, until a low bubbling sound from Sally Bulmer drew Sylvia's attention away from the screen. Sally's eyes were alight with fun, and, when Sylvia looked at her, she burst into a peal of laughter.

'Isn't it the most wonderful rubbish?' she cried.

Sylvia got up and turned it off. 'I'm afraid I rather enjoy it.'

'Then you shouldn't. Oh, for a lark now and again! There's no harm to it in mild doses. But night after night! Good Lord, woman, you've got more to do than that.'

Sylvia would have liked to slip out of the room, but her figure was not made for slipping, and Miss Bulmer's equally large form seemed to fill all escape routes. She was leaning back in her chair, blowing a smoke ring and looking at Sylvia with an amused quizzical challenge.

'It's very kind of you, Miss Bulmer, I know. But I'm not at all a clever person and what appeals to me wouldn't appeal to you.'

'You can't be a half wit. You've run a good number of hotels for a good number of years. That isn't idiot's work. Get out and do things again, Mrs Calvert.'

'I've not been very well, you know. With this high blood pressure, I'm a bit of an invalid.'

'You'll be more than an invalid if you go on in this way. You'll be a nut case. Tele-itis. It's the scourge of our time.'

'It's very kind of you, Miss Bulmer. I know it's your job.'

'Job! I haven't come here as Welfare Officer, bless you. I've come here as woman to woman.'

'Well then, it's even kinder of you to want to help me, but . . .'

'No, not you! Lay not that flattering unction to your soul! It's not you I care about. Or not principally. It's our Harold. As Welfare Officer of Carshall I know how valuable our Harold is to us. He's taken far too much on already without having mum trouble.'

'I see. Don't you think he'll get used to me? He's my son, you know, and I believe I understand him after all these years.'

Miss Bulmer threw herself back on the couch and loosened her cloth coat from her shoulders so that she almost seemed to be in décolletée evening dress again. Her big, dark eyes gazed at Sylvia measuringly. 'Do you? Do you?'

Sylvia said, 'I'll get you some tea.' When she came back with the tray, Miss Bulmer was leafing through *Queen or Duchess*.

'It's rather good. About a girl who is maid of honour to Queen Anne.'

'Queen Anne!' Miss Bulmer laughed dramatically, 'Queen Anne's dead, woman! But Carshall isn't! It's full of life and people and things to do. And problems, as I know. Come out and meet us! Some of us are bores at times, but you'll have lots of fun.'

'I'm not a girl, Miss Bulmer.'

'I know that. But I'll tell you what you are. You're a bit of a juggins.' Miss Bulmer laughed, then looked more serious. 'Why are you living in other people's lives all the time, Mrs Calvert? And what people! Queen Anne who's been dead for centuries, and all that nonsense on television – unreal people, talking unreal twaddle! You know that. You're frightened of something, frightened of bogies, frightened of the dark. Well, you won't get away from it with all that rubbishy pretence. Doing things, meeting people, getting on with the job. That's the answer.' She put down her cup and stood up. 'Well! It's shock treatment. It may or may not work. That's up to you. And I've made myself disagreeable, but somebody had to do it. Good-bye. Sorry for interrupting the tele.' With a peal of laughter she was gone as suddenly as she had arrived.

Sylvia went up to bed. Through the window, in the moonlight, the first sprinkling of green shoots showed on the surface of the miles and miles of ridged earth. The hedges that at intervals cut irregular shapes out of the endless plain were green, and, here and there, white with thorn blossom. Something moving caught Sylvia's eye. Somebody was sidling along by the edge of one of the hedges, keeping close, walking no doubt on a narrow balk – but going so slowly, what was the word? ambling, yet the night air must be cruelly cold. Impossible to tell what kind of person – gipsy? Sylvia drew back from the window at the thought of the gypsy's all-seeing powers. Tramps – who saw them now, or drunkards for that matter either? It looked from the room like a little thin humpbacked old woman. Sylvia made herself watch – superstition would do no good – and the figure crept on, now turning at right angles by another hedge along another field, and so on, until after a quarter of an hour Sylvia could see it no more, for it was swallowed up into the black, empty distances.

She finished the last chapter of *Queen or Duchess* in bed. The Duchess sent for Deborah Forrester and told her that she must stay with the Queen. 'We are bound by a strange bond, the Queen and I. Stronger than you can understand, Mistress Forrester, it will ease my haughty spirit to know that my pretty little Deborah is in attendance on my old friend in all her royal loneliness at Kensington.' And the Queen and Deborah lived out a peaceful and happy time at Kensington, walking in the Orangery or playing a hand of cards. As for the Duchess, Deborah on her visits always found her busy like a child with some new toy – building Blenheim, inspiring poets, teasing Vanbrugh, making her devoted family laugh with her endless witticisms.

Sylvia closed the book with a real bitterness against Sally Bulmer. Because of course it was worse even than that interfering woman had said. Not only was Queen Anne dead, but it had never even been like that. She knew from other books that the Queen had died, with her fourteen children dead before her, surrounded by intrigue, swollen with dropsy, broken by remorse for her treatment of her father; and, as for Sarah, she had ended her days a spendthrift, quarrelsome, crazy bitter old woman whose family hated her and longed to see her dead.

And now Good Friday was here with its hot cross buns and all the shops closed. It rained all day, which was such a shame, for nobody could get out and enjoy themselves. Ray lay late in bed. Mark had gone off on a demonstration march – what weather for it, poor things, even if you didn't agree with them. Judy buried herself in her studies; she was upset because she had wanted Caroline to go to morning service with her at a little old country parish church, but Mrs Ogilvie didn't believe in the three hour service for girls and wouldn't let her daughter attend. Harold's golf was off – he was all too seldom persuaded to take a real holiday out of doors! – so he spent the day with Sally Bulmer, talking over the survey; they were going to make a book out of it. With Geoff Bartley at home, Arthur was able to spend the whole day at 'Sorbetts' playing poker – he seemed never to go to the Cranstons now. Sylvia had finished her library book – some story about divorce and the South of France, not much good; there was nothing worth looking at on tele. But then Good Friday always had been a gloomy day as long as she could remember. Even her mother, who'd been as narrow about religion as they came, never approved of Good Friday – there'd been no service or anything at the Bethesda Chapel. On this wet Good Friday Sylvia had felt so low that she almost picked up the breadknife and made an end of it.

Luckily the weather changed on Easter Saturday. But then Easter was always a cheerful time – something new and something blue! In the old days the children used to have their breakfast eggs on Easter Sundays coloured to their choice – Harold liked pink, Len yellow and Iris always chose violet. On this Easter Saturday evening there was such a cheerful look in Harold's eye that Sylvia, buoyed up by her own post-Good Friday rise of spirits, dared to try to break through the near-silence that had prevailed between them since she had refused to continue her 'little job'. She recalled the coloured eggs of childhood to him, and, in no time, he and she and Arthur were all laughing and sighing over the old days together as they hardly had done in their lives before.

And even when Harold's voice suddenly sounded serious, it was in a warm, friendly tone. 'I don't know whether you'd care to come to church tomorrow. I know we're not a churchgoing family. But I always think Easter is a time when we can all do with a church service, however little we believe. Far more than the conventional Christmas really.'

Sylvia wanted to ask why he thought that, but she decided not to interrupt.

'I don't go to St John's here in Melling. I don't altogether care for the Rector. But I think I can promise you something worth hearing at St Saviour's in Town Centre. Marchant, the vicar there, is quite an unusual man. Rather a controversial figure. You never get any of this dry-as-dust theological stuff from him that's done so much to keep people out of the churches. Quite the contrary. Last Easter he gave a sermon on the eleven plus. A very fair statement of the situation, too; although it put some of the grammar school people's backs up. Anyhow, if you'd care to come I shall be going, and probably Judy too.' Holding his horn-rimmed glasses in his hand he looked at each of his parents in frank appeal.

Arthur was as frank in his responding look. He shook his head. 'No, old boy. I thoroughly respect your views, of course. But I had quite enough of church when I was a kid. I haven't led the life of a plaster cast saint, but going to church wouldn't have improved matters. That I do know. No, I don't know whether I believe that there's anything for us after we've had it in this world, but if there is . . . I say "if", mark you . . . I can't believe the Almighty won't turn out to be a bit of a sportsman. Whatever my vices, they *have* been a man's vices. "Arthur Calvert," he'll say . . .'

Harold had been growing more impatient as his father talked. Now he interrupted. 'Yes. Well, you may be right, Dad. What about you, Mother?' His voice expressed little hope.

'I should like to come very much, dear.'

The effect on her son was electric. 'I'm very glad indeed. We've got off rather on the wrong foot recently, but perhaps on this Easter Sunday we shall be able to make a new start.' He beamed at Sylvia. It's as though I were a prodigal daughter coming back, she thought, and then was both surprised and shocked at the tone of such a thought when Harold was being so genuine.

St Saviour's, crowded with women in smart hats and men in their best lounge suits, looked more than ever like a meeting hall. The blues and violets of the windows seemed less happy to Sylvia now as they cast unearthly, livid lights here and there on the faces of the congregation. Everyone was dressed to the nines. Sylvia almost wished that it had been colder so that she could have worn her leopard hat, but the ruched red ribbon turban looked quite nice.

She found it difficult to concentrate or to feel as though she were in church. Lowering her heavy weight on to one knee and cupping her eyes with her hand in silent prayer as they settled in their seats, she felt quite silly. But the first verse of the hymn for some reason carried her away, although Harold bellowed terribly and Lorna Milton two rows away was quite embarrassing in her descant.

> 'Immortal, Invisible
> God only Wise.
> To Light Inaccessible,
> Hid from our eyes.
> Of all thy great mercies,
> This Grace, Lord, impart;
> Take the Veil from our Faces
> The Veil from our Hearts.'

Already, however, she could feel the congregation rustling and murmuring, Judy whispered 'That's not the vicar, Gran.' And a moment later Harold's voice came more loudly on her other side, 'I'm sorry about this, Mother. I can't think why Marchant should be away at Easter.' Sylvia didn't know the vicar so that she could not sincerely regret his absence. She feared all this murmuring of disappointment must be most hurtful to the feelings of the substituting clergyman. When he made his way to the

184

pulpit, she tried to look up at him sympathetically to help him out.

The preacher was probably not the sort of man to be much affected by atmosphere. He was a very old man with a very long red nose and a rather dirty-looking beard of the kind old King Edward VII had worn. He spoke in a strange, trembling voice, dragging out many of the words with broad Scots vowels as though at any minute he might change from speech to chant. Sylvia could feel the unfavourable effect he produced on the congregation in the rustling and coughing that broke out. Two rows ahead a young couple had been seized with a fit of giggles as soon as he spoke, and their giggling might well prove infectious. Sylvia felt with surprise a bond of sympathy with the grotesque old man; like him, she had no ties with this dressed-up, united congregation of Carshallites. As he spoke on, she was increasingly held by his words.

'Christ is risen. In order that we may know eternal life. In order that we may save our souls alive. . . . It's an awful difficult thing with some of us to tell whether we're alive or no. For being a bustling, hustling busybody – that's not life or no more life than the frugal ant or the hoppitty flea. No, nor building up businesses or rushing to our neighbours with gossip, nor being house proud, nor family proud. You can be all these and your soul may be still no but a wisp of straw. . . .' After five minutes or so of this the congregation around Sylvia became either torpid or distracted – Harold made notes on the back of an envelope, Sally Bulmer lolled and looked back over her chair as though in a box at the theatre, Lorna Milton was reading in the hymn book. Then a sudden comical change in the old clergyman's voice roused them all to attention; the giggles were set off again. An adolescent girl after uselessly trying to suppress her laughter, got up and left the church with her handkerchief to her mouth. 'Aye, but what aboot me, guid Lord' – the voice was the refined squeak of an Edinburgh Judy in a Punch and Judy show – 'I've been awfu' busy all my life, clicketing among my neighbours, doing a muckle lot of guid for others. Aye, and we all know what happened to her – the Guid Lord looked down and never a creature could he see but a wee, wee body bustling hither and yon to nae

185

purpose, wi' a soul like a wisp of straw that was quickly gathered up into the flame and burned. No! Good works'll not save your soul alive. . . . This Grace, Lord, impart! So we ask for Grace to be given to us, for we'll not get it by shouting or fussing and fretting away our souls. No, not all the charity, the social work, as they call it now, can save your soul alive if there's no soul left to save.' Harold was drumming on the chair in front of him now; Sally Bulmer, her face turned to those behind, had assumed a look of patient amusement; Lorna and Chris Milton were whispering to one another. Then once again the old man's strange powers of mimicry startled them back to attention. 'Said the one carlinwife to the other, "Aye, Annie," says she, "I've been aye doing so muckle guid, I've noe had time to set me down and mind who I am." Ah! And she can sit on her buttie to all eternity, for buttie's all she'll have – there'll be no living soul to save. Is there nothing we can do to help us to God's Grace? Indeed there is. The Lord forbid that I should preach to you folks any strait-jacketed Calvinistic doctrine. There's a great deal you can do. You can be toward. You can go out to meet God's Grace. Go out to mind who you are. Go out, not into the busy clamour of getting and spending, nor even into the soothing clamour of good works. No, go out into the dreadful silence, into the dark nothingness. Maybe ye are no but a wisp of straw, but if you go out to face the fire, out through the desert and the night, then indeed may the Lord send the light of his face to shine upon you then indeed may you be visited by that Grace which will save your soul alive. And now to God the Father . . .'

Mrs Marchant, the vicar's wife, a dowdy cheerful-looking woman, was in the atrium among the unvarnished wooden tables and book racks all stacked up with pamphlets each with a clever, eye-catching photograph on its cover. 'I'm so terribly sorry,' she said to everyone, 'Kenneth's slipped a disc. And we had to take what the archdeacon could send us at the last moment.' She repeated her apology like a faulty gramophone, until someone nudged her elbow and made her aware that the old clergyman was standing beside the door like some bedraggled, mangy old goat. 'Oh, Mr Carpenter, so fascinating, so fascinating.

May I introduce Miss Bulmer, our welfare officer? And Mr Calvert, the headmaster of Melling School. And . . .' But the old man did no more than bow his head and rub his dirty old beard against his surplice, so that the poor woman gave up in perplexity. As the little knots of people chattered and flashed smiles in the Easter sunshine, Sylvia knew an entirely unfamiliar urge to action. She went over to the old man. 'Thank you very much. I shan't forget what you said.' His rheumy eyes looked at her quizzically for a moment, as though he were estimating her probable weight. 'Ah! Good! It's all old stuff, I'm afraid.' He shut his eyes against the sun and her talk.

Harold was fiercely outspoken on their way home. 'It's perfectly disgraceful. I know their pay and pensions are ludicrous. But still there are plenty of eventide homes especially for the clergy where old creatures like that can go. I blame the archdeacon. . . . This is, of course, exactly where organized religion has failed. Though I will say for the Roman Catholics that their discipline simply wouldn't allow a thing like this to happen. There were a number of my boys in the congregation and, whether the authorities like it or not, I shall make it quite clear what I thought. How could they respect me if I appeared to condone that sort of nonsense? And vicious nonsense! I suppose few more barbaric doctrines have disgraced humanity than all this rubbish about Grace . . .'

'I found some of what he said rather helpful, Harold. . . .'

'Oh, Gran! That awful voice! And it was so embarrassing. Daddy, I do wish we could go to one of the little country parish churches. There's such a real sense of order and tradition in the worship there.' Harold ignored Judy's plea, but he smiled at Sylvia. 'You don't have to be polite, Mother. As a matter of fact I was thinking of you a lot of the time. Here you are, brought up in that ghastly Calvinistic chapel atmosphere which must have completely scared you away from all religion. Then one Easter you come by chance to church here and you have this sort of stuff served up to you.'

'It doesn't seem quite the same, Harold. With mother's minister it was all damnation and that. But the old man here was trying to be helpful, surely.'

'Helpful! "A wisp of straw gathered up into the flame!"'
Harold's Scots accent was not good, but his rising annoyance was clear.

'I don't think I understood the religious part much, dear. It was more the teaching that appealed to me.' She smiled at her son, and he too tried to repair the now so often mended breach.

'You're too forgiving, Mother, that's the trouble. I suppose a lot of my antipathy to that sort of thing comes from my resentment of the way you were treated as a child. I never knew my grandmother, but I can't forgive her for refusing to see you after you married Dad.'

'We certainly didn't get on very well. But there it is. It's all old stuff, now I'm afraid.'

Arthur was waiting for them at the front door. 'Quick march, the holy brigade.'

'As usual, Dad, you chose the more comfortable *and* the wiser part.'

It had been their original idea to motor out to a nearby teagarden on Bank Holiday afternoon. There was a charming old millstream there, it seemed, and a little private zoo – really more of an aviary plus a few monkeys – that was well worth seeing. First, however, both Ray and Judy cried off – as Harold said, 'There's a surfeit of pleasures for the young nowadays.' Then Arthur decided to toddle down to the Sports Ground and support the Melling Cricket XI in their opening match of the season – 'The Melling lads will wipe the floor with the Carshall louts.'

'You mustn't let your sympathies get too parochial, Dad,' Harold teased, but he was delighted. In the end, what with the accident figures on tele and the unexpectedly hot weather, Harold and Sylvia decided to make it a holiday at home. They sat out on the lawn in deck chairs. Harold corrected the proofs of his new Reader and talked now and again to passing friends. Sylvia dozed off over her other book – she always borrowed two over the holiday periods, one fiction and one non-fiction, this one was Lady Violet Clanpatrick's book *Within an Ace*, that had been talked about so much. ... 'Neither of the Clanpatrick houses was what I would call really beautiful, not like beloved Gaydon where I had been brought up. Hinton Polcourt we used to say was huge and hideous, and Laoirghmile was little and *laide*. However they were Duncan's homes and it was soon clear to me that I should have to learn to love them. After all I was to be mistress of both. . . .' It was not an easy book to get into. When Sylvia woke to the sound of Harold's hailing a friend, she skipped a few pages. . . . 'They called my generation a golden one and I truly think that we were in love with life. Even when years later the big break-up came between Duncan and me and we knew that we were not really suited to one another, we romped through the months of separation and finally of divorce as we had through three fortunes and a thousand parties. On the night the decree was made absolute we had a dinner *à deux* (quails with grapes and brown bread ices) at Quaglino's, and dear Quaggie (what a terrible waste of human life – but war means just that!) thought we looked so happy that he asked if we'd been remarried that day! A month later Duncan's rather enchanting old father died. I had been 'within an ace' again. This time of being a duchess. I can't say that I gave it a thought at the time. There were so many much more exciting things to be. For instance, the first Englishwoman to snub Ribbentrop. This is how it happened. . . .'

Sylvia shut the book. It was neither here nor there. She went indoors and prepared their afternoon tea – tomato sandwiches and some little home-made Queen cakes. Just an ordinary, homely English afternoon tea, but, to her delight, Harold said more than once how much he was enjoying it.

'I'm afraid you had a poorish time with old Sally.'

'My dear Harold, whoever told you about it?'

'She did. She's worth her weight in gold where the average human is concerned. But in every hundredth case or so she fails. And when she does her touch is a bit elephantine.'

Sylvia said nothing.

'Of course, I blame myself, Mother. I suppose it is that I have such a fear of New Town neurosis that I . . . But there's no doubt we've tried to rush you. Shock tactics are all right for the majority of people. They just need that little push. But there is the minority and I think you're one of them. You need to take your own time.'

'I think so, Harold. But Miss Bulmer meant to be very helpful. And she said one or two very good things. About the tele, for instance. It's often more of a drag really.'

'Yes. I should get outside as much as possible if I were you. You can sit in the garden here while the weather's good. And don't worry about calling to neighbours over the fence if you want to. There's no snobbery of that kind, thank the Lord. In fact it's rather the "done thing".' He laughed at the phrase. 'If you *do* want to get out among people a bit, Gorman's Wood is only a step. It makes a very pleasant walk. Or you can take the bus to Sugley Park. It's not far from Craighill. I don't expect we ever took you there in the old days, because Beth wasn't keen on walking. And it still looked rather like a private garden then. But they've made a lot of changes – much of Sugley Manor's been pulled down – I believe they've made it all most attractive.'

Tuesday, if anything, was a finer day than Bank Holiday. Sylvia took *Within an Ace* out into the garden, but she really couldn't get on with it. The high spirits seemed so forced. Of course, life may be all roses for the upper ten, but everything that concerned her at the moment Lady Violet seemed to have left out. She got up and walked round the garden, but apart from a very few daffodils at the foot of one of the sycamores, there was nothing to see. She almost thought of buying a few seeds – just some ordinary annuals – but she was too fat for gardening and anyway Harold might not like it. She did not care to look out on to Mardyke or Higgleton, for passers-by tried not to stare, and then, after what Harold had said, she was unsure whether she should speak to people – but what should she say to them? She stood by the sycamore trees and stared out over the distant green fields. Somewhere far off some machine was doing something or other. She supposed they sprayed everything much more' now – but wasn't it rather early for spraying? She'd forgotten so much. In any case, what is an old woman doing staring at the spraying of fields, and still more, gazing into the empty distance?

She went indoors to choose a book from Harold's shelf – she would go to the Library tomorrow. On the shelf with the Sydney Fox case were a number of other reports of murder trials. Hesitantly she picked out the Haigh case, knowing that she was feeding her own morbidity. Surely it had been in a hotel? She read a little, and it all came so alive to her – the dining-room conversations from one little table to another, the chats over coffee in the lounge, the meetings in the hall, even the hiring of a car at the reception desk. She had never worked in those South Kensington hotels, and the Onslow Court was clearly rather grand, but the trade was not so different from the seaside one. Telling herself that she should not do so, she took the book out into the garden, already reading on obsessively about Mrs Durand-Deacon as she walked out.

'This is my sister, Mr Haigh. My only relative really.'

'Such a charming man, my dear. I think he's retired from the army. But quite young. And such a good business head. He's so interested in my little scheme for plastic fingernails that you've always laughed at. Doesn't think it impractical at all.' And the conversations about the scheme – from the few words in the book they all came pouring into her head: the setting, the tone of voice, everything. 'Now, you know I don't like coffee sugar. Take it away and bring me some ordinary lump sugar. I cannot get them to bring me the right sugar, Mr Haigh. I can't bear all those little bits of coloured sugar. Perhaps I'm old fashioned.' 'No, I think you're perfectly right, Mrs Durand-Deacon. Like a lot of modern inventions, they're a fussy waste of time.' 'Oh, I'm so glad to hear you say that, Mr Haigh. They seem to invent all the things that nobody wants and never think of the simple things that we're all longing for. . . .' Sylvia could hear Haigh's admiring little chuckle. 'Now I have a scheme for making plastic fingernails which nobody will take seriously, but . . .' As Sylvia began to read the reported conversation from the trial, she realized that she had been supplying all the rest herself; but she knew for certain that that was how it had happened, the words, the stirring of the coffee in the little cups, the whisky nightcaps, the interchange of reminiscences coloured up a little to entertain. So that was what people meant by her 'knowing human nature'. Well, then, she also knew into what dark places it led. She could follow into them. Not with Haigh; she could not guess what lay behind that fat-faced, dark-eyed, soft-voiced, smooth urbanity, what horrors jumped out at him from the wardrobe of his small bedroom on the top floor. But Mrs Durand-Deacon – she could follow her every step, in her long-sleeved black semi-evening dress as she made her way up to bed, every breathy step of that tall fat body – the regal, individual but smart hair styles and dress, the slight nervousness before addressing new residents followed by the bright but always reservedly dignified conversation, the charm and the occasional irritability with the servants but each alike in condescension, the determined independence, the physical exhaustion never shown. Sylvia knew what would jump from the big ward-robe in Mrs Durand-Deacon's large first floor room: loneli-ness – black, screaming, strangling loneliness. She saw it looming over the tall white-haired woman in her Persian lamb coat as she got into the hired Daimler on that sunny, windy, fateful morning. She had eavesdropped at all the preliminary conversation, had indeed whispered them like a prompter when the printed pages of the trial's report dried up. 'I've seen the city people, Mrs Durand-Deacon. They've got everything tied up at the end. It only remains to sign the documents. Shall I have them sent straight to your solicitors?' 'No, certainly not. I always see to every-thing myself first.' 'But you'll consult them in fairness to me. Otherwise your sister, your family quite rightly . . .' 'My dear Mr Haigh, if I bothered with my family . . . No, no, I decide everything myself. . . .' 'Well, anyhow, that's the financial side of our little venture. I don't mind saying I shall be pleased to see the back of it. As you know, it's the technical side that interests me. What I confess I'm looking forward to showing you is the little workshop I've bought for us in Haywards Heath. I have a feeling that until you've seen that, you won't really know what a working propos-ition the whole thing is.' . . . 'Dread the discomfort of the railways. Never really recovered from the war. . . . Why not let me hire a car? . . . Harrods . . . charming Sussex countryside. . . .' The yard of the workshop must have seemed bare and empty when, with Haigh's soft voice pouring, she was let in through the wooden gate. . . . Small and poky for her great enterprise now realized, more like a disused junk dealer's yard. The strips of wood, the rusting tools, a cobwebby shelf with dusty bottles, some pails with slops of rainwater, an old enamelled bath on four clawed legs. . . . 'I believe you'd get the best idea of the technical process if you'd just look into this bath where I am at present experimenting. . . .' The crushing snap in her head and then all her unanswered love, all her unappeased loneliness breaking apart into the night black emptiness of space.

Sylvia was trembling when she had read the report of this scene. After that all the horrors and squalors of the acid bath seemed a stupid footnote, the contemptuous dissolution of an unwanted human. And as for the other victims – the jolly dolls' hospital owners with their loved Alsatian, the unknown woman in the army hut, the old dingy Pimlico couple and their young deserter son – their stories roused her only to the sad nausea with which she normally left murder trials unread. She closed the book, opened it again at the earlier pages, then forced herself to close it once more and resolutely returned it to Harold's shelves.

But the story did not leave her. Again and again as she dozed off in her deck-chair that afternoon its details returned to her, and she could only exorcize Mrs Durand-Deacon's demon by walking down to the sycamores and staring out across the country in contemplation that held her own lonely fears.

6. Wanderings Abroad

On the next day she decided to take Harold's advice: out
of doors, but not away from Carshall; she would explore
the country in the town. And here indeed between Melling
and the Industrial Area lay Gorman's Wood, a copse
preserved to enrich and soften the lives of those who lived
on the estate. She did not, as Harold had predicted, find
herself among people. She passed only two schoolgirls who
giggled and stuffed their handkerchiefs in their mouths as
she went by them. She had thought herself fat and old, but
unnoticeably ordinary; now she wondered whether she
could be growing odd looking. But a minute or two later,
around a bend in the path came a little queer old hunch-
backed woman, dressed in a cheap flowered cotton dress
and a man's blue raincoat, and talking to herself. No doubt
it was this old woman who had set the girls off: heaven
knew! with her hump, she was odd and creepy enough to
give anyone the gigglejumps. But what the hump had set
off, her own fatness perhaps had kept going. The thought
was disquieting enough to complete Sylvia's disenchant-
ment with Gorman's Wood. The trees were mostly firs
whose evergreen darkness seemed disappointingly shabby
and dusty, when elsewhere, all around, deciduous trees
were showing their subtle range of colours. The undergrowth was a mass of brambles, bruised and purple from
winter's ravages, just when anemones and primroses and
celandines should have carpeted the ground. But even if
there were some stray clumps of wild flowers in Gorman's
Wood, Sylvia could not find them, for the only footpath
was cut off from the trees on each side by close-meshed wire
fences. To offer this narrow, well-trod, ant-infested way
as some substitute for the ranging, unbounded choice of the
solitude of the countryside seemed to Sylvia such a cheat
that had she been younger and more agile she would have

climbed the fence in defiance of authority to tread down the undergrowth if only in protest. Others had defied the limits, as scraps of paper, cartons, here and there a bottle, two socks, a French letter, and mysteriously an old broken wicker armchair witnessed; but then others were slimmer and younger. After she had walked for a quarter of an hour the brambles gave way to docks and nettles, the firs to elder bushes, and immediately she was out upon the bypass road across which she could see the broad glass arches of the Electrometrico factory. There was nothing more to do but return along the same damned path by which she had come. She came back to 'The Sycamores' quite out of temper.

At supper she said, 'I wonder they don't build on that Gorman's Wood, Harold, instead of Goodchild's meadow. That would be no loss to anyone.'

Harold narrowed his eyes as he answered and his tone was prickly with irritation. 'You may have formed that opinion, Mother, but I hope you won't broadcast it about. As far as the preservation of countryside amenities within New Town areas is concerned – and that's essentially our case – Gorman's Wood and Goodchild's meadow are exactly on all fours. You would do our case a lot of harm by public expression of the opinion you have just stated.'

'I don't know why anyone should take account of your mother's views on local politics.'

'Just because she is my mother, Dad.'

On Thursday she carried *Queen or Duchess* and *Within an Ace* back to the Public Library. From the Town Centre she took a bus out to Sugley Park, Harold's third suggestion for open-air neighbourliness. When she got off the bus and followed the gravel path between shady oak trees and crossed a wooden bridge over a minute stream, she felt hopeful that here she would find some gentle, lively peace. There were golden marsh marigolds growing by the stream's edge, and she caught a glimpse of the bushy grey softness of a squirrel's tail among the oak leaves. The path turned into the park, and there, indeed, as Harold had said, were people. One part of the old garden by the rhododendron shrubbery had been covered in concrete and here were as many children as filled Higgleton Road and

Mardyke Avenue, clambering over swings and round-abouts, playing in sandpits, crawling through a great concrete tunnelled mound that formed the centre piece of the play centre; they slid with whoops down the chute, they swung with screams from ring to ring. She walked on past neat ovals in which newly bedded out plants as yet not in flower were protected in their soggy hollows by a surround of wire hoops. Here around a small ornamental pond with a rock for an island at its centre sat all the young wives of Craighill (though they might just as well have come from Melling) surrounded by babies and toddlers, and competing in their rhythm of happy chatter and contented, silent sewing with the alternate quacking and underwater grubbing of the ducks. Beyond this again she came upon another shrubbery of huge overgrown rose bushes and of tall bamboos, and suddenly she found herself in the backyard of the old manor house.

It was not really picturesque, all red brick and no beams, but still some of those old brick houses – Queen Anne, surely – were said to have lovely rooms, so Sylvia decided to walk round to the front and look in. As she passed the side of the house two young men in dark suits went by her and eyed her curiously, then peering into the first ground-floor room, she found herself looking into the staring eyes of a young woman seated before a typewriter; this young woman said something to three or four others who all looked up and stared. Sylvia hurried on. On the sides of the entrance were a series of name plates: National Assistance Board, Registrar, Corporation and County Council Joint Consultative Committee, Rents Advice Bureau, Maintenance and Parks, J. B. Glamish, Mrs Thurso ring three times. There was also a white painted sign – Inquiries: Ground Floor, Walk In. A stoutish, middle-aged man came out, belching slightly; he put his hand to his mouth when he saw Sylvia, got into a small motorcar and drove away. Sylvia made no inquiries. Not liking to follow the car down the drive because of the curious eyes that no doubt still looked out from the house, she passed quickly by the other downstairs windows, and found herself among the builders' litter. In the next dusty shrubbery she really feared that she had lost her way when suddenly a sign pointed up a rutted drive among rhododendrons to Rectory School – Boys 6-12 girls 6-18. Headmistress: Miss Hurry. Sylvia walked up the drive between laurel hedges. It was such a pretty house, with two bow windows and a small conservatory at the side, but a cruel kind of house to work in as she knew from experience. The place seemed deserted, so she walked round to the back door where the dustbins smelled a little mouldy, and peered in at one or two of the windows. It was all much as she had expected, but a strange gale of memories blew her back into the past; and, when at last she reached the main road again and the bus, she felt more confused than ever, as though she had found and lost herself again in a few moments of time.

Since Easter she had returned from the world of fiction to food and family. Yet as she sat silent at the supper table, she was as effectively cut off from those around her by a thickening fog of memories as she had been by Mrs Harker, Queen Anne and Wardress Webb.

'Well, lovey,' Ray said, 'sulking on your ownio again?'

He had adopted this loving direct teasing as his only means of reaching her.

She smiled absently, 'Yes, I went all round a school.'

'School?' Harold was amazed.

'Did you have your dinner out?' Ray intervened quickly. But Harold repeated, 'School? What school?'

'The Rectory School, dear.'

There was a silence. Then Ray said in despair, 'You do have tactless walks, Gran, you really do.'

'Your grandmother can hardly be expected to realize the scandal of a private school of that type being allowed to trade on misplaced snobberies in a New Town like Carshall. Even of its kind, I believe the school is what Judy would call very crumby. No doubt you can tell your grandmother more about the place, Judy?'

'Oh, it's an awful place, Gran. A frightfully bad education. Mrs Ogilvie says she couldn't imagine who would send a girl there. I mean as soon as she had decided against one of the really good boarding schools, she knew there was only the County High possible for Caroline.'

'Say no more, Judy, or I shall begin to feel sorry for Miss Hurry or Scurry or whatever her name is. Anyway, now you know, Mother. Even the county rejects it.'

Sylvia hoped that she laughed in the right way. 'It was only that it reminded me so much of the Rectory. . . .'

'Rectory? What rectory, Gran?'

'Good God, if your grandmother starts telling all her murky past . . .'

'That's not fair, Grandad. *You're* always telling . . . Anyway, what rectory, Gran?'

Sylvia folded her hands on the table before she spoke. She looked neither at Arthur nor Harold.

'The Rectory where I was in service as a girl, dear.'

'Your grandmother was housekeeper . . .'

'No, Arthur, I was housemaid.' There was a silence, broken first by Mark.

'I'll bet it was draughty . . .'

'Well, it *was* in the kitchen quarters. But the gentry were protected by a green baize door.'

'Did you wear a pretty cap, lovey?'

'Yes, it was rather a pretty one, dear. With long ribbons behind, you know.'

'There's no need to look ashamed, Judy, because your grandmother was in service.'

Judy got up from her chair and flung her arms round Sylvia's neck.

'I wasn't Gran, I wasn't. Honestly I wasn't.'

'Well, if you had been, dear, it wouldn't have mattered. But things were different then, you know. It was at the beginning of the First War.'

'Perhaps Judy looked ashamed because you never told us, Dad,' Mark said, just loudly enough for his father to hear. But Harold decided it was easier to be deaf; he glowered all around him.

These petty but sad family sequences to her outdoor expeditions within the town strengthened Sylvia's growing sense of a futile evasion. Only through the dark nothingness and the dreadful silence, she judged now, could she hope to pass.

One morning later that week, she cut herself two egg sandwiches and set out resolutely to explore the countryside. Yet, once sought, the endless 'Midlands', that lay open before her in such terrible enticement from her bedroom window, proved hard to find. The New Town, though it merged into the country, was yet cut off from it by a system of lanes and roads that turned back on themselves and eventually returned to Town Centre, as inevitably, by contrast, the paths in a maze lead away from its core. Often and again she would follow the lanes that, leaving behind the last primary school's bold colours and even the white pavilions of the last sports ground, passed on between fields of tender young wheat and stretched ahead, it seemed, to an endless rolling patchwork of fields – when suddenly there would appear a familiar green sign white-lettered: 'Footpath to Melling' or 'Footpath to Carshall' or 'Footpath to Darner's Green'. Her fears welcomed the diversion; she knew, indeed, that, if it had not come, she would have found some other excuse – probably the throbbing at her temples, or her shortness of breath – to turn back; yet she also knew that these obstacles only deferred the day when she must go on into the distance. She passed very few people in these walks – a householder with his dog, an occasional young woman pushing a pram; and twice she came upon the crazy old humpbacked woman, though no doubt she had seen her many times before in Town Centre but had not noticed her among the shopping crowds. Both times the old creature was jabbering away to herself, and on the second occasion she said something to Sylvia, who walked quickly on. After four or five days of such frustrated assaults upon the countryside, she came one afternoon upon a signpost that read merely 'Footpath', and, after a sceptical quarter of an hour, she realized that she was at last moving away from the town along a path that was no more than a narrow grassy strip between two sown fields. She had sought it so long that she half expected some miraculous change in her feelings to come about from the discovery, to walk straight into some enchanted land of good or evil, but all that came from that first two hours' walk along the field balks was a laddered stocking and very tired feet, for the surface was stony and bumpily uneven from molehills and deserted rabbit warrens.

She had never analysed what revelation of horror or hope her superstitious awe of the surrounding country expected; or even perhaps thought quite consciously whether she expected any revelation at all. She sensed only that the long familiar sketchy outlines of her grey life had now suddenly so blurred and dissolved that she had altogether lost herself. If she could have hidden herself in the smallest hollow in the tightest nutshell so that from its very pressure, from its very narrowness, she could find some shape in life however small, she would have sought such a cramped cell immediately. But 'The Sycamores', she now knew, was not that prison of peace. As for escape, it too had failed – neither Mrs Harker nor Queen Anne nor Lady Violet nor Wardress Webb could swallow up what remained of Sylvia Calvert; on the contrary, the great comforting engulfing whale of fiction seemed now to have died on her, so that she looked out through its ribs to nothingness; and even that skeleton was decaying into dust from which nothing more came to her than the sweetly sick smell of romantic falsity. Why the flat prosaic countryside should offer such dread, or promise some vague hope through this dread, she had no idea. Since so many of her thoughts now were mere morbid fancies, she thought it likely that this too was simply some such sickly whimsy. Out of the fog in which she moved only one thought about herself came suddenly, clearly and quite absurdly: she remembered the first jumper that Iris had knitted – at the age of about eleven or twelve – a garment so badly strung together, so loose and shapeless, its two-colour pattern so muddled that even the little girl herself had started at once unpicking the wool in order to knit it all over again. It seemed clear to Sylvia that she was that jumper. Perhaps to weave all the threads together again, she needed to return to the country world of her childhood – but even this idea seemed more something she had once been told than any personal conviction.

Yet if in that vague idea of return Sylvia had sensed some slight promise or comfort or happiness, she was soon undeceived. For long distances of her walks she could not have accounted for any scene or object that she passed, neither could she have recalled the trains of thought that distracted her from her surroundings. All that remained was a pervasive depression or a nagging ache of anxiety as from fugitive, forgotten bad dreams. At other times she

noticed every object that she passed with a dreary mono-
tonous clarity: vetches or poppies not yet in bud springing
up every now and again between the rows of wheat; coarse
thistles growing in the banks and on their spiny leaves a
trail of snail slime; fragments of broken shell pressed into
the soil – every petty repeated detail that lay before her
tread. Sometimes more suddenly she would be roused by
a bird shriek to the sharp vision of two magpies swaying
in the wind in a larch sapling, or by a sudden hiss to a tiny
snouted shrew disturbed from its lifelong, unappeasable
search for food. But petty or rare these sights carried no
overtones, merely passed in blank visual succession, leaving
no trace in her memory. On other days again the thoughts
that shut out her surroundings remained clearly with her,
but again with no meaning, no effect but stunning misery;
she would remember only hours of obsessive concentration
on the image of some old or ageing woman humiliatingly
pulped into nullity: Mrs Tyler no longer hotelworthy, that
terrible drawing of the Queen of France in the tumbril,
Mary Stuart at the block, faces reserved and proud and
terrified, faces appealing, chattering, smiling and terrified
all came out from among past memories of residents, and
old Mrs Fox and Mrs Durand-Deacon, and that poor old
countess running like a squawking hen round the execution
block. These obsessive images now brought less and less
panic horror, they only remained with her for successive
days as dead weights upon her spirits.

Only once in that bright warm April of aimless wandering in the countryside did something happen positive
enough to break through her numbed anxiety. She was
walking along a little path between a field and a copse of
firs planted as windbreakers when at a sudden turn she
came on a large ginger farm cat with a young rabbit
dangling from its mouth. Startled from her thoughts she let
out a cry. The alarmed cat crept stealthily away, and then
when she followed it dropped its prey and sped off into the
wood. The rabbit's back had been broken; it lay on the
path with eyes of glazed terror and blood clotting on its
fur; it jerked convulsively. Sylvia bent down with some
difficulty, picked it up from the ground by its cold damp
feeling long ears and quickly snapped its neck. She was

surprised at how easily the knack came back to her from so many years ago. But she left the copse with intense disgust for pity, asked or given. And the disgust remained with her.

No answer had come from Miss Priest. For Sylvia this, too, seemed part of the expected course of things. When daily events passed in random disorder, who would expect the broken half-intimacy of two old women to be re-ordered from the past? It was difficult enough to make the right noises for one's own flesh and blood.

Yet their demands on her remained.

'Mark,' Judy asked at breakfast, 'have the scorers been chosen for the match against the Budgies?'

'Scorers? I don't know. Better ask Jim Forrester. Why?'

'Oh, only that you said I was a good scorer.'

'*I* did?'

'Well, Jimmie Forrester did.'

'He'd say anything to the right girl. And as a matter of fact, you are.'

'I could score for the Mellingerers.'

'Well, go on,' Ray said, 'accept, boyo. You won't get anything easier on the eye. . . .'

'That's the trouble, she'll distract Jimmie. . . .'

But when Judy looked disappointed, Mark said, 'No. We'd be glad. At least I think so. I'll ask Jimmie.'

Harold, who had been opening his letters, now bore down on the conversation. 'You didn't know our ban the bomber was the local ten pin champion, Mother. Scoring for the Mellingerers! Will you sink that low, Judy?'

'Here, mind your language,' Mark said.

'Oh, don't mistake me, I'm delighted to see Judy take an interest in anything local. I suppose the County Ball's been cancelled. . . .'

The sudden disappearance of Judy's normal sulky look when her father praised her attracted even Sylvia's attention. She turned to Harold to see if he had noticed his daughter's pleasure, then she became aware that an unopened letter by his plate was addressed to her. The stamp was a foreign one. She found it at once almost impossible to attend to the conversation.

'Harold, is that a letter for me?'

'. . . unfortunately *I* don't think you should, Judy. . . .'

'Harold, I wonder if that isn't my letter. . . .'

'But the rehearsals were quite a different thing, Daddy. They lasted for weeks. . . .'

'Nevertheless . . .'

'Harold, I believe that letter is for me. . . .'

'I should have thought the whole thing was simply a matter between Judy and Mark. . . .'

'No, Ray, I'm not perhaps what Judy would call a "super" father, but I am . . .'

Sylvia could control her curiosity no longer. The letter was surely from Miss Priest. The reply, now so firmly discounted, seemed to offer some magical answer. She leaned across and picked it up. Harold glanced at her in surprise.

'From foreign parts apparently, Mother. In any case, Judy, the exam is that much nearer and any unwelcome distraction . . .'

'Anything that we do together that doesn't revolve round you is an unwelcome distraction. . . .'

'You have an almost infinite capacity, Mark, for psychological fantasies. Anybody else could see that my whole aim has been to keep the family . . .'

Sylvia gave all her attention to the large round handwriting before her.

DEAR MRS CALVERT,

Of course I remember you. And very well too. For those of us who choose to live our lives in hotels, people like you who give us both comfort and friendliness are rare, memorable, and to be cherished. I am only so glad that you recall our expeditions and my chatter with pleasure. I remember I felt at the time that I had perhaps tried too hard to break down your reserve – I'm that foolish thing, 'a friendly person by nature', which means sometimes that I am a thoughtless and irresponsible intruder. I can say for myself, however, that some part of my motive was good: I knew more than you realized what a hard, backbreaking time you were having keeping your hotel going and I saw no other way of helping. I am very happy to know that I succeeded a little. And, as you have probably guessed, happiness has not been to the fore in my life in these past few months. When one gets as old as I am one spends so much time putting the little pieces together. It's been a wonderful life but it isn't easy to make sense of it all. My religious friends propose different jigsaws, but the pieces never seem quite to fit. I certainly shouldn't have chosen hundreds of noisy, vulgar, inquisitive journalists' voices questioning and intruding on top of the natural sadness of old age. At times it's been almost unbearable. Of course it *has* been bearable because it had to be borne. But now like an old wounded animal I only long to creep away somewhere to lick my wounds and doze in the sun.

Not that any licking can soothe the wound left by my niece's terrible death. I find I can write to you about it, because you never knew her and there is no sense of betrayal. She was all that remained to me of a once large and lively family. My much loved brother's daughter – but also the pitiful result of my brother's unwise upbringing and a precarious mental balance. I only hope that there are few people in the world as unhappy by nature as Theodora was. All I could do for her were a few practical things – to give her a comfortable roof over her head and the constant change of scene and people that her restless spirit seemed to demand. Those things and not to interfere. And what has it led to? For all my good intentions, we have two unthinkable deaths – hers and now the wretched man's. I expect the world has said again and again, 'How much better if the old girl had gone instead.' If only they knew how gladly the old girl would have done so to escape this sordid last act. . . .

The noise of a chair scraping the floor sharply withdrew Sylvia's attention. In any case, Miss Priest's words seemed without healing magic.

It was not Judy, tense and on the edge of tears, nor even Mark, beetroot red and furious, who was walking out this time, but Ray.

'Look,' he said to Harold and he threw the whole weight of his stocky little figure behind the accusing arm he shook at him. 'You've very nearly had it, you know. We stood it when we were kids. We stood it when Mum was ill. We stood it after she died. But if there's much more coming from you, I can tell you now just where you can stuff it!'

Sylvia could see from Harold's face that such an outbreak coming from Ray upset him greatly, and she could understand it; at the back of her own mind she always excused her powerlessness to help in solving the family problems with the thought that in any case Ray could be relied on in his own easy, jollying way to get them through.

Washing up with Judy afterwards, she made a concentrated effort to involve herself, but the girl maintained a bitter silence. At last she turned on Sylvia.

'Perhaps if you'd been a little less intent on reading your letter, Gran, you'd know a bit more about what went wrong. However, that's too much to ask, I'm sure. After all, any news that comes from outside must be terribly important to you. We all know how much you hate living with us here.'

Sylvia could find no reply.

Ray *was* of the party, however, that set out from 'The Sycamores' to the Bowling Hall at Town Centre to watch Mark bowl for the Mellingerers in the League match against Craighill's team – the Bowling Budgies, although Harold, against all family remonstrances, had maintained his refusal to allow Judy to score for the team.

The evening began badly. As they were gathering in the hall before packing into the Zephyr, Judy came downstairs, looking her coolest and prettiest in a tangerine silk dress against which, Sylvia thought, her hair lay like thick gold thread.

'Oh, Judy dear, how pretty!'

'Blondes for ever.'

Her grandparents were enthusiastic. Harold asked, 'And where may you be going, young lady?'

'Oh, it's an awful bore really. It's the first barbecue of the summer of the County Young Conservatives. They're mostly rather awful – small farmers and people. But Mrs Ogilvie says it's terribly important to rally round all the same.'

'Go upstairs and get on with your work.'

Judy taking no notice, passed Harold. He seized her arm. 'Did you hear what I said?'

Sylvia suddenly saw Harold in school blazer in a rage with his sister Iris. Over his head she caught Arthur's eye.

'Now don't be silly, Harold dear,' she said.

'Yes, come on, Harold, old boy, we must cut along.' Each of his parents instinctively took one of Harold's arms and led him out to the car. He accepted the regression, but his face flushed red with suppressed anger as he started the engine.

They entered the bar of the Falcon as though they were

a much larger party, with plenty of talk and laughter to cover Harold's silence until he could regain his temper. To Sylvia's relief, there at the bar were seated Jack and Renee Cranston and old Mr Tucker. She smiled at them and nudged Arthur, 'Look, there's the Cranstons.' He answered with no more than a wave of his hand; while Harold, in his mood, could find nothing to offer but a rather dismal nod. Yet after a little whispering between husband and wife Jack Cranston came over to them.

'Are you coming to see the Budgies beat the Mellingerers tonight?'

Harold bucked up immediately. 'Alternative version, Jack. We're going to see Mark and our lads wipe the floor with the Craighill twitterers. But you don't mean to say that a Melling man like you is backing the opposing team?'

Jack looked judicious. 'Oh yes, I believe in backing the best team. None of that sentimental rot. However, I'll grant you Mark's the greatest danger. The Budgies'll have to watch those strikes of his. But he'll have to watch his follow-through. I know our Mark if he starts to tire.'

Harold smiled, but Arthur said: 'The boy's got a beautiful action. His doubles are going to make rings around the Craighill boys tonight. . . .'

'Oh! You're going to teach us how to bowl now too, are you? Let's see, when were you champion of the BTBA League? 1921? Or could it be that ten pin bowling hadn't come in then?'

Sylvia was wondering whether she'd expected too much of Miss Priest's letter, but the aggression in Jack Cranston's voice forced its way through her reverie. She looked up to see that rarest of sights – a flush of embarrassment on Arthur's cheeks.

Ray said, 'What's it to be, all? What's yours, Gran? Renee? Mr Tucker?' He drew them all in.

Harold said weightily: 'Dad is a natural athlete. I've never known anyone in my life who gets the finer points of a new game quicker. I've no doubt he's mastered the tender art since he's been here, eh, Dad?'

'I've given it a dekko once or twice. Like to see the pretty girls.'

'Oh, I'm sure,' Renee said.

Arthur decided to concentrate on Mr Tucker. 'Hullo, you old scoundrel. Who spread the news of your funeral?'

'Don't you pick on Dad, Captain Calvert. Pick on someone your own size.'

Arthur, man to man, ignored the women. 'How come so long time no see at the bookies, Tucker. I had a good thing for you the other day. Marzipan. Romped home at 60 to 1.'

'Marzipan! Oh, that would have been too sticky for me,' Mr Tucker's laugh echoed miserably round the bar.

Renee put on her version of a posh accent. 'We don't all have private fortunes.' She and Jack laughed in a loud hostile way. 'Your tips come too expensive, Captain,' Jack said.

Looking at Arthur, Sylvia knew from experience exactly what had happened. She made up her mind to settle it all with the Cranstons before Harold could find out. She would have a quiet word with Renee and reassure her that they wouldn't be losers.

'Hullo, Mrs Calvert,' Renee said. 'I thought you were too good for us.' But her tone was friendly.

To her surprise Sylvia found herself saying, 'I've been rather upset lately. Perhaps you've read of this murder in Spain. Well, I knew the aunt, Miss Priest. Of course I wrote to her. But perhaps I expected too much from the answer. . . .'

Renee was entirely bewildered, but their attention was immediately drawn away by the raised voices of the men.

'No, no, no, Harold. Believe me you've got it all wrong. I hadn't looked into it before, but . . .'

'I'm particularly sorry to hear you take this line, Jack. I've always considered you the backbone of New Town life. . . .'

'And I'm sorry to disagree with an old friend, but if what you want is to maintain Carshall as the blokes who started it intended, then there's no question about it. Let Goodchild's meadow go. Anything better than extending the boundaries, making the place geographically larger. That way you *are* going back on the original intention. . . .'

'Oh, of course, it's a choice of evils. I grant you that. But this new housing is needed if we're to get a multi-status community. To accommodate you and Renee, for example, with what you'll be wanting soon.' Harold explained the general phrase in personal terms.

'You can count *us* out for a start! Multi-status community! No, thank you. That's all right for you, Harold. Not to be rude, you like to be – what do they call it? – a trout among minnows. Anyway you're a County Council man. That's quite different. But executive people in industry don't want to live among their work-people and their work-people don't want them there either. No, no, Renee and I'll be moving out to the country as soon as we can find a place.'

Harold took a deep draught of his bitter and wiped his mouth slowly with his handkerchief. 'Then I'm afraid you'll be ratting on a fine experiment, Jack.'

Arthur belched, and leaned on the bar staring through triumphant narrowed eyes at Cranston's discomfiture by his clever son. Sylvia looked round in desperation for Ray. She saw him in a huddle in a corner of the now crowded bar with Mr Corney and two rough-looking youngsters – one had filthy old blue jeans on, and the other, a dark chap, looked as though he needed a good wash and shave.

'Mr Corney!' He was just the one to cheer them all up. She remembered his help at the party. 'Hullo, Mr Corney,' she heard herself say quite loudly across the crowded bar. 'Come along and join us.' The face Mr Corney raised to her call was startled and worried. Before he could reply Ray had shepherded him and their two friends out of the bar. As they left she heard the dark, gipsy-looking one say, 'What's the hurry, Radiance?'

'I'm only glad to think you don't realize the nonsense you're talking, Jack.'

'Jack's not one of your boys at school, Harold,' Renee remarked.

'No, Renee, I should teach him a bit of sense if he were.'

'Now look here, Harold. Cool off, can't you? This business isn't the end of the world. . . .'

'If you're ready, Mother, Dad?'

'Oh, now, Harold, be your age. . . .'

'Oh, don't worry about it, Jack. He'll come round in time.'

The hall, crowded, noisy, brightly lit, was large, but the

match between the Mellingerers and the Bowling Budgies had by competition rules to be played on adjoining lanes ten and eleven, right in the centre of the hall, so it wasn't going to be easy to avoid trouble with their supporters scarcely on speaking terms. Sylvia could see that Arthur smelt trouble, for, after clapping Mark and his captain, Jimmie Forrester, on the back a few times and giving loud hearty advice to the Mellingerers, he moved off down the hall. Sylvia watching him, thought, selfish old thing, he knows his onions; then, seeing that he had transferred his attention to the girls' match, she thought, silly old thing! She was really worried about Harold now. He was talking so much and ignoring the nearby Cranstons so tremblingly. Ray, who had joined them again, seemed preoccupied and made no effort to help. Surfacing up from the depths of her own depressions with a vast effort, she began to ask Harold questions about the game. He showed her the shoes, the balls, a score card, explained the lit-up numbers, showed last season's honour rolls with the Mellingerers' name inscribed. She guessed that his heart was as little in the conversation as hers, but she persisted.

'Is it tenping bowling in all the lanes?' she asked.

Ray beside her whispered, 'Pin, lovey.'

Instinctively she looked into her bag, 'I'm sorry, I haven't got one.' Then, realizing her silly mistake, she blushed and felt unable to say more. She sat then looking so miserable that Ray took her to one of the little spectators' tables and gave her a cup of coffee from the bar. He sat with her, drinking a coke, equally gloomy, and silent, as the booms of the balls and the crackling crashes of the pins brought back to her once more the horrors of the bombing.

'Ray,' she said at last, 'I wrote to Miss Priest, you know. And her reply seemed so ordinary. I don't know what I'd expected. I suppose I'd got things out of proportion. I mean, just because she was involved in a murder story . . .'

'I don't know, lovey. You're right out of my class. I've never known any murderesses.'

She could tell he hadn't listened. He'd come back so soon from his friends, she wondered vaguely if there'd been a quarrel. They sat then, hearing Harold's voice raised in loud, knowing, technical cries.

'A beautiful working ball!... Lovely turkey!... Go for the poison ivy, Mark.' Once he called back to Ray and Sylvia, 'Oh! This lane's a piece of cheesecake.'

Jack Cranston was competing in loud commentary. Ray only spoke once and then more to himself. 'When Dad goes all pop, he certainly goes pop.'

Sylvia felt out of it all. Most of the crowd were teenagers – all this Mods and Rockers! Well, it was easy enough to tell which was which, but so what? as they used to say. There were some family parties at the lanes, but at the coffee bar it was all kids really with cokes and hamburgers. She saw Arthur talking to two girls with no proper make-up, only heavy eyeshadow; they giggled then turned away from him. Silly old thing, she thought, but she feared from the Cranstons' remarks that the old cycle was beginning again – she didn't know how she could get through it all this time, depressed as she was, and with no hard work to keep her mind off things. Mr Corney appeared at the doorway and beckoned to Ray to come out. She sat on by herself – she must look like some forgotten dozy old mountain to all these youngsters, she thought. Every few minutes she could hear Harold or Mr Cranston holding forth; then suddenly there was a general buzz of voices around lane 10 and above the clamour Harold called: 'I appeal against a breach of etiquette.'

She turned to see him, red-faced, pointing at the Cranstons, like somebody on the stage. 'Such continuous distracting comments from spectators constitute a recognized infringement.'

Renee was red-faced and defiant. 'Oh, for God's sake, man, your son's choked his ball, and not surprising with all your shouting at him, but stop trying to find excuses.'

Sylvia could see Mark glowering at his father. He stepped forward, but his captain, a tall fair-haired young chap, held him back. The captain himself addressed Harold. 'If there are any appeals to be made, Mr Calvert, I think I'm the bloke to make them.'

'Well, go ahead and do so then, Jimmie.'

The young man looked hesitant. He stammered, 'I... I'm not too sure...'

'For the Lord's sake, boy, haven't you got rid of that stammer?'

The question put an end to it effectually. 'The trouble is, Mr Calvert, that your behaviour has been just as bad as . . .' Now at last Mark broke forth with a voice that sounded beyond lanes 9 and 12 to lanes 8 and 13 and even to 6 and 14. 'Take your resentment somewhere else then, Dad, but get out of our way.' Harold turned and walked out of the hall. As he passed Sylvia she tried to speak to him, but he strode by her.

She went over to Arthur, 'Harold's gone off in a temper.'

'Oh for Christ's sake! He's not a kid any longer, Sylvia. He'll get over it. What do you want to do? Change his nappies?' He turned back to lane 5. 'That little red-head rolls a beautiful straight ball.'

Later, as the game was ending, Harold reappeared rather sheepishly. When the Mellingerers' victory was announced, he went up to congratulate his son, but Mark turned his back on him.

Arthur said, 'You shouldn't have upset the boy, Harold.'

'Do you mind, Dad? Surely you must have some idea of how ashamed I feel.'

They returned a depressed party. Sylvia didn't know what to do to help. As Miss Priest had written, there's nothing much you can do, except practical things. Going to the kitchen, she found a tin of Ovaltine and came back to the sitting room with a cup all round for everyone. Judy had returned, but there was no sign of Mark.

'Good God, what's that?' Arthur asked.

'Not for me, Mother, thanks.'

'Thank you, lovey,' Ray sat stirring dreamily.

'Oh, Gran, I couldn't, thank you. Not after all that punch.'

'Was it a nice whatever it was, dear?'

'Oh, lovely. The moon was just right for the barbecue. And then we had a treasure hunt with super local clues. Of course, I was terribly lucky, I went in the Trenchard-Bourne's car.'

'Why was that lucky?' Harold asked.

'Oh, you know, Daddy. They have that lovely old

Jacobean house – Rumpett Hall. But they're awfully nice people. Absolutely simple and friendly.'

'My God! That I should have produced a snob.'

Ray tapped with his spoon against his untouched Ovaltine, 'Bed, I think,' he cried.

Sylvia reheated Mark's Ovaltine and put the cup in his bedroom. with the saucer on top to keep it hot.

When Arthur was undressing, she said to him with all the kindness she could muster through her exhaustion, 'Have you got into a mess again, Arthur? Do tell me if you have. We'll manage to pay it off somehow without Harold knowing. And then we can forget it.' He was sitting in one of the mustard chairs, pulling off his vest; the face he raised to her was pitiably old and anxious.

'It can't be as bad as that, Arthur.' He was about to speak, but his doddery hands got the vest caught over his head. He began to swear. Sylvia got out of bed and helped him off with the vest.

'Oh dear, Arthur!'

'These bloody things. I wish I was dead.'

'That wouldn't help, dear.'

Nor did her remark. The moment died away in irritability. The next morning at breakfast, when the telephone rang, Ray ran to it before Harold could get there. When he replaced the instrument, he looked quite relieved. He went straight upstairs. Ten minutes later he was down with a suitcase and Mark's cup of Ovaltine.

'I'm afraid he won't be drinking this, lovey. That was him on the 'phone. He's staying round at Jimmie Forrester's for the moment. I'm taking his suitcase there on my way to work.'

Harold put his head in his hands. 'Whatever I do is wrong since she left us. God knows, I tried to meet him on his own ground, but it's a curse to be a teacher. Poor old, mixed-up Mark! He of any of us so desperately needed a woman about the house.'

Ray looked at Sylvia with a friendly grin and patted her arm. To his father he said, 'Don't upset yourself, Dad. He'll be better at the Forresters' for a bit. He's been wanting to get away for some time.'

One afternoon that May, in the course of her wanderings,

Sylvia was sitting on a bank in the shade of a hazel bush and picking the cleavers off her skirt. She was intent on the task for she had become ashamed of her melancholic rambles in the country and tried to conceal all evidence of them from the family. She jumped with alarm when a woman's voice sounded quite near to her. There, hoisting herself down on to the bank next to Sylvia, was the little humpbacked old woman. Near to, she seemed even older and uglier, with a loose, protuberant lower lip and a wart on her right nostril; but her dark eyes gleamed with lively brightness. To Sylvia's astonishment, after one or two casual remarks about the fine weather and the growing dust in the country lanes, the old woman, her short cotton skirt hitched up above the knee of her wrinkled stockings, began to tell her life story. It seemed to Sylvia to last for hours. At first she found it difficult to attend, her eyes kept travelling to that horrid hump. But as the narrative went on the woman's physical presence was quite swallowed up in her words. Although there were many names of places and people that were unknown to her, and although the woman's singsong foreign accent was not at all easy to follow, she found herself quite carried away; yet when the story was ended, she felt only torn and sad.

THE OLD WOMAN'S STORY

'Do you know that I shall be seventy-six in August? Yes, I was born on the 11th of August 1887. It seems hard to believe that I am so old. And very few people do believe it. "No, you cannot yet be sixty, I am sure, Mrs Kragnitz," the greengrocer told me only the other day. "And you are *so* active." But then, of course, I had such a healthy, strong childhood with everything that money could buy. And the child makes the woman, as you will read in Grillparzer, however hard the later years may be. Oh yes, everyone remarks on how young I am looking. Except that Edna. She is my niece – my nephew's wife – no relation by the blood. And sometimes Jerzy also – when he wishes very much to please her. That is why I am walking so much all times and weathers. To keep out of her way. When Jerzy is there she cannot attack me, but at other times. . . . I won't say to poison my food, that is too fanciful. Although these peasants do so, you know, my dear. Oh yes, I have known many cases in Poland and in Pomerania and in the Urals. Even in China, where the respect for the old is remarkable. However, she is better than the other one. So I must live my life out with her – a creature that has never even read a book. But I take care – I say always that I have survived the British Army and the Gestapo and the Ogpu and the Japanese, so I don't intend to be put to death by Edna.

'I was born near Cracow. Do you know that town? Very beautiful! Not at all as the rest of Poland. When I went with my husband to Italy for our honeymoon – to Florence and Siena, but I knew it already. It was just Cracow come alive again. You must know that in that time Cracow and the countryside where we are living – all is Austrian. Not really, of course; really it was and it always has been Poland. And we were Polish, you know, although we lived under the Hapsburgs. But people like my uncle Ladislaw would not have anything to do with them. He would not speak to any of them – not to an Austrian or to a Russian or to a Prussian. "But there are such charming Austrians, my dear fellow," my father said. "Let them leave our Poland and I will see all their charms," my uncle replied. He cared only for Poland and he was quite right. I know that now. I should be there too. What matters about all these Governments? Conservative, Socialist, Communist, Imperial and Fascist. I have seen them all. They go. It's the place where you were born. That's what counts, my dear. As the great Count Tolstoy says – this is my homeland. But my father was a different kind of man. A very good Catholic, but a practical man. "The Austrians are the best that we shall get," he said. And so he accepted them, even worked with them. He held a position in the Commission of Forestry near Lake Morskie Oko – that is the Black Lake, a very deep lake. And we moved in the best Austrian society. At Zakopane once I skated with the Archduke Ferdinand. There were no winter sports then, of course. Oh no!

'And then I had to go and marry a Prussian! You're laughing already, I see. A protestant from Pomerania! You may imagine the horror of my family – oh yes, and also of Willibald's family. My father liked Willi at first, of course, when he was just a visitor – they hunted together and talked of trees and trapping. But to marry! Even though the von Kragnitzs were an excellent family, older, more illustrious than the Adamowiczs I must say – a Junker family. My father refused to see me, but it was not serious to him, I was only the girl of the family. It was more terrible for Willi – his father cut him off from his will. Fortunately he had some money from his grandmother. So we went to Italy for our honeymoon and then to the East Griqualand to help make the New Germany overseas. Do you know where East Griqualand is? I am sure you do not. Why even at Hamburg when I boarded the ship, there was a lady in the hotel, "Be sure to visit Milos," she said, "Milos is indispensable." She thought I spoke of Griechenland. And she was a German! Willi was quite shocked to think a German woman should know so little of her own Empire. But then the Hamburgers are very stupid – *Dumm wie einer Hamburger* – it was well known. We started with an ostrich farm. In those days, as you will remember, everything was ostrich feathers. Later woman – capricious woman, that is how Lermontov describes us – changed her mind. And so all the ostrich farmers lost their money. But by that time we Germans had been made to go from Africa, so it did not concern us.

'I must tell you in all honesty that I do not at all like ostriches. They are greedy and stupid. But we must make our life very often with such creatures, as you know. And they suffered when Hitler came, the poor ostriches with their heads in the sand. The life was hard and rather lonely, especially when the War came and Willi had to leave me on the farm. But I was good to our native boys and they were good to '*die Polsche Frau*' – I imagine they just could not say '*Polnische*'! What they liked was to hear me singing Polish songs. I think it was all the little s's hissing like little snakes in the Polish language that pleased them.

'The British took our farm, but they sent us home to Germany free of cost. I can stay if I wish but of course the wife must go with the husband. I did not feel so very grateful, but I didn't know then how often in my life the

British would come forward to pay my fares. Willi's father was dead, but his mother received us. She was a little old woman, rather humped, do you say? but very powerful in spirit. It was not more than a year before they quarrelled, she and Willi. Everyone was poor in Germany and then she tried to live in the old way with all the peasants and great feasts with raspberries when the neighbours hunted wild pigs. Willi got very angry and said that was not the way that Germany would rise again. He started to read books and such things that the old lady did not like – Red books that were lent to him by a friend in the University at Königsberg, a very clever man, a *lektor* in *Handelsgeschichte*. So then they quarrelled very fiercely. "A house ruled by a woman is a mockery of law." Do you read Strindberg? I know him only in translation. So we went away. I was glad because I did not like to live there in those big cold rooms "amid those dark forests and gloomy lakes" as Mickiewicz says in our great national poem.

'So then we went first to Königsberg and then to Berlin. Everyone there was so very poor. That was the great inflation time. Willi had only a little work in a bookshop, but we had a room near the Tiergarten and we were very happy. I must tell you that Willi had become a communist. I can see that you are surprised – a von Kragnitz, a former Kolonialbürger, a communist! You hardly believe me, I think. But so things were at that time, everybody was changing their views. "The lion brays and the ass roars", as the old saying is. Our little room was filled now with people all day, talking and smoking and shouting against the Weimar Republic. The floors were covered with pamphlets and lampoons. But I was happy making coffee – acorn coffee you will laugh to hear – and on special days sometimes I would serve some *Torten mit Schlagsahne* or a little *Kompott* to all the shouting comrades.

'But the cloud was not long in coming. A brown cloud! A cloud of brown shirts! I think now sometimes that Willi was secretly much pleased by Hitler's speeches. But his path was already chosen. It was a Party member. And quite an important man. And you do not leave the Party, you know. Already in 1933 the call came one night for us to leave Germany. I remember it was a very cold night and we had the two children. I put the little top coat with its fur collar on to Britte, but little Dietl had no coat. I could not find it anywhere in our room. So, imagine! he travelled all the way, yes, through Poland and Czechoslovakia and Roumania and Bulgaria (for we had to go by a secret route) many, many days, until we came round to Moscow, with only a little jersey. In Moscow everywhere was snow, although the golden roofs of the Kremlin gleamed. But roofs will not warm a little boy of six years, however golden. Yet as the old Russian fable says – "the little fox is too inquisitive to catch cold". At Moscow Willi joined us. And then began a long new life. Moving about Russia while Willi is being trained for party underground work in Germany. And I too learned something – to boil the samovar and to make blinis. At last in 1939 we were right down to the Chinese border. And glad for it too, for life was less dangerous then at the frontiers than in Moscow. "He stands about the throne today, tomorrow he is swept away!" I don't remember where the lines come from. Is it Pushkin? And then Willi must go to Moscow, and, with him, Dietl who is now nearly twelve. I never saw them again. That is the price Stalin pays to Hitler – to be rid of some German comrades. Not important ones, of course; Willi was never important. But even we the women, the useless women, must be swept away too – "if the blossom dies, the beetles fall with it." I learnt that later in China. Do you know I didn't understand how it could be until one day in a little village in the mountains near Peking I was sitting and the almond blossom was falling round me and with the blossoms many hundred little blue and green beetles banging on the ground. So must sayings have their sense, I think.

'But the little beetles got away this time. An official, a very upright man helped us across the border. He wanted to ask his price from Britte, but he had to content himself with the old mother. Just the situation of Schnitzler's comedy, you know – but not for me so much a matter of laughter. However we were to be in the way of luck. In Sakhalin we met many White Russians, former aristocrats. I thought that they would poison us – such things do happen, you know. The remains of a German communist!

but not at all! There was one old general – he heard our name – "But I hunted the pigs in your husband's forests" – he knew nothing of Willi, only of his family – "I was an honoured guest in your husband's riches, you must be honoured guests in our poverty". So we lived there some years – all samovars but no blinis. All the time war was around us. Yet strangely it did not touch us. "I heard the guns, I saw the fire; I drank my tea and played at dice", as your own Byron says. And then all of a sudden the Japanese put us on the move. Hundreds of miles, hundreds of miles each day. The sick and the old died on the road – my Britte died of the typhoid – her lips were swollen like puddings. Then I almost died too. There I could find nothing to live for. We were put to Hong Kong. Do you know here at Carshall, Mrs Rickard? No? She is friend of Edna. She asked me, how do I find the Zoo at Hong Kong? I answered her I found it all the time, nothing else. I was shut up. And then came the British. The British with their files and their records. Who are you? Where do you come from? Where is your family? For the British and the French, it is always the same – where is your family? And what am I? I am Russian, for Willi was at the last with a Russian passport. But I don't want to be Russian and the Russians don't want me. As the play says, "Thank you, gentlemen, I am content to be myself." But nobody knows who that is. The von Kragnitzs are swallowed by the Russians and the Germans don't want those born in Poland, and the Hapsburgs are no longer. But the British find out. Oh no, they are not to be refused an answer. Your family is in Warsaw, they say. And it is quite true, my brother Andrezj is in Warsaw – only he is dead and his wife too, and his daughters. But the British are not to be put off. It seems that my brother has sons – Dzislaw and Jerzy – who fight in the battle of Britain and are not killed. "The eagle soars, swoops on its prey, and lives to swoop another day." Those are the lines of an old poet which I read when I was very small. And now Dzislaw is in Johannesburg. So the old woman must go to Johannesburg, but the British will pay. Do you know Johannesburg? A terrible town, not a town at all, no river – a mine. And Dzislaw is married with an Afrikaaner – Cornelia. You laugh already at the name?

But you will not laugh at the woman, the big, fat, blonde *mevrouw*. She sits all day, eating and shouting at the native boy. No books in the house! From the first day I make rows with her. I remembered my native boys in East Griqualand and how I sang them Polish songs. But in Riverdale, that is where we live in Johannesburg, oh very smart, a vulgar suburb, there is only one native boy who lives in an outhouse in the garden behind the poinsettias. And Cornelia does not like me to sing to *him*. And then suddenly they say that Willi was a communist and I must go. But the British are very just. If I cannot live in Johannesburg, then they find another nephew for me. And in a New Town it does not matter that an old woman was once married to a communist. I can stay with Jerzy here. And with Edna. So there is my life.'

As the old woman's tale had progressed, her English had grown more and more difficult to follow so that at last Sylvia had to strain to catch the words. When it was ended there was a long silence. 'I've never been out of England. I really only know foreign people from the hotels I've worked in.'

'So I should suppose.' The old woman sounded quite sarcastic and her eyes had grown sharp and hard.

Sylvia resented this remark. How could the old woman know she'd been in the hotel business when she'd never let her get a word in edgeways? After a moment of mumbling the old woman got up. Sylvia noticed the hump again, but almost worse the eccentric dirty clothes all held together by safety pins.

Unintelligible though most of the old woman's story was, Sylvia felt a wondering respect for someone who'd been through so much. The vision of the woman's dirty, ragged skirt remained with her as one of the warning horrors of those days. Yet there the woman was – a picture of what got served up to women in this world; and, since the least we can do is to stand by one another, Sylvia tried once or twice to speak to her again. But the old woman, her story told, avoided Sylvia. So there it was and just as well really.

She described the old woman to the family and it appeared that she was a very well-known figure locally.

Both Ray and Judy called her by the name which was used by all the schoolchildren – old Humpy. But only Harold had any information about her.

'She's been one of the banes of Sally Bulmer's life. Apparently her children or whoever it is she lives with are a model couple. The girl's a hardworking little cockney and he's one of the decent Poles. It's really very good of them to put up with it. There have been all sorts of shindigs. The old lady's quite round the bend – accusations of poisoning and heaven knows what else! Sally offered to get her into an old people's home, but they wouldn't hear of it. So she does her bit by going round there and listening to the old woman's stories. She says they would make another Arabian Nights and they're never the same from one week to another. Though no doubt, as she says, there's a substratum of truth in it all. The rulers of the world can't disregard the speed limits without causing casualties.'

The old parson had said keep on through the darkness until you come into the light. But, no doubt, he had left out all those like the old woman who kept on through the darkness and through darkness and through darkness and hadn't come out anywhere; that was no part of his message. Or those like Miss Priest, who walked bang out of a long bright day into the blackness of night.

As Sylvia continued her aimless moochings, the May weather grew especially warm. People began to hope for one of our freak good summers, the sports grounds were filled; Harold ordered all classroom windows to be kept open; Ray bathed each evening on getting home before he joined in Carshall's crowded social life; Miss Castle told Judy and the other A level candidates not to be rattled by the heat; Muriel Bartley wore a bikini in the garden; Sally Bulmer showed bare arms; even Lorna Milton shed her excess woollies; and the farmers complained of drought. Only Arthur seemed unaware of the heat, though his eye caught with pleasure the summery look of the girls of the New Town – indeed in the warm evenings the streets of Melling, as of all Carshall, offered up an endless dalliance of youth.

Warned by spells of giddiness or of sudden shortness of breath, Sylvia took her walks at a slower pace, rested more under the hedgerows, made her sandwiches last out for two or three little snacks in this or that shady lane or wood. She set out earlier, telling herself that to explore further at slower pace, she must give herself more time. But where further was she seeking to go? On occasion she would find herself at some unfamiliar country pub with a small green table and chair set up before a bed of wallflowers or tulips, or she would come upon an unexpected pond overhung by willows in which the boatmen scudded over the green slimy weed and the first tips of yellow lilies showed above the water level. Yet even by these distinctive landmarks she stood unsure whether or not she had been there before, or, just when she knew that she had not the landlady would say 'A soft boiled egg you said last time, I think.' But she told herself that at least she'd gone 'further afield'.

So Sylvia didn't brush the face powder off her jacket, she didn't clean her brown suede shoes, she didn't mend the tear in her skirt, she didn't wash the eggstain from her blouse – or rather, she often didn't do these things. For, although she already saw herself a jumbo-size Humpy without the hump, Judy said one evening, 'Caroline Ogilvie saw you right over at Burpitt on Wednesday, Gran. They were out there riding. She said you looked dressed for Oxford Street.' So that was all right really; or rather, judging from Judy's tone, it wasn't. And again with the shopping, the many little household jobs – you could get away with it once, take people in twice, paste over the cracks three times, but in the end you were bound to fall into lies and little secret hiding places, into inventing conversations that you'd never had in the shops.

So, on through that lovely May, heavy with lilac scent and with the sound of nightingales at midnight from despised Gorman's Wood (the town planners certainly knew their onions), Sylvia carried her heavy body and her heavy thoughts about the fresh green fields without more than a passing notice from home or abroad. In the last days of the month the air grew intolerably heavy with stale, hovering warmth which had collected in every corner during the many past windless weeks. Sylvia's vague glooms were startled now and again by random rolls of thunder. How tired and scratchy everyone seemed!

One afternoon about four o'clock – time to start thinking where she had come to and how to get back again – Sylvia sat on the edge of a copse in the shade of a high gnarled elm tree. The world appeared to be absolutely still; and, on looking round at the trees behind her, she could not see a ripple in all the far-stretching ocean of green leaves, patched in contrasts of near black and softest jade as the strong sunlight chanced to strike them. Only the growing host of midges spiralled ceaselessly in shimmering cones around her; and even from these there came not the slightest sound. Far on the horizon, across the fields away from the wood, clouds were gathering, shapeless as yet and light grey-white. She sat, keyed up to the coming storm, yet uncertain whether to flee the lightning or the rain. Under the trees or out into the fields? The first quiet rustling in the leaves grew louder as the wind surged towards her; with it came immediate and intense memories of other storms – of pressing her face against the hard rock in terror as she sheltered in a cave near Minehead, of making a sudden, frightened rush towards the French window at Bognor to shut out with heavy curtains all sight of a storm's terrors, of shamefacedly covering the steel knives on the dining-room sideboard at Paignton. She knew at once that she feared the lightning, however remote its dangers, more completely than the Flood itself. As though to confirm this knowledge a forked tongue whipped out and cut the sky above her; she was almost on her feet before she heard the bang and roar that followed. Stumbling across the ridges of tender wheat – a farm girl's remembered sacrilege – her bucket bag clattering against her side, locks of mauve-white hair falling from under her wide-brimmed straw hat, she saw before her a vast field which offered no threat of treacherous shelter. The clouds by now had swollen up from the horizon, swollen and broken into huge lowering black, fog yellow and smoky-grey shapes. Soon they would burst and drench her, but at least she was safe from the lightning that flashed and cracked on every side. But not from her terror of it – a terror inspired in the main by the thunderous roars with which the lightning made its threats. All the pressed in, tight packed nervous terrors of the past months burst out with the storm's explosion; yet at the same time all wandering fragments of nightmare came together in one sudden overwhelming flash and roar. Whatever it was had found her, driven her from cover, and now would strike her down. She ran, stumbled once, fell, cut her hand upon a stone, with difficulty raised herself, pushed back her hair with her bleeding hand, then ran again, calling – she heard herself with fogged amazement – 'Arthur! Arthur!'

It was only as the rain began to fall, swamping the world, that through its clatter she could hear a voice screaming, not in words, but in sheer terror. Turning, she saw that where the field sloped away to her right, one tall crumbling, leafless, ghostly-fingered oak tree had been left to decline and fall in its lonely sovereignty over the landscape. There, clinging to the tree trunk, with face pressed close to the lichened wood, the little girl might have been guardian in a game of grandmother's steps, if it had not been for her hysterical, agonized yelling all on one high note of panic. Sylvia had just time to speculate whether with those strange knee-length shorts and close-cut hair this was indeed a little girl, before the child's real danger drove out every other thought from her mind. There was scarcely a second's interval now between the vivid flashes and the bangs. Leaving one shoe behind as she waddled-ran across the field, she seized the child's arm and tried to drag her away from the tree. Screaming with renewed terror, the child clung more closely to the trunk. 'You must come away from the tree, dear. It's dangerous there.' Sylvia found at last a soothing, maternal calm voice. Memories of Iris flooded through her to steel her will. In a minute the child yielded and now in turn she pulled the fat stranger back into the open field. There, herself shivering with the cold drenching rain and with shock, Sylvia held the small trembling girl to her until they seemed to merge into one sodden mass. And then, whatever it was struck too late, as a jagged blinding flash zigzagged across the field and the rotten oak went down in a moment's flame and a long plume of funeral smoke.

The striking of the tree shocked them into calm. Almost immediately the lightning ceased, the thunder only rumbled away some miles off, even the rain fell less heavily for a while. Crouching down low over the flooded ground, Sylvia talked to the child in reassurance.

'It's all over now, dear. We must take you back home. Where do you live?'

'I'm Amanda Egan and I live at Murrel Farm, Clivett Saint Creeting.'

To Sylvia's surprise the child's voice was American.

'Where is that, Amanda?'

'Why, it's here of course. And I'm usually called Mandy.'

'Oh, I'm sorry.'

'That's all right. You don't know me. So how could you tell what I'm called? Here, we'd better get out of this before it rains hard again. All the water's falling off your hat on to your nose.' Amanda was now very talkative.

'But where do we go?'

'Why, home, of course. Least, my home, that is.' She pointed into the distance past the smoking tree, over the slope.

'But you said you lived here.'

'No, I didn't. I said this is Murrel Farm. And so it is. My daddy owns all this around here. For miles and miles.' Quite suddenly she was silent and then she began to sob almost noiselessly. Sylvia found her shoe, then took Amanda by the hand.

'Come on,' she said.

The incongruous soaking pair set off down the slope into the valley below. Amanda only ceased her sobbing once, and looked up at Sylvia.

'You were scared.'

'Yes I was, dear.'

'I thought you were. It must be awful to be so big and to be scared.'

7. A Wonderful Summer

'Oh Lord! Please! You don't have to be polite. It's just not furnished at all really. That old four-poster was my idea. But I know it's just a fake. All the rest is junk. God rest Timbo's aunt's soul, but she collected junk like her teeth collected all that terrible green moss. No, the whole place is a mess.'

There were faces that Sylvia thought she could make and those that she knew she could not; any sustained face of polite disagreement was quite beyond her. She did not even try to make it. In any case Mrs Egan didn't seem to need the stimulus of a reply.

'But how *do* you make these old beamy houses look right anyway? Do you bring *out* the beams or do you suppress them? Miss Warner that taught interior decorating in school was always talking about bringing out or suppressing something. But she never said anything about beams. I guess she'd never heard of them. What do *you* do about beams?'

The pains in her legs which Sylvia had managed to ignore during her many weeks of walking had intensified cruelly during the night. She did not know how to bear the weight of the little breakfast tray. She said, 'My son's house is very modern.' She could hear her words jerking out from the corner of her half-closed mouth. Mrs Egan frowned, 'Isn't it awful? I don't understand you at all. We've been in this country a year and I still can't understand half of what people say. God knows, after living in Victoria for a year, British speech ought to be easy. But I guess in Victoria they're just so British that . . .'

Such a lot of it Sylvia couldn't really follow. Victoria certainly didn't mean Victoria Station, but that was about as far as she could interpret. Not that she was able to give proper attention to Mrs Egan's words. The excitement of the previous day's events still exhilarated her; yet the surface of her mind was dulled and apathetic. And then how to explain? She couldn't in fact. You can't say to a complete stranger: I had a very slight stroke in your house last night, and, although my speech is returning, it's still not quite right. She contented herself with a smile and hoped that the resulting pull on the muscles of her face did not mean that she was making too grotesque a grimace.

If it were so, Mrs Egan didn't seem to notice. Instead she sat down on a chair facing Sylvia's bed as though she had decided that the time had come for a good long chat.

'I'm keeping Mandy in bed today.'

Sylvia would have smiled to herself if it hadn't been too soon after the last smile for her unwilling facial muscles. For except that her hair was worn in a small coil and that there were two deep furrows in her forehead and that she was so tall, Mrs Egan might have been deputizing for her little girl – in the same kind of open-necked white shirt and the same kind of knee-length jeans.

'Anyway that's such an awful school: I just make every excuse to keep her at home. She won't learn anything here, but what she learns *there*! It's terrible! And Miss Hurry is so awful! What do you think she made the poor kids learn last week? Some game called "Pooh Sticks". They all had to sit around a smelly pool and hum. One kid nearly got drowned. Honestly I think the primary school would have been better. But when Timbo digs his heels in . . .' Despite everything – exhaustion, stroke, painful legs – Sylvia felt curiously happy lying there with this strange lanky girl – she was no more than a girl – talking at her. As the stream of words flowed on, she became increasingly forgetful of the tray's weight or the painful jabs in her calves. She only wanted to close her eyes and feel the comfort of Mrs Egan's presence rather than to register it. She didn't want to sleep, just to close her eyes; but with a stranger. . . . And then Amanda came running into the room.

'I don't want to stay in my bed, Mummy. I want to get into her bed.'

Yesterday's near-boy was dressed in the softest, most feminine ankle-length nightgown of cornflower blue muslin.

Her mother considered a moment, but she didn't consult Sylvia.

'Well, all right, go ahead.'

'But I can't with that awful heavy old tray.'

'That's rude, Mandy. Mrs Calvert hasn't finished her breakfast.'

'She has too.'

'Yes, really I have.'

Mrs Egan removed the tray.

'Why are you talking funny?'

'Now that *is* rude, Mandy.'

But none of it seemed to matter to Sylvia as the small girl wriggled in beside her.

'You're wearing Mummy's nightgown.'

'Oh now, Amanda, for heaven's sake. She saves your life and you bawl her out because she didn't bring her nightgown with her.'

'I do usually bring my own night clothes when I go away to stay.'

'Well, I should hope so,' Amanda laughed, but she held Sylvia's hand tightly. 'Doesn't she say funny things, Mummy?'

'I don't stay away for the night very often.'

'Well you will now. You'll stay here very often. Because you saved my life.'

Mrs Egan said very seriously, 'Now if you think carefully about that, Mandy, you'll see it's a very conceited thing to say.'

The small girl seemed to consider.

'Well, everybody else can say it even if I can't. Anyhow, you don't have to stay here just 'cause you saved me. Wasn't it awful, the crash of thunder? And weren't we scared? No, you must stay here, you've got a very nice face.'

'Now, Mandy, that's personal and silly. Oh, I don't mean "silly". How awful of me! You *have* got a very nice face. I didn't notice it at first. I just thought of you as the wonderful person that had saved Mandy's life. And then I looked at you and thought, "she has a good face, too". Not that someone who saved Mandy's life would have a *bad* face. Now we're beginning to talk about Mandy as though she wasn't worth saving. Which she is too.'

Mrs Egan came over and hugged her daughter passionately; then she kissed Sylvia full on the lips.

'We just want you here whenever you can come. And stop overnight, of course, if you want to.'

'That's very kind of you, but my home is so near. And then I've got all the family to think of. . . .'

'They didn't seem to be falling all over themselves. . . .'

Sylvia rushed in to cover Mrs Egan's evident embarrassment, 'Captain Calvert's not young any longer, so he couldn't come all this way to fetch me. And my son Harold was out. He's very active with this Goodchild's meadow business.'

'Goodchild's meadow! Oh, Lord!'

'Why? Do you know about it?'

Mrs Egan didn't answer. Instead she said, 'I'm sure they wanted to come. They just knew it was better for you to rest up here for the night. And they were right too.'

'She can't rest much while you keep talking to her, Mummy.'

'Oh, Lord! Isn't it awful? She sounds just like *the* American child. Don't you let Timbo catch you talking in that awful I love Lucy way, Mandy.'

'Well, you're not like Lucy, Mummy. You're far too tall. You're more like that cop that was courting her.'

'Jesus God! She never used to be like that. It's the fault of that awful school. It's so British. She has to act this way in self-defence. Anyway she's right. I ought to be on the job.'

'Yah! What job are you on this morning?'

'Don't be rude, Mandy. Anyhow right now I've got to make a whole raft of sandwiches. They're spraying. And that makes Timbo *really* hungry. Do you know they've got ten men to do that spraying? Isn't that the British for you? You'd think it was the whole state of Kansas instead of a few hundred acres or whatever it is. Do your men like French dressing?'

'Oh, don't make anything for them, please.'

'But they asked themselves for around lunch-time.'

'Oh, they shouldn't have done. It's only because Harold's working that he has to come and fetch me then. But he could have sent a taxi.'

'What, to fetch his wounded mother from a strange house! That would have looked well. How are those lesions, by the way?'

'Lesions?'

'Those cuts on your thigh.'

'Oh, they're all right. But you shouldn't! Cooking for my family after all the trouble I've given you.'

'Look! For the husband and son of the woman who saved Mandy's life I'd stay up all night baking cookies from now to Thanksgiving.'

She got up and left them. Mandy squeezed Sylvia's hand.

'I guess *we* can talk now!'

But in a second her mother's long solemn face peered round the door.

'What were you doing out on that big field anyway?'

'Oh, I walk a lot. But little Mandy . . . ?'

'Oh, Mummy and I go for miles, don't we?'

'I guess we have walked a lot in this place, though I never walked as much as a block at home. But I've promised Timbo . . .' She stopped. 'You must rest.'

Sylvia felt no wish to rest. There were so many things to think about that it was easy enough to dismiss all of them and concentrate solely on this comfortable sense of being made a fuss of. So many things happened in this house that she couldn't agree with – knee-length jeans, spoilt children, being kissed on the mouth – and she felt happy with all of them; it seemed wisest not to think further.

'Making sandwiches! That's all she does. That and salad dressing. There isn't enough here for her to do.' Mandy sounded grown-up and solemnly critical.

'A farmer's wife always has something to do, Mandy.'

'How do you know?'

'I was born on a farm. My mother never stopped working. There were always jobs.'

'Like what?'

'Well, there was the pig swill to mix.'

'If you mean hogs, we don't have them.'

'Then there were the eggs to collect. That meant a regular old hide and seek. And then they had to be washed. . . .'

'I should hope so. But that's all done by the graders. Anyway what do you mean hide and seek?'

'Well, you could never tell where they'd lay. I remember one old brown hen, she'd lay like as not in the nettles one week. And then just when we'd got used to that, she'd lay in the hen-house to fool us.'

'Were they *loose*? Do you mean they went round the place as they pleased?'

'Yes, they'd run all over the farm. . . .'

'Oh!' Mandy paused in thought. 'Well, ours don't.'

'Then there was the milking and the separating and filling the churns. And sometimes we'd make cheeses. . . .'

'Cheeses! Oh, well, maybe *they* do too. I don't know. The milk's all taken by the Co-operative.'

'Then sometimes there'd be ducks' eggs to collect.'

'Ducks' eggs! Why, they're the most dangerous things to eat. Everyone knows that. They give you amoebic dysentery or something.'

'Oh, I don't think so. They're a bit rich, of course. But they make a nice change. And then there's fruit to bottle and jam to make.'

'We don't eat jam. I guess Mummy bottles. Doesn't that sound funny? But that's only a few days in the year.'

'Well, then there's hoeing.'

'What's that?'

'Weeding in between the rows of wheat and that.'

Again Mandy considered. 'I think that's done by machines. Yes, of course it is. Anyway, Mummy doesn't go out in the cornfields. What else?'

'There used to be gleaning. But I suppose these days . . .'

'Gleaning ! That's in the Bible. About Ruth. Did you go gleaning?'

'Oh yes. On some farms they used to let the village women come in to glean. But we couldn't afford to lose it. No matter how hot it was, we would all set out. Five of us there were and Mother and Aunt Betty. You had to go ever so slow or you'd miss something. Like grandmother's steps it was.'

'What's that?'

Sylvia laughed. 'Haven't you ever played grandmother's steps?'

'No. My Grandmother's still in Victoria, but she's going to live in California as soon as Grandpa's estate is settled. She hates Victoria.'

'One of you is chosen to stand with her face to a tree. And then the others creep up on her. She has to count five or ten, I forget which, and then she may turn round. And if she catches anyone moving, they have to go back to the beginning. They mustn't move at all. The fun was the funny positions you had to keep. My brother Ted kept right on one toe for it must have been five minutes. I can see it now, like a ballet dancer. Then he fell in the mud.' Sylvia shook the bed with her laughter.

Mandy looked at her a little suspiciously. 'I wouldn't have thought that was so funny for him.'

'Nor it was. Not for any of us, especially me, if you'd known my mother. But mostly we were too busy to get into real trouble. Gooseberry picking. Now that was a job. . . .'

'Are you still talking? Oh, for Heaven's sake, Mrs Calvert, I don't mean you. I mean Mandy. It's getting on for a quarter of twelve.'

'Oh dear! They'll be here soon. And I'm not dressed, not even up.'

'Well, what of it? I suppose they can drink Scotch and wait as well as other men. Now, Mandy, let Mrs Calvert get up and dress.'

'But Mummy, do you know all the things she did when she was little?'

'No, dear, you can tell me this evening.'

'Well, let me tell you some of them now. Please. Only the ones beginning with G. Gleaning, and grandmother's steps, and gargling with salt and water and goose-feather plucking, and playing gooseberry . . .'

'Playing gooseberry! I'm sure Mrs Calvert never did that.'

'I'm afraid I did once.' To her surprise Shirley Egan waited for her to go on. 'It was at Lady Pembroke's at the hospital when Arthur, that's Captain Calvert, started courting me. There was another girl worked there – an Irish girl, Annie her name was. A nice girl but a bit backward. She was walking out with a Canadian, he'd been hit in the stomach. He was good-looking but he talked rather big. Of course a lot of the Canadians turned out to be bad lots. Well, we were to go out, all four of us, over to Weymouth. Quite an expedition in those days. Then Arthur had one of his bad turns. I didn't want to go. But we'd booked the excursions and you couldn't waste two tickets. Of course if Arthur hadn't been courting, we'd have taken another young chap along. But as it was I had to play gooseberry. And it wasn't a nice day's outing at all, I can tell you. Not with what that Canadian was after. He was trading on Annie being a bit simple, of course. He could have killed me for being there. But I stuck out if only to help the poor girl. Once he got so wild, he started shouting at me. Arthur was furious when he heard about it later. I was afraid there might be a fight, which could have meant a court martial of course. Though mind you, they were officers . . .'

'Shirl! Shirl!' Mr Egan's deep bass, very grand English voice interrupted a reminiscence of Sylvia's about her honeymoon with Arthur in the New Forest – 'Arthur doesn't believe me to this day, but I know it was the same pony . . .'

'Shirl! Shirl!' The voice was loud and carried all over the house.

'Well, come on up, Timbo.'

Outside the door Mr Egan said, 'It's twelve thirty, darling. What's happening about lunch?'

'Oh, Lord! Well, come on in.'

'Is that all right, Mrs Calvert?'

Sylvia said yes, but her voice was drowned by, 'Come on in, Daddy!' 'Well, of course it's all right, Timbo. Do you think I'd tell you to come in if it wasn't?'

He came in – more handsome even than Sylvia had remembered from her exhausted pain-fogged vision of the night before – so tall and fair with deep-set blue eyes and a scar on his chin.

'This *is* Mrs Calvert's bedroom, Shirl.'

'Oh, Timbo, and you bandaged her thigh last night. I don't know. The *minds* of the British!'

'That was professional, darling.'

'That wars profesharnal,' Shirley's imitation made Mandy laugh.

'Wouldn't you know right away, Mrs Calvert, that he'd taught school? Yeh, that's what he was doing when I met him. Geems mastah at a boy's public school in Victoriah. Oh, very British. Thank the Lord his aunt died and left him this place. So he could quit. I don't say I'm crazy about Britain. But Victoria! I used to think Vancouver was bad enough when the engineering company sent Dad up there. But Victoria! Oh, boy! No, I guess if it can't be home it may as well be Murrel Farm.'

'Now we've had your piece, Shirl, I'll say mine. I was rather glad too. Teaching little boys is a disgusting job. They smell so.'

'Oh, for Heaven's sake, Timbo, you'll do something terrible to Mandy, like putting her off boys. . . .'

'I don't think little boys smell, Daddy. At least there is one boy at school, Marcus Campkin, who does smell a bit. He smells like . . .'

'I don't think we want to hear how Marcus Campkin smells, Mandy. Now go down and get lunch ready, Shirl. You're a slattern. And you get back to your own bed, Mandy. If you're well enough to come into someone else's room, then you're a double slattern to be in your night-gown.'

Mrs Egan got up and lifted Mandy out of Sylvia's bed. 'Off we go.' Turning at the door she said to her husband. 'Mrs Calvert's son, who's coming to pick her up, teaches smelly little boys, darling.'

'Oh, Lord! Said the wrong thing, did I? I'm sure it's not at all the same kind of teaching, is it, Mrs Calvert?'

'Oh, don't worry about Harold. He often laughs at himself.' Sylvia hoped this was true.

'Often laughs at himself? Whatever for?' Shirley Egan was puzzled. 'Oh, I see what you mean. Yes, and Mrs Calvert thinks Canadians are a bad lot too.'

'Shirl's determined to make mischief between us, Mrs Calvert. But don't worry, I shan't be Canadian much longer. I'll be back to British in three months' time.'

'Oh dear! I only meant in the Great War, and I'm sure it was only those noisy few.'

'After saving Mandy's life you have *carte blanche* to mean anything you like.'

'To come and land myself on you and then to say things . . . I didn't know. . . . What a thing for a guest to say.'

'Look, Mrs Calvert, get this clear. Shirley and Mandy both like you. As far as I'm concerned that's all that matters. It's the only criterion I make for guests in this house.'

He gave her such a friendly smile that for a moment she almost thought he too was going to kiss her. She knew she wouldn't have minded.

'Oh, God! That's them,' Shirley turned to her husband: 'We're very pleased to see Mrs Calvert's family, darling.'

'Well, of course. It's just that nothing's . . . Oh, shut up and come on down and talk to them.'

As they went from the bedroom Shirley asked: 'What shall I say if they want to come up?'

'Tell them I'm all right and that I'll be down very soon.'

From the passage Tim Egan's voice carried, 'If *they* want to come up? Really, darling, they're her family, not the plumbers.'

'Well, they might as well have been plumbers last night. . . .'

Sylvia tried to hear no more, but her sense of well-being was complete when Shirley's highest note floated up the stairs to her, 'I'm going to spoil her a little. That's what I'm going to do.'

She didn't even try to tell herself that Mrs Egan meant Mandy.

For all that, it was a full minute before anyone was conscious of her arrival in the big parlour downstairs. Harold was holding forth to Tim Egan, and Arthur, with Mandy, now swathed in a thick blue dressing-gown, on his knee, was telling one of his stories to Shirley. Sylvia felt a pang of jealous fear that perhaps he had already taken over the little girl from her. The next second Mandy had clambered down from her perch and rushed towards her.

'Here she is! Here she is! There was smoke too, wasn't there?'

'Yes, dear.'

'Well, when *he*,' pointing at Arthur, 'was nearly struck by lightning there was only flame. That's what *he* says.'

Sylvia felt a rush of relief and with it a sudden affectionate

234

warmth for her husband and all his old tricks. She walked across and kissed him on the cheek. He was genuinely moved, she thought, as he held her for a moment. Then he turned back to the Egans, and there were tears in his eyes.

'Thank God! Old Sylvia's all right.' His voice trembled. 'I don't want to go through another night of anxiety like last night, thank you,' he patted Sylvia's arm, 'but I'll be all right – don't worry.' Sylvia looked away. Some of his old tricks were a bit much. Happily he was quickly absorbed again in the story he was telling Shirley. 'So this old magistrate cove looked down at me through his spectacles. "You appear to be a pretty disreputable sort of fellow," he said, "but you've done a deed of great bravery." I couldn't help smiling to myself, but I simply said, "Thank you, your honour." It never does, you know, to argue with the law, especially in this country.'

But Sylvia was drawn away from Arthur's exploits by her son's attentions.

'So you're a heroine, Mother. I'm very glad of it. Very glad.'

He kissed her on the forehead and smiled across to Tim Egan at the little tableau. Tim didn't smile back.

'Do you realize, Mother, that Egan leases Goodchild's meadow? I've just been trying to explain to him what an important chap he is. The Committee's been trying to get in touch with him for months. We'd hoped to get him along to a meeting, but these farmers are so busy. However, as he's on our side anyway . . .'

'That's it.'

'We're demanding a Public Hearing from the Ministry, you know.'

'Oh, you're *those* people. . . .' Shirley cried.

Tim interrupted Shirley, 'I'll freshen your drink, Calvert,' and he moved off with Harold's glass. As Tim seemed intent on his duties as host Harold addressed the room at large.

'That Carshall people should have good farmland well-farmed running through the centre of their conurbation lies at the basis of everything the New Towns stand for.'

After a silence, Shirley said, 'Well, if sincerity can raise mountains . . .'

'Remove,' Tim said, 'or better still level.'

Shirley giggled. Sylvia realized that up to that moment she had not heard any of the Egans laugh.

'Our neighbours the county and the farmers don't seem so keen on Carshall New Town.'

'Oh, the county! Aren't they ghastly?'

'I'm not devoted to them as a class,' Harold underlined the mock moderation of his words, 'but it's the positive aspect I want to stress. The artificial division between town and country. . . .'

'Look, I think I'd better make things clear. I'm appealing for the right to keep my lease of Goodchild's meadow purely out of sentiment. And not my own sentiment either. My aunt's. The land had belonged to her family for centuries and when the New Town came along it almost broke her heart. However the fact that the architect's plan allowed for the survival of this strip of meadow, even though it was only on a lease, was something. It seems absurd, but I understand how she felt. All the rest, Murrel Farm and Oakhurst, belonged to my uncle – he was a rich man anyway. But this was what my aunt had brought to him on her marriage. And so I'm willing to offer a piece of good land from here in place of Goodchild's meadow, which by the way is only passable grazing. It's quite insane, but it makes up for all sorts of bad conscience which is my own personal affair. And if I don't win the appeal, well I shall have done my best.'

There was a silence after this speech too. As Shirley had covered up for Harold, Sylvia thought she ought to say something now – a woman can often tide over these tensions.

'I don't think anybody could say fairer than that.'

But Harold was unappeased. 'Well, I shan't give up hope of bringing the wider issues home to you. We'll send you the literature we've got out.'

'He's going to send the literature, Timbo. We'll surely read that, Mr Calvert.'

As they left Mandy said, 'What time will you come to-morrow?'

'Oh, you've had enough of me to go on with.'

'No, we haven't, have we, Mummy?'

'I wish you would come, if you can. I'll come and get

you in the car. I don't want Mandy going back to that school for a while. Not after that shock. If you could be with her . . . I'm just so busy on the farm. Besides, I'm just getting so I can understand every word you say, which is more than I do with most British.'

'That's 'cause she's not talking funny any more.'

Sylvia blushed with pleasure at the confirmation of her own guess.

'Well, really, I don't know . . .'

'You'd better make up your mind to come often, Mrs Calvert. You're Mandy's latest craze. And then Shirley likes to see people. The right people that is. She doesn't see too many these days. You heard her view of the county.'

Harold said finally, 'Mother will look forward to it, won't you?'

'Well, you seem quite a favourite with them, Mother,' he told her as they drove back to 'The Sycamores'. 'This may be very important. It's been impossible to get in touch with these people before and I can't feel even now that Egan is as strong a support as I'd like.' He added, 'We're glad to have you back safe and sound though.'

'Pretty little girl that, but spoilt. Why the hell they wanted to toast the sandwiches, I can't think.'

'It's the American way, Arthur.'

'They're Canadians actually, Mother.'

'Well, dear, Mr Egan is. But Mrs Egan comes from the United States, I believe.'

But Harold couldn't agree. 'I think you'll find they're Canadians.'

Whatever they were, throughout those warm, sunlit June and July days, Sylvia found them wonderful company, not least wonderful because it was she they called on to entertain them, to surprise them. And, in surprising them, she often surprised herself.

It was the fiction that she was at Murrel Farm only, or almost only, for Mandy. And in the first weeks for whole afternoons the fiction would reign. She and the small girl would set out for country walks together; but they never went far. Long country walks were out of the question; neither Shirley's anxieties nor the small girl's remembered fears nor Sylvia's own physical powers would allow them to go further than the kitchen garden or the paddock. The stroke, that might have seemed an inevitability to Sylvia in her days of depression, a savage beast camouflaged amid the sad, grey flora of her melancholy world, had struck her now in her new-found happiness as a warning, as a challenge to survive. She ceased to fuss herself about her health, but she took more care than she had ever done in her life before.

The long walks were out, Sylvia's corpulence even allowed them the happy excuse of a joke: between Mandy and her it was quite agreed that if fat people walked too long in the heat, they just melted away like candle grease.

For Mandy, walking between the box hedges, freeing a blackbird from the nets over the currant bushes, helping to pluck asparagus, helping to pick strawberries, just helping, were all activities that demanded a constant transfusion of Sylvia's childhood memories – all to be retailed to her mother with quick-fire wonder: 'Do you know, she used to think you could tell who liked butter by putting flowers under their chins?' 'Do you know, she wore a pinafore and a straw bonnet, and donkeys wore bonnets too?' 'Do you know, her mother used to put a peeled onion in her ear if she had the earache? Isn't it awful?' 'Do you know, she knew an old woman that had drunk soup made of mice to cure a cold?' Do you know, do you know? Sylvia once coming into the room and hearing Mandy talking about her, thought suddenly, 'I'm the fat lady in the fair'; but happy fat lady if she was loved so much.

It was all in the telling and retelling for Mandy. Real buttercups picked in the paddock and held under her chin soon palled; Sylvia trying to recall the few real names of wildflowers she had once learnt from Mrs Longmore, early renounced her efforts, for Mandy only wanted to know 'What did *you* call them?' Grandmother's steps remained a constant favourite in anecdote, but failed entirely as a game played before the walnut tree, even with Shirley enlisted to swell the team. Sylvia had not known she could remember so much about her childhood, and not only her own but Ted's – 'Do you know what? Her brother Ted went to sea and nobody knows if he got drowned or not!';

and Bertie's – 'Do you know, her brother Bertie went to Australia and nobody ever missed him, isn't that terrible, not to be missed?'; and Violet's – 'She had a sister called Violet whose nose was always running, wasn't that horrible, but she isn't dead like the others, she lives in Leeds'; and Rosie's – 'She had an awful sister called Rosie who was mean as mean.' Yet she did remember them more and more – memories that came from she couldn't really tell where of long, happy summer country days, or so they turned out to have been as Mandy picked them up in wonder and turned them over and handed them back for more detail and more wonder.

These childhood days retailed to Shirley by Mandy then became even more wondrous and sweeter, for Shirley, to Sylvia's surprise, was a mother careful to extract the smallest grit from the knowledge her child digested. 'I don't think Mrs Calvert meant that her father actually kicked the cat, dear. Though heaven knows we all want to kick things sometimes,' or again, 'Mrs Calvert's mother *talked* about hellfire, dear, like lots of people did in those days. But it was only a way of speaking. I expect we say a lot of things that'll sound pretty funny fifty years from now.' She explained her view directly to Sylvia. 'I know kids have to have a lot of roughage in their food, but I think there'll be time enough for all the other kind of roughage later on. And that *doesn't* mean I want Mandy to play "Pooh Sticks" or any awful whimsy like that.'

Her own tastes in Sylvia's reminiscences were more adult. She couldn't hear enough about hotel life in England: 'Eight maids slept in one room? The old people get reduced rates by agreeing to give up their rooms in the summer? It's not *true*! I don't believe it! Well, I guess we have the same kind of thing at home, I just don't happen to have run into it. And yet again I don't *believe* it! . . . No medicine bottles allowed on the tables! For heaven's sake, what was it, a convalescent home? Chamber pots in every room! They had to carry them downstairs! Bread and dripping for the staff supper – well what's *that*? . . . It has all got such an awful, grey *British* sound. "*Private* Hotels"! Why do they have to be private anyway? Isn't that typical? And so like Victoria. Can you blame Mother for deciding to sell everything and go to California as soon as Dad died? She writes me, "I just can't wait to get to Monterey and thaw out a little! . . ." Oh my God, just think of those hotels.'

Sylvia was driven to laughing self-defence. 'You wouldn't give me a very good reference as a manageress.'

'Oh, you! I know you were wonderful. I can't imagine anyone I'd rather have manage me. It's just the set-up. Though sometimes you make me mad! You let them just trample all over you. Well, it's not going to be that way now.'

Sylvia protested at all this praise. 'I really did nothing, you know, just a job,' and, 'You'll be giving me a swelled head and that'll never do.'

But, in fact, she never felt in danger from Shirley Egan's praises any more than from Mandy's wonder, for she didn't really take any notice of what Shirley said; she just let herself relax in the affection which was given her; after all Shirley was almost as much a child as Mandy. She was a little more scared of Tim – catching his English eye at times, she felt as though unwillingly they were in some plot together.

Then one evening he announced that he would drive Mrs Calvert back to 'The Sycamores'. She couldn't think what to say to him; he seemed so ill at ease.

'That oat field's coming on well.'

'You won't always be a seven-day wonder like this, you know. Mandy's a kid. And . . . Shirley's a very enthusiastic person.'

'Oh, of course, they're bound to get tired of me. But you don't mean that I'm coming too often.' Her throat had constricted. But it was he now who was horrified.

'Good Lord! No! Don't get me wrong. Shirley's the loyalest person you can imagine. If you're in with her you're in for life. I only meant that . . . well, you won't mind if the red carpet's replaced one of these days by the ordinary rugs.'

From that moment she was no longer afraid of him either. That he should prove to be such a child as to believe her to be so simple.

'As long as my gabble amuses them . . . But if it didn't . . . well, you don't know what you've all done for me.'

'What you've done for us would impress most people more.' She didn't protest. They weren't the kind of people you had to make polite noises with. And, as a matter of fact, Sylvia felt no great sense of imposing on them. It was true that she talked as she had never done before, but that did not mean that either Mandy or Shirley were silent. They had the power – she couldn't think how – of talking and listening and asking questions all at the same time. Of course, they were young; she could hardly expect to have their energy. It was good enough that she kept up her own end and enjoyed it.

As Tim had predicted and as she had expected, in the second week of July the situation changed. Perhaps it was that for a few days the beautiful warm weather gave way to a strong south-west wind driving squally showers before it. Mandy, who could not go out, suddenly showed a passionate affection for Miss Hurry, the school, and all the children in it.

'Well, you can't go back this term, because there isn't any term to go back to. They've shut down until the fall.'

Mandy then changed her tack to her general isolation from other children.

'I don't like being an only child. It's bad. Always being with old people.'

'Oh, not that again!'

But Mandy was stuck fast in the groove of an old record that Sylvia had not heard before.

'You had lots and lots of brothers and sisters, didn't you, Mrs Calvert? And you had a very, very happy childhood.'

'There were many hard times.'

Mandy gave them both a challenging look. 'Hard times aren't so bad when you've someone to share with.'

'God in Heaven! She's gotten hold of a Shirley Temple script!' In fact, she didn't stay with it long. The next day Sylvia came up to the farm, Mandy was friendly and more polite than usual, but she was busy all the afternoon with games of her own. Once or twice they heard her singing, 'Hard times aren't so bad when you've someone to share with,' to a wailing blues tune she'd invented for herself.

The incident, however, pricked Sylvia's conscience. 'You know, I *didn't* have a very happy childhood,' she was sitting mending the hem of one of Mandy's dresses. 'In fact it wasn't happy at all. I don't know how it is that Mandy's got that impression. I never thought . . . I suppose I just didn't want her not to like the stories I told her. But now I'm afraid she's got such a false picture. You see we were very poor and Father's was a very small farm and bad land and then he drank. They were both disappointed really, he and mother. Oh, it wasn't anybody's fault. But being the eldest I got the brunt of it. I couldn't have told little Mandy what my childhood was really like. I suppose I should have said nothing. But you mustn't think I lied to the child.' Sylvia talked on hoping Shirley was going to say something, but she didn't. She came to an abrupt halt and there were minutes of silence.

'You see, people say that the old farm ways were better, but . . .'

'People say? Awful people!'

'Well, I suppose we lived nearer to the land but . . .'

'But it was kind of muddy.' Shirley stubbed out her cigarette.

'This is going to be hard for a kid of seven to understand. How about if we say nothing about it? I don't think Mandy's going to be the type to do a lot of research on British farming conditions in the days of good Queen Vic . . .'

'I'm not quite as old as that.'

'Well, whenever it was. Queen Mary or who.' After another silence she said, 'It seems kind of jesuitical doesn't it. Not telling Mandy, I mean. But there you are that's wonderful Britain for you. But we ought to talk about you. Weren't you ever happy as a kid?'

'Oh, it wasn't as bad as all that. Yes, it *was* pretty bad sometimes. I don't think I really knew how bad. Except that once I spent a wonderful happy morning . . .' She told Shirley about that hot morning of 1911 and about Mrs Longmore.

'What a b-i-t-c-h.'

'No, not really. I don't think she knew what she'd done. We were the poor, you know.'

'What's that got to do with it?'

'Well, the poor in those days . . .'

242

There was again some minutes' silence before Shirley spoke.

'You frighten me, Mrs Calvert. You're so vulnerable.'

'Oh, I shouldn't be hurt like that now. I know being old's childish, but it's not the same as being a child, is it? And a poor child too. People say the poor are tough. And, of course they put up a good front. But I think it's very easy to hurt poor people. It's not like that now though. I'd like to see our old rector's wife trying to talk to the people in the New Town like she talked to my mother. Oh yes, it was bad to be poor in those days. Very bad. There was always the fear of being sold up. They were bound to be hard and quick-tempered. Mother and Father, I mean. I see that now. Mother could forgive you anything but trying to get away from it. Oh, she was wild when I left the Rectory and went to Lady Pembroke's – it was a hospital and all that far off and for officers! Although of course I was only in service still. But she took the whole war like that – with land-girls on the farm. And then the last straw came when I married Arthur. She put it on to his swearing and gambling. But it wasn't that really. It was my starting the boarding-house of my own. Poor Mother!'

'Oh, Lord! I don't think people have the right to be that grouchy. Why, that way the world could never change. You had a right to happiness even if she couldn't have it. I don't know whether you found it?'

Sylvia answered quickly to that.

'Oh, I've been too busy to think about that. Of course there have been bad times. Terrible ones. When the police told me that Iris had been killed by that lorry, I thought I'd scream and shout the house down and I wouldn't have cared if the world had tumbled with it. I always felt closer to her, you see. She liked things neat and then, although she was only fourteen, she looked after the house as though it were her own. She said she'd like to be a nurse. Of course she was too young to know really. But you've no idea the strangers that crowded into the house. I suppose they always do with accidents. I couldn't care for appearances, I just cried and cried.'

'Good Lord! of course you did. What else would you do?'

'Well, nobody wants to give themselves away before strangers.'

'Oh, nuts! Who cares about strangers? Anyway what do you mean "give yourself away"? That's how you felt, isn't it? What did you want them to think, that you didn't care if your daughter *was* killed?'

'No, of course not. But making a scene never does any good.'

'Making a scene? I don't think I understand. Oh, you mean letting yourself go. Well, for God's sake, why not? If that's how you felt.'

Sylvia tried to explain.

'You don't want to make a fool of yourself, do you? As Arthur always says, "You've got to be one up on other people." And you can't be that if you give yourself away.'

It was clear, however, that Shirley didn't really understand. Not that she didn't have clear views on many of Sylvia's family problems when they came up in the course of conversation. For instance, she set Sylvia's mind at rest about Mark's leaving home; she was so certain that he was right – 'Good for him!' And again she gave a reason at once for all the tension between Harold and Judy. 'Well, *of course* she fights with him. She's in love with him. Seventeen? I guess I was finally fixed on boys by then, but around fifteen I was completely overboard about Dad. She's a little late, but after all this is Britain.'

On the whole though Sylvia kept off 'The Sycamores' at Murrel Farm just as she said little about the Egans when at home. One of the happiest features of this new routine had proved to be the easing of life at 'The Sycamores'. She no longer felt the guilt of her unhappiness, the strangeness of her long desperate walks coming between her and her family. She carried the shopping and the roster duties (now so increased by Mark's absence and Harold's preoccupation with Goodchild's Meadow) without any sense of strain; she sat in the evenings reading or watching tele without any sense of melancholy. The pleasure that came from her afternoons at the farm lasted all that day and into the next. Of course there were tensions still but she was not their cause.

It was only to be expected that Judy would be keyed up

with those vital examinations right on top of her. Harold, too, had so much to do, but he did seem exceptionally touchy. It was Arthur who worried her most. Yet she did not dare as yet to risk her new-found happiness in order to meet all his familiar troubles half way. She contented herself by doing as good a part by him as she could and laying up strength to face the inevitable rainy day.

There was certainly no inclination on the Egans' part to obtrude upon 'The Sycamores'; but Harold was more restive about Sylvia's double life.

'Does Egan say what *he* thinks the Ministry's decision is likely to be, Mother?' he asked once or twice, and when she answered, 'I don't see much of Mr Egan, dear, and Mrs Egan and I only talk a lot of women's natter, you know,' he said, 'I hope these Egans aren't making use of you, Mother.'

The difference in approach was very clear when the question of her birthday came up. It had never occurred to her that anyone would mention this late July event. Sixty-five was nothing to rouse anyone's interest; it's not even a round number. And yet she found herself offered two celebrations.

'Have you got your Chinese kimono or whatever they call it back from the cleaners, Mother? You'll need it on the 23rd.'

Sylvia had a special face that she'd perfected over the last months for Harold's jokes when she couldn't quite see their meaning.

'Foxed, eh? Well, it is a bit difficult. Because, of course, the 23rd isn't your birthday. But it's the nearest day to it that the Bartleys are free. Muriel wanted us to go ahead without them, but they've been so good at having Dad there for cards since the Cranstons became so impossible. In any case I thought you'd like another woman at the party.' His voice sank to a mumble, 'Family occasions haven't been ideal lately. We miss Beth.'

Then he brightened up again, 'Ah, but of course, you want to know why Chinese. Well, I thought we'd go to Chen Fu's. We're all too busy at the moment to cook except you and it's no fun to cook your own birthday dinner. Besides, I've told Ray to tell Mark he'll be welcome. I suppose he won't refuse to wish his grandmother many happy returns. I'm perfectly happy to see him, but as long as "The Sycamores" is not good enough for him to sleep at, I'm afraid it's too good for him to use as a casual restaurant. However, Chen Fu's is very good. People are often surprised that the New Town's only restaurant should be Chinese, but Beth didn't agree at all. She always said it was quite logical, since Chinese cuisine is about the only decent thing you can't prepare at home in the average modern kitchen. I would have left the whole thing as a complete surprise, but I thought you might like to invite your farming friends. Egan really ought to meet Muriel. After all, she's the woman who's trying to save his meadow for him.'

Sylvia said she would ask Shirley, but she doubted if they would leave Mandy at night. 'I've been baby-sitter for them once or twice, but I can't help out this time.'

Harold didn't laugh. 'You'd better not tell me any more about the way that child's spoilt or I shall begin to regret that you saved it from the fires of heaven.'

She had guessed Shirley's excuse correctly or nearly correctly.

'Isn't that nice of Mr Calvert, Timbo? But Mandy just hates being taken out at night, so I'm afraid we'll have to say no. It would be kind of silly to come to your birthday party without her. How about if *we* give a birthday picnic the next day? Mandy would like that. You can take the day off, Timbo, and provide champagne.'

'I don't know if . . . That would be a Thursday, you see, and Mark and Ray at any rate wouldn't be able . . .'

'Oh, I had thought just you and us,' Shirley sounded stunned. She hesitated but more it would seem for Sylvia's agreement than in any consideration of change of plan. Sylvia, though a little guilt-striken, was quick to accept.

'Oh, goody! We'll go to what-you-may-call-it, that olde worlde place by the river. Mandy likes that. It'll be lots of fun.'

Sylvia's pleasure was only marred by a certain shame that she looked forward so much more to Shirley's improvised outing than to Harold's carefully planned dinner.

There was such a muddle about the table when they

arrived at Chen Fu's that they stood for quite five minutes. Sylvia had plenty of time to look around her. It was rather a small room but this was made up for by the brightly coloured Chinese décor. The paint work was scarlet with thick gold Chinese squiggles embossed on it. The lighting was subdued and intimate except for the big central Chinese lantern which was emerald green with scarlet tassels and a pattern of some scarlet figures – fish or something – that moved slowly round the light. The hushed lighting made it difficult for Sylvia to see everything, but you could tell that the two pictures on the wall were Chinese because they were long and thin and without frames; they, too, were in bright emerald with some black marks, perhaps also fishes, or maybe birds. Clearer were two big coloured photographs of a town that looked like America – all skyscrapers – but Ray said it was Hong Kong or Shanghai or Singapore or somewhere. There were also two big coloured photographs of girls, one in an emerald green dress with a purple flower, and the other in a strawberry pink bikini with an apricot-coloured carnation over one ear. Only when you looked the second time did you see that they were not ordinary pin-up girls but Chinese. It would all perhaps have seemed a bit too brightly coloured, if it hadn't been for the subdued lighting. Even then it needed dressing quietly for, as poor Muriel Bartley must have soon felt. She was wearing a very tight purple sweater and a very tight daffodil yellow tweed skirt, and had put on her heaviest lilac eye shade. Really Sylvia could hardly bear to look at her in that setting of scarlet and emerald.

Arthur, on the other hand, had his old eyes riveted to Muriel's breasts, which seemed to Sylvia to dominate the restaurant like two huge plums. It was lucky Muriel was the sporty type, Sylvia thought, for when he was in a silly mood he had no sense of shame. But either Muriel was out of sorts or else she wasn't such a sport when it came down to it – she loosened her sweater the little that she was able to and turned to Arthur.

'Do you mind, Captain Calvert? This isn't the Windmill, you know.'

Her tone was quite sharp. She moved away from him and

whispered in her husband's ear as they waited for Harold to settle the question of their table.

There was no easy solution to seating. The dozen tables at Chen Fu's were arranged six to each side of the room, in intimate dark recesses with back-to-back seats. They were ideal for parties of two or four, but difficult for the Calvert party of eight.

'Well,' Harold said to his waiting guests, 'it seems we have to split up. I suggest Judy and Mother with me, Ray and Mark with Dad over the way there. Then a Bartley apiece. Geoff, you'd better be at Mother's table, and Dad'll look after Muriel.'

'I'd rather Muriel sat with us, Harold. Park yourself here, Kid,' Geoff indicated to his wife the place where Judy was about to sit.

'Very well,' Harold was puzzled. 'You go and sit with your Granddad then, Judy.'

'Yes, come here, Judykins. We'd rather have the rose-bud, wouldn't we, Ray? These tables are a bit small for the last rose of summer.'

'Please, Daddy, I'd rather stay at your table.'

'What do you mean? There's no place . . .'

'Please, Daddy, please.' Judy's voice was quite hysterical.

'Let her do what she wants, Dad. She's just finished a week's hellish exams.'

But if Ray was concerned for his sister, Sylvia had no thought for anyone but Arthur. She could see by the way his hand trembled as he appeared intent on the menu that he was feeling one of his rare shames.

'I don't see why I shouldn't be allowed the honour of sitting next to Arthur even if he is my husband. I don't often blow his trumpet for him. But in all my sixty-five years I've never met a better story-teller and I can't think of better company for my birthday.' As she made her little speech she moved across and sat down beside him. She was quite out of breath with indignation. She took his hand under the table.

'Well?' she said, 'Wotcher, cock?' It was one of his favourite expressions.

'Wotcher, Liza.'

Heads close together, they studied the menu and laughed

at the names. Arthur was particularly pleased with the entry 'Chou Sai Ho Fun (Fried Rice Sticks)'.

'Fun Sticks!' he whispered to Sylvia. 'Those'll just about suit Betty Big Bubs.' And when she managed through her laughter to hush him, he said, 'I was just warning the missus off the bit of fun they offer here.'

Everybody looked so silent and solemn that Sylvia felt the devil raised in her. She giggled and whispered as she'd hardly done since they'd been courting.

'Carry on all and don't mind us. Pity Arthur didn't bring his pig-tails.'

But the party remained obstinately silent until Mark tried to help out.

'Some of the names are pretty grim certainly, Gran. Goo Yoo Luk!' He laughed, but even then the others only smiled faintly. After their earlier treatment of Arthur it made Sylvia feel wild. Very much the little ladies and gentlemen they all were with their posh foreign restaurants! Well . . . the lot of them, even Mark, putting them at their ease; what business of his was it? She and Arthur weren't ladies and gentlemen and never had been, but just because they were old didn't mean they couldn't get a kick out of life.

She said loudly, 'Oh, it isn't just *any* of the names, Mark. You want to look again. Fun sticks! We girls'll have to be careful of them, won't we, Mrs Bartley?'

Ray started to giggle, but turned his laughter into a cough. Then when Arthur had joined her in a good wheezing laugh, they announced their intention of ordering from the side of the menu headed, 'English Fare.'

Later, seeing Harold's face, Sylvia felt a bit contrite because after all he'd gone to all this trouble and expense for her. But really that Soapy Sam stuff made her sick! However she did ask to taste his sweet and sour pork and pronounced it excellent. She also drank liberally of the vin rosé he ordered, although it was sour enough to give you the gripes.

'I'm awfully glad you were able to come along, Geoff,' Harold had given their orders and his voice was now loud, bright and formal: it seemed to Sylvia that he was officially opening the proceedings and placing all their earlier unsuitable talk as prologues off the record. 'You're not

249

easy people to get hold of with all the social life you lead.'

'Don't look at me, Harold, look at her ladyship. She's the one who carts us out every night on these soup and fish larks. I told her the other day, "What we bought a house with two lounges for, I don't know". To keep her famous dolls in, I suppose. I'm a simple stay-at-home chap, you know, underneath the mask.'

'And what a mask! Did you ever see such pouches under the eyes, Harold! He could carry his loose cash in them.'

'What about all those poker nights, Geoff? You're at home then. I look on "Sorbetts" as a sort of do-it-yourself casino.'

'Oh, we haven't had a poker game for over a month,' Muriel's mouth snapped as she said it.

'But Dad's been . . .' Harold was bewildered. He looked across the room towards Arthur, but the old man had begun a long story to his grandsons. 'I must have misunderstood him. He will miss your poker games though, especially since the Cranstons have turned so funny.'

'I shouldn't criticize Renee and Jack too much if I were you, Harold. I'm sure the remedy's in Captain Calvert's own hands.'

Geoff intervened, 'No, you're wrong, Muriel. Once bitten twice shy. I'm not starting that poker game up again, not even if the Captain's famous dividends start paying. What is it? Tin mines in Tooting or copper in Camberwell? I always forget.'

Looking at Harold's perplexed face, Sylvia found it difficult to believe that he hadn't cottoned on at once. But then, of course, it was years since he'd had first-hand experience of Arthur's ways. Well, he'd got a shock coming to him. Meanwhile she set herself to move to Arthur's defence. After all, whatever he'd done she wasn't having him got at in public. But she needn't have worried, Arthur had taken over his own case. Ignoring the Bartley's remarks, he raised his voice to include the whole party in the anecdote he was telling Mark.

'No, he's a very good fighting man, your Chink. We had a few labour-detachments of them with us in Flanders, you know. And they spoiled for a fight. Not like our ancient and honourable ally the Pork and Cheese. I was in charge of a crowd of Hun prisoners of war at the time. Order to protect them. Protect my Aunt Fanny! Well, the Boche 'planes came over – it was late in '17 – and straffed these poor bloody Chinks to hell. The next day I was sitting in the mess when the sergeant comes in, "Major Calvert, sir. Come at once. The Chinks have run amok!" 'Course when I came out the German prison compound wasn't there. Blown to smithereens. Just a bit of wire and guts left. The Chinese were quite open about it, "German killee Chinese. Chinese killee Germans." They'd chucked a couple of bloody bombs at them. The colonel went mad when he heard about it "You must make an example of them, Calvert," he said. "If you'll excuse me, sir", I told him, "I'll do no such thing. You can't blame them. It's their philosophy." Well, the long and short of it was that we had a hell of a row, but I managed to get the thing taken to higher ranks. In the end – laugh this one off – it got up to the C.-in-C., and gor blimey, if he didn't come down on the side of yours truly. "Calvert's perfectly right," he said, "it's the Chinese philosophy. It's all in Confucius." That's their equivalent of Jesus Christ, you know.'

'No, I'm afraid I didn't know, old man,' Geoff smiled at the others. 'We're not all as full of information as you, you know.'

'Well, you know now, my friend. Very just chap the C.-in-C. I always got on very well with him.'

'Oh yes,' Geoff laughed, 'we know. You and Lord Kitchener were like that,' he held up two fingers together. 'Swopped marbles as kids.'

'I'm afraid your knowledge of the war that made the world safe for you is a bit deficient. Kitchener was dead. He was, by the same token, one of England's greatest men. But he'd been drowned by Lloyd George in '16.'

'Oh, I say,' Muriel cried, 'we *are* going back to school. Don't forget Geoff's only a common cockney boy.'

'Dead! Well, that wouldn't stop him, would it? So many of your pals have done their best work when they're dead. The Captain was telling us last month about what he did for Bonar Law in the General Strike. Of course it was way before our time. Then it was fire-watching with Douglas Haig. Well, even I smelt a rat there.'

'Yes,' said Muriel, 'Lord Haig. The poppy man, you know. He'd been dead for years when the war broke out. . . .'

'So I looked up this Bonar Law bloke,' Geoff went on. 'Well, if he *was* in the General Strike, he must have looked a nasty mess, he'd been in his grave four years.'

Sylvia looked to Arthur. It wouldn't be the first time she'd seen him shrug that sort of thing off. But by her side sat a shrunken old man, like a humped wet rooster. His dejected look seemed to silence everyone; even the Bartley's hostile jeering notes faded away into the air.

'And how is Mark?' Sylvia asked. Despite everything, and apart from her concern for Arthur, she felt in high spirits.

Geoff Bartley seemed to feel the need to atone to the company. 'I've been hearing big things of you, Mark. Old Mackie talks of you as one of the white hopes of Electrometrico.'

'He won't much longer. I don't think I'm stopping there. I've almost made up my mind to join the Hunger Relief Committee. Perhaps in one of the North African countries.'

'Good for you!'

Mark looked surprised as the rest of them, for the exclamation came from Sylvia in an almost exact imitation of Shirley's accent. She wondered at herself, for she really knew nothing about it. It was just that Mark didn't bother to fit in with all this smug lot.

'I'm glad you're happy about it, Mother. Good God! Mark. Is this what your friends the Forresters have encouraged you to? Let Jimmie Forrester go. I should admire him for it. No doubt he's an excellent sales representative, but they can be spared. But if people like you, trained technicians, give up, we shan't have any surplus with which to feed hungry Africa. For God's sake, man, where's your logic?'

'Your Dad's right, you know, Mark. Look, if you go on at Electrometrico, from what I can make out from old Mackie, you've got a good chance of coming out a three thousand a year man. All right! Feed hungry Africa *then*. That's how I've done it. God knows all Muriel and I do for charity. Orphans, blind, cancer, old folks, you name it, we've given to it. But I made my lolly first.'

'That isn't quite what I meant, Geoff, but . . .' Harold said.

'No, Geoff, you don't understand. Mark's an idealist. After all he's only taking after you, Harold. You oughtn't to be so down on him.'

'Yes, I don't know whether Harold's the best example for the boy, Muriel. No offence, Harold. But you do let things run away with you. At the moment, for example, you're being an awful bloody fool, in my opinion.'

'Now Geoff, you know you promised me not to bring that up. Anyway it's confidential.'

'All right, I know, darling, but I think it's our duty to say something to Harold. Well, look how Muriel's taken the lead. But there's such a thing as going too far. . . .'

'Count me out on this, Harold, I don't agree with Geoff. I'm on your side. Though it's only right perhaps that he should warn you.'

'It's like this, Harold. You don't want Carshall to lose the meadow. And you're right. But Jock Parsons and all the local outfit don't agree. And they're not going to like it better for hearing it from a County Council man. And the County Council aren't going to be happier to have one of their men getting in wrong with the Development Board. They've quite enough quarrels of their own on their plate. . . .'

'The truth is, Harold, since Geoff has gone so far, the Education Committee's more than concerned about it already. I don't know that I should tell you, but as one of the school governors . . .'

'Is that all? Oh, you don't have to worry, they've told me already. It seems that in the County Education Committee's opinion my misguided zeal over Goodchild's meadow threatens to undermine much of the valuable goodwill that I've built up in the fifteen years that I've been Headmaster at Melling. The cheek of it. . . .'

'It is only their opinion, Harold. They've a right to that,' Muriel spat bean shoots over the table cloth in her excitement.

'They've a right to say nothing. It's a matter of personal

conscience. Anyway I'm apparently only undoing the good work I was responsible for in the first place. All right, it's entirely my own affair.'

'Oh really, Harold, as Governor . . .'

But Geoff, vigorously shaking soya on his prawns as the spoke, silenced his wife. 'No, Muriel, it's nothing to do with rights and wrongs. It's simply a question of your own future, Harold. You're tops as Headmaster. Everyone knows that. But nobody's indispensable. Apart from anything else, think what a loss it would be to Carshall if they moved you.'

'Goodchild's meadow's a cause on which Beth felt very strongly.'

'Mother wouldn't have wished you to risk your job, Dad.'

'How very little you know your mother, Ray. She would never have given way to common blackmail.'

Suddenly they were all urging caution on him. And then into the middle of their din Harold's fist crashed down on the table, making the dozen or so dishes rattle and splash.

'I don't want anybody's advice, thank you very much. If nobody believes in principle any longer, I do.'

His tone was so fierce that they were all silenced. Muriel drew herself up straight in her chair and speared a water chestnut delicately with her fork.

'Well, Judy, how did the exams go?'

Judy seemed to Sylvia to have turned into a young woman overnight when her exams ended. She answered Muriel in the grandest way. 'Not at all badly, Mrs Bartley, thank you. There was one beast of a question in the French paper about Corneille; the Unities and all that.'

'Oh, I don't like the sound of the unities, whatever they may be. Do you, Geoff? The things they teach at school these days. Still, I suppose a nice long holiday now.'

'Yes, I hope to go to France. A friend of mine, Caroline Ogilvie, knows of a marvellous French family near Blois – De Clamouarts. They have an old family chateau. It looks quite heavenly from the photos. People say that as long as you go to the Loire, it doesn't matter about the sort of family you stay with. But as Mrs Ogilvie says, that would be all right if it was simply a question of accent. Everyone knows that the purest French is spoken in Tours. But there's still the whole question of the nuances of the language. You can only get that from really good families. The De Clamouarts speak the French of Racine.'

'That should be extremely useful to you in the France of today.' Harold had found an outlet. 'The appalling snobbery . . .'

But the new Judy, as Sylvia saw, was not to be easily beaten.

'You just aren't up to date, Daddy. De Gaulle's France is much nearer to the seventeenth century. . . .'

'There's no need for clever debating points. You know perfectly well what I mean.'

'It isn't a debating point. That's exactly the illusion the English have had about De Gaulle all along. And look what it's cost us. . . .'

'I'm not discussing politics. I'm merely saying that I don't intend to pay large sums for my daughter to spend her time with a lot of French snobs who haven't even grasped that they've had a Revolution.'

'Oh, Daddy, really . . .'

They were as close now and as separated from the rest of the party in their quarrel, as Sylvia and Arthur had been in their jokes.

Both Ray and Mark groaned.

'And people ask why I left home!'

'Go on, lovey, it's your birthday, make them stop.'

To Ray's surprise, Sylvia said loudly, 'They're lovers' quarrels, aren't they really? Judy's probably a bit in love with her Dad. It's a phase that lots of girls go through.'

The remark silenced Harold and Judy for a moment, and, indeed everyone else too. Then as an afterthought, Sylvia laughed and said, 'And Harold's playing hard to get?'

Ray exploded, 'Lovey!'

Mark guffawed.

Harold decided to treat it humorously, 'Go on the De Clamouarts or de Clamooers, Judy. I don't care whether they speak the French of Charlemagne. I'm not having it said even by my venerable mother in her cups on her birthday that I'm playing hard to get with my own daughter.'

Muriel summed it up, 'She's getting proper shocking in her old age, isn't she? But there you are, a birthday has its privileges.'

So they all drank Sylvia's health. And to please Harold and thank him for the dinner, she agreed to try a plate of lychees and cream, although when it came she had the greatest difficulty in getting the stuff down; if there was one thing she couldn't stomach it was anything jellified, and jelly with stones!

It was Judy's comment that really upset her.

'I'm pleased Daddy's come round, of course. But I don't know where you picked that idea up from, Gran. I'm surprised at anyone with your good sense accepting all that. Sex is such a terribly easy answer to everything, isn't it? Miss Chapman was telling us in essay-period last term that Freud was never analysed himself. So the whole thing falls to the ground really.'

Sex! As if she'd meant anything of the sort; and she was sure Shirley hadn't: It really made her wonder what sort of mind Judy had got under that prim little miss exterior of hers. No wonder she made such a hullaballoo when Arthur came out in his birthday suit. The sooner the girl had a boy friend she thought, the better, if that sort of thing was on her mind all the time.

Ray and Mark suggested a drink at 'The Falcon' to round off the evening with, as their share of the treat. Muriel excused herself because of a rotten headache that had come on suddenly; she always seemed to get one at Chen Fu's, it must be the smell from the kitchen. Shepherded by an anxious Geoff into their Humber, she said her thankyous and good-byes and many happy returns with her head back on the tartan seat cover and her lilac eyelids closed.

'They had gone all royal tonight, hadn't they?' Ray said to the disappearing big black car.

Again to Sylvia's surprise, Mark of all people said, 'Poor old Geoff! I shall never marry one of those dolls that get themselves up like tarts. They give nothing when it comes to the point.'

Harold took the remark broadmindedly. 'I think that's a bit crude, Mark, but there's something in it. God knows

Muriel does everything she can to fill her life and I respect her for it, but there's a basic dissatisfaction somewhere, hence all these imaginary aches and pains.'

'Neither she nor Geoff Bartley can take anything on the chin. They haven't a sporting instinct between them.' Arthur was quick to make the point.

But Harold had given up the Cranstons for Arthur's sake and that was enough.

'You're a bit inclined to think that nobody's a sportsman but yourself.'

'My dear boy, I've had a very long experience of the card tables and I know Sheeny sharpers when I meet them. . . .'

'The Bartleys are not Jewish, Dad, and even if they were . . .'

'I don't care what they are,' Judy said, 'I wish Muriel would learn *some* idea of colour. What did she look like?'

Something snapped in Sylvia. 'Oh, shut up all of you. They came to my birthday party and I think they're very nice people.' It wasn't strictly true, but she couldn't stand all this belly-aching.

Things went better in 'The Falcon'. Harold met an old boy of Melling School with his new wife; Arthur found Mr Bolton to talk racing with; Ray and Mark joined up with a party of young friends who'd dropped in for a drink before going to the Mecca; even Judy chatted happily with a younger girl in the party who'd been at the County High until last year. Sylvia sat back with a glass of white port and let herself be comfortable as she thought of the next day's picnic.

She was reflecting how nice it was going to be to have a talk with Tim, although she still felt a bit shy with him, when she saw Mr Corney come into the bar. He was obviously looking for someone. His quick little black eyes seemed to search every corner at once. What a nervous little chap he was, she thought. She caught his eye and he came over.

'Well, Duchess, and how does your grace come to be in this humble hostelry?'

'They're giving me a birthday party, Mr Corney.'

'Sweet seventeen and never been kissed.'

'No, sixty-five, I'm afraid.'

'What, "sixty-five and still alive"? Well! Oh dear, what have I said? Better luck next year, then it'll be sixty-six and out for kicks.'

'Oh dear! No. Much too late for that. But there's life in the old girl yet.'

He was silent. He really seemed quite absent-minded and his eyes still searched round the crowded room.

'Had your holidays yet?'

'What me? Oh no. We're going to Cannes, or at least I hope we are.'

'We?' Sylvia gave him a teasing look.

'Ray and another young chap. Why, hasn't Ray said anything? Well! Funny that! It's the third year running. It's ever so gay in Cannes. Just the place for three bachelors gay.' He gave Sylvia a look she didn't know how to take.

'There you are. All you young people. I've never been out of England.'

He was still only half with her, so she added, 'Ray and Mark are over there with the youngsters. Go and join them.'

'Me? I don't know any of Ray's posh friends, here or in London.'

'Of course you do. That's Priscilla White, the blonde who played the wife in *Look Back in Anger*. And that's Terry Knowles, the good-looking dark boy. Don't they make a handsome trio? A dark and two fair. Like that ad for beer. He played Cliff, that was Ray's friend in the play. They were very good together.'

'So I hear,' he said sharply.

'Didn't you see it then?'

'Oh no. Much too highbrow for me. I'm Ray's low friend, you know.'

He looked so dejected that Sylvia couldn't cope with it.

'Well, let's *both* go over and talk then.'

Ray was a bit off-hand with Mr Corney. 'You know Wilf Corney,' but he didn't say the names of the others.

'Well, I hear it's the Duchess's birthday party.'

'That's it, Wilf,' Mark answered for his brother, 'We're all blown out from Chen Fu's rice.'

'Oh! Chen Fu's. Did you Foo Yung Dan? That's the one I go for.'

He giggled.

Ray burst into a laugh, then scowled. He turned his back on Wilf Corney.

'You know, Pris, I still think Dad directed it wrong in the third act when you come back. He had me right upstage...'

'What goings on!' Mr Corney's smile was malicious. He turned to Terry Knowles. 'I hear you and Ray are doing the piece next time without Miss White.'

Terry Knowles was puzzled. 'What do you mean?'

'They almost played it without me this time.' Priscilla White commented, 'We'd better get going, Terry, if we want to be there for the spot prize.'

Mr Corney bent over Ray and whispered, but when Ray backed away, he said sharply, 'I only thought you'd like to know Pete was here.'

'Are you ready, Ray?'

'I don't think I'll come after all, Pris. I need an early night.'

'Oh, well, you asked yourself. You changing your mind too, Mark?'

But Mark wasn't. He joined the party.

'Why don't you go with them, Judy?' Sylvia asked.

'Because they haven't asked me, Gran,' she whispered.

She looked as though she could have killed Sylvia. A moment later when the dancers left Harold came over.

'Everybody ready for home?'

'Be nice to Judy,' Sylvia said to Harold on one side, 'they've all gone off to a dance without her. Except Ray, that is. He's tired.'

When she looked round Ray was leaving the bar with Wilf Corney. To Sylvia's pleased surprise Harold took his daughter's arm. 'Would you hate a post-mortem, Judy? Or would you like to tell me about your papers? The schoolmaster in me longs to hear.'

Arthur, as he left Mr Bolton, was in less easy mood. 'You'll fix that for me tomorrow morning then.'

'I don't know, Arthur, I can't say. Don't count on it.'

'There's another bastard,' Arthur said as they went to the car.

Sylvia tried to revive their joking mood as they sat in the back. Her contentment was reinforced by the sight of

Harold and Judy chattering so easily in front. But Arthur didn't respond.

'You seem bloody pleased about everything.'

It riled Sylvia. 'As a matter of fact, I am.'

Arthur went straight upstairs to their room. To avoid facing him immediately, Sylvia laid the breakfast table and smoked a cigarette. As she came out of the dining room, Harold's head appeared round his study door.

'I wonder if I could have a word with you Mother. It's about Dad.'

Oh Lord, here it comes, she thought, before I'd settled it all. The Bartleys or the Cranstons must have spoken.

'He seems to have quarelled with the Bartleys now as well as the Cranstons. But that's his affair. What I am concerned with is what he's doing with his time. . . .'

'I'm afraid he just mooches, Harold. You know what Dad's like. He has his ups and downs.'

'Very expensive mooching. Only the other day he came to me and said he was short . . .'

'Oh, Harold, it's too bad. After all you're doing for us. . . .'

'Oh, I don't say it was a lot. But quite enough considering he has nothing to do.'

'How much *did* he borrow, Harold?'

'I didn't mean to tell you of it. But he had ten pounds from me.'

'Ten pounds!'

'Yes. I can't think what he does with it.'

'Can't you? If you've nothing more to say to me, Harold, I think I'll go up to bed.'

'I only want to know what we should do, Mother.'

'Do? After all these years, dear, I don't think there's much to do about it.'

She left him before he could say any more.

Arthur was in bed. Only a pale light from the waning moon outlined the objects in their overcrowded room. Sylvia decided that it would be better to speak in this half-light.

'Arthur dear, I'm sorry about the way those Bartleys talked. But there's nothing we can't put right, I'm sure.'

He began to snore loudly.

'Arthur! You're not asleep, I know. I'm only trying to help you. But I can't help you if you won't help me.'

The snoring grew louder. She wanted to laugh at his childishness, but she feared to offend him and then they would get nowhere.

'How much do you owe? To the Bartleys and the Cranstons, I mean. And to anybody else in Carshall. Let me know it all. I don't want to have to go to them and ask. And we certainly don't want them going to Harold. I've got something put away in the Post Office. You had all the gratuity the hotel gave me for the debts at Eastsea, but there's what I've saved . . .'

He sat up. 'That's right. Throw what you've bloody well done for me in my face.'

'I didn't mean to bring it up, Arthur. It slipped out. But do let me settle this. We've not got so many years left, dear, that we can afford to be miserable. Oh, I know I've been like a wet blanket since we got here, but we could start again.'

In the end he told her. It was more than one hundred and fifty pounds, and, God knew, if it was *all* he owed, this would be the first time he'd come clean. It would make a tidy hole in her savings, but it would have to be faced sooner or later.

'I'll pay them all as soon as I can draw the money out.'

'What do you mean, *you'll* pay them? Very nice that'd look, Mrs Calvert graciously pays her husband's debts.'

'Nobody will look at it like that, Arthur. Anyhow, I'm afraid that's how it's got to be.'

'So you don't bloody well trust me even with a few quid.'

'Oh, Arthur! I don't know how you can say the same things again and again after so many years.'

He grumbled and even shouted at her, but she did not give way. It was lucky she felt so on top of things, otherwise she wouldn't have had the energy to hold out.

'And I suppose you'll tell young master Harold of your wonderful generosity. You and he are a fine pair.'

'I promise you, Arthur, that Harold shan't know anything about it.'

'That's one thing I'm not standing for. That bastard

261

looking down his nose at me. Can't even part with a tenner without a bloody Sunday-school lecture.'

Sylvia laughed, 'I know he's a proper skinflint in some ways. But he's generous in others, dear. Try not to mind it here too much, Arthur. I know things haven't gone well for you this last month. It's a shame after you've tried so hard to fit in. But we just haven't got the money for cards and horses and that.'

'If I had a bit of capital, Sylvie, this last month I could have covered my losses and come out with a small fortune in the end.'

'I'm sure you could have done. But there it is, we haven't got any capital. But things needn't be too bad, you know.'

He rolled over in the bed. 'I'll tell you this, Sylvie, if it wasn't for you, I wouldn't care a damn if I went tomorrow.'

A moment later he was snoring. This time she knew it was genuine.

As she got into bed she stubbed her toe on the bed leg. She should have put on the light. As it was, everything had slipped away once more in Arthur's meaningless sentimentality. Anyhow she felt happy enough these days to give more time to Arthur! – if her time had only been what he wanted, which it wasn't.

It turned out that they were not to be just the Egan family for the picnic, because Mandy had invited Marcus Campkin to join them. He was a plump little boy with huge round dark eyes. To the grownups he said nothing but a scarcely audible, 'Thank you very much, Mrs Egan,' or 'If you please, Mrs Calvert'; but as he and Mandy played on the river bank or among the stumps of a recently cut larch wood near by he seemed never to cease chattering; the further from the three adults the louder his voice sounded in injunctions and commands. Mandy in his presence became obstinately off-hand with her mother and Sylvia, but she sought again and again to show off her father in all his splendour.

'Well, what do you know? So she finally chose Marcus Campkin. None other. I guess smell still counts for a lot at that age. Not that I can smell anything.'

'Shirl! For God's sake, darling.'

'I said I *couldn't* smell anything, Timbo. That's not rude.

Anyhow, good for Miss Hurry. I take back a lot of what I said about that school. I guess I believe too much what I read. I was sure Mandy was going to get taken up by some awful gym mistress or whatever they call them.'

'Shirl! Darling!'

'Well, that's what they do at these public schools for girls, isn't it? But to come back with a boy friend at seven. That's quite something. I know he seems a kind of a dope. But you can't tell with British men. You don't know what Timbo was like, Mrs C., when I first met him. "Ackcherlah I was hoping to work in timbah when I came to Canadah." You should have seen Dad's face. That's when we first called him Timbo.'

'And what about you? "Shirley's a kind of lovely field poppy, Mr Egan."' Sylvia had to laugh at Tim's American lady's accent.

'Oh! For Heaven's sake! That was aunt Pearl. She's nuts.'

They had brought a chair of red striped canvas and steel for Sylvia so that she sat a little above them as they lay on the rug – Tim stretched out flat, Shirley propped with cushions. As they talked Shirley's hand found Tim's forearm and paddled in it with her fingers; later Tim stroked her neck with the back of his hand. Sylvia felt happy that they accepted her so completely, or rather that they had no care for whether she was there or not. After a quarter of an hour Tim fell asleep in the hot sunshine.

Shirley whispered, 'Are you all right, Mrs C? Would you like the Sunday paper? I've got to read this book. Mother sent it weeks ago. She's mad about it. I can't keep writing her that I haven't got around to reading it yet.'

Then she concentrated with frowning solemnity on the large book she had propped against her knees.

Sylvia looked at the papers, but the sense of what she read ran through her head without leaving a trace in her memory. She breathed in the smell of wild mint that came from the bank where the children in their play had smashed and bruised the leaves. She tucked some pages of the newspaper round her legs, for there were midges about. She watched for a while a team of red ants jerkily carrying the sun-dried corpse of some larger insect – it looked like a grasshopper – across the bumpy ground. She wondered if one afternoon she and Arthur should go to the tea-garden at Herley Ford. She remembered suddenly another tea-garden near Eastbourne where they kept monkeys in cages. But all that sort of thing, bringing things to the countryside from foreign places, and gardens too really, and clock golf and so on – they only spoilt the peace of things. She fell asleep.

When she awoke Tim was unpacking the picnic basket – chicken and champagne and fresh peaches. They really were spoiling her. And so they seemed determined to do, for all of them came out of their separateness and embraced her with talk and good wishes and healths and demands for reminiscence of her birthdays. True, when the food had been eaten and the champagne drunk, Shirley returned to her book. But Tim was not accepting this.

'Come out of that. You don't understand a word of it anyway.'

'I do too. It's a kind of new way of life based on Eastern thought and, oh well, it's lots of things. I guess you'd call it eclectic.'

However, after she'd read a couple more pages she shut the book.

'Yeah, well, I don't think it's the way of life for me.'

After that each produced a present for Sylvia – Tim gave her a silver cigarette case, Shirley a huge bottle of Chanel No. 5, and Mandy a leather needle case that she'd saved up for and chosen herself. Marcus Campkin, fired by their example, found a small bag of lozenges in his pocket and presented them to her very formally. Tim put his arm round the back of Mandy's legs and drew her to him.

'*You* wouldn't be here if it wasn't for Mrs C.'

Shirley added, 'That's right and no one's going to forget it.'

These were surely speeches to round off the occasion, although, in fact, they ended the afternoon in playing snap and beggar-my-neighbour.

August brought intermittent rain that year. Sylvia could not but think of the families at the seaside stuck indoors in their hotels and lodgings. She pitied the landladies and manageresses. She counted herself well out of it. Of course, that was exactly why so many people went abroad nowadays. Ray came back from Cannes nicely bronzed. Mark was said to be in Yugoslavia. Judy wrote that the Chateau la Miraillière was all she had dreamed of, and the De Clamouarts all she had hoped for. Harold clearly found that the school holidays weighed heavily upon him. He told Sylvia twice that this would be the first year in which he had not gone away with Beth – there had always been some conference, or there had always been Shakespeare at Stratford. He couldn't consider leaving Carshall this year, however, with the Ministry decision expected from day to day, indeed already characteristically overdue. Sylvia tried to talk with him, and she prepared all sorts of surprise dishes for his meals, but she knew that she could not do much.

With Arthur she could do little more. First she had freed him of the anxiety of his local debts. Muriel Bartley and Renee Cranston had taken her repayment of what was owed to them very differently. Muriel said, 'Of course we would never have *lent* money after we'd promised Harold. You know that. But we did think he'd pay his card debts. You're the one I'm sorry for. Mind you, there can be no question of starting up the poker game again. Well, you heard what Geoff said. I mean if only for the old boy's sake. I'd never have started if I'd realized what a curse cards are to him.' She offered a drink, but Sylvia didn't have time to stay and hear any more.

Renee said, 'I hoped you'd never know, but Jack said you had guessed. I suppose we shouldn't have lent it really, but the old boy's got such a way with him, although he does rile Jack at times. Oh, I'm so glad we can forget it. I hate unpleasantness. I'll write straight away and ask him to bridge.' But though the bridge games were resumed, it was clearly never the same. They played at the most twice a week. On some other evenings Sylvia took Arthur off to the cinema at Old Carshall by taxi and they ate afterwards at the Trust House. It seemed worth the expense. Each time Arthur cheered up a little over dinner, but the outings fell rather flat. Most of the time now he mooched about Town Centre, and often for days at a time he stayed in bed.

She still spent some afternoons up at Murrel Farm, but far less often because of the weather. In any case she had so much to do at home. She had decided to turn out all the rooms at 'The Sycamores' in turn, while that tiresome roster was suspended – it was a fallacy to suppose that modern houses didn't collect dust. She had her reading to catch up with and she still liked to watch tele of an evening if there was anything specially good showing. Once or twice on rare fine afternoons she took a walk by herself, but not too long a walk, because she had been to see the local G.P., Dr Piggott, and he had told her that she must take the slight stroke as a warning not to overdo it. However, she found that even a stroll round the buildings always provided something to watch – children on swings or chutes, young people playing tennis. She got talking to a number of people who turned out to be near neighbours. Renee Cranston drove her out for a whole afternoon to look at some old houses that were up for sale. She remembered and tried out an old recipe of her mother's for damson cheese, and very nasty it turned out to be. Time seemed to pass so quickly.

Into this pleasant hurrying calm there fell suddenly the bombshell that everyone had so long awaited: the Minister advised the Development Board to refuse Tim Egan's offer of alternative building land. Goodchild's meadow would now be developed as a medium-priced housing estate as soon as Tim's lease fell in at the end of the year. Harold made only one comment when he heard the decision.

'I'm glad that Beth isn't alive for this. It would have killed her.'

Sylvia thought that she would have killed anyone who laughed at that moment. He rallied from the blow by devoting all his energies to persuading the Committee that a grand protest meeting might save the day.

At first Sylvia was prominent in his plan of campaign; it was to be her function to rally the Egans to another attack on entrenched bureaucracy. But Tim showed a steadfast determination not to go over the top.

'Sorry, Mrs C, I'd do a lot for you, but I told Mr Calvert what I was prepared to do about the meadow. I've fought Aunt Lilian's battle. We've lost and quite frankly I'm only too glad. I'm not Aladdin to wish to exchange good land for bad if I can help it.'

She tried to explain how seriously Harold took the whole thing. He listened very politely, but repeated that he could do no more. In the end Shirley had to weigh in.

'Look, if Timbo says he won't do it, he won't do it. He may be right or he may be wrong, but he won't do it. I know my Timbo.'

When Harold rang Murrel Farm himself, he must have been rather roughly choked off, for he was in a bad temper with Sylvia for the rest of the week.

Taking some shirts that she had washed for Ray into his room, she tried to rouse him to share her anxiety over Harold's state of mind.

'Dad's a fighter. No, sorry, lovey, that's balls. I got so used to hearing Mum say it that I almost believed it when I was a kid. No, Dad hasn't the sense to come in out of the wet. But let him have his protest meeting and be refused again and he'll come round. It'll take a little time. We'll suffer a bit here and the kids at school next term'll have hell. But even headmasters have to recognize some musts.'

'But, Ray, he gets so excited about it. I'm afraid he'll have one of those breakdowns that seem so common now.'

'Look, lovey, I'm a simple textile designer not a psychiatrist. Now, don't look so worried. As far as I can I'll hold his hand at the Monster Rally. There! Does that satisfy you?'

It had to. But she wasn't alone in her fears. One evening Muriel Bartley arrived. She refused a drink.

'All right, Harold, you win. I've persuaded Herbert Raven to agree to the protest meeting. We've got Carshall Community Centre. So we can get seven hundred in.'

Harold, beaming, kissed her on the cheek.

'Yes, that's all right, Harold. Though you oughn't to have your own way like this. And I don't believe it'll make a damned bit of difference. But we'll see. I shall take the chair. And Raven will kick off for our side. Now, here's what you won't like. You won't speak.'

'What! Rubbish! I shall say whatever I choose. It's a public meeting.'

267

'Well, you won't speak from the platform. And I shan't call you from the floor. The Education Committee's been on to me again. They're worried stiff. And they've some reason. You've made a lot of enemies in the town over this. And that bitch Lorna Milton's seen to it that tongues have wagged. The Committee say they've written to you again.'

'The Committee have behaved abominably. After all my years of service, they've even stooped to veiled threats.'

'Oh, Harold dear . . .'

'You stop out of this, Mother. If your precious friend Egan . . .'

'Don't bully your mother, Harold. She feels as I do that we can't see a brilliant man muck up his career out of obstinacy.'

Arthur's expression when he came in at that moment was appropriately depressed. But he was not with them. He ignored Muriel and walked up to the window. He looked out gloomily. 'Well! If this something rain goes on there won't be any play at Old Trafford. That I *can* tell you all. And I've got a bet on with a chap that the South Africans'll be out first innings for less than a century. No play, no bet. Just my bloody luck.'

Harold wheeled round on his father. 'I wonder if you've had any thought in your life that ever went further than your own little ego?'

'Don't speak to me like that. I've been pushed around enough as it is . . .'

'I'll speak exactly as I choose. I provide you with a roof over your head and you come here and quarrel with all my friends and borrow money from me and God knows what! It doesn't seem to occur to you that somebody else will have to pay for it all. My name is mud now in this town. I'm not even considered suitable to speak from a public platform.'

To Sylvia's distress Arthur did not shout back. He stood with his jaws working, but no sound came from him.

'You'll be so ashamed later, Harold, to have spoken to your Dad . . .'

'Well, really Harold, fancy talking to the poor old chap like that. As if he had anything to do with it. Don't worry Captain, Harold doesn't know what he's saying.'

'Would you mind keeping out of my family business, Muriel?'

'Oh, don't be such a pompous ass! You'll be grateful to me one day for saving your job for you.'

Sylvia ran after Muriel down the front path.

'I just wanted to say thank you very much.'

'Oh, that's nothing, Mrs Calvert. A fat lot of use I've been. You ought to get him to see a doctor though.'

'I wish I could. But I can't talk to him. I don't think anybody can. This Goodchild's meadow business has made him impossible.'

'Oh, Harold! I didn't mean him. Silly bugger! Pardon my language. No, I meant the old boy. He looks terrible.'

Sylvia couldn't bring herself to talk to Harold, so she went straight up to her room. Arthur was sitting there, reading the evening paper. Muriel was quite right: he looked quite off colour, wrinkled and yellow, like an old tortoise.

She poured out two strong whiskies from the bottle she kept in the wardrobe.

'Cheer up, Arthur. Don't worry about him. You ought to have given him more hidings as a boy. He's been too well cushioned all his life.' She chuckled, but Arthur didn't respond, although his head shook a little as he read.

She could find no way to hit back on Arthur's behalf except to tell Harold that she would not be coming to the meeting. He looked at her so fiercely that she thought he was going to hit her, but he got up and walked out of the room in silence.

It was Arthur's unexpected resignation that kept her anger with Harold alive. Yet she felt distressed to be cut off from either of them when each seemed so troubled. She took refuge in underlining Ray's promise to be with his father.

'It's just as well you'll be with him, Ray. I'm not going to be there, not after the way he spoke to his Dad. I don't care how he takes it.'

'Nice friendly lot, aren't you, love? It's like Mum used to say, "There's no parents and children in this house, we're all just friends." Clever old Mum as usual.'

Sylvia had never heard him speak in such a sarcastic tone, but she wasn't going to give way.

Yet in the end she did. It was Shirley's doing. She had telephoned to know where the meeting would be held and when she heard that Sylvia was not attending, her amazed disagreement nearly broke Sylvia's ear-drum.

'Oh no! You've *got* to go! I don't care what he's said. He's standing up for what he believes in and you ought to be there. Yes, I know what Timbo said. And he made a lot of sense. Timbo always makes sense. But Mr Calvert isn't looking for sense, he's looking for supporters. Well, of course he's been awful to all of you. He *minds* about this. Good God! There aren't too many people over here who'll make a noise about anything. So good for him. Look, you've got to be there. I guess I'll come with you just to make sure you don't run out on him.'

The hall was packed except for the front row, reserved no doubt for V.I.P.s. Sylvia, sitting in one of the outer seats with Shirley, thought she would never be able to spot Harold in this great array of backs that converged towards the platform.

'But it's beautiful!' Shirley said looking round.

'I believe it's quite famous. People come from all over the world to see it – architects and that, you know. We call it The Oyster.'

'We?'

'People in the New Town, I mean. I don't quite know why.'

'Because it's shell-shaped, for Heaven's sake. But it's beautiful. I just love those smooth black panels and acres of glass. And the ceiling! Do you know what that is? Red Cedar. We've got whole forests of that in Oregon. My! You ought to be proud of this.'

'There are a lot of fine modern buildings in the New Town.'

'Well, I guess so. I can't think why I go on marketing in that awful olde worlde Carshall. I guess because Timbo's Aunt Lilian hated the New Town so much. But this is a lovely hall.'

Looking round it, Sylvia felt quite proud.

'Ah, here the speakers come,' she said. 'That's Muriel Bartley sitting in the middle.'

'She certainly intends to be seen, doesn't she? Where in hell did she get that green and red material? And that neckline! It's warm in here, but not that warm.'

But Muriel was speaking.

'All of you will have heard the sad news ... don't run away with the idea that your Committee's efforts were wasted ... our little job to keep alive the right to protest ... make clear to the Ministry ... state our case once again if only for the record ... strength of local opinion must give the red tape Johnnies a warning ... call on Herbert Raven.'

Sylvia only followed in part, for her eyes were seeking Harold. She might, it was true, miss the back of his head – there were so many dark heads with balding crowns; but Ray's strong sunburned neck with his hair almost golden from his holiday, she was sure she couldn't fail to see that.

Mr Raven wasn't a very impressive man – tall and thin with a mop of wiry hair standing on end and a big Adam's apple jerking up and down above his open-necked shirt. His slow cockney voice was high in note and adenoidal in tone.

'Ladies and gentlemen. You may perhaps feel that this meeting is something of a post mortem. But your Committee felt that we owed it to all of you who contributed so generously to the campaign to give some account of how your money has been spent – what has in fact been achieved despite this very disappointing decision of the Minister. . . .'

Suddenly, so that Sylvia's heart missed a beat, there was Harold, standing in one of the gang-ways, shouting.

'Nothing's been achieved! It's all ahead of us.'

There were whispers in the audience, some titters and a few hand-claps.

'I'm very grateful to our friend Harold Calvert, who has done so much for us, for his very sound observation. It is all ahead of us. We may have lost this time, but not again.'

'Shame! Shame!'

Even from her seat Sylvia could see that Harold was shaking as he shouted.

'I'm afraid my friend Harold Calvert didn't altogether understand me. . . .'

'I understood very well. You've ratted.'

271

But Muriel's hand was shaking now as she rapped on the table.

'Order, please. Let Mr Raven tell us . . .'

'We don't want to hear a pack of lies. I demand the right to speak, Madam Chairman. The aims of this Committee are being totally misrepresented. . . .'

'Now, my dear friend, that is just not true. But if I may continue with my speech, perhaps that will become clear. It is sometimes said that if the mountain will not come to Mahomet, then Mahomet must go to the mountain. But your Committee has brought Mahomet here to you. Yes, we've got our P.R.O. Jock Parsons here to explain to you why the Development Board has made its decision. Now I think that to have made the powers-that-be feel that they owe us an explanation is a great achievement in this bureaucratic age.'

'Then you're a fool!'

'I'm not going to argue with you, my friend. I would point out though, that to prevent free speech hardly furthers the cause we both have at heart. Now Jock Parsons is not the sort of chap to listen to professional grousers or belly-achers, he's a realist. He's come here because he recognizes that your Committee . . .'

'He knows he can fool you any time he likes. That's why he's come here. . . .'

There was some more clapping and some woman shouted, 'Well said, Mr Calvert.'

But there were more cries of, 'Shut up!' and 'Sit down!'

Muriel seemed heartened by this, for she smiled and almost winked at the audience. 'Now you shut up, Harold, and let Herbert speak. You can have your say later. I'm sorry to talk in such an unconstitutional way, ladies and gentlemen, but it's the only way to talk to our old friend Harold Calvert when he blows his top.'

Sylvia was trembling so that her knees knocked against Shirley's: Shirley put an arm through hers, took her hand, and held it, pressed tight. Harold, muttering, sat down on the gang-way step. A young usher whispered to him, but Harold turned his back. The rest of Mr Raven's speech continued uninterrupted. Sylvia was too agitated to catch more than a little of what he said, but it appeared that he thought the Development Board would never again make any big changes in planning without consulting public opinion in the New Town. He sat down to a good deal of applause. Before Muriel could speak, Harold was on his feet.

'Madam Chairman, ladies and gentlemen, I would like to make it perfectly clear that so far from having achieved a victory, the Committee have sold out all along the line...'

But Muriel banged so loudly with her gavel that Harold's words were inaudible where Sylvia was sitting.

'Will you sit down, please,' Muriel had returned to her official voice. 'I shall throw the meeting open later. Meanwhile I call upon Mr Parsons.'

Jock Parsons rose in the front row – burly, bluff, farmer-like in broad tweeds.

'Madame Chairman, I am very glad to have this opportunity . . .'

But now Harold was shouting again something that Sylvia could not hear, for immediately there were calls of 'Sit down!' and 'You'll have your chance later' from every corner of the hall. Muriel was banging; Mr Raven protesting; Mr Parsons smiling patronizingly at the uproar in the hall. Muriel signed to the young usher who took Harold's arm. Harold shook him off angrily. For a moment Sylvia feared he was going to hit the man. She half rose, but Shirley restrained her.

She cried out 'Ray! Ray!' and Shirley said, 'Oh, Lord!'

As if in answer Mark appeared from the other side of the hall; scarlet in the face, he glared at everyone; he took his father's arm and led him to a still empty seat at the end of the front row.

Jock Parsons began again. 'As I was saying, I'm very glad to have this chance to put before you some of the reasons why the Development Board . . .'

But Sylvia could not attend, for a young policeman was now on the platform whispering to Muriel. If the police interfered with Harold, she felt sure that she would lose control. Muriel appeared, however, to be pointing far over Harold's head into the audience, up towards where she and Shirley were sitting. Then the policeman disappeared. She forced herself to listen to Jock Parsons.

'Now the Board have always felt very strongly that if the town must develop and change – for development means change – then the principles on which the pioneer architects and planners of Carshall worked should always be respected, but . . .'

Once again Harold was protesting. She could hear him call.

'That's a lie!'

But she could not see him, for Mark seemed to be holding him in his seat. At that moment the young policeman loomed over her, his young boy's face very solemn.

'Mrs Calvert?'

When she nodded he handed her a piece of folded paper. As she opened it, she heard Jock Parsons saying with a chuckle, 'We haven't always believed that the best people to teach us our business were the servants of the County Council, but we're always open . . .'

As she read the note, she could hear Harold shouting and protesting.

He had risen and Mark was with difficulty preventing him from throwing himself at Jock Parsons.

'I must go,' she showed the note to Shirley.

'Oh, my poor Mrs C. Now come on. I'll run you home.'

As Sylvia stumbled along the gangway past the two rows of seats behind her, a hand came out and caught her arm.

'For God's sake, woman, you're surely not running out on your son now!'

It was Shirley who explained to the indignant Sally Bulmer that, 'Mrs Calvert has to go right away. Her husband's very sick.'

Back at 'The Sycamores' a police constable was waiting in the hall.

'One of our men found the old gentleman wandering on the motorway. He seemed confused . . .'

But Sylvia cut him short. 'Where is he now?'

'We took him up to his bedroom. We went to the wrong room first, but we could soon tell by the agitation the gentleman showed. Dr Piggott's with him now . . .'

Arthur lay in bed. His face, for long now so yellow and shrunken, was flushed. He was mumbling and picking with the fingers of one hand at a fold in the sheets. She went straight over and kissed him. His eyes moved slowly to focus on to her, but he didn't seem to recognize her, although he mumbled more quickly and excitedly.

Dr Piggott's curly-haired boyish earnestness had left her unimpressed when she had consulted him on her own account a few weeks earlier, but her new will to live had made her more attentive to his warnings than she would have been ordinarily. Now, as soft-voiced he reassured her that Captain Calvert's little stroke, little seizure really, if that wasn't an old-fashioned term, should not cause her alarm, she saw him as one of these young doctors in tele-serials; and, seeing him so, dismissed at once him and the serials from her serious consideration.

'It was unfortunate, of course, that he should have been taken ill in the open street like that. His mind was inevitably confused and he wandered on to the highway; then the police came into it and the whole thing wears a more alarming aspect than is really necessary. A good rest in bed and a bit of attention will soon put him right again. For the time being at any rate.'

Sylvia didn't believe a word of it. Of course, as a doctor he knew best, but then he didn't know Arthur, hadn't seen the course of his life in this last year. She did, and had, and she knew that it was all up with him, that he would die.

'Thank you, doctor. If you'll wait while I get rid of the policeman, I'll be back and then we won't keep you.'

But, as she was speaking, the noise of people thumping about in the hall almost distracted her from what she was saying. And then the curious unexpected sound of sobbing. That should have been herself, not whoever it was, and who could it be? Surely not the policeman.

Her sudden sense that Arthur was dying released in her such a flood of conflicting thoughts and feelings and memories, that when she reached the hall she could not remember why she had come downstairs. To find the policeman, of course; but there was no policeman, only a woman who came towards her and embraced her.

'Oh, you poor, poor thing.'

It was Shirley Egan – she had quite forgotten her; she drew back from the embrace.

'How is he, Mrs C?'

'I'm to be with him. You'll excuse me, I must go back to our room.'

She moved away.

'Mrs C, there's something else you'll have to know. Mr Calvert's come back home. He's pretty sick, I think. He broke down at the meeting. His son's with him in there.' She pointed to the study.

'Thank you for telling me. I'll ask the doctor to see him.'

Shirley seemed surprised, but she only asked, 'What can I do to help?'

It was Sylvia's turn to be surprised. 'Oh, nothing, thank you. You're very kind.'

'I'll call you in the morning.'

'Thank you.'

'If you need anything at all, just call us, and Timbo or I will be right down.'

'Thank you.'

'And – and – Mrs C, don't hold it in. Let yourself go.' But Sylvia was already on her way upstairs.

8. Harvest

When she told Dr Piggott about Harold, he said, 'Ah!' and then, 'I've been expecting something of the sort ever since his wife died. He took it all much too well. Then he came to me because he hadn't slept for months. But would he take a sleeping pill? Oh no, that would be a confession of weakness. You're an obstinate family, aren't you? Did he seem at all hysterical?'

'I didn't go in, doctor. He's got Mark with him and I was needed up here.'

The doctor's surprised, open mouth reminded her of the goldfish at Renee Cranston's. Everyone appeared to be surprised at what she did; herself she was surprised that at such a time she noticed their reactions – but then she seemed to notice everything nowadays. Luckily she need not take any account of the opinions of others, for her own feelings told her now so clearly what to do.

'Well, like it or not, he'll have to have a sedative tonight.' At the door he turned. 'Now don't overdo it. If the Captain needs lifting at all, get one of your grandsons to help you. And for the rest, we'll see. I'll find out what the District Nurse can do.'

She sat close to Arthur, trying to make sense of his jumbled, distorted talk. From time to time she wiped his sweaty forehead and neck with eau de cologne tissues, or stroked his hair, but touch seemed to bring her no nearer than hearing. He was less restless and flushed now, and his mumbling died away into tight, scraping breaths. Although the sound was more familiar – herald of so many bouts of bronchitis – she longed to shake him, to force some connexion between them before he slid into sleep that somehow she feared might be his last. Common sense and kindness were stronger than her fears and she watched him fall asleep with all of a professional nurse's satisfaction. As he slept she gradually became aware of the patterns and lines and wrinkles that crossed and recrossed his cheeks and his neck. Glistening with beads of sweat, the furrows were outlined and highlighted with the exaggerated clarity which recalled to her the effects she too often got on the tele-screen when she turned the wrong knobs. "Do not adjust your set – Do not adjust your set" – but she had no set to adjust.

She awoke to see Mark looking at her from the doorway. 'You were asleep!'

Someone else shocked! But to him she felt some need to offer defence.

'I'm not a young woman, Mark, you know. And it's very late. What is the time?'

'A little after two. Dad's sleeping now. How's Grand-dad?'

'He's sleeping too. So that's all right.'

She wanted to laugh. Pulling herself together, she could see by the twitching of his mouth that so did he.

'Where's Ray, Mark?' and she wished immediately that they'd had their laugh together. But it was too late: Mark's face had set in a sadly solemn mould.

'That's what upset Dad most. I mean Ray's not being at the meeting. I've had to pretend that he'd be back at any minute, because I couldn't risk the shock this might give Dad.' He handed her a sheet of paper covered in Ray's handwriting. 'I saw it in time to suppress it.' Sylvia puzzled out the crabbed hand.

Sorry, all, but I've gone to London for Good. You'll probably know why tomorrow. Don't think too hard of me. *I'm not in trouble as far as I can tell.* But after what's happened to Wilf I can't stay on in Carshall. It's a bugger, but there it is. And I've let you down, Dad, about the meeting. But Mark'll be there and he's worth twelve of me. Anyway, good luck and don't care about it too much. Damn the lot of them!

She put the note down on the bed table.

'I don't understand it, Mark. Why should Ray be in trouble?'

Mark looked at her for a moment so carefully, as though she was something he was pricing at a shop. But then he looked away again.

'I don't know, Gran. But whatever it is you can be sure Ray's in the right.'

'Yes, of course, dear. I just don't know. What's happened to Mr Corney anyway?'

Now Mark glared at her challengingly. 'I rang Wilf Corney's lodgings. He gassed himself last night. His landlady said Ray had rung this morning, so he must have known.'

'Oh, the poor man! Wasn't there anyone he could turn to? He always seemed so full of life, Mark.'

'Well, he isn't now.'

'No dear, but, well, I think *I* understand how easily it could happen. Poor Ray! No wonder he was upset. They were such good friends. It must have been too awful for him not to be able to help. But he should have told us . . .'

'You're not to blame him whatever happens, Gran. Ray's the best of the lot of us. I can tell you that.'

'Blame him! Of course, I shouldn't. Why, Ray's been wonderful to me. Better than anyone here. I mean . . .'

'That's all right. I'm glad you know it. He's taken all of us on. And we have to stand by him now if he needs us.'

'But of course, dear. I don't understand but . . . Only surely you should have shown your father that note. If he's worrying where Ray is, on top of everything else, I mean.'

'At the moment Dad can't think of anyone but himself. Except Mum. Oh, I can understand how it is. But if he reacted to Ray's troubles in that way, I think I'd walk out on him. And just for now, at any rate, I can be useful here, so I don't want to . . .'

'I see, dear. Well, as I said, I'm not as young as I was and there's going to be a tiring time ahead of us. I think I'll go off to bed now. I'm a light sleeper. If your Granddad should wake, I'll hear him.'

She could tell that he was as glad to end the conversation as she was. It was never any good discussing important things late at night when you're tired and strained, was it?

Arthur in the morning seemed a bit dopy. But she could

understand a little now of what he said, though his voice was very weak. She had to help him hold his cup of tea to his mouth.

'If I've got to be fed like a bloody baby, the sooner I go the better,' and when a drop of tea slopped on to his pyjama jacket, 'Bloody cow,' he called her. But she'd known he'd be fretful. She also knew that Dr Piggott would feel satisfied with his prediction of recovery. And Arthur, of course, brightened up for strangers.

'I've got to be all right for the last Test, Doctor.'

'What? Are you playing for England then, Captain?'

'I could still make circles round these blighters. I've never seen such a lousy team as this season's lot.'

'The old chap's going along very nicely. But *you* mustn't overdo it. I've spoken to Nurse and she'll look in twice a day for the time being.'

He appeared almost as satisfied with Harold's condition.

'He only needs a rest. He's still harping a bit on this Goodchild's meadow. But I've told young Mark to distract his mind over this week-end. As soon as the Captain's better, I think Harold ought to take a holiday before term starts. Though mind you, once he gets back into the swim . . . Anyhow, I think he'd like to see you now. I've told him to stop in bed a couple of days. After all, he's a reading man. . .'

But Harold didn't stop in bed. As Mark and Sylvia were relaxing over a cup of coffee in the kitchen, he appeared, fully dressed.

'I'm sorry to hear about Dad. I looked in to see him, but he was sleeping. Piggott says he'll be up and about in a few days. Quite frankly it's a blessing in disguise. It'll keep him out of mischief. And we can't afford any of the old man's little tricks at the moment. I shall have my hands quite full enough putting some guts into that Committee.'

He reached out for a ginger nut and stuffed it hungrily into his mouth so that he appeared to speak through a deadening blanket. 'Some people might say I'd gone about things in the wrong way last night. But I've thought about it seriously and I'm quite sure I did the right thing. Both Raven and Muriel needed blowing up. I shall go over to "Sorbetts" this morning and I don't mind saying that I'm certain I shall find a very chastened Muriel when I get there.'

He glared defiantly at his son and his mother, then: 'Any news of Ray?'

'No, Dad. But you can be sure that he's just gone away for a few days on business.'

'Gone away for a few days at a moment like this? Without any warning? Well, he can stay away. Your mother and I never asked anything of you children unless your heart was in giving it to us. And that goes for everyone as far as I am concerned. If people don't feel as strongly about the iniquitous way the Corporation's behaving at the moment, well, of course, they're perfectly entitled to their opinion. Goodchild's meadow is not the centre of the universe, but at the moment it happens to be the centre of mine. As long as that's understood all round, I daresay we shall get along all right.'

He gulped down a cup of coffee as though to give them time to reply, but no answer came.

'It was very good of you to come back here last night, Mark. But there's no obligation on you whatsoever to stay here. Indeed I suppose you must be getting your inoculations or what-have-you for abroad. To which of these under-developed countries are you giving your services? I should have asked before.'

'I'm not leaving Carshall, Dad. I've got my H.N.C. with endorsements. No more Tech. As a matter of fact, when it came to the written, I realized how much . . . I mean you were right, Dad, they seem to think I'm cut out for this. And certainly when we were in Mostar and Sarajevo I didn't seem to get on too well with the Serbs. Priscilla White – she was with our party – said she'd never seen anything more like the traditional Englishman abroad. Mind you, I think if we'd been in Zagreb . . . they say the Croats are altogether easier. But then as Pris says, if you're going to do famine relief work you can't pick and choose. Anyway I can't go back on it now. I'm entered at the Institute. So with any luck, Gran, in a few years your spotty grandson will be Mark Calvert, A.M.I.E.E. . . .'

His voice died away. Harold was abstracted.

'Good, old man, jolly good. I'm sure you've done the right thing.'

Sylvia felt the heaviness of the silence. She gave Mark a kiss on his pimply cheek. 'I'm so pleased, dear, so very pleased and proud.'

She trusted that he couldn't detect how far away from him her thoughts were also.

'Thank you, Gran. Anyway, that means I may as well shift back here, if it suits you all right, Dad.'

Harold didn't answer, he was glaring into the distance. Sylvia felt that she couldn't answer for him.

'So I'll just pop round to the Forresters and pack my things and I'll be back to help with the dinner. Don't you budge, Dad. You ought to be in bed.'

Harold spoke bitterly when Mark had gone. 'In bed! I wonder if it occurs to any of them with their feather beds of security and ladders of opportunity and hire-purchase homes and the rest of the clap-trap, that some of us have to keep awake however much it hurts, to see that the whole pleasant dream doesn't vanish overnight . . .'

Sylvia was used to Harold's speeches being difficult to follow as he packed down the tobacco in the bowl of his pipe and sucked and puffed between every second word. But at the moment he seemed to her as confused as Arthur. He began to pace up and down the room.

'Not that I'm putting the whole blame on the young. Far from it. Look at last night's exhibition. I've known Herbert Raven a long time and he's never had any real guts, but I didn't dream in my worst moments that he'd sink to last night's depths. It will give me a good deal of satisfaction to obtain a vote of no-confidence in his chairmanship. And it can be done. It's just a question of rallying the right group. I've been far too led away by friendship. I'm a funny chap, Mother, I'll go on trusting and trusting, but when finally my eyes are opened, then nothing in heaven or earth will move me. And so that bitch Muriel Bartley's going to find out. Dad's got a lot of faults, but I'll give him his due, he saw through her pretty quickly. Of course, I know what'll happen, she'll make an appeal to her friendship with Beth. Well, that won't wash with me. If Beth had lived, Muriel Bartley would have stayed in the sort of subordinate positions she's capable of filling in public life. Good God! When I think of all Beth did for her and the way she's treated me . . .'

Sylvia could see no way to stop the ever faster and more angry flow of words. But luckily the bell rang.

'I think that's probably the District Nurse, dear. Anyway, I must just see after Dad. Now don't you move from here until you've had your lunch.'

But far from moving, Harold was already seated in an armchair. 'I've never asked for thanks, only for a little loyalty.' He didn't seem to be speaking to her, so she went to the front door.

It was indeed Nurse Hepburn, bright and Scots with a flat-cheeked face like a bannock and an underhung jaw. Sylvia hoped that her jollying-along, domineering manner wouldn't grate on Arthur as it did immediately on her. However they wanted her assistance and they must pay for it.

She went into the bedroom to prepare Arthur for Nurse's arrival. He was not asleep but he refused to open his eyes. She shouted at him. Then one eye opened to glare malevolently at her. He managed to get out some words with wheezing and straining.

'Where the hell have you been? I might have been dead for all you care. And you can tell that ruddy cow of a nurse to stay out. . . .'

The violent words sounded pathetic in his weakened voice.

'Och, we're in a difficult mood, aren't we? Well, that only shows that we're well on the way to making a recovery. In fact, we're a bit of a fraud. . . .'

Sylvia waited for an explosion, but there was none. Arthur shut his eyes again.

'Have we had a wash today?'

Nurse Hepburn signalled to Sylvia to leave them. She felt quite guilty at deserting Arthur, for as the nurse began to assemble the basin and soap and talcum powder, she looked like one of those inquisition people with their instruments. Sylvia picked up Ray's letter and went downstairs. She had another duty in her mind.

Sure enough, as she had expected, Harold was still sitting in the armchair. As she came in, he stood up and began immediately. 'I hope you don't suppose, Mother, that I've asked anything of them. Neither Beth nor I have ever asked anything. We were simply content that they should find some fulfilment in life. That was quite enough reward for us. . . .'

'But Harold, dear, think of Mark's news. Just what you wanted. Think how well he's done. Beth would have been so pleased and proud, I know. Do say a word to the boy, Harold, when he comes back.'

'Judy, Mark, Ray. Not one of them that hasn't thought of themselves. Mark's quite content to return because it suits him. All right, if he wants to use the place as a hotel. And Judy, too, when she's not staying away with her grand friends. But Ray, I must say I never thought . . . Well, he can stop away now. I . . .'

Sylvia stamped her foot violently on the floor. 'Oh, shut up, Harold! I, I, I. You don't deserve to have such good children. I don't know a nicer lad than Ray. He's in some sort of trouble, and all you can do is to go on about yourself. They spoil you! "Dad mustn't be worried." Mark hasn't even shown you this.' She put Ray's note in his hand. As he read it, Harold burst into tears, great gulping sobs like a small child out of control. They came to her from the past – the occasional, sudden uncontrolled sobbing of Harold or of Len. She'd always told them that the Calverts didn't go on like that; that making an exhibition of themselves wouldn't help them; they must be manly like their Dad. Now she put her arms round Harold and held him tight to her. Being a fat feather-bed is of help for once, she thought; and it's too late now, my girl, you should have done it years ago; he doesn't want his mother now, he wants . . . As Harold's sobbing became less violent, what he wanted did in fact pour forth.

'Oh, God! Mother, how I miss her. We weren't just any ordinary marriage – she was everything to me. And they don't care. Not any of the three of them. They don't miss her. They're glad she's dead.'

'Now, Harold, they're growing up, that's all.'

'I can't get through to them, Mother. It's all a thick fog. I hate them. They hate me. And I promised her, promised that I'd keep us together. I've let them all go. They can't talk to me. I feel as though I was walking through a dark tunnel, I work and work to try to get out of it that way.'

'You can't, Harold, not really, I think. Not once you're in it.'

'Good God, Mother, I'm not a coward.'

'I didn't think you were, dear. But that doesn't really help. You have to go on through it.'

'And supposing there's no end to it?'

'It's a bit of luck if there is, I think. At any rate, it was for me. Otherwise, without luck . . .'

She could only hold him tightly. But she was not surprised when his loneliness and panic refused any further comfort. He suddenly wrenched himself free from her embrace, so that she was pushed back against the chair. Once again she thought, Lucky I'm a feather-bed. He shouted, 'For God's sake, leave me alone!'

Once again she thought – You're too late, my girl, he needs someone else than you, thank God.

They must have looked a tableau of misery, for when Mark came in on them, his face set into a self-conscious grin.

'I don't know why your brother Ray's misfortunes should amuse you so much.'

Sylvia saw suddenly how subtle the unhappy are in finding means to hurt others.

Mark's anger was loosed on her. 'You silly old fool! Why on earth have you always got to meddle?'

'I meant . . .'

There was no point in saying what she had meant, but she replied to Mark: 'Mark, both your father and I want to know how to help Ray.'

'Why have I been kept out of this, Mark?'

Suddenly Mark's normal slight stutter turned to an agony of incoherence. Red in the face, he was reduced to banging his chest with his fist as though to force out the words. Indeed they came out in a rush.

'Ray's never liked girls. If you couldn't see, he couldn't tell you. And you're not to say anything against him.'

Through her own puzzled thoughts, Sylvia could watch Harold's body stiffen and yet she could sense that he was at last a little relaxed in his cage of misery.

'You mean that he's homosexual.' He sounded deliberately casual, but his surprise would out. 'Ray! He's so popular, so good with everyone. . . . Oh, well, it's not the end of the world. I'm not entirely Victorian, you know, Mark. But I don't know that *you'll* want to hear all this, Mother.'

'Why shouldn't I? If it's to help Ray. . . . Oh, you mean because he's a homosexual – I never knew how to pronounce it before, but you see the word so often in the papers and books and things nowadays, don't you? I don't know. I hadn't thought of it connected with anyone I love. But there it is, we'll *have* to think about it now, won't we? Don't look so worried, Harold. I'm an old woman, not a child. You're being like Arthur. How shocked he was when I said what it was – what men did together. One of the sisters told me when I was in service at the hospital. She put it very crudely. I think she did it on purpose. It upset me rather. But then years later there was all that trouble with young Vic, the porter at Lowestoft, and I had to see it differently because he needed help. You wouldn't know about that – you and Len were just kids and my main thought was for you not to find out.'

She could hear herself telling it all to give them time, especially to give herself time to get ready for whatever it was that had happened to Ray.

Mark showed a letter to them both. 'You'd better read this. He left it for me at the Forrester's.'

Sylvia, leaning over Harold's shoulder read aloud: 'Dear Bumface. . . .'

'That's the name he always gave me. I called him . . . well, that doesn't matter anyway. It was a secret.'

Sylvia didn't read aloud any more.

I'm off up to London. For good. A lorry bloke got pinched last week that was one of our lot at the transport cafe. He was done for nicking off the lorries. But they've been down at the cafe questioning everyone. Prowse had a word with me, 'just a friendly word of fatherly advice' – two-faced old sod! I never had anything to do with this bloke. My chums aren't the sort to shoot their mouths off. It was Wilf I was worried for. You know what he's like. And now they've frightened him so much he's stuffed his stupid head in the oven, silly bugger! If I stay here I shall hit one of the bastards and that'll do no one any good, not even poor bloody Wilf. Anyway I see it all clearly now. I can't live here – the greatest in Carshall, the lad they all love – and don't suppose I don't like it, not just being the greatest, but Carshall, the whole set-up far better than you. If I was normal, that is, but then I'm not. Geoffrey's been telling me this for ages. It's only London that'll work for us. Anyhow the point is I've got to get out now. And that leaves you and Gran to hold the umbrella over Dad. And he needs it badly at the moment. As I told Gran he'll never come in out of the rain himself. So I've sold you the pass. Anyway with the managing directorship a certain carrot in the future, you can afford to carry the load, boyo. Congratulations by the way. We ought to have celebrated. *And don't worry about me.* I'm not in trouble yet. And with good luck in London I shan't be. Geoffrey's address will find me.

The address was in Bryanston Square. Sylvia, looking at Harold, guessed that much of Ray's letter was as mysterious to him as to her.

Mark, mistaking their incomprehension, said apologetic-cally,

'It all sounds a bit too hearty, doesn't it? But he's under great strain. He wouldn't put all those things ... I mean about managing director and that stuff, he knows as well as I do that I've only made the first step. . . .'

Harold brushed this aside.

'Of course he's under strain. He's by no means sure that he's not in trouble. He's whistling to keep his spirits up. And if he is in trouble, doing a bunk gives the worst possible appearance.'

'Poor Ray! Poor Mr Corney!'

'Yes, Mother, I'm sorry for that too. He wasn't a bad little chap, but he was always a queer fish, you know. Lorry drivers! Nicking! Prowse may well have warned Ray. What a world to get into! All this stuff about the police, though, is a pity. I'm not blaming Ray, but he's lost his sense of proportion. I'm going down to see Inspector Prowse myself this afternoon. We're good friends and if Ray's in trouble with the law, I shall soon get an idea of it. If not, he must come back at once. I don't know who this Geoffrey is. . . .'

'Geoffrey Lawshall – he's a London friend of Ray's, Dad. He's in the rag trade too.'

'Ah! ... Well, he's given very bad advice. This isn't a

London suburb or a cathedral town. If a community like Carshall can't help a decent chap like Ray to make a more normal life for himself, then we've failed. We want him back and we want him with the family. I'll have no narrow-minded censoriousness in this house. Oh, I don't mean you, Mother, you've taken it very well. I'm going to have to work over-time with term coming on, this business of Ray's and galvanizing the Committee into life again.'

Sylvia saw Mark flinch at the word 'Committee'.

'You'll put Ray first, dear, won't you?' And she looked across at Mark to give him hope. 'I must go up and relieve Nurse Hepburn. If Dad hasn't strangled her already.'

But she needn't have worried. Arthur's voice was still very weak, yet in slow, halting tones he was busy chaffing the nurse.

'Reeling down Sauchiehall Street every Saturday night and psalmsinging with the meenister next morning. Bloody hypocritical race! How do you expect any of them to get into the First Division?'

'I don't know anything about football.'

'She doesna ken a muckle thing. . . .'

But the Scots accent was too much for him, he ended in a wracking fit of coughing.

'Now, you'll not say another word. That'll teach you to speak against Scotland.'

But even pain didn't hold Arthur back on such an occasion.

'Whatever its faults it produces very bonnie nurses. I'll say that for the land of the heather.'

'Och! You're an awfu' flatterer.'

Nurse Hepburn seemed to grow more Scots under his charms.

'Well, Mrs Calvert, I must awa' noo and get ma dinner. But I'll be back again to keep you in order, Captain, aboot six o'clock. And now, Mrs Calvert, if we could have a wee word ootside aboot the Captain's medicine.'

Once in the passage Nurse Hepburn assumed a mourning face, but Sylvia resisted her example.

'Well, he seems in good spirits, Nurse.'

'Aye. It's a good thing. It's best for them to go out that way.'

'But Doctor Piggott thinks he'll be well again in no time.'

'Och! Then he will be. The doctor knows best.'

'I think you should tell me what *you* think.'

'I don't think anything, Mrs Calvert. I'm just the nurse. But. . . . Well, with these strokes, you can get quite well. But he's an old chap, and never a strong one. All we must hope for is that he'll not linger a long time after the second stroke. They tend to come in threes, you know.'

'Yes, I did know that.'

She came back into the bedroom full of a tenderness that frightened her. Before Nurse Hepburn's declaration her belief that he would die had been her own secret. Now she felt for him as someone to be protected against the world's knowledge. He lay with his eyes closed. She stood over him and stroked his cheek. He opened his eyes.

'Yes, yes. I know. I'm a goner. But I don't know why *you're* looking so glum. When I'm down you're up. And this time I'm going down for good.'

He said it so much as a statement of fact that she couldn't tell what bitterness there was in it. She went on automatically stroking his cheek for a few seconds, and then suddenly drew away her hand. Her tenderness seemed like an insult to him now. It's you who've overdone the slush this time, my girl. She sat down to sort it all out.

Although Arthur went off to sleep, she asked Mark to bring her a boiled egg up to their room. She would never now let Arthur wake up alone.

'Dad's gone off to see old Prowse. I don't think he can harm Ray and he may do some good. Certainly it seems to have pulled him together.'

'Yes, dear. He wants so much to be of use to you all. That's the trouble. Oh, I know it's silly. You're grown men now. He'll have to see it sooner or later.'

They sat for a few minutes in silence.

'Now that Dad's out, and if you're all right, I might go out myself. I arranged to meet Pris . . . and some others. It's such a fine Saturday. And we'd thought . . .'

'Off you go at once.'

But he'd hardly left when she heard the door-bell, and on going to the door, his voice.

'Who is it, Mark?'

He came upstairs and whispered. 'It's old Bulmer. She wants to talk to us. She's in a state about Dad.'

'Oh dear. I can't leave Arthur now. . . .'

'She seems so serious. I think we should see her.'

'Very well, dear. But she'll have to come up here and talk quietly so as not to wake your Granddad. Anyway, you go off, I can see her on my own.'

'Of course not. Dad's just as much my job as yours.'

Going back to Arthur, Sylvia thought, Why do we all have to be so much each other's jobs?

Certainly Sally Bulmer had made Harold hers. She disposed quickly of her respects to Arthur's illness by tiptoeing up to his bed and peering at him, for all the world as though he were some rare butterfly that might take flight at the first creak of her heavy bones. Then still on tip-toe and smiling at Sylvia as though she were the proud owner of the rarity, she sat down and whispered,

'He's not done for.'

Sylvia wondered how Miss Bulmer claimed to know this and what business it was of hers anyway.

'Harold Calvert's too useful to Carshall and too good a man to be downed by a lot of talk. He made a fool of himself last night, but more shame to those who let him do it. Yes, don't look away, Mark, I mean you. By the way, I hear it's to be room at the top after all. Congratulations. And the rest of his family. Oh, I don't blame you alone. We all let him down. That fool of a woman Muriel Bartley's been on the phone to me already. "I ought to have let him speak from the platform. I thought I was acting for the best." Twaddle! I believe poor old G.B.S. is out of fashion, isn't he, Mark? But he was wise in his generation – "Hell is paved with good intentions." Well, I gave her a piece of my mind that might have brought real green shadows to her eyes. And Lorna Milton! "I suppose our Harold will be running to a doctor now for sick leave, leaving the management of the school to Chris again." If your man managed you for a bit, he'd show himself a man for once, I told her. But there's still a lot of work to do stopping tongues.'

'We've been kept very busy here.'

'Oh, Lord, I know, Mark. Rabbits in your hutch. That's

why I'm here. To light a cracker or two under your tails.'

She stared at Sylvia, but Sylvia stared back at her, only indicating Arthur as her natural priority with a slight gesture of her hand.

'Troubles never come singly. You're old enough to know that, woman, but it won't do you any harm. Better for you than Wardress Webb.' She broke into a laugh, then put a finger to her lips to urge silence in the sick room. She took Sylvia's hand.

'Don't take any notice of my barking. You're doing a fine job. But we must stop the tongues wagging. That's the first job.'

'If only Ray were here. He knows everyone and gets around so much.'

'Hm. Maybe it's as well your brother isn't here. If you're writing to him, give my love, and tell him from me, if he can't be good, to stop away. We've only just missed a nasty bust-up as it is, from what I can make out.'

'I don't know what you mean.'

'Oh, comeity come! As if I haven't dealt with Ray's kind all my working days. I like them on the whole. But I've always said the same to them, 'It's a stupid law but it's there. So if you can't be good, be careful.' Of course, they never are. Oh no, he's better off in the big, bad city.'

'Now Miss Bulmer, Mark doesn't know what you mean and I'm sure I don't. You talked about tongues wagging . . .'

Sally got up from her chair. She stood regally in front of them.

'My dear people, in case you don't know it, I am a social worker. We have our professional ethics, you know. We honour the confessional like a priest or doctor, and as carefully. Did you really suppose I should say anything outside these four walls?'

When she had gone, Mark said, 'Isn't she awful?'

'She's been very good, Mark. Not many people, you know . . .'

'Yes, of course. But I said, isn't she awful?'

Sylvia nodded, 'I'm afraid she is. Awful.'

Then they both burst out laughing.

Indeed it was almost a jubilant evening. Arthur was well enough to take a little supper, and even Nurse Hepburn urged Sylvia to leave him alone at dinner time. Down in the dining room Harold announced that Ray was in no danger from the law.

'Prowse said very frankly that Ray had got into unwise company. He gave me quite a talking-to as Ray's father. But he thinks Corney was the source of the trouble, and that in the right crowd of young people Ray should soon put the whole thing behind him.'

'I don't think it's quite as simple as that, Dad.'

'No, no. I realize that, Mark. I'm not an entire fool, but I wasn't going to say anything that would put Ray in wrong with the police. No, I think he's got seriously to consider having some decent up-to-date treatment. But first he must come home. I've drafted a friendly letter this evening urging him to come back at once.'

The pencil draft took some deciphering, but they got the main drift of what he read to them.

I have seen Inspector Prowse and you have no reason to be afraid that you're in trouble although it's pretty clear to me that you've been very unwise. I only blame myself that you never felt able to come and tell me of your difficulties. If you had, what was probably only a passing phase in every adolescent's life (I seem dimly to remember some "crush" as we called them on a golden-haired, cherubic junior boy – now no doubt a hoary father of five – in my own school days) need never have assumed the exaggerated proportions in your life that it has now. Anyway, come home, I do beg you. Sexual choice is a small, often exaggerated part of life. The pleasures, ideals and memories that unite you to your family and to your friends here at Carshall are so much more important than this one barrier that now seems to loom so large in your life, your ever loving Dad.

Harold sat back. 'I've done my best. I can't do more.'

It seemed easy now to Sylvia to put her hand on Harold's shoulder and press it rather than to answer. She looked across at Mark. He too said nothing, but smiled at his father.

'Well, if everybody's satisfied, I'll make a fair copy and post it this evening.'

Harold went off to his study. Sylvia stayed to help Mark with the washing-up. He was too eager to communicate his own good news to comment on his father's letter.

'I went round to Alan Rodger's before supper. I admit

old Sally B. had me a bit rattled about Dad. But Alan says there's as many approve of what Dad said as don't. And as to his outburst, he's looked on as an excitable, clever chap. Alan's doing the report in the *Mercury*. He read it to me. It simply says, "Mr Calvert, as one would expect, protested vigorously and eloquently against what he believed was a mistaken decision." So much for old Bulmer's crackers. We've still got our tails. Mine's a bit singed but . . .'

Sylvia was still laughing at this when she answered Shirley Egan's 'phone call.

'Yes, he's a little better, thank you, Shirley. Yes, and Harold, too.'

'Oh, I'm so glad. Timbo and Mandy send love.'

'Oh, thank you.'

'Well, it's good to hear you laughing, anyway. Let me know if we can do anything. And when shall we see you?'

'Oh yes. Thank you.'

Sylvia was still chuckling as she rang off. She only registered Shirley's question later that night.

The luminous dial of her watch told Sylvia that it was half past three when she woke next morning with an urgent need to go somewhere. The demands of her bladder were so irregular and frequent these days, but, there you are, that was one of the penalties of old age. Arthur, propped up by pillows, was in one of his deeper sleeps; his breathing sounding as it so often had for so many years of his life, like an agonized last gasp. She crept out of the room and left the door ajar, even so she feared she must have woken him, for, from the lavatory, she could hear him moving in the bed – a sound now rare, he usually lay so still. Then as she hurried back across the passage, there sounded a loud and heavy thud; and she entered the room to see him lying sprawled on the rug beside his divan bed. She went to lift him, but he lay so heavy and inert that she had to call Mark and Harold. Together they got him back into bed, but apart from his prolonged sharp breathing and the flicker of his eyes, his whole trunk was motionless. He had suffered his last, paralysing stroke.

Some hours later, around eight, with doctor and nurse in attendance, he died. As Harold said more than once, 'In the circumstances no one but a monster would have wanted the old man to live on.' Although this was not a thought that came often to Sylvia that day. She had known enough deaths – who hadn't at sixty-five? – to go through the routine of undertakers, telegrams to Ray and Judy, choosing a wreath, answering phone calls and all else as though she had done it all before in some dream. By the afternoon only physical exhaustion warned her of the strain she was undergoing.

'I shall just go and lie down for half an hour, Harold, dear.'

'Of course, Mother. You'd better use Ray's room for the time being.' She was puzzled. 'Ray's room? . . . Oh no, dear. I've always shared a room with Dad.'

She looked at Arthur's white face above the sheets. They had somehow smoothed out most of his wrinkles. After closing his eyes, Nurse Hepburn said that he looked peaceful, but to Sylvia he looked only dead.

Kicking off her shoes, loosening her belt, she flopped down on her bed. Her gorge rose, so that for a moment she thought she would vomit, then awful retching, rending sobs welled up in her so that her fat body was shaken again and again. She tried deliberately to recall, to cling to, those few happy secret times they had known together; but a desperate grief closed in upon her, grief for all the years and years that had been nothing or worse than nothing, for tenderness dried up and tenderness drained away into indifference. For more than an hour she lay there, pressing her face close into the pillow, stifling her frantic crying that no one must hear, as wave followed wave and knocked her down again, punishing her for shyness, prudery, laziness, selfish bitterness, failures she couldn't name.

Nobody spoke of Arthur in the few days before the funeral. Harold said, 'Now, Mother, you've got to take it very easy.'

Mark said, 'There's a girl, Gran.'

Shirley on the phone said, 'You poor, poor darling.'

Ray sent a telegram from Milan ('Ah, that's why he hasn't got my letter yet,' was Harold's comment): 'Unable make funeral, with you lovey all the time.'

The De Clamouarts anxiously telephoned that Judy, on

a bicycle trip in the Midi, was not to be contacted and might they present their most esteemed condolences to *Madame veuve* Calvert.

Wreaths came from Sally Bulmer and the Bartleys and the Egans and the Cranstons, from the British Legion and from Arthur's Regiment. Sylvia in protest, found herself telling stories of Arthur, repeating his stories, desperately keeping his name alive, so that Harold and Mark and some of their friends looked at her once or twice in embarrassment.

At the cemetery, after the coffin had been lowered, Shirley Egan appeared from behind the knot of mourners, around the grave and took Sylvia into her arms.

'Don't mind them, honey. Don't mind anybody. Just let it go.'

How could Sylvia explain there in public that she *had* let it go, that it was over? Shirley was such a good girl, but Americans *are* different, she wouldn't understand. It was quite a mercy that to Sylvia's surprise, Priscilla White was also there. All in black, nudged forward by Mark, she led Sylvia away from Shirley to the waiting car. Sylvia could see from Harold's expression that he shared her surprise at the girl's quiet invasion of the family. For a while after the ceremony, back at 'The Sycamores', she kept up her chatter about Arthur. She could have kissed Jack Cranston when he said, 'Yes, I don't suppose I'll ever meet a better sportsman than the old chap.'

At last, battling against the tide of their talk, she gave up her efforts in shame for them and went to her empty bedroom. She lay down and slept for more than three hours.

It was not until two days later that Harold remarked, 'It seems sad to say it, Mother, but one can't help thinking Dad's was a wasted life. He had genuine ability and considerable personality, but he never settled to anything.'

'Settled to anything! Harold, how can you? A man who went into the war as a normal, healthy young chap and came out with rotten lungs.'

'I didn't mean to sound hard, Mother. But millions of men were in the war. Not only the First War. We fought a war too.'

'Oh, *your* war, Harold! Sitting behind a desk! No, forgive me, dear, I shouldn't have said that. You did very well. But your war sent you to a teacher's training college, gave you education. Dad's war gave him disabled officer's pension and told him to find a gentleman's occupation even if he wasn't one. How could he settle down? He didn't know whether he was coming or going. Oh, I've thought about it so much, Harold. We all laughed at Dad, at his tales and his boasting. But what could he be? At least he was a character.'

'It's very generous of you to say all this, Mother, considering the life he led you.'

'Oh, don't make any mistake, Harold. I'm not going to pretend. Arthur said that when he was up, I was down. And he was right. I shall be better off without all the worry he gave me. But what a thing to have to say after all those years. And then a lot of it was my fault. I was so pleased with our boarding-house, and he wanted better. You see, I don't think he ever knew what a great thing it was for me marrying him – an officer – and then to have my own guest-house, when all I'd ever known was washing the front steps and carrying jugs of hot water up four flights of stairs. We started out on different floors, Dad and me, and I'm afraid we always stayed on them. That was our lives. And then they say "the good old days"! No, you're quite right, Harold, to be proud of Carshall.'

Harold took her hands in his. 'My dear Mother, it's extraordinary that you should . . .' He spent some time in filling and lighting his pipe. . . . 'But I don't know why I should be surprised.'

'I sometimes surprise myself, dear.'

Harold looked at her with affection, but the look grew more absent.

'I shall be glad to hear from Ray, or better still to see him. Milan! Beth and I went right up to the parapet of the cathedral. I can't think why *he's* gone there, can you?'

In a few days they knew. Ray's reply came from London. It was full of gratitudes to his father both for his love and for his understanding, to all of them, especially to Gran at this rotten time for her. He hadn't expected such affection and confidence, although he ought to have known. . . . His not doing so showed how little he measured up to them. But he did most deeply and gratefully thank them. Yet the answer must be a definite no. It just would not work. Of course he'd been very happy in Carshall. If he were not as he was . . . but he was. And it was no good. Things might run along all right for a while. But there was always the sense that people were talking, the strain of pretending. And in the end what? To have no kick in life except running risks. That was how Wilf had been this last year or two. He couldn't bear the thought of it. As it was he had a real hope of making a happy life with Geoffrey. Geoffrey had wanted him to join him for the past three years. He was lonely in the Bryanston Square flat, wanted Ray's skill in the business. That was why they had been in Milan – for a textile exhibition. There were great prospects and new interests. . . . More his own boss. The flat was very posh. Geoffrey said to tell them they were to come and stay whenever they liked. He couldn't come away yet, for it was a small business and he owed it to Geoffrey. . . . Worked late – nine or even ten some nights. . . . Please, please understand how grateful he was, grateful yet certain . . .

Sylvia and Mark waited breathless for the storm. And it broke.

Harold took Ray's letter and very deliberately tore it into small shreds which he then threw into the wastepaper basket.

'I don't intend to act the Victorian heavy father. But I don't want another word said about that young man.'

'Oh, Dad, don't be absurd.'

He wheeled round on Mark and shouted, 'Did you hear what I said? If he hasn't the guts to try to come to terms with life after my letter to him, I wash my hands of him.'

'Oh, Harold, you're talking about Ray. You can't wash your hands of someone you love.'

'Someone I *did* love. You may not be able to, Mother, but I can. "So grateful to us, so fond of Carshall." It would have at least been more decent if he'd left that sort of pretence out.'

'But, Harold, I'm sure Ray is very fond of Carshall. He fitted in here so well, if he hadn't been . . . And as to talk, he's quite right. I've heard some already. It wouldn't be a happy life for him with gossip of that sort.'

'I suppose you agree with your grandmother.'

'Yes, Gran is quite right. Even Pris had heard something, I'm sorry to say. And Ray's right too. Of course I'd wish things different. My own brother! But he knows whether he can change or not. And if he can't, we ought to be grateful to him for not running risks in the town where we live.'

'Oh, you may be sure he won't run risks. A good job and a smart London flat. It makes me sick. No one can say that I'm narrow-minded. I've long said the law's antiquated. But to trade on his abnormalities. Living with some rich old man.'

'That's nonsense, Dad. This bloke Geoffrey Lawshall can't be a year older than me, if that. It's just a small family dress business he's inherited.'

'I don't know anything about that. People in that sort of world are old for their years, you know. But for Ray to live on somebody!'

'But, Harold, he isn't. Why should you object to his getting a good job? I'm a woman and if I can forgive him for not caring about women, I should have thought you . . .'

'Your attitude rather disgusts me, Mother. Apparently you don't care that your grandson's a little whore. Well, I do.'

'Whore! Really Harold, you're talking rubbish. How can a man be a whore? I've no patience with you. I'm not staying to listen to any more. But I'll tell you this, if nobody else goes to stay with Ray, I shall. He's been a lovely boy to me.'

Nor did Judy's letter to the family help. It made light of Arthur's death – "Poor old Granddad. He was one of the old school, wasn't he? I've been thinking of you a lot, Gran, but at least he didn't linger on. Mrs Ogilvie's father lingered on and on *for four years*' – and rather light of the loss of Goodchild's meadow – "Poor Daddy! And you had worked so hard. Oh, do think of moving somewhere where people appreciate your sense of what's worth fighting for a bit more than at awful Carshall." The rest of her letter was full of a young man called Alistair Courtenay who was staying at the De Clamouarts. He was tremendously clever and witty and up at Balliol and one of the Devonshire Courtenays. He spoke simply marvellous French and had written a parody of Chateaubriand that even Madame de C., who was terribly critical, said was brilliant. Oh, and she'd heard from Nottingham and there was a place for her next term, but she wasn't going to say yes until she heard from Somerville. She did hope so much for Somerville because Alistair Courtenay said it was the *only* women's college in Oxford from the social point of view.

Yet the ominous words 'Committee' or 'meadow' that Sylvia and Mark dreaded to hear remained unspoken. Harold, indeed, was unrecognizable in his moody silence. He got up each day a little later, mooched about the house, sat with an unlit pipe in his mouth and stared into space, often retired to bed before supper. It was like Arthur when his luck was out at racing. Not a second time, Sylvia thought. She remembered Arthur's phrase – 'Not on your nelly!'

But she thought bleakly that Mrs Milton's contemptuous prediction to Sally Bulmer might well come true. Then one morning, shopping in Town Centre, she saw Muriel Bartley turn suddenly into a doorway ahead of her. Whatever Muriel's motive for avoiding her she would not let her get away with it.

'Thank you very much for sending that beautiful wreath.'

'Oh! Mrs Calvert. I didn't see you. We were so ... Geoff and I felt perhaps ... but then after all that silly business ...'

'Arthur was hopeless over money. That's all there is to say about it. But surely that isn't why you avoided me just now?'

'I didn't avoid. I just ...'

'Now, Mrs Bartley!'

'Well, all right, I did. I thought after the way I'd messed up things for Harold at the meeting, that I should hardly be the Calvert family's favourite girl.'

'Oh dear! How these silly misunderstandings grow. We all made a mess of that business, especially Harold. The

New Town's a fine place, but he wants to make an ancient monument of it, I'm afraid. Good heavens, Mrs Bartley, he's lucky to have such good friends.'

'Well, I have tried to make up for it. I've squashed all these silly rumours as soon as I've heard them. And I've had a real go at the Board of Governors and the Education Committee in case . . .'

'You all spoil him.'

'I think it's been of some use. Everyone admires him so much. He could have them eating out of his hand again tomorrow. But now I ring the school secretary about his talk to the Parent-Teachers' Association next week and she tells me he's not answering the telephone. Is he ill?'

'No. He's not ill. He's. . . . What is this talk? I haven't heard anything about it.'

'It's for the Parent-Teachers' Association. It's rather one of my pets. He's to talk on his work for backward kids. You know all about that.'

'Not very much, I'm afraid.'

'Well, you ought to. Harold's a genius. A lot of these teenage kids owe it to him that they can read at all. And he'll tackle a job when everyone else has given up. Parents were coming to this talk of his who normally never show a moment's interest in their kids' schooling. If he knew some of the names I've had in – the Marleys, who've had three kids on probation at one time, and Mrs Scarfe who can't read or write herself. "My Les wouldn't have his job if it weren't for Mr Calvert. And now he's bringing our Doris on nicely. My old man said anyone who can bring our Doris on. . . ." I wish he'd heard her. And now if he doesn't turn up!' She looked at Sylvia hopefully.

'It's up to him isn't it, Mrs Bartley? You've done your best.'

Sylvia sat in her room reading *The Blokes at the Back of the Class*. It seemed a funny sort of title to give such a highbrow book. She couldn't make much of it – mnemonics and *Gestalt* and emotive conceptual barriers – but then it was intended for teachers, not for the blokes themselves. It was so like Harold that – talk like a dictionary and then throw in a bit of slang to show there were no hard feelings. She gave up *The Blokes* and turned to one of the Readers. She felt rather absurd at first, sitting reading kids' books with pictures and photos and the words split up. But she read all four Readers at one sitting, with increasing fascination.

Looking at Harold's pouting miserable face that evening after dinner, she wondered to herself how he could know so much about modern kids. And then she said it.

'I don't see how you know all that, Harold, about the ton-up boys, Dick and Bill and about the girl who worked at Woolworth's – I mean about all what they do at the cafés and Meccas and so on. And about that girl Lolo who worked that mixing machine in the chocolate factory?'

'The Readers are designed for Dick and Bill and Lolo and kids like them. That's why the stories are about their lives. They want to read about the things they know.'

'Yes, I see that, but how do you know about them?'

'They're my life, Mother. The people I see all day. Or rather the boys and girls I see every day are going to be them. But what on earth's put you on to the Readers?'

'Oh, just that I ought to have known long ago what you'd written. The pictures are good, aren't they? When I think of what we had as kids. "Pat has my hat." "Pat is fat." "That is Pat's hat." No wonder your Uncle Ted never learned to write properly. All his letters home when he was at sea were written for him. And your Aunt Violet! She wouldn't thank me for telling you, but when I saw her last – she must have been thirty – she was running her finger along each line of *Home Chat* and mouthing the words. And they weren't complete fools. But some of the kids you speak of in that book sound more as though they were simple. . . .'

'Yes, a good part of those I'm concerned with in Chapter Four are E.S.N. The core of my work though is with illiterate teenagers – many have low I.Q.s – but their handicaps are primarily emotional or environmental or both.'

As he talked she knew it was no good listening. He turned it all into his usual grand-sounding words. But she knew now why they all admired him. He must have talked for twenty minutes or so with increasing excitement; but it was all theory.

'I'm supposed to talk next week about all this to the parents. Why don't you come along?'

'I think I've had the talk already, dear.'

He took it well. 'All right, Mother. Anyway you wouldn't be allowed in – only parents or teachers.'

The talk was a success, everyone said; and it served its purpose, for Harold started the term with gusto. Muriel Bartley rang Sylvia to congratulate her.

'You're a dark horse. I thought you weren't going to do anything about it. Now Harold tells me it was you who roused him into giving his talk. It was a bit over their heads. But he was marvellous with them in the discussion afterwards. It's easy to see who's going to hold his hand from now on.'

It was pointless to argue with Muriel, but her heart sank. She hadn't retired to take on Harold. But she needn't have worried, for Sally Bulmer was on the scene.

'He's back at school and in fine form. But he needs more than running a school for his energies. I'm going to get him going on the survey again.'

And so she did.

Soon she was a familiar figure at 'The Sycamores' in the evenings. She and Harold had got down to a complete re-thinking of their approach to the questionnaire, she told Sylvia. And indeed it seemed to her that they were exactly doing that. When she joined them for tea and biscuits at bedtime one evening she found that Sally had got down on her knees on the study rug and was busy sketching out what she called the status/emotion chart on a huge sheet of cardboard. How she managed her pencil with her big bosom in the way all the time Sylvia wondered. Harold was on all fours as well, helping, as though they were playing bears.

Sally looked up as Sylvia came into the study.

'Ah! There you are, you dear woman. We've got work for you. How would you like to manage the oldies' questionnaire? A visit out to the eventide home. Matron will have them ready with their little answers . . .'

'I should hate it, Miss Bulmer. I didn't give up managing hotels to manage people. I want to put my feet up.'

Sally would have answered, but Harold was impatient for her attention. 'Look here, Sally, I don't think question eight will do – it's altogether unsubtle.'

Down Sally went to wrapt attention, up came her huge tweed bottom to Sylvia's view.

There's no room in one house for two big bums. She watched their heads in close discussion. Bears and squirrels!

Now for her last move but one. She only looked forward to finding a place of her own. Somewhere near Town Centre, if she could get it. That would be a good centre for operations. Operations! What a gloom she could be! She chuckled aloud. Harold looked up.

'You're in good form these days, Mother.'

'Yes, dear, I think I am,' she said.